SHADOWHUNTER

'When he left, it was as if he'd taken some monumental decision. He looked . . . ' she fumbled for the words, 'grim, but in some way—satisfied. It's the only way I can describe it.'

'I'm not with you. What do you mean?'

'As if he'd decided on some sort of revenge, or thought of some way of getting even with Gunnar, or the KGB or whoever sent him here.'

'What sort of revenge?'

'I don't know. He'll find a way. Philip hates Russians, you know. He'll do something. I don't know what. Fire a missile at Moscow? Is that possible?'

She'd meant it as irony, but started when she saw the shock on Andrew's face.

'He couldn't! It's the wrong sort of boat, isn't it?' she gasped. 'What *could* he do to them, Andrew?'

'I shudder to think.'

SHADOW-HUNTER

Geoffrey Archer

ARROW

First published in Arrow 1990

9 11 12 10

First published in Great Britain by Century Hutchinson Limited 1989

Arrow Books Limited
Random House UK Ltd, 20 Vauxhall Bridge Road, London SW1V 2SA

Random House Australia (Pty) Limited
16 Dalmore Drive, Scoresby, Victoria 3179

Random House New Zealand Limited
18 Poland Road, Glenfield
Auckland 10, New Zealand

Random House South Africa (Pty) Limited
PO Box 2263, Rosebank 2121, South Africa

Random House UK Limited Reg. No. 954009

A CIP catalogue record for this book
is available from the British Library

Papers used by Random House UK Limited
are natural, recyclable products made from wood grown in
sustainable forests. The manufacturing processes conform to
the environmental regulations of the country of origin.

ISBN 0 09 960380 2

Printed and bound in Great Britain by
Cox & Wyman Ltd, Reading, Berkshire

To Eva, Alison and James,
for their encouragement

CHAPTER ONE

Wednesday 16th October.

The restaurant was Greek. Kebabs and non-stick rice, washed down with retsina. Plymouth had a dozen like it; the evening trade was good in a navy town.

The watchers sat outside in a car, wishing they were inside so they could catch something of what the man and woman said to each other, but there'd been no spare table.

For a week, the two men from Special Branch had been shadowing the big blond man who claimed to be Swedish. The man had chatted up a young submariner in a pub, asking questions about nuclear propulsion that were too intelligent to be casual.

Up to now there'd been nothing; a dreary circuit of bars and dockside dives. Sometimes the man had drunk alone, just looking at faces. Sometimes he'd feigned drunkenness and joined in the raucous banter of the sailors, but there'd been nothing they could call a contact.

Clearly the man was searching. But for what? Information? Secrets? Or just companionship?

For most of the week the Swede had stayed in cheap lodgings. Then, that morning, he'd gone up-market – checked into the Holiday Inn. The receptionist had welcomed him as a regular client.

Now he'd met a women, a classy one at that, judging by the way she dressed. Someone else's wife, they'd guessed. She'd come separately to the restaurant, kissing him as she sat down. They'd been given a table by the window, easily visible from the watchers' car.

'If this job had been important, they'd have given us the gear and we could hear what Blondie's saying,' one of the watchers grumbled.

'Don't need to hear it,' the other replied. 'He's talking dirty. That's what the hotel room's for.'

Nearly ninety minutes passed. Concentration was flagging.

'Hey, look!' one of the policemen snapped. The woman was agitated. She was clutching her head in her hands, her shoulders shaking.

'She's blubbing.'

They saw the Swede grab her hand but she pulled it away.

'Talking too dirty, you reckon?'

'Hang on! She's moving.'

The woman stood up, then scrabbled on the floor for her bag. The man reached out, trying to pull her back. He glanced round, embarrassed.

The door opened and the woman ran into the street. Disoriented at first, she pulled a handkerchief from her bag and dabbed at her eyes. Then, darting a look over her shoulder, she turned right and ran down the street.

The Swede stayed inside and called hurriedly for the bill.

'She's got a car, look. A Golf. You follow her – I'll take Blondie.'

The watcher closed the passenger door and slipped into the darkened entrance of a newsagent's shop. His companion started the engine and moved off in pursuit of the woman.

Three minutes passed before the tall foreigner emerged into the street. He looked around briefly, pulled a cigarette from a pack, and lit it. For a split second his gaze rested on the doorway opposite. Hand and cigarette hovered for a moment.

Casually he turned and walked up the road, passing one pub, but pausing uncertainly outside another. The watcher was in the open now. He kept moving, knowing he'd been seen, but perhaps not yet recognized for what he was.

The Swede pushed open the door to the lounge bar. The watcher gave him a few seconds' start then crossed the road and followed him in.

The lounge was packed. No sign of him. The policeman eased through the crush to the bar, looking all around.

He reached the counter and his eyes met the Swede's, inches away, grey-blue and hard as nails.

'Can you watch this for me? I must take a leak.'

The blond pointed to his pint of lager.

'Sure,' replied the watcher, unprepared.

The Swede elbowed his way to the gents'.

Did he know? Was his cover blown? The policeman dithered for just a moment too long.

He shoved through the crowd, drawing complaints and threats. Inside the toilet a cold wind blew through the wide-open window. Outside he heard a motorbike roar away.

'Sod it!' Blondie had been a professional after all, and he'd lost him.

* * *

Thursday 17th October.

It was weeks since Commander Andrew Tinker had worn a cap and the soft leather band felt like the steel hoop of a barrel. At sea submariners ignored naval formality, but heading back into harbour after six weeks on patrol, uniforms were brushed and smoothed, ready for the world of normal people.

'Funny smell.' Tinker sniffed, stepping clear of the hatch and stretching. He leaned his elbows on the edge of the tall, slim fin. The joke was an old one.

'It's called fresh air, sir . . . ,' the watch officer fed the expected line.

The early morning sky was grizzled, but there was no rain. Andrew gulped at the offshore breeze, rejoicing in its scent after weeks of confinement in conditioned air. As they rounded Penlee Point into Plymouth Sound, he could taste its sweetness; his senses peeled away the layers of smell – woodsmoke, wet grass, sea-weed.

It was like being released from sensory deprivation, every nerve newly sensitized. The gentle flapping of the bridge ensign was like a whip-crack to his ears, the light wind on his face seemed to tug like a gale.

He was pale; they all were after weeks without sunlight.

However, a few brisk walks on the moors would soon bring the colour back.

The conning tower stood thirty feet above the casing. Dark green water washed like liquid glass over the fat, blunt nose of the submarine and away to the sides. There was no sound, no vibration from the powerplant deep below the surface. The black shape probed and the smooth sea yielded effortlessly to its penetration. Brutal. Phallic.

Eyes fixed on the parting of the waters, his thoughts turned to sex. They could afford to now that he was going ashore. He'd learned to suppress such feelings at sea. Within hours he'd be home; Patsy would be waiting for him.

'About forty minutes 'til we're alongside?'

'That's right, sir. First line ashore at 08.00 – that's if *Truculent*'s cleared the berth in time. We should see her any minute.'

The lieutenant raised a heavy pair of binoculars and focused on the distant cranes of Devonport dockyard. The towering roof of the triple drydock dominated the view. At that range the black fin of their sister ship heading for sea would be difficult to spot against the vertical lines of the harbour side.

HMS Truculent was almost identical to Tinker's own *HMS Tribune*; a few pieces of equipment on board differed. Despite his eagerness to be home he envied *Truculent*'s captain. Commander Philip Hitchens was heading for the north Atlantic for biennial NATO exercises. This autumn the manoeuvres were being held closer to Soviet waters than ever before. Tinker enjoyed war games – stalking the massive American aircraft carriers and 'sinking' them with salvos of simulated torpedoes and missiles. It was a shame the patrol schedules had favoured Hitchens rather than himself. Hitchens would never admit to enjoying something as serious as war, even when it was just a game.

'Steer two-nine-zero. Revolutions for five knots!' Andrew ordered into the bridge microphone. They were passing north of Drake's Island, the Hoe to their right

10

dominated by the disused lighthouse known as Smeaton's Tower.

'Got her, sir! She's just coming through the narrows.'

Andrew raised his own binoculars and followed the line set by the lieutenant. It was the *Truculent*, all right; and there was Phil on the bridge. The set of his head was unmistakable.

'Great sight,' Andrew whispered as the *Truculent* picked up speed towards them, bow-wave foaming.

'The best there is,' the young lieutenant concurred. 'A five-thousand-ton black mistress! That's what my girlfriend calls this beast.'

'Jealous, is she?'

'Hmmm. But they like to be jealous, don't they, women?'

Andrew didn't reply at first. He was very young, the lieutenant.

'Planning to tie the knot, are you?'

'No, not me. Not ready yet, sir.'

Truculent was less than half-a-mile ahead, aiming to pass a hundred yards to port. Tinker raised the binoculars again; the finely-chiselled face of Philip Hitchens stared straight ahead from the conning tower, cap pulled firmly down against the wind.

'Come on, Phil,' he breathed. 'Give us a wave. You're not making a movie!'

The two commanders had shared a 'cabin' at Britannia College, Dartmouth, and their careers had progressed in an undeclared spirit of competition.

It surprised Tinker they'd remained such good friends. Hitchens was so straitlaced he was a curiosity. He had breeding and style, yet often seemed overwhelmed by the responsibility of his work. His handsome features should have made him a 'ladies' man', yet Andrew had never known him make a pass at another woman, despite his own wife's questionable fidelity. Tinker found the mismatch of appearance and character intriguing.

Andrew saluted as the two black hulls passed one another silently.

'The bugger!' Tinker growled. 'He's not even acknowl-edging! Come on, Phil! What's the matter with you?'

To ignore the salute of a fellow warship was very bad form in navy protocol. Tinker sharpened the focus of his binoculars. His friend of twenty years was studiously ignoring him.

'Something we said, sir?' the lieutenant suggested blandly.

Within the hour they were alongside the jetty in Devon-port submarine base, astern of the lustrous black hull of a sister boat just out of refit. Standing on the casing ready to welcome aboard the Captain of the Second Submarine Squadron, Tinker realized how tatty his own vessel had become. The black paint had lost its sheen and there were patches on the fin where sound-absorbent tiles had pulled away, the adhesive softened by weeks of immersion. *Trib-une* would need a spell in the dockyard before her next patrol.

'Good morning, sir.' He saluted briefly.

'Morning, Andrew. Welcome home!'

Captain Norman Craig had eight nuclear-powered sub-marines in his squadron. He was responsible for the well-being of the boats and their crews.

'Lovely day. Let's get below for a chat. Won't keep you long.'

Tinker followed him down through the hatch and into the wardroom where the stewards were pouring coffee. De-briefing was routine at the end of a patrol. The wea-pons and mechanical engineers would hand over reports on defective equipment so the mechanics at the shore base, *HMS Defiance*, could put it right. Personnel pro-blems would be raised, and gossip exchanged, but the session was always kept brief. The members of *Tribune*'s crew who were due to take shore leave would want to get home.

The briefing over, the two men crossed the quay towards *HMS Defiance*, the Captain hurrying to keep pace with Andrew's longer stride.

'Patsy picking you up?' Craig asked. Andrew looked at his watch.

'She'll be teaching. Home for lunch, I expect.'

'My car can take you back if you want.'

'You sure, sir? That'd be great.'

'The driver can't spend *all* day polishing it! It'll give her something to do. What time do you want to leave?'

'In about an hour? That'll give me time to complete my paperwork.'

The black Cavalier was driven by a WRNS, a plump girl with rosy cheeks and a warm Devon accent. As she swung the car expertly out of the suburbs of Plymouth and into the country lanes, they talked of the fortunes of Plymouth Argyll football club, of which both were fans. But the more she talked the slower she drove, which grated on his nerves, so he pulled a folder from his briefcase and pretended to read.

Coming home always made him anxious, gave him a fear that his domestic life might have changed radically while he'd been away.

The lanes grew narrower as they approached the village where he and Patsy had lived for the past four years. They'd had four different homes; appointments had moved him round the country, but they'd determined to settle in the West Country. Two limestone cottages knocked together had created a home large enough. The three children were away at boarding school; eight-year-old Anthony was just experiencing his first term of separation from his parents. School had started five weeks ago, so Patsy had handled the boy's last-minute tears on her own.

The red Devon soil glowed in the midday autumn sun. The car turned into a narrow lane and dived between banks and hedges. Soon it wound its way into the village of Yealmsford.

The vicar stepped out of the tiny post office carrying a newspaper, looked at the naval registration of the car, peered to see who it was, then waved in recognition.

He'll be getting me to read the lesson again before long,

Andrew thought. The vicar said he had a voice that made the congregation sit up and listen.

The Tinkers were well known in the village and Andrew was a celebrity. To command something 'nuclear' carried kudos in this part of the world.

Patsy was out. It irked him she wasn't there to greet him. She taught in the mornings at the village primary school, but should have been home by now. He carried his small grip into the house – a submariner takes few possessions to sea.

The emptiness of the cottage alarmed him. With all the children away at school now, there were no toys littering the hall. He put his bag down and called out. No answer. Where the hell was she?

Then he heard her car.

'Oh, you're back!' Patsy looked startled, as she came through the doorway. 'I wasn't sure when you were coming. Have you been here long?'

She dropped her briefcase in the hall and hugged him. Her copper-coloured hair brushed his cheek; it smelled of shampoo and the cigarette smoke from the school office. He squeezed her and lifted her feet off the ground.

'I missed you,' she purred, the way she always did.

'Missed you too!'

'You didn't! You had your boat to play with!'

'Not as much fun as playing with you!'

She pushed him away with a forced smile. It was stupid, but she always felt shy when Andrew came home. To cope with his long absences she'd made herself unnaturally self-sufficient. His homecomings were like the arrival of a stranger.

'Have you had lunch?'

'No, and I'm starving.'

'I'm not sure what there is. You can come shopping with me later!'

He followed her to the kitchen. He was used to this; whenever he returned from patrol, Patsy seemed to feel the need to 'house-train' him again.

'It'll have to be a sandwich for now. With the children away, I haven't been stocking up.'

'I was worried something had happened. It's so quiet in the house . . .'

'I know . . .'

She looked pained. She would never tell him how lonely she felt at times.

'How was Anthony when you took him to school?'

'He howled all the way there, and I howled all the way back! But he's fine now. I got a super letter from him this morning. We can have him home for a weekend soon. He's dying to see you.'

Andrew watched her work. With Patsy having her own job, her own friends, and being life's mainstay for their children, he sometimes felt himself an outsider.

'I saw Sara this morning. She looked dreadful,' Patsy said, slicing bread.

'Hitchens?'

She nodded.

'She's having problems with Simon. He's going to be thirteen soon and still hasn't got used to boarding school. His headmaster's accused him of vandalizing microscopes in the biology lab. Sara's worried he'll turn to arson next!'

'That's appalling! Philip sailed today. He ignored my salute! Not like him at all. Perhaps he was worrying about Simon. Last thing you need when you're going to sea.'

'Last thing a *mother* needs at any time,' she stressed pointedly. 'Particularly Sara. You know how unstable she is.'

'Over-emotional, that's all.'

'You fancy Sara, that's your trouble!'

'I just feel sorry for her. She's not so good at coping as you are. And I have to take an interest. Simon's my godson.'

'Ohh! Well remembered!' Patsy mocked. 'When did you last even see him? Last year? Year before?'

'Oh, come on . . .'

'Sorry. That wasn't fair. Here's your sandwich.'

She passed him a plate and they sat down at the kitchen table. 'I'm afraid we're out of beer.'

She smiled apologetically.

'Welcome home!'

★ ★ ★

Commander Philip Hitchens had seldom experienced claustrophobia, but now the cabin felt as narrow as a coffin, as *HMS Truculent* hummed towards the Atlantic depths.

For eight hours after leaving Devonport, Philip had hardly left the control room. Inshore waters were the most dangerous, and avoiding collisions took maximum concentration. He didn't trust the watch; all young men, their minds wandered when he wasn't around.

They'd kept at periscope depth in the Channel; the sea was calm and visibility good. The sonar produced a jumble of tanker traffic, confused by echoes from the sea-bed, but he could see the ships clearly enough through the periscope up to five miles away.

Keeping busy had served another purpose, too; to distract his mind from the nightmare of the past three months, a personal nightmare of duplicity, the depth of which he had yet to fathom.

Now it was evening. South of Ireland, they were away from the shipping channels. Time to leave it to the watch. He withdrew to his cabin, to his solitary hell. Once there, he sat hunched at the foot of his bunk like a child. It was the furthest he could get from his work-table, from the framed photograph of Sara. Every time he looked at her picture, the shock, the misery, the pain engulfed him anew.

Betrayal! The word echoed in his mind like a slamming door; not just her – the bastard Russians, too!

He'd thought of putting the photograph in a drawer so as not to look at her, but ruled it out. Everything had to stay normal; no one must know. His cabin was also his office, visited by others. Family photographs were like icons in officers' quarters. Their absence would be quickly noticed.

He couldn't stop thinking of her. The night before they'd sailed he'd stayed on board, unable to sleep, knowing she was seeing that man again. She'd promised it was to say goodbye, to tell him they'd never meet again. But did he believe her? *Could* he believe anything she said, any more?

As for Simon – he couldn't imagine, didn't dare think, what his future would hold now. His son was the one restraint on what he planned. But he was at a good school; they'd see him right. Nothing must stand in his way.

There was a debt to be settled, vengeance for a past wrong, a terrible wrong which transcended all other considerations.

'*Captain, sir! Officer of the Watch!*'

The tannoy loudspeaker above his desk startled him.

He leapt up from the bunk and clicked the microphone switch.

'Captain!'

'*Sound room's got a sonar contact. They think it's a trawler, sir.*'

'I'm coming now.'

His cabin was just yards from the control room. He was there within seconds, glad of the distraction. Trawlers were the bane of submariners' lives in coastal waters. Fouling their nets could mean the early end of a patrol.

He headed for the navigation plot. The submarine's position was being provided by SINS, the Submarine Inertial Navigation System, a gyroscopic device that had proven remarkably accurate.

The navigator and officer of the watch was Lieutenant Nick Cavendish, a twenty-five-year-old on his first patrol with *Truculent*.

'Depth?'

'Seventy metres, sir. Thirty metres under the keel.'

'Should be okay at this depth. What's the contact's bearing?'

'Ten degrees on the starboard bow. Range unknown.'

He stared at the chart. They were approaching the edge of the continental shelf west of Ireland. A few more hours and the sea bed would drop thousands of metres, giving them all the water they could want to avoid hazards trailing from the surface. The chart showed no obstructions for miles.

'I need more sea room. They're bloody long, those trawl wires. Officer of the Watch, come round to 210.'

'Aye, aye, sir. Helm! Port thirty. Keep course two-one-zero.'

Best to take no chances; trawl nets were undetectable until their hawsers scrapped the acoustic tiles off the casing, by which time it was too late.

'Anything else on sonar?'

'One other surface contact up to the north-west, very distant. Sounds like a tanker. No submarines, sir. And none expected for the next twenty-four hours, according to the intelligence sitrep.'

Philip shot a glance round the control room. In the centre, the oiled steel periscope shafts glistened in their deck housings. About a dozen men, ratings in blue shirts, officers in white, were concentrating as the boat manoeuvred. The planesman at the one-man control console operated the stick that 'flew' the submarine through the water, marine engineers monitored gauges for the trim valves and propulsion system, and seamen, some of them not much more than eighteen, peered at the amber screens of the tactical systems.

Those who caught the captain's eye looked away quickly. They didn't like him much, the men of *Truculent*, but they respected him, and that was what mattered. He'd need that respect when the crunch came in a few days' time.

Across the room at the weapons control console, the weapon engineer officer, Lieutenant Commander Paul Spriggs was talking to a rating. Hitchens liked Spriggs; the man was crisp and concise in the way he handled his men, everything by the book. Spriggs would be vital to him at the end, a WEO who wouldn't question orders.

Philip hovered by the chart table, pulling out the sheet for the north of Scotland and the water between Iceland, the Faroes and the Shetlands. Known as the GIFUK (Greenland, Iceland, Faroes, UK) Gap, this was NATO's underwater front line, a strategic barrier through which Soviet submarines should not be able to pass undetected on their way to the central Atlantic.

A ridge of sand, mud and rock ran between the land masses, along which the US Navy had laid a string of hydrophones known as SOSUS, SOund SUrveillance System, able to detect the passing of almost any submarine. Sonar-equipped surface ships and aircraft patrolled above, to complete the barrier.

Truculent was taking part in Exercise Ocean Guardian, which involved over a hundred NATO ships and submarines, practising the reinforcement of Norway and control of the Norwegian Sea.

'Are we going tactical on the transit, sir?' asked the WEO. 'See how many Yank skimmers we can zap before they get a whiff of us?'

'Certainly not!'

Heads turned at the sharpness of Philip's reply.

'Sorry, sir,' Spriggs mumbled. 'Thought that was the plan.'

'No,' Philip repeated softly, conscious of his overreaction. 'We've got to avoid any risk of detection. We're blue at first, as you know. But then we go unlisted.'

Paul Spriggs frowned. He'd attended the pre-patrol briefing in the Northwood headquarters of Flag Officer Submarines, along with the captain and the first lieutenant; that briefing had certainly put them playing 'blue' (NATO) first, but by midweek they were due to switch to 'orange' (enemy). There'd been no mention of their going 'unlisted'. That meant some sort of secret mission, usually intelligence gathering deep inside Soviet waters.

'Will you be briefing us on that, sir?' he asked edgily.

Hitchens felt his face begin to flush. They were staring at him.

'Yes, WEO. In due course,' he answered curtly.

He stepped into the sound room adjoining the control room. Cordell, the tactics and sonar officer, was listening intently on headphones. Three ratings sat at panels controlling glowing green video displays. Here, the myriad sounds of the deep detected by hydrophones spread round the bulbous bows were translated into vertical patterns and gradations of light, unintelligible to the uninitiated. One of the ratings stood up from his seat and crossed to a cabinet to change the laser disc on which every sound detected was recorded in digital code.

'Got a hiccup with sonar 2026, sir.'

Lieutenant Sebastian Cordell had removed his headphones.

'Processor's gone barmy. The CPO's going to change a board, see if that cures it.'

The 2026 was the processor for the second sonar array, a yellow plastic tube over a hundred metres long, filled with hydrophones, towed a thousand metres behind the submarine. The computer for analysing the sounds it detected was highly sophisticated, and had developed a fault.

'How's that fisherman doing? Still tracking it?'

The possibility of the trawl net slipping like a sheath over the nose of the boat haunted Hitchens.

'We think she's passing clear astern, sir. Shouldn't be any risk of fouling now.'

'Thank God. You'll keep me informed on the 2026? I want a report on it.'

'Of course, sir.'

People seemed to be staring at him. He'd keep moving; didn't want them reading his face to see what he was thinking.

He passed back through the control room, heading aft, telling the officer of the watch he was making his rounds.

He sensed a conspiracy around him. Of silence. They knew about Sara!

They'd heard gossip ashore. Must've done. In the pubs. Perhaps some had even heard that sod of a chief petty officer boasting about how he'd screwed the captain's wife!

How would he have described it? Bonking? Poking?

Anger made his head swim. He put out a hand to steady himself as he made his way to the tunnel that crossed the top of the reactor to the machinery spaces beyond.

When the penny had dropped just a week ago, it was like a blow to the stomach. He'd taken Simon, home for the weekend, shopping in Plymouth for construction kits to take back to school.

Strolling down Market Avenue, Philip had vaguely

recognized CPO Terry from years before. He'd remembered the face, but not the name – until Simon called out, 'Hi Reg!' He'd sounded so pleased. The CPO had grinned at Simon, then glanced uncomfortably at Philip.

Surprised the boy should know Terry, it had been a minute or two before he'd asked about it.

'Just someone I know . . .' had been Simon's reply.

He'd felt panicky, suddenly aware how little he knew about his son's life. The boy was away at boarding school for most of the year, and when he was home for the holidays, Philip was more often than not away at sea. But why should he know Reg Terry?

He'd pressed him to say where they'd met.

'At home. He used to come and see us sometimes, me and Mummy.'

A door had suddenly opened into a world he knew nothing about.

Philip reached the airlock and turned the bar-bell handle that withdrew the heavy bolts securing the outer door. He was almost exactly in the middle of the submarine, forty metres from the dome of the bow-sonar, forty more from the end of the cowl that housed the silent propulsor at the stern.

He closed the outer door behind him and opened the inner one. He was now standing on top of the reactor. Beneath his feet the controlled uranium reaction generated enough power to serve a town of 50,000 people, the potential of the nuclear radiation to destroy his body cells held back by thick lead shielding.

There was no sound from the thousands of gallons of water being boiled into high-pressure steam below him. Millions of pounds had been spent on research into silencing the powerful pumps that circulated the cooling water through the reactor core, pumps whose reliability was essential to the life of the submarine.

He passed through into caverns packed with the machinery that drove his boat and generated the megawatts needed for its electrical systems.

Those who saw Philip greeted him smartly. The work of the men 'back aft', essential to the silent operation of the boat, was not considered as 'macho' as that of the weapon crews 'forrard'. Philip was conscious some COs tended to ignore the mechanical end of the boat, which was physically separated from the forward section by the reactor compartment. They may not like him, but he wouldn't be guilty of that.

Did these men know about Sara? What if they did? He must act normally, show no sign of weakness. His authority mustn't be questioned.

In the officers' quarters forward, Lieutenant Commander Paul Spriggs had returned to the cramped cabin he shared with the wiry first lieutenant, Lieutenant Commander Tim Pike. The first lieutenant was second in command – the executive officer and 'general manager' of the boat.

'Tim, at the ops briefing at Northwood . . . ,' Spriggs began.

'Mmmm?' Pike put down the nuclear propulsion manual he'd been studying for forthcoming promotion exams. 'What of it?'

'They said "free play", didn't they? Defined areas of sea, but we can do whatever we like within them?'

'Well, they didn't say we couldn't. But it's supposed to be a fast transit up to the Lofotens.'

'Yea, but if the opportunity's there, it's okay. That's what I said to the old man, but the silly sod jumped down my throat.'

'What? Our own dear warm-hearted Captain? You astonish me.'

'He was really narked. Then he went stomping off on an inspection.'

'Must be that time of the month. Mind you, they could have said something different to him afterwards. He had another session with FOSM later.'

'Did he? I didn't know. That fits what he said, that we're going unlisted.'

'Unlisted?' Pike frowned.

'You didn't know either?'

'He . . . er, hasn't seen fit to brief me yet.'

'Bloody hell, Tim! You're his second-in-command!'

Pike smoothed the ginger stubble he called a beard, his pale grey eyes betraying the wounded pride that came from being deputy to a man who trusted no one.

'I'm sure he'll tell us "in due course", Paul.'

' "At the right time", you mean.'

' "When we need to know".'

'You've been reading the rule book again!'

Pike shrugged. 'I've been through this before with Hitchens. Made an issue of it once. Wasn't worth it. He went out of his way to be bloody to me for weeks afterwards.'

'You don't surprise me. But tell me: you've worked with him longer than I have – how do you rate him as a skipper?'

'He knows his stuff. And he's the one with the most gold stripes. That's what matters when the chips are down. If I had a run-in with him, the men with scrambled egg on their hats would back him up to the hilt. They'd drop me like a lump of shit!'

* * *

Friday 18th October.

Vice-Admiral Feliks Astashenkov looked round cautiously as he entered the arrivals hall at Moscow's Sheremetyevo airport. He was not in uniform and had flown from Murmansk under a false name. The plane had developed an engine problem at the start of its taxi run; the passengers had had to wait on board for three hours while an Aeroflot mechanic repaired it.

As one of the *Vlasti*, the 'powerful ones', he was unused to such demeaning treatment. The Deputy-Commander of the Soviet Navy's Northern Fleet was entitled to better than that. But the message from the Soviet leader, delivered to his home by a courier, had insisted on maximum secrecy for their meeting.

At Murmansk Airport a KGB guard had recognized him. It was inevitable that someone would. He'd slipped the man ten roubles, told him he was Moscow-bound for a weekend with his mistress, but that his wife thought he was on a fishing trip. The policeman had passed the note across his mouth. His lips were sealed.

The silence he'd bought was to keep the journey secret from the Northern Fleet Commander, Admiral Andrei Belikov, rather than from his wife. Belikov was just a vassal of Admiral Grekov, Commander-in-Chief of the Soviet Navy, who'd been at odds with Nikolai Savkin, the new Soviet leader, from the moment he'd taken over.

They told Astashenkov he'd be met at Sheremetyevo and taken to the rendezvous. He elbowed his way through the crush, impatient at the willingness of his countrymen to accept such conditions. Astashenkov felt apprehensive. He'd been given no reason for this unorthodox summons to Moscow. He'd met the General Secretary on several occasions, admired his energy and reforming zeal. Nikolai Savkin was of his own generation, a man with the vision to press on with change even though the birth pains of the new, competitive Soviet Union had become intolerable to many of his countrymen.

Comrade Savkin was in need of friends, no doubt about that. Was that why he'd been summoned? But why him? It was in the factories and the Politburo that Savkin's support was waning. The armed forces had stood back from the arguments over the economy. And why call for him at this precise moment, when a massive fleet of NATO warships was assembling a few hundred kilometres from the Soviet coast for 'manoeuvres'? At a time like this he should be at his headquarters in Severomorsk, studying intelligence reports, ready to take action if the 'exercise' turned into something else.

'Comrade Vice-Admiral . . .'

The touch on his arm was casual, as if someone had merely brushed against him.

'Please follow me.'

It was the courier who'd delivered Savkin's message. Dressed in a brown parka with a fur-lined hood, he moved through the crowd slowly enough for Astashenkov to follow with ease. Not once did he turn his head to check; to anyone watching, the two men would appear unconnected.

They stepped outside. It was after eight in the evening and dark, and the October air had a nip of frost. The

Admiral spread the gap between himself and his escort. Ahead was the car park; Astashenkov fumbled for keys, as if he had a vehicle of his own to go to.

The messenger stopped by a battered yellow Volvo estate and opened the door on the driver's side. Astashenkov paused, placed his overnight bag on the ground and began to feel in his inside pockets, while looking around to see if he was being observed. The passenger door of the Volvo was pushed open. He climbed in.

They drove for nearly half-an-hour, the courier making it plain he had no wish to talk. Astashenkov had spent several years of his career in Moscow, but the part of the city through which they travelled was unknown to him. He suspected that the driver was making the route circuitous in order to confuse him.

They stopped in an old quarter. He followed the driver into what would once have been the townhouse of a prosperous merchant. Feliks was mystified; all this subterfuge for a meeting with the Soviet leader? What was going on?

Inside it smelled damp, as if seldom used. An oil heater burned in the hall. A guard emerged from the front reception room, carrying a sub-machine gun. The escort removed his parka and helped the Admiral off with his coat. Then he led the way upstairs.

Savkin seemed smaller than Astashenkov remembered, as if the burden of a national crisis had begun to crush him. At the sound of Astashenkov's entrance, the General Secretary of the Soviet Communist Party and President of the USSR stopped in mid-pace across the room.

'Ah, Feliks! A tired, impatient victim of air travel! And they always call it a "technical" fault, don't they?'

The smile looked forced. The pure white mane of hair looked as if it had not seen a comb all day.

'They wouldn't let us leave the plane! We were like pigs in a pen.'

'All the more reason for me to be grateful that you came.'

'It was my duty, Comrade General Secretary.'

Savkin's eyebrows arched momentarily. 'Duty' was

25

such a subjective concept. Where would the Admiral feel his 'duty' lay once he'd heard what Savkin had to say?

'Come and sit down. I must apologize for the room.'

He waved a hand dismissively. The walls were faded and peeling, marked with dusty rectangles where paintings had once hung. A heavy pedestal desk in one corner was half covered with files from an open briefcase. Savkin led the way to a green, leather chaise longue, and sat himself in the high-backed armchair opposite.

'The house belongs to the Pushkin. It's not used much, only for storing spare exhibits. My wife's cousin is curator of the gallery, so my link with the place is personal rather than official, which means it's clean – no bugs. And the guards here are my men. They'll bring us tea in a moment. Now, remind me. When was the last time . . . ?'

It was a gambit. Savkin would remember perfectly well. Such urbanity did nothing to calm Astashenkov's unease.

'It was June. At Polyarny. *Podvodnaya Lodka Atomnaya*. The nuclear patrol submarines – your inspection.'

'Of course.' Savkin nodded. 'It was a good turnout. Very impressive. Fine technology. The efficiency of your men was so vibrant you could almost touch it.'

'They were on their best behaviour. You must be used to that.'

'Yes, but you can tell when it's just show . . .'

There was a tap at the door, which had been left ajar. It was the guard bringing the tea. Conversation lapsed until he had left the room.

'Now. Why do you think you're here, like this?' His tone of voice was condescending, keeping the Admiral at a disadvantage. He would be asking a lot from Astashenkov, but did not want to appear to be a beggar.

The Admiral shrugged. There was no point in prevaricating.

'I really don't know. It might be that you require some service from me which would not win the approval of my Commanding Officer . . . ?'

Savkin smiled drily. He'd wanted a forthright reply. It saved time.

'And if that *were* the case . . . ? If neither Grekov not Belikov were to be involved?'

'Then it would be a difficult decision. I should need to understand why.'

'Of course.'

The grey eyes studied the sailor. Astashenkov recognized in them the flicker of uncertainty and weariness.

'Let me ask you something,' the General Secretary said. 'I've gained the impression, on the few occasions we've met, that your interests stretch wider than just naval matters. That *perestroika* has caused you some excitement; that you welcome it. Am I right?'

'It's my duty to be politically aware . . .' Feliks stalled.

'Yes, but you know I'm talking of more than awareness, Comrade. I'm talking of *commitment*.'

Astashenkov looked blank. Savkin would need to be more explicit.

'The changes on the farms and in the factories, and in the public services – making our people more responsible for their labour, and rewarding them individually – is a process I believe you support in principal, Feliks. But that process, as you know, is now at its nadir. People's lives have become harder, but not yet better. Faith in the policy has crumbled. It's no secret that the Zhiguli car factory has been on strike for two weeks because the enforcement of new quality standards has cut the workers' bonuses. What *is* still a secret, however, is how fast the strikes are spreading. Within two weeks, fifty per cent of our industrial production may be at a standstill.'

Astashenkov let out an involuntary low whistle.

'Yes. It's as bad as that,' Savkin was pleased he'd been able to startle the Admiral. 'And the strikers are supported by the majority of the Party. The *Nomenklatura* can hear the death-rattle of *perestroika*, and plan to finish it off!'

'But then what? A return to the old ways? They must know that's impossible now.'

'Is it? Are you sure?'

Astashenkov sensed he had been trapped.

'Well . . . , I'm only a submariner. I've no real understanding of economics . . .'

Savkin was not satisfied with that answer. He waited for Astashenkov to continue.

'It seems impossible to me. If we're not to be at an economic disadvantage for ever, we must produce at a price and to a standard that will enable us to compete worldwide. To return to a system of quotas without accountability . . .'

He knew he sounded if he were parrotting one of Savkin's own speeches. But it was what he believed.

'So you think we must continue with the policy? *Perestroika* at any price?'

Astashenkov breathed in deeply and let out a sigh. He sensed a noose tightening.

'It's what they accuse *me* of,' the General Secretary persisted. 'The *Nomenklatura*. They say it's my vanity, that I can't admit the policy is a failure.'

'Not all the *Nomenklatura*, Comrade General Secretary.' Feliks himself held one of those appointments which had to be approved by the Party.

Savkin frowned. Impatiently he pushed his fingers through the straggling white tufts at his temples.

'Feliks, I need to know how far you yourself will go, in supporting me?'

* * *

An hour later, Feliks Astashenkov stood outside one of those slab-sided apartment blocks that fill much of Moscow's suburbs. Savkin's courier had dropped him at the end of the road, as he'd asked, and he'd walked the last few hundred metres to Tatiana's flat. He was badly in need of the fresh air, which was cold enough to numb the end of his nose. What Savkin was planning had shaken him to the core.

He'd telephoned Tatiana the day before, to check she would be at home that evening. Opportunities to see her were so infrequent nowadays, he seized them whenever they arose. But now, as he stood looking up at the lighted windows, trying to remember which one was hers, he regretted making the rendezvous. Solitude was what he needed, not the distracting company of his mistress. He wanted time alone, to consider what Savkin had asked him to do. Not a word of his meeting would he be able to share with Tatiana. No one must ever learn from him what had been said that day.

She'd sounded edgy on the telephone, affecting indifference to his proposal to visit her. Feliks knew what that meant. His affair with her had started when he had been posted to Moscow three years earlier but since his transfer to the Kola Peninsula eighteen months ago, they'd not spent more than a dozen days together. He'd known it couldn't last. For the second time that day, he approached a rendezvous with trepidation.

★ ★ ★

Saturday 19th October.

Devon, England.

Andrew Tinker had been home for two days. He opened his eyes and looked at the bedside clock. It was just after seven a.m.; there was no hurry.

It was the birdsong that had woken him. At sea, he was accustomed to the dull roar of the ventilation system, to being awakened at any time by a call from the control-room and dropping off again easily. But here the persistent trill of a blackbird defeated him.

Patsy's naked body radiated warmth beside him. His first night home had been difficult. It usually was, with both of them tense from suppressing their feelings for so many weeks. Last night had been different, however.

He turned on his side; she had her back to him.

'Mmmm. Hello, stranger,' she mumbled.

'Hel-lo.'

'Are you the same stranger who did such lovely things to me last night?'

'That rings a bell . . . ' Andrew chuckled.

He kissed her neck. She smelled muskily of sweat and perfumed bath oil.

'Can you prove it?'

'Maybe. There's only one way to find out!'

★ ★ ★

'I'm going to do bacon and eggs,' he called to Patsy, who

29

was in the shower. 'Just to show you there's more than one thing I'm good at! Like some?'

'Put like that, how could I refuse . . . ?'

He was just dishing up when the telephone rang.

It was Norman Craig.

Andrew caught Patsy's eye across the kitchen and gave her a thumbs-down sign. Craig meant work.

'Hello, sir. Good morning to you.'

'I'm desperately sorry, Andrew. Pasty'll never speak to me again. But I'm about to ruin your weekend. If it's any consolation, I'm in the same boat, but I've been tied up since yesterday.'

'Sounds serious. What's the problem?'

'Look, I'm not being unreasonable, but I simply can't tell you anything over the phone. You understand. But if you could meet me in my office at about ten, earlier if you can make it, I'd be eternally grateful. It's bloody important. I wouldn't be disturbing your leave if it weren't.'

The captain's voice had developed an edge.

'No, of course not. I'll be on my way in a few minutes.'

Andrew replaced the receiver.

'What do you mean "you'll be on your way"? Where are you going?'

'To *Defiance*. To Craig's office,' he replied.

'Oh hell! When will you be back?'

'I don't know. He wouldn't say what it was about.'

'It's not fair. You've just got home, and now this . . .'

He poured them some coffee and began to eat fast. He would have to change into uniform if he was going to the naval base.

'Ring me, will you? When you know what he wants?'

'Sure. But I'm bound to be back by lunchtime.'

* * *

HMS Defiance was a building of concrete and brick. On the first floor Tinker pushed his security pass into a turnstile which let him into the administrative sector. The ground floor was packed with workshops; *Defiance* was primarily the maintainance base for the Squadron. As its

Captain, Norman Craig described himself as 'working from an office over a garage'.

'Oh, well done. You made it,' Craig remarked, ushering Tinker to the small sofa, while looking at his watch. 'Sorry I was cryptic on the blower, but this one really is a stinker. Bloody Sovs. Let me get you a coffee. NATO standard?'

'No sugar, thanks.'

'I've boiled the kettle. Shan't be a mo.'

Craig slipped into the clerk's office next door. None of the staff was in on Saturday. He returned, carrying the mugs.

'Now . . .' he began, dark eyes concentrating on Andrew. 'You're an old chum of Phil Hitchens, aren't you?'

Tinker nodded.

'You know his wife Sara?'

'Well, yes. We've been friends a long time. Their boy's my godson.'

'Of course. Well, she's in a spot of trouble.'

'Really?'

'In fact, I think we all are.'

Andrew frowned, wishing Craig would get to the point.

'Yesterday evening, I had a visitor. Chap from London. Security. Actually wore a trenchcoat, would you believe! There's someone they've been keeping an eye on, apparently. Claims to be Swedish, but they've discovered he's about as Scandinavian as Josef Stalin!

'Anyway, this man lives in London but does business in the West Country. That's *his* story, anyway. MI5 heard about him from the local Special Branch who'd been called in by our own security staff here at Devonport. They'd been tipped off by a young sailor, who met this so-called Swede in a pub and wasn't too happy about the sort of questions he was asking. The sailor's a marine engineer, on nuclear propulsion. He's a good lad. Did the right thing in reporting it.

'The Branch boys started tailing the man. On Wednesday night, something happened which made them call in MI5. They showed the London men a photo, but they had nothing on him.

'Then, by pure chance, MI5 got a tip-off in London. A couple of foreigners had done a bunk from their home in the middle of Wednesday night. They showed our local boys' picture to the neighbours and it all fell into place. They instantly reckoned the Swede was an illegal, a Russian undercover agent. Ten out of ten for sharp thinking!

'The fellow had quite a circle of naval friends in pubs around Plymouth, but it seems he was still building up confidence and hadn't asked too many clever questions yet.

'Anyway . . . , to cut a long story short – that incident on Wednesday. The watchers saw the Swede meet a woman in a kebab house in Plymouth. They seemed to know each other *intimately*. Lots of holding hands and whispering. But the woman got upset, and left without finishing her meal. One of the watchers followed her home. Can you guess who she was?'

Andrew's frown deepened.

'You don't mean Sara Hitchens?'

'The very same.'

'Bloody hell!'

'Exactly. And the reason MI5 decided to call on me yesterday is that when they raided the house in London they found the couple had left some bits and pieces behind. Including some of the little knick-knacks you get given free when you work for the KGB! The Swede *was* a Russian spy. Confirmed.'

'Shit!'

'Exactly. And we're in it. Up to our necks!'

'So, you're saying Sara was having an affair with a Soviet spy?'

'Correct. Not the first little dalliance, by all accounts. There'd been gossip about her among some of the wives, so I'm told.'

Andrew felt the back of his neck prickle, uncomfortably aware that the gossip was well-founded.

'But Sara can't know anything important,' he stated briskly. 'What would a KGB man hope to get from her?'

'Apart from a good time, you mean?'

'Yes, well . . . it doesn't quite make sense, does it?'

'I put the same point to MI5. They seem to think the man had only just started spying. Still feeling his way around, as it were, seizing any opportunity that presented itself. And one day, there was Sara. Do you know what she used to do when her old man was off on patrol? She used to go on her own to restaurants and pubs, sit at a table all by herself, and see who she could pick up.'

'I don't believe it!'

Poor Sara. Still desperate for affection, Andrew thought.

'It's true. She admitted it. Told MI5 that was the way she'd met the Russian. Said it usually worked a treat. Navy town – full of presentable young men, all a bit lonely, looking for female company . . .'

'What's happened? Has she been arrested?'

'No. Adultery's not a criminal offence. She denies utterly that she ever said anything to her lover. Anything secret, that is. There's nothing to charge her with.'

'But if she didn't know anything of any importance, and denies telling him anything anyway, why are you so concerned? Why . . .'

'Why have I dragged you in here on a Saturday morning? Quite simply because I'm far from sure that Sara told MI5 the truth. Normally, I'd agree, she wouldn't be much use to a spy, but in the last few days something may have happened to change that.'

'What do you mean?'

'She told the police that Philip had found out about her affairs and they'd had one hell of a fight.'

'Oh God!'

'In a situation like that, things get said. Things you wouldn't normally let on about, but in the heat of the moment . . .'

'When did you say you heard about this?'

'Yesterday.'

'Phil was at sea by then, so he wouldn't have known that the boyfriend was a spy?'

'Presumably not, since Sara claims she was convinced the man was a Swede.'

'So, you're worried that in the middle of a domestic

row he might have blurted out some state secret that she could later have passed to the Russians? Bit unlikely, isn't it, sir?'

'It's the timing that matters. The date when the row happened. As far as I can work out it must have been just after his ops briefing at Northwood.'

'But that sort of detail, he'd never bring it up in a screaming match with his wife!'

'It would only need *one* detail, Andrew . . .'

'Like?'

'Like exactly where he was going . . .'

The penny began to drop.

'They had something special on?'

'Precisely. *Truculent* wasn't just taking part in Exercise Ocean Guardian.'

'Can you say what it was?'

'I don't even know, Andrew. Just that it wasn't an ordinary mission.'

'I see . . . So, you want me to try to assess the likelihood of his having given something away? Because I know them both. Is that it?'

'I want you to go and see her. She may open up more to you than she did with the police.'

'Now, wait a minute . . .' Tinker cut in. 'In what capacity? Am I the Navy, or a friend?'

'Both. A special ambassador chosen because of your personal links with the Hitchens family,' Craig sounded unfortunately pompous. 'You're concerned for her welfare, and so is the Navy. And concerned for Philip, of course.'

The last point was the key consideration for Andrew. He pictured himself at the start of a two-month patrol, and wondered how he would cope if his own marriage had disintegrated days before he'd sailed.

CHAPTER TWO

He went home to change first, not wanting to look conspicuous by arriving at Sara's house in uniform.

Patsy was so consumed with curiosity he felt compelled to tell her something, but he'd been sworn to secrecy on the security angle.

'Look's like Sara's been a naughty girl. Picking up men in pubs. Philip found out, and did his nut,' he explained with forced levity.

'Doesn't surprise me,' she answered coolly.

'No? You knew about it?' He hoped the anxiety wasn't noticeable in his voice.

'The odd rumour, nothing more. Sara doesn't socialize much with other Navy wives; she's never come to terms with being wedded to one of you lot. And Philip's the last sort of man she should've married,' Patsy snorted.

'That's true.'

'He's an emotional cripple. Probably wears his uniform in bed!'

'Come on! He's not that bad.'

How often had he heard himself defending Philip?

'You watch out for Sara this afternoon. There's many a time she'd have got *you* into bed, given half the chance.'

'Rubbish!'

He thanked God she'd never guessed. It had happened just once – a mistake which had been safely buried until now.

'What does Norman Craig want you to do about it, anyway?'

'To find out what sort of mental state Philip was in when he left home. To make sure he's safe.'

'And a bit of marriage guidance, too?'

'Maybe. Might make a career of it when I leave the service,' he joked as he set off.

★ ★ ★

35

It was fifteen minutes' drive to where the Hitchens had their home, close by the river Yealm. The old, grey, limestone parsonage was a far larger house than they needed, but Sara had been determined they should buy it. With its large open fireplaces and an apple orchard, it was the English country home she'd never had as a child – the one she'd longed for as she accompanied her diplomat father from one strange place to another.

The village was pretty, with a river frontage and boats lying in the mud at low tide. The house was on the outskirts, and a little isolated. The Hitchens had few friends in the village; Sara was not good at the small talk of neighbourliness.

As he turned into her drive Andrew felt nervous, unsure how she would react to his visit. It was two years before that they'd had the briefest of affairs.

Philip had been at sea, and he at home on leave, just like now. Sara had rung him up one day when Patsy was at school and begged him to meet her, at a remote spot on the moors where they wouldn't be seen.

He was flattered and intrigued. Sara spelt danger, and it had excited him. Under normal circumstances, commonsense would have prevailed and he'd have said 'no', but her call had coincided with a blip in his own relationship with Patsy, a silly argument over money. She'd been furious with him because he'd bought a new car, instead of re-equipping their tatty kitchen. She'd hardly spoken to him for days.

Andrew had kept that rendezvous with Sara on the moors. Two days later they met again, on a warm afternoon in an Indian summer, and made love in the heather.

Sara was watching from a window as his car entered the drive.

'Andrew!' she greeted, as she opened the door. 'Surprise, surprise!'

Her pale lips smiled but her eyes were tense and suspicious.

'I was just passing . . .'

'No, you weren't! You end up in the river if you "just pass",' she retorted.

Suddenly she embraced him, and buried her face in his shoulder.

'I'm awfully glad you came,' she whispered. Her breath smelled of wine.

Then, just as suddenly, she broke away again and led him to the living room, where a south-facing French window looked across the orchard to the river.

'Why are you here? Is it official, this call? You know what's happened?'

'Yes. I'm sorry. It sounds a mess. Craig told me.'

'And he sent *you*?' She raised one eyebrow cynically. 'How thoughtful of him.'

'He knows I'm a friend. Of both of you,' Andrew hedged. 'He thought I might help. He's very concerned.'

She studied him for a moment and her waif-like face softened. Her thin mouth twisted mischievously.

'It's all your fault, you know. If you hadn't taken fright and we'd stayed lovers, I wouldn't have bothered with other men!'

'I'm not sure how to take that!'

'As a compliment, you oaf! Or a joke. I have to joke about it now and then. Otherwise, I just cry.'

Her face crumpled and she turned away.

She ran her fingers through her straight, chestnut hair.

'What're they saying about me?' she asked, turning to face him. 'Be honest!'

'I don't know who you mean by "they",' Andrew hedged again.

'Them. The Navy.'

'Well, if a sailor's wife runs around with other men while her old man's at sea – it's, er . . . it's frowned upon.'

She laughed at his restraint.

'And when one of the woman's lovers turns out to be a Russian spy,' she said, her voice rising in hysteria, 'then I guess the Navy shits itself!'

'You can say that again!'

'But . . . I didn't *know* he was a spy!'

She dropped onto a sofa and clamped her arms round her stomach as if it hurt her. She shook her head, her hazel eyes widening with disbelief.

'I can't believe all this.'

She reached for a packet of cigarettes.

'Inside, I don't feel I've done anything wrong. I can't accept that it's all *my* fault.'

She drew at the smoke as if it was oxygen, and coughed.

'Look, there's a bottle over there. Pour a glass and fill mine, would you?'

He handed her the drink and sank into a chair opposite.

'Why *did* Craig send you?'

'To try to find out exactly what's happened, I suppose.'

'*Why* it's happened. That's the question. Isn't anyone asking that? Some dreadful man from London – MI5 or something – came here reeking of cheap aftershave and B.O. Never even wondered *how* people get into this sort of mess. Don't *any* of you realize what it's like to have to share a husband with the fucking Navy?'

'Come on, Sara!' Andrew snapped. 'You knew what Philip did for a living when you married him.'

'I was only nineteen, Andrew! I'd only left school the year before!'

They both looked down at their drinks. Sara shivered.

'Sorry, there's no fire . . . It's chilly enough for one. We were hoping to put in central heating next year. But it's so expensive . . .'

'Don't worry. I'm not cold.'

There was an awkward pause. Andrew eased forward to the edge of the chair. There was one question he wanted answered above all others.

'Does Philip know? That you and I . . .'

Her eyes softened. She was remembering, as he was, the warm wind that had rustled the bracken around them as they'd lain on the moors that afternoon two years ago.

'No. He doesn't know,' she answered eventually.

She looked down at her hands. Was she lying? Andrew couldn't tell.

'How much do *you* know?' she asked suddenly. 'They told you about Gunnar, obviously?'

'Craig didn't say a name. Just that the man claimed to be Swedish.'

'That was feeble. I knew from the start he wasn't.'

'You knew? How?'

'I spent three years in Stockholm as a child, remember? I told you – I must've done. I told you *everything*,' she grimaced. 'No wonder you went off me so fast!'

Andrew laughed, but only for a moment. Sara pulled a crumpled handkerchief from her sleeve and blew her nose. Her voice had sounded bitter.

'Gunnar said he came from Stockholm. But he only knew the tourist places. He stopped talking about it once I said I'd actually lived there.'

'So, where *did* you think he was from?'

'I don't know. It didn't really matter at the time. We all pretend things. *I* told him I was divorced.'

'But didn't it occur to you that his interest in you might not be *entirely* romantic? A man with a false identity, you with a husband in the Navy?'

'Not at first, no. It did later . . .'

'Oh? Why was that?'

'Well, as we got to know each other, we kind of peeled away the layers of deception. It was a game, really. I told him I knew he wasn't what he said he was, and he told me he knew I had a husband in the Navy.'

'Did you ask him how he knew?'

'Just said he could tell. Knew the type. I'm not unique, you know,' she rounded on him. 'Navy towns are full of unhappy wives.'

'And what did you tell him?' Andrew prodded. 'Did you say, for example, that Philip drove a nuclear submarine?'

'Well, yes, I did. It's not actually secret, you know,' she retorted. 'But after that, Gunnar kept asking about Philip's work. So I began to think he could be spying for somebody.'

'What did you tell him about Philip?'

'Nothing, Andrew! Nothing of any significance, anyhow,' she insisted, blowing a plume of smoke at him. 'I'm not stupid. At least, not in that way. Anyhow, I don't know anything about Philip's work, except that he spends six months of each year inside a black metal tube.'

'You *do* know things, Sara,' Andrew cautioned. 'Dates. When he goes away, when he comes back.'

'Anyone can stand on the Hoe and watch submarines go in and out of the dockyard.'

'But they can't tell one from another. They don't know if it's the same boat that goes out in the morning and comes back in the evening, or if it's two different boats.'

She shrugged and stubbed out the cigarette.

'But if you guessed he was some sort of spy, why didn't you tell someone? The police?'

She shook her head.

'How could I? What the hell would I have said? "Excuse me officer, but the man I'm having an affair with may be a Russian spy; could you investigate, but please don't tell my husband?" Don't be daft.'

She slipped off her shoes and pulled her knees up to her chin.

'I can see what you're thinking. And I don't blame you. You can't understand. You'll never be able to. But I'm going to try to explain it, just for my own sake.

'Being married to Philip – it's like doing something by halves. You know me; I always want everything, all at once, all the time,' she said ruefully. 'But Philip's only here half the year; when he is home, his thoughts are only half with me. I want him to pay *me* some attention!' she exploded. 'To do something with *me* that's exciting, or unpredictable. And when he doesn't, I find myself longing for him to go away again.

'And yet I do love him – sort of. He can't help the way he is, and he *is* reliable, honest. . . .

'But that's not enough. I'm left feeling so *empty*. And when Simon went away to boarding school, that was it. I couldn't cope with it any more. So I found a way. A way of staying married to Philip, keeping a home for Simon, and of filling the emptiness.

'There were . . . other men . . . after you, and before Gunnar. Most of them were nice, kind while it lasted, not interested in a long-term commitment. It was manageable, you see? Everything under control. Philip didn't know. I wasn't hurting anybody – except myself occasionally.

'So, you see, even though I had suspicions about Gunnar, I couldn't tell anybody. The whole thing would have come crashing down . . .'

'Which is exactly what's happened now,' Andrew said drily.

Sara took his words as a reproach. Her mouth turned down and her face hardened.

'But you can't accept it – the way I feel – because you've got a wife who *does* manage, who divides herself up, one bit for you when you're there, another for her job, and another for the children. Her life's like a time-share,' she concluded bitterly.

'Okay. Some women aren't cut out to be married to sailors,' he conceded. 'And you're one of them. But, for the moment, it's academic. You're in trouble; Philip's in trouble; the Navy's in trouble. So let's not think about the reasons why it's happened; let's just try and sort it out.'

She threw her head back, the sinews of her neck taut with despair.

'I've killed him, Andrew . . .' she whispered, eyes beginning to brim with tears.

He froze.

'If you'd seen his face . . .'

She clamped a hand over her mouth to prevent herself crying. Her bravado had suddenly evaporated.

'It was terrible when he found out. He went to pieces . . . I didn't know he could be like that . . . All that emotion – it'd been there all the time. And I never knew . . .'

'What d'you mean, you've killed him?' asked Andrew, shaken.

'Inside,' she sniffed, tears running down her face. She made no attempt to brush them away. 'He *trusted* me . . . ,' she whispered.

Andrew looked away awkwardly and ran his fingers through his hair. *He trusted me too*, he thought to himself.

Sara was a pitiful figure, her shoulders shaking with sobs. But it was Philip Andrew had most need to be

41

concerned about. He pulled a clean handkerchief from his pocket and passed it to her.

'There are some details . . . , things I need to know,' he coaxed. She dried her eyes and blew her nose.

'When did all this happen, exactly? By the time the security people got wind of things, you'd already had the bust-up with Philip and he'd gone to sea. Is that right?'

'Yes,' she sighed. 'Everything fell apart about a week ago.'

She wiped her remaining tears with her fingers, leaving streaks on her face.

'Philip found out first about another man, someone called Reg Terry. I'd got very close to Reg and let him come here at weekends sometimes, when Simon was home from school. Stupid of me. Last weekend Philip and Simon went shopping in Plymouth, and they just bumped into Reg. Simon greeted him like a long-lost friend, and suddenly Philip began to click. Next day, he started asking questions. He just went on and on, until I got so angry I just told him everything and said it was all his fault.'

'You told him *everything*?'

'Almost everything,' she corrected herself, carefully.

Andrew's unease grew.

'What exactly did you tell him about Gunnar?'

'I told him my present lover was a Russian spy,' she whispered, stroking back some hair that had stuck to her moist cheek.

It had been at that point that Philip's temper had finally snapped.

He'd lashed blindly at her, punching her with his fists. The high-necked pullover she now wore concealed several purple and yellow bruises.

'For God's sake! You told him that? What did he say?'

'He went berserk. Knocked me round the bedroom. Then he stopped. For a time he didn't say anything. Just stared out of the window. Then he told me to try to remember everything I'd ever said to Gunnar about him, about the Navy, about our family. As I told you before, there wasn't much . . .'

Her voice tailed away.

Suddenly an alarming question occurred to Andrew. If Philip knew about the spy, why hadn't he said anything to the police, or to Captain Craig at the submarine base?

'Did Philip say anything to you about going to the police?'

'No. He didn't want anyone to know about *my shame*, as he called it. Kept asking me which of our friends knew. I said I hadn't told anyone. That was true.'

'But did he say he was going to do something about Gunnar? There must've been something. He wouldn't have left it. Not if he really believed Gunnar was a spy.'

Andrew put down his glass and leaned forward, hands clasped, elbows on his knees. Sara was holding back further tears. Her lip trembled. She was scared.

'I don't know what he was going to do. He made me swear I'd end it with Gunnar. That's what I was doing when the police saw us in the restaurant. But Philip hardly spoke to me again. He behaved like a robot. And on Wednesday morning he went to the boat.'

'Did he say anything to you about the patrol he was going on?'

'Nothing. He never did.'

'No mention of where he was going?'

'Heavens, no!'

Inwardly Andrew sighed with relief. Craig's prime security worry seemed to be unfounded.

'Why do you ask? Where *is* he going?'

Her voice sounded alarmed.

'I don't know,' he answered stonily.

She stared into his eyes, trying to read his thoughts.

He stared back, trying to imagine the hell Philip must've gone through, discovering what sort of wife Sara had been to him.

'He *had* decided to do something about Gunnar.'

Her voice cut through the silence that had descended on the room.

'What d'you mean?'

'I don't know, exactly.'

She rubbed her forehead, trying to order her thoughts.

'When he left, it was as if he'd taken some monumental

decision. He looked . . . ,' she fumbled for the words, 'grim, but in some way – satisfied. It's the only way I can describe it.'

'I'm not with you. What do you mean?'

'As if he'd decided on some sort of revenge, or thought of some way of getting even with Gunnar, or the KGB or whoever sent him here.'

'What sort of revenge?'

'I don't know. He'll find a way. Philip hates Russians, you know. He'll do something. I don't know what. Fire a missile at Moscow? Is that possible?'

She'd meant it as irony, but started when she saw the shock on Andrew's face.

'He couldn't! It's the wrong sort of boat, isn't it?' she gasped. 'What *could* he do to them, Andrew?'

'I shudder to think.'

Two minutes later Andrew drove away, his mind in turmoil. He hardly noticed the shabby Ford Escort parked in a gateway fifty yards up the road from the Hitchens' home.

Behind the wheel a dark-haired man in his twenties appeared to be taking a nap.

Andrew put his foot down and headed for the naval base. Philip Hitchens had to be got off the *Truculent*, and fast.

* * *

HMS Truculent was in her element. By Saturday afternoon her huge black hull was sliding silently through dark waters west of the Hebrides where the Atlantic is over two thousand metres deep.

Cruising north at eighteen knots, *Truculent* had stayed a hundred metres down for nearly twenty-four hours. Above and below, water layers of different temperature created acoustic barriers. The submarine moved in a 'shadow zone' where the risk of being detected by surface ships was minimal. That depth was also good for detecting other submarines. With her sensitive towed sonar restored to working order, *Truculent* could hear other boats over a hundred miles away if conditions were right.

The executive officer, Lieutenant Commander Tim Pike, had completed his rounds, looking for gripes to deal with before they became a problem or a danger. There'd been few. *Truculent* was a well-run submarine.

The control room watches lasted six hours, the tactics officer (TASO) and the navigator (NO) alternating as watch leaders.

Pike had little to do at that stage of the patrol, with the sea around them so deep and so empty.

He came into the zone for promotion in a month and was using his spare time for studying. He'd already passed the course to command a submarine, aptly named 'The Perisher'; if you fail it you have to leave the Submarine Service for good.

He'd commanded a diesel sub for two years after that, but was now lining himself up to take charge of an SSN.

'Day-dreaming again, Tim?'

The weapon engineer, Lieutenant Commander Paul Spriggs, nudged his arm.

'Yeah. Wondering what's in store for us.'

'This patrol, you mean? The captain's special orders. Hasn't he briefed you yet?'

'Nope. Not yet. I expect he will soon.'

'On the other hand . . .'

'He may not.'

'Exactly. Something's up with him. You've noticed how preoccupied he is. Hardly speaks at meals. Only smiles at my jokes out of politeness.'

'We all do that, Paul.'

'Oh, really? How extremely depressing.'

His chubby face looked genuinely perplexed. He pushed back the dark hair that fell across his forehead.

'But you're right,' Pike agreed. 'He doesn't seem to be with us on this trip. I might try to draw him out later. We've got a communications slot coming up in fifteen minutes. Perhaps he'll get a "family-gram" that'll cheer him up.'

'Be safer to write him one yourself!'

Tim Pike pulled a long face and crossed the cramped

control room to the navigation table. Three paces and he was there.

'Where are we, Nick?' he asked the navigator who was duty watch leader.

'Here, to be exact.'

The young lieutenant pointed to a cross on the continuous pencil line he'd drawn on the chart.

'The SINS puts us northeast of Rockall and west of the Vidal Bank. In about an hour we should alter course to zero-four-zero to keep us in the deep water east of Rosemary Bank.'

'We'll need a little dog-leg for a communications slot before that. Almost due east? What do you think?'

The navigator pulled out a chart with a different scale, showing their position in relation to the British Isles. To listen to the signals from CINCFLEET at Northwood, they used a long wire antenna that floated just below the surface so as not to reveal themselves to watching radar. To receive signals they had to align the antenna by pointing it towards the transmitter in the north of England.

'Almost exactly one-one-zero. Done this before, sir?'

'Once or twice. I expect you'd like an Omega fix, too?'

'Certainly would. What's the time of the comms slot?'

'18:00 to 18:30. We'll be at four knots and sixty metres.'

'Right.'

Cavendish plotted the details. The wire would also pick up low-frequency signals from Omega coastal navigation beacons. He'd get a position fix to within a mile, enough to confirm the inertial navigation system hadn't drifted. For a more accurate fix they'd need to poke a periscope or satellite receiver above the water, and risk revealing their presence.

Pike slipped out of the control room and rapped gently on the door frame of the captain's cabin. A curtain hung in the doorway, and Pike heard a hurried scuffling behind it.

'Yes?'

He pushed aside the curtain. Commander Hitchens was at his desk.

'Good evening, sir. We're proceeding as planned in

deep water at eighteen knots. We have a broadcast we're scheduled to monitor in about thirty minutes. With your permission, sir, I'd like to reduce speed to four knots, bring her up to sixty metres and deploy the floating wire.'

'Any other submarine activity?'

'Nothing at all, sir. We'll check the surface picture before we deploy the wire.'

'Very good. Carry on, Tim.'

'Er, one other thing, sir . . .'

'Yes, what is it?'

'I was wondering if sometime this evening might be an appropriate moment to discuss our mission profile.'

Hitchens fixed Pike with his unnervingly blue eyes.

'Sorry. Not yet. I'll brief when the time's right.

'From Wednesday we're dropping out of the exercise. Special op. I'll tell *you* that much, but it's not for general knowledge yet. This one really is very sensitive. You'll have to trust me.'

'Oh. Right. Okay then, sir; I'll carry on if I may.'

'Yes, please. And make the pipe to the ship's company, will you?'

'I will, sir.'

Pike returned thoughtfully to the control room. There was nothing he could put his finger on, but something wasn't right with his captain.

Philip closed his eyes and held his breath.

Damn it! Pike's request had caught him by surprise. He should've been ready for him, and he wasn't.

He ran through their brief conversation. It had been okay. He'd handled it. But he had to be prepared for next time, have an answer for their questions.

He expelled the air from his lungs.

Philip needed the men under his command. He was driving a nuclear-powered, hunter-killer submarine – one of the most deadly weapons-systems in the world. Those bastard Soviets would soon be finding out just how deadly, he told himself. But he couldn't operate it on his own. Co-operation and obedience from men like Pike and Spriggs would be vital if his mission was to succeed.

47

Philip knew what he had to do. That much was clear. How to manage it, however, was a different matter. There was still time to think the details through. Until Wednesday he'd follow the exercise brief. After that, he'd be his own master.

The loudspeaker clicked. Pike's voice boomed forth authoritatively.

The 'pipe' was heard on loudspeakers throughout the submarine. The broadcast to update the crew was made at least twice a day, a communication essential to team spirit on board.

The first lieutenant spoke for two minutes, telling the 130 men on board of the day's sonar contacts. They'd included a school of whales.

He talked of the upcoming communications slot, knowing some of the crew would be expecting the forty-word 'family-grams' that kept them in touch with their homes. He ended by reading the menu for the evening meal.

The next pipe – that'd be the time, Philip decided. Start to prepare them for what was to come. Little by little. Step by step.

His eyes strayed to the photograph he'd doggedly kept on his desk, to preserve his mask of normality.

He looked at her image and his guts turned inside out again. He closed his eyes tightly. Would he ever be able to look at Sara's picture without wanting to kill her?

She'd been everything he'd dreamed of when they'd met fifteen years earlier. He'd been serving on a *Swiftsure* class submarine at the time, circling the globe as part of a military sales drive. They'd gone ashore in Hong Kong, to a reception at the British High Commission. Their host had been accompanied by his stunningly pretty daughter – Sara. He'd fallen in love with her instantly.

Sara had glowed that evening; as they circulated socially, her eyes reached across the room to him like a lighthouse beam. Excitement had almost choked him. Until then, apart from brief relationships, the only woman in Philip's life had been his own straitlaced mother. Sara was vivacious, sensual and provocative; if his mother had ever had such qualities, she'd successfully repressed them after

48

the trauma of her husband's disappearance. In Hong Kong he sensed he'd finally met a woman with the power to cut through his shell of inhibition, and free him from the dour restraint of his upbringing.

His mother had tried to prevent their marriage. Nineteen was far too young for a girl to marry, she'd declared. He'd ignored her, terrified that if he didn't bind Sara to him quickly he'd lose her to someone else.

Now he'd lost her anyway.

They'd been immensely happy together for their first two years. He'd had a shore-based job in Scotland, and the sense of personal liberation he'd hoped for became a reality.

Then he'd been given a commission at sea. Sara had been devastated by the separation and had applied intense emotional pressure on him to change his job. Philip had retreated into his shell, as he had learned to do as a youth when pressured by his mother.

Her face smiled at him from the frame. Deceptive, cruelly deceptive. Laughing eyes. Laughing at him? Mocking him?

In the control room, Pike hung the microphone back on its hook and bowed theatrically to the navigator.

'All yours, Pilot!'

Cavendish raised an eyebrow at the mock courtesy, then turned to the helm.

'Ten up, planesman. Keep sixty metres. Revolutions for four knots.'

The rating at the controls pulled back on the controlstick and watched the gauge. The deck began to tilt as the hydroplanes lifted the nose of the submarine. Pike grasped one of the overhead cable-ducts to steady himself.

'Sound room. I want a check for surface contacts!' Cavendish called.

'*Aye, aye, sir!*'

HMS Truculent came up fast from the depths, passing through the thermocline which had refracted their faint sound downwards, keeping them hidden from listeners on the surface. Her speed dropped from eighteen knots to four, at which it was safe to trail the wire antenna without breaking it.

'Lev:l at sixty metres, sir,' the helmsman called.

'Deploy the wire.'

On the outside of the fin a small aperture appeared, and the VLF antenna began to unreel. Black plastic strips trailed from the wire to disguise it as seaweed.

In the sonar compartment the tattooed hands of the ratings tuned their acoustic processors to the new sounds of surface ships, or 'skimmers', as they were known.

Sensors outside the hull analysed water temperature and salinity and fed the data into a computer which predicted the refracted paths that the sounds would follow through the water.

'Cavitation on port bow, chief!' shouted one of the junior sonar ratings. Chief Petty Officer Hicks looked over his shoulder at the VDU, and confirmed it.

On the green 'waterfall' display, low frequency 'spikes' of sound detected by the bow sonar showed as overlapping vertical stripes. Hicks counted them.

'Two shafts. Six blades. That's *Illustrious*,' he announced with confidence. The last intelligence report had told them the British aircraft carrier was in the area.

'Range and bearing?'

The rating keyed in additional data from the towed array. Bearings from the two sonars were triangulated by computer.

'Range, 32.4 miles, bearing 039, Chief.'

The CPO pressed a button which transferred the data to the Action Information panel in the control room. There the carrier appeared on the tactical display as a triangle – a friendly target.

'*What about her escorts?*' demanded the officer-of-the-watch through the intercom.

Eyes scanned the screens and ears strained at headphones.

'Nothing else registered, sir,' came the eventual reply from the CPO.

Sound in water seldom travels in straight lines. *HMS Illustrious* had at least two frigates keeping her company, but *Truculent* couldn't hear them. The sound waves from the warships curved downwards away from the surface, then curved up again many miles distant, to a so-called 'convergence zone'. *Truculent* was in just such a zone for the carrier's noise signature to reach her, but not yet in one for the frigates.

Hicks stood up, desperate to stretch his legs. He stepped into the control room, leaving the sonar ratings to plot the remaining contacts – distant trawlers fishing the edge of the continental shelf around Scotland.

He crossed to the Action Information plot, and yawned as he watched it begin to fill with contacts from the sound room.

'Keeping you up, are we, Hicks?' Pike quipped.

'Off watch in an hour, sir. Boring day! Once we'd finally sorted out the 2026, there's been sod-all to do.'

'Did you report that to the captain? He wanted to know.'

'Yes, sir. Have no fear.'

Pike looked at his watch. Time for the broadcast. He stepped into the communications office as Cavendish ordered the final manœuvre to align the boat to receive signals.

'Planesman, steer one-one-zero, revolutions for four knots!'

At three sites inside Britain, enormous Very Low Frequency transmitter arrays, masquerading as civilian wireless stations, broadcast a constant stream of information for submerged submarines. Weather and intelligence reports are transmitted as routine, on an hourly cycle, backed up at fixed times with specific messages for individual submarines.

The communications room was tightly controlled. Only those with top security clearance could enter the tiny cabin next to the control room. From floor to ceiling, racks of equipment left little space for the signals officer and radio operator.

The young, black-haired sub-lieutenant in charge ran his own plastic security card through a slot on the cipher machine, then punched out a personal code number on a numeric key-pad. Nearly all signals traffic was in code, but the laborious task of enciphering and deciphering was done electronically.

The teleprinter began to chatter. The radio operator leaned over to check that the transmission wasn't garbled.

'Faroes, force ten,' he read. 'Grey-Funnel Line'll be chuckin' up!'

'You can feel it down here,' Pike pointed out as the submarine heaved gently with the surface swell sixty metres above them.

'Glad you volunteered for submarines?' Sub-Lieutenant Hugo Smallbone grinned, knowing full well the torrent of complaint his remark would release.

'Didn't fuckin' volunteer for *submarines*! Told to come here, wasn't I? The one soddin' boat in the Navy that's not supposed to communicate, and I get the job of radio operator!'

'At least you're not chucking up!'

'Prefer that to bein' down here. The money's what keeps me in this branch.'

The sub-lieutenant smiled patronizingly. He stood up to tear the first sheet from the printer.

```
ROUTINE 191800Z OCT
INT SITREP AT 1730Z
RO6 F229 F84 59.20N 008.50W
S 37 W HEBRIDES
```

'So that's where they think we are,' commented Smallbone at the reference to S 37 which was *HMS Truculent*.

R06 was *Illustrious*, the F numbers her frigate escorts. The position given was timed for half an hour earlier.

A string of chart references followed. They marked the last known positions of two Soviet *Victor* class nuclear attack submarines, and three AGIs – Soviet intelligence-gathering trawlers.

The teleprinter bell rang twice.

'Ah! Something for us,' remarked Pike.

He peered more closely at the dot matrix print tapping out across the page.

IMMEDIATE. S 37. SECRET. COMMANDING OFFI-

CER'S EYES ONLY.
CONFIRM RECEIPT BY SSIX AT 2000Z. FOSM.
INSERT COMMANDERS KEYCARD FOR MESSAGE.

'Here you are, Bennett. Got some work for you. Satcom at twenty hundred.'

'P'rhaps they've found me another job . . .'

'No chance!'

The sub-lieutenant tore the sheet from the teleprinter, placed the top copy on a clipboard and took the carbon. As he left the wireless room he added, 'Look smart. I'm getting the captain.'

'A satcom will *not* be popular,' Pike frowned. 'We're just about in range of the "*Bears*" here.'

'*Bear*' was NATO's code name for the big Soviet *TU–95* long-range maritime reconnaissance bombers which patrol the Norwegian Sea to track NATO warships. With Exercise Ocean Guardian underway, they'd be mounting extra missions. Raising a satcom mast above the surface could get *Truculent* spotted by the *Bear*'s radar.

Hugo Smallbone was in awe of Commander Hitchens. A rather immature twenty-one-year-old, he found almost anyone over the age of thirty intimidating. He nearly collided with Hitchens as the captain hurried from his cabin.

'That for me?' Hitchens asked, indicating the signal in Hugo's hand.

'Sir. It's just come in.'

He handed it over and watched Hitchens' face, expecting annoyance. But the expression in Hitchens' eyes was one he'd never seen there before. Panic.

'Thank you, Hugo,' Hitchens whispered, controlling himself quickly. Then he spun on his heel and went back into his cabin. 'Be right with you,' he muttered over his shoulder.

The sub-lieutenant hovered in the corridor. He could hear the soft clicks of the combination lock on the captain's safe, as Hitchens opened it to collect his security card.

'Still here?' Hitchens remarked, surprised to find Hugo hadn't moved.

'Let's get on with it,' he continued briskly, leading the way to the wireless room. 'Bloody nuisance, this need to transmit. Last thing we want.'

'That's what the first lieutenant said, sir . . .'

'What? You've told him about this signal? What the hell do you mean by it?'

'He was in the wireless room, sir . . .'

Hitchens thrust the sheet of signal paper under Smallbone's nose.

'Can't you read, boy? COMMANDING OFFICER'S EYES ONLY. Don't you know what that means? No one's to know about this signal except me!'

'Awfully sorry, sir . . .'

'You'd better watch your step, son.'

Smallbone flushed purple. He felt hurt and indignant. The captain was talking nonsense. The confidentiality applied to the message they had yet to decode, not to the preamble requesting confirmation of receipt.

In the wireless room, Hitchens slid his keycard into the deciphering machine, then tapped out his personal code on the numeric key-pad.

'I'd like you all outside,' he ordered as the teleprinter began its work.

Pike returned to the control room. Able Seaman Bennett glanced at the sub-lieutenant as they moved to the passageway; sensing the thunderous atmosphere, he said nothing.

The printer stopped. Philip ripped off the paper, including the self-carbonizing second sheet. He folded the pages into a small square that fitted his trouser pocket and pushed past the radio operators, heading back to his cabin.

'Whew!'

Hugo Smallbone spun back into the wireless room, before the control room watch could notice his beetroot face.

The teleprinter was chattering again. Messages for crew members. He busied himself with the intelligence reports.

When he calmed down he'd take them to the watchkeeper, so the charts could be updated.

Philip placed the signal on his desk.

COMMANDER HITCHENS.
DUE YOUR UNFORTUNATE DOMESTIC SITUATION, IMPERATIVE YOU TRANSFER TO SHORE. BRIEFING TEMPORARY REPLACEMENT COMMANDER TO CONTINUE
TRUCULENT'S PATROL.
SEA KING WILL RENDEZVOUS WITH YOU AT 1600Z. SUNDAY 20TH. POSITION N58.50 W06.30.
PLSE CONFIRM BY SSIX 2000Z TODAY.
FLAG OFFICER SUBMARINES.

They knew, despite Sara's promise to tell no one. The bitch! She'd betrayed him again!

What had she told them? He re-read the signal.

'Unfortunate domestic situation'. They weren't giving much away back at Northwood.

Had she told them about the Soviets or just the personal bits? In either case they all knew the worst part, knew how she'd humiliated him.

But why? Had she sensed what he intended to do? Were they trying to stop him?

Who would she have spoken to? Craig probably. There was no one else she knew. Craig would have passed it up the line to CINCFLEET.

The questions echoed in his head like prayers in a cathedral. There was one which came back from the recesses of his mind where he'd banished it. Why, *why* had she done what she'd done? What was it he'd failed to give her that she needed?

Lonely. She'd told him she felt lonely . . .

That wasn't enough. Other men's wives were lonely, but they didn't parade themselves like whores in public places? Didn't soil their bodies with other men's – stuff.

The trembling started again. An uncontrollable shaking that engulfed him whenever his mind re-ran those desperate shouting-matches with Sara, those moments of awful revelation.

He'd raged at her and she'd fought back with a taunt – the name of a man she claimed had been the first of her lovers. Someone he'd known closely for twenty years. A name that would hurt him more deeply than any other.

He'd laughed at her – called her a liar.

Andrew her lover? Not possible. They'd trained together, served together on their first commission as sub-lieutenants, stayed friends ever since. Andrew was Simon's godfather, for heaven's sake! The idea was ludicrous. Wasn't it?

There'd been times in the past week when Philip had wept like a child. One moment he longed for someone to confide in, the next that no one should ever know.

He stood up angrily now. He had to snap out of it, put those nagging questions out of his mind, concentrate on the matter in hand.

The signal – he had to respond to it.

Tim Pike gave orders for the VLF antenna to be recovered into the fin. Their time-slot for monitoring the broadcast was over.

'Steer course zero-two-five. Ten down, keep two-hundred metres,' Cavendish instructed. 'Keep revolutions for ten knots. Increase to eighteen when the antenna's wound in.'

That could take half-an-hour.

A leading seaman was doing duty at the chart table. Two strides and Pike stood beside him. Two strides could get you anywhere in the control room.

'Have you plotted the data from the int. brief?' Pike asked.

'Yessir. The closest *Victor* is here, sir.'

He pointed to a box drawn some seventy miles south of them.

'He'll be listening for the *Polaris* boats coming out of Faslane. Then there's another *Victor* 'bout four hundred miles northeast. On the other side of the Faroes-Shetland gap. A couple of AGIs fifty and seventy-five miles away, and that's about it.'

'I see. So we're well out of range of their radar. Aircraft

are the worry. And we don't know where *they* are. My guess is they'll be keeping track of the skimmers. The nearest to us is *Illustrious*, isn't it?'

''Sright, sir. Just about here.'

He pointed to a circle near the Faroes.

'He'll be down to ten knots with the gale up there,' Pike commented, checking the weather report. 'We'll start catching him up if we don't watch it.'

'He's still miles away, sir.'

'Yes, but I'm thinking of the Bears. They'll be searching a good hundred miles all round *Illustrious*, so we'll need to keep our distance. I'm going to slow down a bit.'

He spun on his heel to face the helm and found himself face to face with Cavendish.

'Nick, I'm worried about Bears . . .'

He explained the problem. The navigator nodded.

'Keep revolutions for ten knots!' he instructed.

'Why are we so slow?' Philip had entered the control room, his face betraying no sign of his private agony.

Pike took him to the chart table to explain his plan.

'I've been thinking about the satcom, sir. In an hour we'll be here.' He prodded the chart with a finger, pointing out the positions of the Soviet boats and their own. 'Should be the best place to avoid being spotted when we transmit.'

'What's the sea state?'

'Force six. Gusting seven . . .'

'Going to be uncomfortable. Have to get the mast high to avoid the waves breaking over it.'

'Gets worse further north.'

'Mmmm. We'll give it a try, then. I'm about to draft the signal. Send the wireless officer to my cabin to collect it in ten minutes, will you? The message will be brief. Very brief. And Tim –'

Hitchens pulled his first lieutenant to one side, out of earshot of the others.

'That signal that came in – we've got new orders. Top secret. The most sensitive operation I've ever known. I can hardly believe what they're telling us to do.'

'Oh?'

'I'll brief you as soon as I can, but it may be a few days yet. I'll have to tell the crew something soon; thought I'd do it tomorrow, on the pipe. Have to keep it vague, but they'll need to know we're on a special op.'

'Will you be giving new course instructions, sir?'

'Stays the same for the moment. As planned. Different tactics, though. CINCFLEET says the Yanks are not to know what we're doing. Got to get across the SOSUS array without them hearing us.'

That wouldn't be easy; the hydrophones on the sea-bed between the Faroes and Shetlands were remarkably sensitive. The American controllers of SOSUS would be expecting them too, and would listen out for them.

'One other thing, Tim. Listening to the signals traffic – it'll be a bit irregular from now on. We'll be going fast, so no trailing of the wire. We'll use the satcom mast when possible, but because of the sensitivity of the stuff coming in, I can't have anyone but myself seeing the signals traffic from now on. I'll have to clear the wireless room when the mast's up. Commanding officer's eyes only, you see.'

'Is that really necessary, sir?'

'Yes, it bloody well is! I wouldn't have said so otherwise! I'll distribute whatever I can, of course. Intelligence, met., news reports. But it may not be much. That's all.'

Hitchens turned on his heel and left the control room.

Pike's jaw dropped.

'Bloody hell!' he breathed.

CHAPTER THREE

Sunday 20th October.

Sunday morning brought relief to the small group of media personnel on board the US aircraft carrier *Dwight D. Eisenhower*. The gale had subsided in the small hours; they'd had no idea a ship of 90,000 tons could roll so much. The three members of the television crew pooling pictures for the four American networks had been seasick to a man.

The *Eisenhower* was about three hundred miles south of Iceland, heading northeast, the flagship for the eighteen American warships taking part in Exercise Ocean Guardian.

The six members of the media pool had been flown onto the ship from Reykjavik the previous evening, smacking down onto the carrier deck in a Grumman Greyhound Carrier-Onboard-Delivery (COD) aircraft. For all the journalists it was their first visit to a big carrier and the COD flight the most hair-raising journey they'd ever made.

Tightly strapped in to rearward-facing seats, the passengers had felt genuine terror as the almost windowless twin-turboprop aircraft was buffeted by gale force winds and manoeuvred sharply to line up with the bucking deck. Even the aircrew had looked scared; they knew what they were supposed to do if the 'controlled crash' of a landing went bad and the plane slipped from the deck into the sea, but they also knew the chances of surviving such an accident were slim.

One of the journalists had thrown up as soon as his feet touched the carrier deck, and the usual briefing on arrival had been postponed.

Now the six were seated in the half-darkness of the '3

deck' briefing room, listening to the public information officer, Commander Polk. Vu-foils illustrated his talk.

'Good-day, gentlemen. Hope you're feeling okay now. I just want to tell you something about Exercise Ocean Guardian, so's you get the big picture. The starting point for the game is this: a huge world power, which has no name but whose national language is Russian, is assumed to have threatened NATO – Norway in particular. Enemy surface ships and submarines are breaking out from their bases on the Kola peninsular. We have to do something about it. We've got eleven NATO navies with 122 vessels taking part, which makes it the biggest we've ever done.

'Now, we have two jobs to do. The first is to ensure we can control the sea line of communication – SLOC for short. The SLOC is the route across the Atlantic along which American reinforcements would be shipped if Europe were threatened by the Warsaw Pact.

'Right now, warships from the US and from European countries including Spain and Portugal are securing the SLOC for convoys – down here.'

Commander Polk pointed rapidly from the Southwest Approaches down to Gibraltar, and westwards across the Atlantic.

'What you are on board today, gentlemen, is the flagship of Striking Fleet Atlantic. The task for this group is to take control of the sea and the air, right up to the Arctic Circle. The *Eisenhower* is now here, just south of Iceland. And we're headed here.'

The journalists' gaze was directed at the most northerly tip of Norway.

'What we're doing this year is something new. We're taking this little tub, 90,000 tons of her, right up to longitude 24 degrees East. Now that's in the Barents Sea, and the Soviets like to think of those waters as their own.

'Gentlemen, the second main purpose of this exercise is to show the Russians and ourselves that we have the power and the motivation to get right up into the Arctic and stop them, if they try it on.

'We've got three jobs to do; to back up land-based airpower with our own combat planes in order to defend north Norway; to locate and destroy enemy surface ships and submarines trying to take over the Norwegian Sea; and to get their missile subs before they can scoot under the ice, and nuke our families back home.'

The correspondent for the TV networks raised his hand to interrupt.

'Aren't you gonna be a pretty big target for the Soviets to hit, if you go right into the Barents?'

'Sure. That's why in past exercises we've not gone further north than Westfjord.'

His pointer landed on the Lofoten Islands some four hundred miles south of the northern tip of Norway.

'And if this exercise was for real, we sure as hell wouldn't put a carrier up there until the air and sea threat had been minimized.

He turned back to the vu-foil map.

'There are two main threats. Aircraft we look after ourselves; submarines – we have a British Royal Navy Anti-Submarine-Warfare force ahead of us, moving north in the Norwegian Sea. The *HMS Illustrious* Task Group provides the first ASW screen; we provide the second.'

He looked at his watch. They had to get moving. He could give them more later. First he had to brief them for the photo-opportunity which had presented itself that morning.

Admiral Vernon Kritz was proud of his ship, and proud of the role it played in containing the Communist menace. He was glad to have the media on board, so they could tell the world just how good his ship was. But this morning something extraordinary had happened that had made him doubly pleased.

Without their realizing it, he would deploy the media like one of his own weapon systems. What they would show on breakfast television back home was going to make those soft-heads on Capitol Hill choke on their granola. 'It's time to trust the Russians' was their cry. The hell it was!

The Admiral had summoned his PIO, while the media group were being given their breakfast, and told him what

61

the photo-reconnaissance aircraft had spotted at first light. When he'd seen the pictures of the Soviet freighter and its deck cargo, the commander had blasphemed in astonishment, then apologized hastily, conscious that the Admiral was a deeply religious man.

'Don't tell 'em exactly what they're gonna see,' Admiral Kritz had cautioned. 'Let 'em think they're getting the first close-ups *anyone's* seen. They'll get a kick outta that!'

All the print journalists and stills photographers were bundled aboard one SH-3 Sea King helicopter, the television team aboard another. The outing was described as a 'photo-opportunity' to get aerial shots of the *Eisenhower* and of a Soviet ship that was passing them in the opposite direction about ten miles away.

'It's a merchantman,' the PIO commander explained. 'But we treat all Soviet ships as hostile. Even if they're not warships, they're sure as hell spying on us.'

The helicopters took off and flew in tandem, one hundred yards apart.

The television correspondent wore an intercom headset so he could tell the pilot of his cameraman's requirements. Their first request was for a couple of circuits of the *Eisenhower*.

Satisfied they'd shot the carrier from every conceivable angle, the helicopter banked away to the south to fly low and fast towards the Soviet freighter's position, which had been radioed to the helicopter from a Hawkeye radar plane circling overhead.

'She's some sort of container ship, 'bout twenty thousand tons, called the *Rostov*. We believe she's headed for Cuba, but don't quote me . . .' the commander shouted above the grinding whine of the helicopter's machinery.

'How do you know that's where she's going?' the correspondent bellowed back.

The commander put his finger to his lips conspiratorially.

'Not allowed to tell!'

The cameraman had been sitting with his legs out of the open side-door while filming, a safety harness buckled round his chest attached at the other end to a hook on the helicopter's roof. But the wind was bitterly cold, and the crew-chief closed the door again for the transit to the next location.

There was little room inside. This was an anti-submarine machine, packed with sonar screens, control panels, and a massive winch for dunking the heavy sonar transducer in and out of the sea. There was a nauseating reek of hot oil.

'Okay . . . We got the Sov on the nose,' the pilot's voice drawled over the intercom. 'We're comin' up astern. We'll pass left of her then turn right across her bows, and come back the other side. Okay?'

'That'll be just great,' the correspondent answered, tapping his cameraman on the shoulder to be ready.

The crew chief slid back the big square door and the cold blast of air took their breath away. The tail of the Sea King sank as the pilot slowed to fifty knots. The grey-green sea surged a hundred feet below, the wind whipping white streams of spray from the wave caps.

To their left the black hull and cream superstructure of the freighter came into view. The correspondent pointed at it unnecessarily; the cameraman was already filming. On the funnel a red band bore the hammer and sickle. They'd need a close-up of that; the correspondent saw the cameraman's fingers press the zoom button. Good boy! He didn't need to be told.

Rusting red and orange containers were stacked on the outer edges of the deck, forming a corral with a space at the centre. There was something stored there. Fin-like objects, cocooned in pale fabric.

The helicopter reached the bows of the freighter and turned across them, giving the cameraman a long, continuous shot, showing the ship from 360 degrees.

'See that stuff in the middle there?' the correspondent's voice crackled in the throat microphone. 'Can't see what it is. Can you?'

'Look like wings to me,' the pilot answered.

'Like what?'

'Wings. Aircraft wings. Could be MiGs. With the rest of the planes in the boxes.'

'Shit man! We gotta get a closer look at that!'

'I can go round again if you want, but I can't get closer'n two hundred and fifty feet. Otherwise the big man has me against the wall for harassing the Russians!'

'Let's try it!'

The correspondent put his lips close to the cameraman's ear and told him to focus on the cargo in the middle of the deck. A raised thumb signalled he'd understood.

They repeated the circuit but came no closer; the shape of the cargo still could not be defined. The cameraman shook his head and shouted into the correspondent's ear, 'Get him over the top!'

The journalist nodded.

'Look, we got a problem,' he reasoned to the pilot. 'We have to be able to look right down on the deck from overhead . . .'

'No way, bud!'

'Look, that ship's going to Cuba! If she's carrying warplanes, that could threaten the US of A! That's something the American people should know about!'

'You want to get me thrown out the Navy?'

The correspondent turned to the PIO who was not wearing a communications set and was unaware of what had been said.

'Commander, you've got to help us . . .'

Shouting slowly, word by word, he explained their need to be certain of the Russian cargo. The commander pursed his lips and shrugged. He took the headset and began to talk to the pilot.

Looking through the open doorway they could see some of the *Rostov*'s officers gathered on the bridge wing looking up at them with binoculars. One had a camera and was taking photographs.

The commander grabbed the journalist's arm.

'Okay. You got your shot,' he shouted hoarsely into his ear.

The correspondent clamped the headset back on and clipped the microphone pads to his larynx.

'So, we're okay with that now, yeah?' he asked cautiously.

'I got new orders. It's his arse gets kicked now, not mine. But I still can't fly over that goddam Russian. But see here! I'm just gonna move up ahead and practise a hover. Now if that ship decides to steam right underneath my hover – that's his problem!'

'That's real neat!'

The helicopter banked to the left and the nose dipped to accelerate. Five hundred yards ahead the pilot pulled it sharply up into a hover, one hundred feet above the waves. He swung the nose round so that the side door looked directly back at the Soviet ship bearing down on them. The cameraman switched on and adjusted his focus.

The second SH-3 with the stills photographers on board flew parallel to the ship, but turned sharply away when it saw the first machine hovering in its path.

As the ship passed beneath them the correspondent's excitement mounted. The cocooned deck cargo revealed itself indisputably to be what the pilot had said; the wings of jet fighters. As the ship's bridge passed below, dark uniformed figures could be seen waving and gesticulating furiously.

Ten minutes later they landed back on the deck of the *Eisenhower*. The TV crew hurried below to prepare their tapes for transmission to New York by satellite. With help from aircraft recognition manuals provided by the PIO, they concluded the wings were for MiG-29 fighters, aircraft considerably superior to anything the Cubans had at present. They counted twelve individual wings; that meant six fighters.

Admiral Vernon Kritz appeared reluctant to jeopardize the secrecy of his ship's location by allowing the TV and newspaper men to transmit their reports, transmissions which could be detected by Russian satellites and spy planes. But eventually he allowed himself to be persuaded, and the media men set up a small gyro-stabilized satellite dish on the flight deck, in good time for the material to be turned round for the morning news programmes back home.

★ ★ ★

Andrew Tinker caught the early flight to London. Patsy had grudgingly driven him to Plymouth airport after an early breakfast.

She'd scowled for most of the previous evening, after he told her he'd been ordered to take command of *HMS Truculent* so that Philip could be brought home.

'It's not bloody fair!' she'd railed. 'Home for three days, and now you're off on patrol again! You'll be gone for weeks!'

She could well be right. He hadn't told her the real reason Philip was being brought back, simply that the Navy took domestic upsets pretty seriously.

'And so they should,' she'd answered. 'Damn Sara! If she couldn't have her affairs discreetly, she should've taken up pottery instead!'

At Heathrow, Andrew was met by the driver to Flag Officer Submarines. The black Granada slipped easily through the light Sunday morning traffic to Northwood. Forty-five minutes after touching down, he presented his identity card in the guardroom of the combined NATO and Royal Naval headquarters.

He was directed straight to 'the hole', the deep underground bunker that houses the operational command. Further identity checks, then he was through the heavy double doors, and down the steps to the Submarine Ops Room.

Flag Officer Submarines was Rear-Admiral Anthony Bourlet, a short, peppery man who had overall command of the Royal Navy's thirty nuclear and diesel-powered attack submarines.

'Very grateful to you for coming, Andrew,' he welcomed, grabbing him by the arm and leading him into his own small office next to the ops room. 'Alarming business, this.'

'We'll probably find when we get him back that it was all in Sara's imagination,' Andrew replied. 'I can't really believe Phil would do anything daft.'

'You're an old friend, aren't you?'

'Since Dartmouth.'

'Mmmm. Now look. This is what we've arranged. We've signalled Hitchens that he's to rendezvous with a helicopter off the Western Isles at 1600, and that he's to be replaced on board. He's acknowledged the signal, so with a bit of luck the scare'll be over by this evening.

'You'll leave Northolt in a 125 at 1300 hours for Stornoway. That's where you'll pick up the helicopter. The 125 will wait and bring Hitchens back here. When he's safely in our hands, we'll get the security boys in and find out what's at the bottom of all this. All right so far?'

Andrew looked at his watch. It gave him barely two hours to get briefed on *Truculent*'s mission.

'Fine, sir.'

'Now . . .'

Bourlet's voice sank lower.

'What you don't know is that Hitchens was given a special briefing before he left. A secret task for the exercise which is terrifyingly sensitive. The C-in-C shat himself when I told him the Russians had been sniffing round Philip.'

Andrew's eyebrows shot up. Craig had told him of a special mission, but not what it was.

'You'll know about the new "Moray" mines . . .'

'Of course. Remotely programmable microprocessors, incredibly clever target selectivity – laid in deep water they launch an underwater guided-missile that can penetrate even the heaviest Soviet double-hull.'

'Precisely. And at the first threat of war with Russia, and politicians willing, you lot would be told to lay them outside all the main Kola submarine bases.'

Andrew's jaw dropped.

'And that's Phil's mission?' he asked, stunned.

'To try it out. To try slipping through their ASW screen, get right up to the Kola Inlet and fire water-shots to simulate laying the mines.'

'Wheew!'

'Not the sort of job to give a man who's facing a personal crisis.'

'You can say that again! A hairy enough job for anybody!'

'The Yanks are in on it, too. They've tasked one of their *Los Angeles* boats to do the same thing further east, at Gremikha. As I'm sure you realize, the point of doing this in the middle of a big exercise is that the Russians'll probably be running a big ASW screen in the Barents. They'll be looking hard for our boats, and we need to know how good they'd be at finding us if we had to do it for real.'

Andrew nodded. It was almost routine for Allied submarines to probe Soviet waters on intelligence-gathering missions, but such operations were invariably conducted when the Soviets were known to be at a low state of alert. Going in when the Northern Fleet was mounting a full-scale anti-submarine sweep would be another matter.

'What's the time scale on all this, sir?'

'Well, there's a cover plan, obviously. He's scheduled to play "blue" in the exercise until Wednesday, and then switch sides. He then has five days supposedly acting on his own, playing "orange"; in reality he has that amount of time to get in to Polyarny and out again. I keep saying "he", but of course it's "you" now. Think you can do it?'

'I'll have a bloody good try, sir,' Andrew replied, trying to look more confident than he felt.

'The key thing is to be damned careful not to get caught. The last thing we want is an international incident with one of our SSNs trapped in a Russian fjord. At the first sign of your being detected – withdraw. Get well away from their territorial waters.'

'There's one problem, sir. I know about the Moray mines, but I don't know anything about the tactics for them.'

'No problem. *Truculent*'s the trials boat for the weapon system. Paul Spriggs is the WEO on board. Knows the mines inside out. And Tim Pike's the first lieutenant, so you couldn't ask for a better team.'

'And they know all about the mission?'

'Umm, well, probably not. Hitchens was alone at the

special session here, and he was told not to brief his crew until the last possible moment. "Need to know", and all that. There's still a good chance of CINCLANT getting cold feet and calling off the whole caboodle. And of course it's political, this one, too. Number Ten and the White House had to give the okay, in the same way they would in a real "time of tension". With President McGuire still feeling his way in foreign affairs, he might well pull out.'

Andrew looked at his watch again and gulped. In just a few hours he was due to take command of a boat full of strangers and head north for one of the trickiest patrols of his career. He felt desperately ill-prepared.

'I'd better look at some charts, and see what you've got in mind, sir.'

'You certainly had. Come along.'

Admiral Bourlet led Andrew along the subterranean corridor, their rubber-soled shoes squeaking on the polished floor, to the SSO room – Submarine Special Operations.

This was the most secret room at the Northwood headquarters. Only a handful of men and women ever entered it – even its very existence was known to only a handful more.

* * *

Washington DC.

Shortly after 10.00am in Washington, the Soviet Ambassador's car drew up outside the State Department at Foggy Bottom, escorted by police outriders, sirens wailing. All morning the television news programmes had been running and re-running the pictures of the Soviet freighter, the close-up shots of the fighter wings carefully cross-edited with file footage of MiG-29 aircraft in action.

The Ambassador was received by the Deputy-Secretary for US-Soviet Relations, the most senior official available at short notice on a Sunday, and ushered to a reception room on the sixth floor.

'My government has instructed me to protest in the strongest terms,' he began with grim solemnity. 'The incident in the North Atlantic this morning was outrageous.

69

A Soviet freighter called *Rostov*, on innocent passage on the high seas, was harassed without provocation by two helicopters from the American nuclear carrier *Dwight D. Eisenhower*. One helicopter passed directly over the ship at mast-top level. It was only by means of a sudden change of course that the captain of the cargo ship was able to avoid a collision. Look. Here, I shall show you . . .'

From his briefcase he pulled out two 10 × 8 black and white prints and placed them on the table. The photographs had been well taken; they showed the deck-derricks of the ship with the US Navy helicopter almost touching them and, in the foreground, crewmen on the bridge with arms above their heads as if protecting themselves from an expected collision.

'My government finds such aggressive behaviour by the United States Navy to be quite incompatible with the more relaxed relationship that has existed between Moscow and Washington in recent years, particularly since it has occurred at the start of Exercise Ocean Guardian, in which your warships will rehearse provocative NATO war plans almost within sight of the Soviet homeland. I am instructed to inform you that General Secretary Savkin is deeply disturbed by this event, and will not let the matter rest.'

The Deputy-Secretary feigned polite indifference to cover his embarrassment at being unbriefed on the affair.

'Thank you for your visit, Mr Ambassador. We shall look into this, and will give our answer to the matters raised in due course. May I express the hope that this incident doesn't prevent you enjoying the rest of this sunny Sunday, sir?'

He stood up and extended his hand. The Ambassador took it without a word, then gathered up his briefcase and turned for the door.

'Have a nice day, sir,' the Deputy-Secretary breathed to the Ambassador's back as he left the building.

Outside on the pavement, a handful of newsmen had gathered, including two TV crews. The Ambassador's press spokesman moved amongst them, handing out copies of the official protest and the photographs.

70

The Deputy-Secretary chewed at a thumb-nail. It was a set-up, he was sure of it. He'd watched the morning newscasts; the networks had done well to get their video on the air so fast. But the Soviets had matched that speed with their stills. To do that, the Russian ship must have been supplied with a professional photographer, a darkroom, a facsimile machine and a satellite terminal. Not the normal equipment of a Soviet merchantman, surely?

The Navy had walked into something. Goddam military and their club feet! And the Defence Intelligence Agency still hadn't answered the request for information that he'd lobbed in as soon as he saw the pictures. He had some 'phoning to do.

* * *

Moscow.

Dr Tatiana Gareyeva's apartment, in one of Moscow's anonymous residential areas, had a sad air about it and smelled stale. Ornaments on the shelves and tables had been collected over the years for sentimental reasons rather than for their intrinsic attractiveness. The furniture looked cheap; it had outlived its initial purpose to be used as a stop-gap until she could create a new home – with a husband.

Tatiana was over forty now, and time was running out. Standing by the window looking out on the bleak concrete landscape where thousands lived in similarly cramped homes, she turned to look at Vice-Admiral Feliks Astashenkov, slumped in an armchair watching television.

He was no use to her any more. Any dream she may have had of making their relationship permanent had long since evaporated. He was a hindrance to her now; his sudden surprise visits a few times a year would be an embarrassment one day if she ever met a real suitor.

She caught a glimpse of herself in the mirror on the wall opposite. Her hair was flecked with grey; her eyes which once had sparkled blue now looked grey as well. Her face, once pretty, had filled to a dull squareness; her body was thickening towards an eventual shapelessness.

And Feliks? Age had not improved him either; he was

developing the heavy jowls and flabby waistline that came from the excess of good living since his promotion to Vice-Admiral.

When they'd first met, they'd loved each other with a passion. She'd almost convinced him to leave his iceberg of a wife and marry her instead. But the whiff of promotion had come his way – and his wife's brother was on the General Staff. . . .

And now? This weekend was the last they would see of each other. Both knew it but neither had said it. Feliks had tried to pretend nothing had changed, but his words had been hollow.

Tatiana turned away again to stare through the big square of glass. She had her work; a paediatrician would always be needed. But working in the Soviet health service had become no easier, despite the lipservice paid to reforms. Reductions in spending on military programmes had still not found their way through to the civil sector. Hospitals and clinics were still chronically short of drugs, dressings and equipment.

The medical problems were worsening, too. More babies were being born dependent on the heroin that had hooked their mothers, and the stringent tests being imposed on the profession meant hundreds of doctors had been sacked for incompetence. Good for the nation's health in the long run no doubt, but it created a shortage of doctors for the time being.

She'd have to make the best of her career; if she could find no love in her life, it would be all she had left.

The music for the opening of the evening news bulletin *Vremya* blared tinnily from the television. The sound was a relief to her. Feliks had said he would leave after the news, to catch the late flight back to Murmansk. She was going to drive him to the airport.

Feliks' eyes had been fixed on the screen for what felt like hours, but his mind had been focused elsewhere, on the real reason for his coming to Moscow that weekend, his meeting with the General Secretary. The more he thought back on it, the more his disquiet grew.

He'd made a promise to Nikolai Savkin, a promise to

help him, yet without any clear idea what it would involve. He understood Savkin's need for a foreign distraction to cool down the internal debate over *perestroika*, but what was his own role to be? The General Secretary had simply told him that sometime in the coming weeks he would call him, make a request for some special service, something undefined but which would be essential to the survival of the reform programme.

Feliks was afraid. He had to admit it to himself. He'd made an open-ended commitment. If things went wrong and Savkin went down like his predecessor had, then he, Feliks Astashenkov, would go down with him.

He glanced guiltily at Tatiana. He'd revealed nothing to her of his talk with Savkin, and because it had occupied his thoughts completely that weekend, he'd talked to her hardly at all. The fire of their affair had gone out anyway. It would soon be over; they'd say goodbye – he'd pretend it was *au revoir* but they'd both know it was *adieu*.

Suddenly he sat forward, startled. The television was reporting a speech made by Nikolai Savkin at a collective farm that afternoon. The video showed the General Secretary gesticulating angrily. Intercut with his words were the same photographs that had earlier been presented to the State Department in Washington, the *Rostov* being buzzed by American helicopters. The pictures showed the ship's crew ducking in terror before the American war machines. Library footage rolled, of US aircraft carriers catapulting bomb-laden fighter planes into the sky.

It was a disgraceful example of old-fashioned American imperialism and aggression, Savkin declaimed, which did not bode well for US–Soviet relations. It was a clear sign of the hostility intended by the NATO Exercise Ocean Guardian which had just begun – the largest and most provocative NATO exercise ever conducted right on the edge of Soviet waters.

Feliks was gripped by a sensation close to terror. It was beginning to dawn on him how far Savkin was preparing to go.

* * *

Scotland.

Andrew Tinker studied his watch with growing anxiety. It was already five in the afternoon. The helicopter should have found *HMS Truculent* an hour ago.

Strapped firmly into the canvas seat in the back of the Sea King, Andrew felt his legs going numb. The hard aluminium seat frame pressed against the underside of his thighs, stopping his circulation. Every few minutes he would shift his position, but what he needed was to get out of that infernal machine. They'd been airborne for one-and-a-half hours.

'Perhaps the rendezvous co-ordinates got scrambled in the signal from CINCFLEET,' he suggested, pressing the headset microphone against his lips.

'We're in the right place, I can assure you,' came back the tart voice in his earphones.

'Navaids are working perfectly. So's the VHF and UHF. If he'd surfaced anywhere within fifty miles of us he'd have heard us calling.'

They'd taken off from Stornoway in the Western Isles half an hour before the rendezvous. Despite the gale blowing and the turbulent seas, it should have been a smooth, routine manœuvre. Boat and aircraft would link by radio minutes before the deadline, and as soon as the submarine surfaced, down would go the winch-wire with Andrew on the end, to come up again a few minutes later with Philip.

But there'd been no sign, no hint that *HMS Truculent* intended to keep her appointment.

What did it mean? An accident? Highly improbable. A misunderstanding? Almost impossible – Philip had acknowledged the signal. Keeping out of the way to dodge a Russian submarine? None had been reported in the area.

Suddenly, Sara's words came back to him. *Philip hates the Russians – he'll have his revenge.*

A nightmare was beginning to unfold.

'Have you talked to Stornoway again?' Andrew demanded, his anxiety growing.

'Two minutes ago. They've told FOSM. Northwood

says there's been nothing from the boat. We've got fifteen minutes' fuel before we have to head for land.'

Andrew hated helicopters; the noise, the vibration, the smell of hydraulic fluid all gave him a feeling of claustrophobia he'd never experienced in a submarine. The Sea King they were using was an anti-submarine version, almost filled by tactical control panels, and a heavy, black winch for dunking sonar into the sea.

Clad in a dayglo red 'once-only' immersion suit, he was squeezed into a folding seat between the winch and the fuselage. Rubber seals gripped tightly round his wrists and his neck; the watertight suit would save his life if they ended up in the sea.

Andrew pressed the 'transmit' switch on his headset cable.

'Let's call it a day. He's not going to turn up,' he called above the gearbox whine.

'Bit worrying, isn't it? Will they start a search?' the pilot responded.

'Shouldn't think so. Submariners change their plans all the time. He'll turn up.'

He was trying to sound reassuring, without success.

What the hell would they do now?

'Back to Stornoway?'

'Yep. Feet dry as fast as you can make it.'

He needed to get Admiral Bourlet on the line, fast.

* * *

HMS Truculent.

The invisible five-thousand-ton bulk of *HMS Truculent* was some two hundred miles northeast of the helicopter's position, her captain the only man on board who knew they'd missed a rendezvous.

For most of the past twelve hours Philip had stood in the control room, hovering nervously between the tactical displays and the chart table. He was desperate to get his boat into the deep waters of the Norwegian Basin, where a submarine could disappear with ease to run fast and free.

But their progress north had been halted by their need to cross the SOSUS barrier undetected. The chain of hydrophones stretching along underwater ridges from Greenland to the Shetlands would be sure to mark their passing unless they resorted to deception.

SOSUS was linked to a processing centre in South Wales, and the data could be presented within minutes as hard intelligence information at headquarters in Norfolk, USA and Northwood, UK.

Philip guessed the hounds would be rapidly unleashed once his masters knew he was out of their control. The Faroes-Shetland gap would be the obvious place they'd start looking for him; he didn't want to give them a head-start by revealing his position.

His first thought had been to hide amongst the noises generated by the aircraft-carrier *Illustrious* and her frigate escorts, but they were too far ahead, and would already have crossed the SOSUS barrier before *Truculent* could catch up.

So he'd decided to hug the continental shelf and pray for a merchantman to happen past. Throughout Saturday night they'd lurked, listening, west of the Orkneys. Philip had slept fitfully, leaving orders for the watch to wake him the moment a suitable decoy appeared.

Sunday morning came and went, with Philip finding it increasingly difficult to contain his fear of entrapment. He'd been on the point of making a run for it through the gap; to hell with the risk of being detected. If he was fast enough, he might slip away into the Norwegian Deep before the surface ships and the Nimrods could be marshalled onto his trail.

Then soon after lunch had come the breakthrough he was waiting for. A Russian fish-factory ship was heading back to Murmansk from the Scottish coast, laden with sprats and mackerel. The heavy thump of its diesel engine and the uneven beat of its imperfectly-milled propeller provided the screen of noise he needed.

To compound the deception, Philip ordered the trailing of a noise generator, a slim canister towed astern which transmitted a broad band of underwater noise, to swamp the discrete frequencies from the submarine which could identify it to the SOSUS system as a *Trafalgar* Class boat.

Philip crossed the control room to the chart table.

'How're we doing?'

Nick Cavendish was ready; the captain had asked him the same question every thirty minutes since lunch.

''Bout twenty miles northeast of SOSUS. Still at twelve knots, with the Soviet fisherman two miles to starboard.'

'Where's the *Victor*?'

'Last reported about one hundred miles north, but that was yesterday, sir. We're short of fresh intelligence.'

'Okay. Let's dump the noise generator, and head due north. Get down into the deep water and do some listening.'

'Aye, aye, sir.'

'Stretch our legs a bit. Once you're sure we're out of everyone's way, we'll stick a mast up and pick up an int. broadcast.'

'I'd like that, sir.'

Ahead lay the vast, empty waters of the Norwegian Basin, 3600 metres deep in places. Deep down, *Truculent*'s towed sonar array came into its own. If the Soviet *Victor* was anywhere within a hundred miles they'd have a good chance of finding her.

Cavendish gave the orders for the new course and depth. He set their speed at fifteen knots, fast enough until he had a better idea what other submarines might be sharing the waters with them.

He stepped into the sound room to look over the shoulders of the sonar ratings as they checked their waterfall displays. In the deep sound channel into which they'd descended they heard no trace of other submarines, just the squeaks and groans of countless krill. The *Victor* must have moved on.

Back in the control room he decided it was safe to put some distance behind them.

'Make revolutions for thirty knots!' he ordered. 'Maintain depth two-hundred-and-fifty metres.'

Their own sonar would be deaf at that speed, but he'd risk it for half an hour. He clicked the intercom to report the change of speed to the captain.

'Very good. Carry on,' Hitchens approved.

*

Thirty minutes later Cavendish ordered a return to fifteen knots. They were now over forty miles from the SOSUS barrier.

In the sound room the ratings scanned 360 degrees around the boat. Still no trace of man-made noise in the ocean depths.

The time was shortly before 1800 hrs. He'd checked with the wireless room; at 1814 there was a satellite transmission scheduled. Any submarine listening could take in the latest intelligence and news reports in a thirty-second burst of compressed data, together with signals directed at individual boats.

'Captain, sir! Officer-of-the-Watch,' Cavendish called into the intercom.

'*Captain!*'

'No contacts in the deep channel, sir. Propose to come up to sixty metres, and clear the surface picture. If nothing's around, I'd like, with your permission, sir, to return to periscope depth, raise a mast and take in the broadcast scheduled for 1814, sir.'

In the pause that followed, Cavendish imagined Hitchens studying his watch.

'*Sounds good. I'm coming to the control room, but carry on.*'

Cavendish swung round to the blue-shirted planesman.

'Bring her up to sixty metres, Jones.'

The rating pulled back on his control stick, keeping a careful eye on the angle-of-ascent gauge.

They came up fast and levelled out at a depth where they could hear the sounds of surface ships, hidden from them before by the temperature gradients which separate surface sounds from those of the deep.

Somewhere up here was the *Illustrious* task force, but Cavendish calculated the ships should be well north of *Truculent*, closer to Iceland, preparing to sweep the seas for submarines ahead of the *USS Eisenhower* battle group.

'*Control room! Sound Room,*' the loudspeaker crackled by Cavendish's ear.

'Go. Control Room.'

'*No contacts on sonar, sir. Surface clear.*'

78

Cavendish smiled with relief. Philip Hitchens joined him at the bandstand, behind the planesman.

'Did you hear that, sir?'

'Yes, I did.'

He looked at his watch. 1805.

'You can proceed to periscope depth. I'm going to the wireless room.'

Hitchens moved awkwardly across the control room, as if conscious the men were watching him. How many of them knew about the controls he'd imposed on the communications procedures?

He'd told sub-lieutenant Smallbone the previous evening that all future communications would be for his eyes only.

The burst transmission of digital data from the satellite would be recorded on magnetic disk, then fed through a processor to be printed out in real time.

'As soon as you've got the stuff printing, I need you out of the room, I'm afraid,' Philip reminded them briskly.

Smallbone and the operator Bennett nodded at him sullenly.

'I'm sorry. Not my idea. Orders from CINCFLEET,' Hitchens lied smoothly. 'Everything set now?'

'Sir,' Smallbone acknowledged.

Hitchens peered at his watch for the third time in a few seconds. He couldn't conceal his nervousness and spun back into the control room.

Cavendish was raising the forward search periscope.

'ESM?' Hitchens snapped.

'Negative, sir. No contacts.'

The Electronic Support Measures mast was the first to be raised whenever they closed with the surface. Its sensors were designed to detect radar transmissions from ships or aircraft, transmissions that could spot their periscope or radio mast.

Cavendish completed his all-round look.

'No visual contacts, sir. Sea-state five.'

Hitchens studied his watch again. 1814 precisely.

Philip stomped back to the wireless room. The disk-drive chattered as it filed the data.

'Transmission complete, sir,' Smallbone reported.

Philip turned on his heel and called into the control room.

'Officer of the Watch, down periscope, and take us deep again.'

Hugo Smallbone shuffled awkwardly out of the radio room, and stood outside the door, hands clasped behind his back as if at parade-ground ease.

'I'll press the tit for you then, sir?' Bennett growled.

'Yes, please.'

The rating did so, then scuttled from the room with exaggerated haste as the printer began to pour forth its data. Philip slipped inside and closed the door.

Lieutenant Commander Pike stepped into the control room having just completed his rounds. He spotted the wireless operators hovering awkwardly outside in the passageway.

'So, he's really doing it,' he murmured to the OOW.

'Didn't doubt the captain's word, did you, sir?' Cavendish retorted.

Pike raised one eyebrow in reply.

'Ten down. Keep two hundred metres,' ordered Cavendish. 'Steer oh four oh. Revolutions for eighteen knots.'

He looked at the control room clock. Just over half an hour until the end of his watch.

For Sunday's evening meal, the galley offered corned beef salad or 'oggies' – Cornish pasties – and chips.

Philip ate early, the steward bringing him a tray to his cabin. He wanted to be finished with his meal and with sifting the signals by the time the watch changed at 7 pm. It was the time he'd chosen to make the pipe; to give the men their first clue as to what he planned.

The signals were easy to sort. The intelligence reports he'd pass to the watch leader; the family messages and the summary of the world news he'd give to the first lieutenant for distribution. Those he placed to one side. He slid the messages for other submarines included in the burst transmission into the bin at his feet.

In front of him was the message he'd dreaded, the one he'd had to prevent the crew from seeing.

FLASH 201814Z OCT.
FOR: EXEC. OFF. HMS TRUCULENT.
FROM: FOSM NORTHWOOD.
RESTRICTED.
NEED IMMEDIATE EXPLANATION WHY YOU
FAILED TO MAKE RENDEZVOUS 1600Z TODAY.
ESSENTIAL YOU COMMUNICATE HF/SSIX
SOONEST.

They'd addressed it to Tim Pike, trying to by-pass him. Sent it without special code, so the whole fleet could see it. Clumsy. By making it so open they'd hoped to get the message through. They were wrong. It merely showed they had yet to realize what they were up against.

He smiled but with little satisfaction. He had no wish to take on his masters. Circumstances had forced him into it.

He carefully folded the signal and placed it inside the wall safe.

He waited until ten minutes past the hour, so the men would be settled in their mess decks or at their watch posts, then he stepped briskly into the control room, checked the navigation plot and the power settings, and unhooked the microphone that would broadcast his words throughout the boat.

'Do you hear there? Captain speaking. Just an update on our situation,' he began, hoping the tremble in his voice would not be noticeable. 'We're well clear of the Faroes-Shetland Gap now, and very shortly we're going to put on a bit of speed. Our destination is still somewhere in the north Norwegian Sea, but I can't be specific at this stage.'

He swallowed to moisten his throat, and turned away from the men in the control room so they couldn't see his face.

'I have to tell you that our orders have been changed since we left Devonport. It may well be that we no longer take any part in Exercise Ocean Guardian – that's not quite clear yet. The thing is, there's a bit of tension brewing between the Russians and NATO, and . . . er . . . we've been put on alert for a very special and very sensitive mission. Can't tell you anything about it at all at the moment; CINCFLEET has classified it Top Secret – Commanding Officer's eyes only. But, I *can* tell you what was on the BBC World Service news this evening – I've just had the summary through on the satellite.

'Earlier this morning there was an incident some way north of here, involving helicopters from the US aircraft carrier *Eisenhower* and a Soviet cargo ship called the *Rostov*, carrying MiG fighters. The Russians are apparently accusing the Yanks of threatening their ship. Mr Savkin, the . . . er . . . Russian leader, made a very provocative speech this afternoon, accusing NATO of all sorts of things, particularly slagging off this exercise that we're involved in.

'Now, it's not entirely clear what he's up to, but CINCFLEET isn't taking any chances. So, I've been given my orders. I hope to be able to give you some details in a day or two, but in the meantime please just take my word for it that whatever we do, there's a good reason for it. That's all.'

He made to hang up the microphone, but snatched it back again.

'Just one more thing. The video tonight, according to the first lieutenant's list, is *Gorky Park*. That's all.'

At the chief petty officers' table in the ratings' mess, CPO Hicks turned to Gostyn, the propulsion chief, knife held up in mid-air.

'What the fuck was that all about?'

'Not good news. Not good at all.'

In the wardroom six officers sat round the table, stunned into temporary silence. All eyes turned to Tim Pike.

'You heard the captain. I can't talk about it, can I?' he growled uncomfortably.

* * *

Northwood.

Rear-Admiral Anthony Bourlet paced like a caged rat up and down the floor of his office overlooking the main gates at Northwood Royal Naval Headquarters. Andrew watched him uncomfortably.

'This is bloody ridiculous! Something must have gone wrong with the boat. I can't believe a commander in Her Majesty's Navy would deliberately flout his orders and take off into the wide blue yonder on a personal vendetta! A man would have to be mad to do that.'

'That's just the point, sir. He may be. Some sort of breakdown.'

'They'd know. On the boat. The other officers would realize something was wrong, and sort him out, take command or whatever.'

'Eventually, yes. But how long would it take, sir? I'm no expert, but if Philip just appeared slightly odd, it wouldn't be enough reason for the executive officer to take over. If Pike misjudged it, he'd be on a charge of mutiny.'

'Mmmm,' the Admiral growled. 'What could you get away with on your own boat, Andrew?'

Bourlet stopped pacing. Fixing both hands on the desk, he leaned bulldog-like across it. The broad band of his Admiral's insignia glinted gold against the dark blue of his uniform sleeves. He'd commanded surface ships as a younger man, never a submarine.

'What d'you mean exactly, sir?'

'If you took it into your head to sink half the Soviet Navy, could you do it? Could you actually launch the torpedoes?'

Andrew smoothed down his thick, dark hair, and frowned, taken aback by the question.

'Well, that's the job of the weapon engineer.'

'Of course. But could you convince him to do it?'

Andrew reflected for a moment.

'It'd be bloody difficult. If we were firing a live round against a real target – there'd be a dozen men involved at least. It'd be war. Everyone on board would have to know.'

'Could you, as captain, convince them to do it?' Bourlet pressed. 'Tell them you'd received secret orders, a personal briefing, CO's eyes only? Something of that sort?'

Andrew expelled his breath through pursed lips, then shook his head.

'It'd be pretty impossible, sir, with the Harpoons or torpedoes. There'd have been signals, targeting data and so on. That stuff wouldn't be CO's eyes only.'

'Then we shouldn't have too much to worry about . . .'

'But if he's got mines on board. That could change things . . .'

Bourlet winced at the confirmation of his own fears.

The intercom on his desk buzzed twice. He pressed a key.

'Yes? What is it?'

'*Sub duty ops officer to see you, sir. Says it's very urgent.*'

Andrew got to his feet.

'Do you want me to wait outside, sir?'

Bourlet held up a hand.

'Send him in.' Then looking up at Andrew, he went on, 'Stay here. This may well be relevant.'

The duty operations watchkeeper entered, the same lieutenant who'd been directing Andrew's efforts at Stornoway earlier that afternoon.

'It's *Truculent*, sir. We think we may have had a trace of her.'

The young man's face was flushed – alarmed even.

'We've been comparing the SOSUS data with the radar surface picture from a Nimrod at about 1700 this afternoon. The SOSUS detected a Soviet fishing vessel heading for Murmansk, apparently in company with a trawler. Two surface vessels. But the Nimrod radar only saw one. The factory ship. No other trawler. We suspect the other noise was a submarine using a decoy, and *Truculent*'s the only one it can be, sir. Nothing else in the area.'

Bourlet shot a glance at the clock.

'God preserve us! That was four hours ago. You're absolutely certain?'

'Only explanation we can think of, sir.'

'Still no signals from her?'

''Fraid not, sir. And we're repeating our signal to her every hour on the broadcast and on the SSIX. She can't be listening.'

'Well, let me know instantly if there is anything.'

The operations officer left, and Admiral Bourlet turned to a large chart of the north Atlantic which covered one wall.

'Sod it! He could be anywhere within a hundred miles of the barrier by now. Even further by the time we get a Nimrod up to look for him. Sod Phil Hitchens! And sod bloody Sara Hitchens!'

Bourlet had been Flag Officer Submarines for two years, and had his eye on the promotion ladder. His tenure of office at Northwood had passed with remarkable smoothness. This sort of crisis was something he could do without.

The system was supposed to spot unstable personalities and weed them out before they could do harm. Hitchens had slipped through the net; ultimately that would be seen as *his* responsibility.

'What the hell's he up to, eh? What exactly did he say to that tart of a wife, before he sailed?'

'I don't think he *said* anything. She just sensed he was going to do something. I know what she means, sir. I've known Phil for longer than Sara – we joined the Navy at the same time, shared a cabin at Dartmouth. He – he can be pretty intense at times. Most of the time, in fact, when I think about it. I don't have many memories of him being really relaxed, having a good time, that sort of thing.'

'Bit of a bore, you mean?'

'He has been called that, sir. Some people find it difficult to tolerate his seriousness; he can be quite obsessive, particularly when it comes to the Soviets. Something of a cold warrior.'

'Nothing much wrong with that. Don't trust the bastards meself, despite the Gorbachev reforms and all Mr Savkin's charm. Still, holding views like that is one thing; planning to start your own war is quite another.'

He stared up at the chart again.

'Come over here and tell me what you think he's up to.'

Bourlet pointed to the Faroes-Shetland gap.

'From there to the Kola, what're we talking about? Twelve hundred miles?'

'Something like that, sir.'

'How long would it take him? A couple of days?'

'That'd be pushing it. He'd sprint a bit, but then probably want to drift so he could use his sonar. Doesn't want to go crashing into anything on the way.'

'Unless he's feeling suicidal.'

'Well, even if *he* is, the rest of the crew won't be, and they'll want to observe normal procedures. They'll stick to the water they were allocated at their briefing.'

'So that gives us *some* idea of where to look.'

'They're pretty big areas, but we can make a guess at it.'

'We'll have to. Now, what'll he do about communications?'

'My guess is he'll stick a mast up from time to time and take in a satellite. He'll want the intelligence data, if nothing else.'

'In that case our signal to the first lieutenant might have got through by now.'

'Unless . . .'

The same thought had just struck them both. If *Truculent*'s crew listened to just one transmission they would immediately know their captain was disregarding orders, and they'd be justified in seizing command. Hitchens must have thought of some way to prevent that.

'In this case . . .'

'Hitchens may have taken steps . . .' Bourlet completed the sentence. 'Pah! How on earth can we say that? We're assuming the man's behaving rationally and irrationally at the same time. God, this is ridiculous. It's like blind-man's-bluff in a lunatic asylum!'

A silence fell, and both men turned their eyes to the top of the chart, the Barents Sea and the Kola Peninsula. The Kola Inlet harboured one of the largest concentrations of warships anywhere in the world, including nearly fifty per cent of the Soviet Union's entire submarine fleet. If Philip Hitchens was bent on revenge, that was where *Truculent* would be heading.

'The special mission he had, sir? To simulate mine-laying. Can I get it absolutely clear? Did he have warshots on board? Live mines?'

'Mmmm. Four of them, I'm afraid. Just a normal weapons load.' Then, after a pause, 'You think he could persuade his WEO to lay them?'

'He might. The point about the Moray mine is that it's designed to be laid in an inert condition *before* a war starts, and wouldn't actually be activated until the start of the conflict. As you know, sir, it can be activated by a sonar transmission from a submarine, a surface ship, or an aircraft, anytime up to a year after being laid.

'He'd have to prepare his groundwork. But as long as no one suspected he'd lost his marbles, he might just convince his WEO they had orders to lay the mines in peacetime.'

'Believing the weapons wouldn't be activated until there was a crisis . . .'

'Exactly, sir.'

'Now the crunch question. Could Hitchens activate the mines?'

Andrew swallowed hard. He'd remembered a detail from Philip's career.

'I've a horrible feeling he could, sir. He trained as a sonar officer. Knows that sonar system inside out.'

Bourlet stared at him unblinking.

'Then he's got to be stopped.'

Suddenly the Admiral stood up and pulled his uniform straight.

'Come on. We're going down the Hole.'

With that he marched for the door; Andrew pulled himself to his feet and followed.

Outside, the night had become crisp and clear, with a half-moon high in the sky. As they hurried down the slope, two young WRNS coming towards them saluted smartly. Admiral Bourlet didn't give them a second glance. Unusual for him – he had a reputation as a bit of a lecher.

At the control post at the bottom of the entrance ramp, the Royal Marines security guards checked their identity badges and cleared them. The two men hurried through the heavy steel blast doors, and down to the first level airlock. The atmosphere in the bunker was kept at positive pressure to protect the occupants from chemical weapon attack, or nuclear fallout.

Four flights down, they entered the long corridor that led to the Operations Control room. The OPCON was dominated by a giant wall-screen; rows of computer terminals were manned by operators wearing headphones. This was the control centre for Exercise Ocean Guardian; all NATO naval operations in the Eastern Atlantic were directed from here.

Bourlet passed through it into the smaller Royal Naval control room beyond. The three men on duty scrambled to their feet.

'Relax,' he ordered. 'This is Commander Tinker, captain of the *Tribune*. He's here helping me with the *Truculent* problem. Now, what I'm about to say is Top Secret – UK Eyes Only. Not a word outside this room, understood? None of those NATO people must know.'

'Sir.' The three men nodded.

'We appear to have an SSN not responding to signals at the moment. Don't know why,' he lied. 'We've got to find that boat and discover what's up. Now what've we got in the *Truculent*'s area?'

The duty officer tapped at his keyboard and a map appeared on his screen.

'*Illustrious* is north of the Faroes, sir, with three escorts,' he announced, reading off the data. 'But *Truculent*'s probably 200 miles east of her. Bit too far for her helicopters to do anything useful. Two more ASW frigates are working a screen nearer to Iceland, so they'll not be much use either. Nor will the three "O" Class subs in the northern North Sea. The one boat that could help is the submarine *Tenby*; she's right up off North Cape.'

'What about maritime air?'

'One Nimrod MR2 from Kinloss is doing a search just inside the Arctic Circle. Currently tracking a *Victor 111* and a *Tango*. A second Nimrod is on barrier patrol between the Faroes and Shetlands. We could divert her, if we knew where to look.'

'Andrew, what do you think?'

'Anybody got a chart?' Tinker asked wrily. 'One of those paper things. I can't work from a screen!'

The duty officer pulled one from a drawer and handed him a pair of brass dividers.

Andrew calculated. It would be five hours after *Truculent* crossed the SOSUS barrier before the Nimrod could be on station. One hundred and fifty miles was the most the boat could have covered in that time.

He measured the dividers against the latitude marks on the side of the chart, then laid the points on the paper.

'If he's taking a straight line towards North Cape, the Nimrod'll have to lay a barrier a hundred miles wide to have a chance of finding him.'

'Get those co-ordinates and ask the Air Commander if we can divert his Nimrod,' Bourlet ordered. 'Now, what else is there on the ground?'

'The Americans' main force is still well to the west, sir, but they've got a *Los Angeles* boat way up north under the ice, keeping an ear open for the Russian BNs.'

'Mmmm.'

'The Norwegians might be able to help, sir. They've got a couple of *Oslo* frigates on anti-submarine duty off Trondheim Fjord.'

'No. The Norwegians couldn't keep a birthday party secret, let alone this sort of problem. No. *Tenby* looks our best bet. She's playing "orange", isn't she?'

Bourlet directed his question at the duty officer. The lieutenant commander nodded.

There had to be something he could do, Andrew thought. He knew Philip better than any of them. He might be able to talk sense into him if he could just get near enough.

'Just a thought, sir,' Andrew ventured, beckoning the Admiral to move out of earshot of the others. What he was about to suggest would commit him further than ever. He was glad Patsy couldn't hear him.

'Go on,' Bourlet growled.

'If I could get on board *Tenby*,' he whispered, 'and we managed to track *Truculent*, I could call them on the underwater telephone. Might be able to get Philip back on the rails. If not, at least I could alert the crew.'

'It'd also avoid our having to brief *Tenby* by signal, which wouldn't be bad. Mmmm. Got any other commitments at the moment?'

'Just shore leave. Patsy'll probably threaten divorce, but I think I can cope with that.'

'Won't be the first time, I'm sure. That's not a bad plan. How would we get you on board?'

They turned back to the duty officer.

'We want to get Commander Tinker on board *Tenby*. How do we do it?' Bourlet asked.

The lieutenant commander pointed to his computer screen, showing the northern tip of Norway.

'Tromso would probably be your best bet. We could order *Tenby* to approach the coast. There's a Norwegian Air Force base there with Search and Rescue helicopters.'

'How long to get to Tromso from here?'

'Depends what you're flying in, but about four hours in something like a 125, I'd say.'

'Mmmm. I'll need to clear this with the C-in-C, but it sounds the right plan. Get it started, will you? Alert *Tenby* that we may need to change her plans, and keep her close to Tromso. Don't give her any details or explanations at this stage. And check with the Norwegians, to make sure they can give Andrew a lift. Finally, book a 125 for tomorrow morning. I'll confirm everything later this evening, after I've talked to the boss.'

The duty men saluted as the Rear-Admiral and Andrew left.

'Got a cabin booked in the Wardroom?' Bourlet asked, after they'd stepped out into the crisp night air.

'Yes. I wasn't expecting to get back to Plymouth tonight, whatever happened.'

'Give my apologies to your wife. Feel free to blame me

for everything. I'm quite used to it. And, look: let the Wardroom hall-porter know where you are, 'cause I'll want another word. I'm just going down the road to Admiralty House. The C-in-C's having a dinner party, but he knows what's going on and is expecting me to call. I shouldn't be more than an hour.'

Andrew watched Bourlet's squat figure stomp up the ramp towards the main gates, then he turned left towards the accommodation blocks of the 'Wardroom' – the shipboard term the Navy used for the officers' mess, which at Northwood amounted to a good-sized hotel.

'You're much too late for dinner, sir, but they'll do you a sandwich if you're quick,' the hall porter greeted, looking at his watch.

Andrew realized suddenly how hungry he was. The only meal he'd had all day were the sandwiches the RAF had provided on the flight to Scotland.

He'd intended to ring Patsy right away; he took a step towards the coin-box telephone on the wall opposite, then hesitated. She'd have to wait, or he'd miss the only meal he was going to get; the way things were going, he couldn't be sure when he'd see the next one.

Rear-Admiral Bourlet had sent his driver home for the night, so took the wheel of the black Granada himself. Admiralty House was less than a quarter of a mile down the road, a substantial red-brick house at the end of a tarmac drive.

A white-jacketed steward emerged from the front door, and pointed to a parking space.

'If you'd care to wait in the study, sir, I'll tell the Admiral you're here. They're just finishing their coffee, so you've picked a good moment,' he chirped as he ushered Bourlet into the house.

The Commander-in-Chief of the Fleet was two ranks higher than he was, but as far as Bourlet was concerned, Stewart Waverley should never even have made Vice-Admiral. The man wasn't so much a sailor as a politician, with his eye on the First Sea Lord's job followed by a seat in the House of Lords.

He waited five minutes in the small study. Shelves lined with volumes of Who's Who, directories of key personnel in the media, and recent political biographies confirmed Bourlet in his prejudices about the man.

'Hello, Anthony,' Waverley greeted curtly. 'Hope this won't take long. I've got the editor of the Telegraph here this evening. What news of the *Truculent?*'

He was tall and elegant in a white dinner jacket, his straight, dark hair held in place by a sheen of oil. His breath smelled of claret and good brandy.

'The news is bad. For God's sake, don't give it to the Telegraph.'

Waverley scowled in irritation at the unnecessary piece of advice.

'There's been no word from her,' Bourlet continued, experiencing a perverse pleasure that what he was about to say would spoil the C-in-C's evening.

'But we think she's been detected. Crossing the SOSUS array between the Faroes and Shetland, about five hours ago. Pretending to be a trawler. I've diverted a Nimrod to look for her.'

Waverley blanched.

'What . . . what on earth's going on in that boat?'

Bourlet explained further, and watched the C-in-C's expression freeze as the implications sank in. When he'd finished, Waverley leaned back in his chair and stared at the ceiling.

'This is appalling!' he exploded, after what seemed like a full minute of silence.

'I'll have to brief the First Sea Lord; he'll need to tell the Secretary of State tonight. This thing's going to explode. The PM'll be horrified. I'm having lunch with her at Downing Street tomorrow. Wants me to tell her all about Ocean Guardian. The Russians have lodged a formal complaint, calling it "provocative". You'll have heard on the news all that business about the Americans buzzing a Soviet merchantman bound for Cuba with MiG-29s on her deck? And the furious speech Savkin made this afternoon?'

'I haven't heard any news – been a bit busy . . .'

Waverley didn't hear him, his mind running on what he would say to the Prime Minister.

'If we've got a rogue submarine heading into the middle of all this, it'll be like tossing a lighted match onto an oil spill. You will find her, won't you?'

'Sir, I don't know. If Hitchens doesn't want to be found, he'll make it bloody difficult for us. We've got to face it, unless we can divert every ship and plane involved in Ocean Guardian to help with the search, we may not be able to stop him doing whatever he intends to do.'

'Good God, man! We can't do that! The whole world would know what's happened. A *Royal Navy* nuclear submarine out of control? A *British* officer threatening a private war with the Soviets? This must never get out! You've *got* to stop him! I'm making you personally responsible for the operation. Set up a small command staff, give it a code name, and use your judgement. I'll look after the politicians – leave them to me. You just get Hitchens back in line!'

Waverley stood up. His hands were trembling.

'And now I've got to go back and entertain my guests without the editor of the Daily Telegraph suspecting anything!'

Andrew dropped three coins into the payphone, and dialled. He looked at his watch. It was nearly eleven o'clock.

'Hello?' Patsy sounded breathless when she eventually answered.

'Hullo, darling. It's me. Were you in the bath or something?' he asked.

'No, I've been out. Heard the phone when I switched off the car – came running in. Hence – breathless.'

'Been somewhere nice?'

'Hardly. Parents' Association meeting. Bleagh! Usual stuff; anxious fathers wondering why their eight-year-olds aren't being taught Shakespeare. Where are you? I thought you'd be at sea by now.'

'Plan's changed. I'm at Northwood. Can't talk much. Just to say things are getting complicated. I still expect to be away for a while, so I shan't be able to call you for a bit.'

'It's still this business with Philip?'

'Yes, but I'm on a public phone, so I can't go into details.'

'Well . . . , all right, but when are you likely to be back? Have you no idea? The children'll be home next weekend. You must be here then.'

Her voice sounded strained, angry even.

'I just don't know. A few days probably, that's all.'

'But it might be longer? Andrew, what *is* this?'

'Look, I'll ring you again when I can, but I may not be near a phone. Could you do something for me?'

'What?' she asked suspiciously.

'It's Sara. Could you keep an eye on her? Make an excuse to talk to her?'

'What about?'

'Well, you know – things. She'll be pretty worried. And she hasn't got anyone to talk to.'

'Hasn't she? I thought she had a knack of finding people . . .'

'Patsy!'

He cursed the constraints of talking on an open phone line.

'Darling, I can't explain any more. But please do it. Say hello to Sara, will you? It's *deadly* serious. And I chose that word carefully.'

There was silence from the other end, just the clicks and the hiss of the line.

'Oh,' she said, eventually. She sounded startled. 'Oh, all right. I'll look out for her.'

'Good girl. And if she says anything which you think is important, then go and see Craig and tell him to pass it on to FOSM.'

'How will I know what's important?'

It was a reasonable question, but on the open phone he couldn't explain.

'You'll have to use your loaf, love. Now I've got to go. I'll see you . . . sometime.'

He wanted to be reassuring, but knew he had failed.

'Be careful, won't you?'

'Don't worry. Bye now!'

'Bye. I love you, by the way.'

Andrew replaced the receiver, but left his hand resting on it. Could he have explained any better? Should he ring her back?

'Ah, there you are!' Admiral Bourlet's gravel voice boomed across the reception area. 'Let's go into the bar for a moment. Just time for a nightcap.'

He led the way in. Only a handful of officers were drinking, most of them young and unattached. They stiffened at the sight of an Admiral but Bourlet waved at them to relax.

'What's yours?'

'That's kind of you, sir. I'll have a horse's neck.'

'Make that two,' the Admiral told the barman.

They retreated with their drinks to a far corner of the bar, where two large, leather armchairs remained unoccupied.

'Right,' Bourlet began softly. 'The plan goes ahead as discussed this afternoon. I'm giving it the codename "Shadowhunt". Trying to find a "*T*" class boat that doesn't want to be found – it's pretty apt.

'Waverley's given me carte blanche. Ops have talked to the Norwegians and they're ready to help. *Tenby*'s been signalled and is on her way to a rendezvous with you. She's got no clue what it's about, of course. You'll have to use your discretion how much you tell her.

'The RAF'll be ready for you at ten-thirty at Northolt. They want you there fifteen minutes before that. You've got your passport with you, I hope.'

'Yes, sir. It's in my bag. Standard kit. There is one thing I thought of, though. My job as I see it, apart from finding *Truculent*, is to talk to Philip on the underwater telephone. The trouble is, I'm bloody worried about what to say. I mean, it's a bit like dealing with a gunman in a plane full of hostages.'

'Damned good point,' the Admiral growled. 'And I know just the person you need to talk to. Young friend of mine . . .'

He cleared his throat noisily and rippled his eyebrows to indicate he was about to be indiscreet.

'Surgeon-Commander Rush – Felicity Rush. Fleet psychiatrist. Based here at Northwood but travels all over the place dealing with mental problems. Delightful girl. Here . . .'

He reached into an inside pocket and pulled out an address book.

'Look, I happen to have her home number – can't imagine how.' Bourlet smirked with self-satisfaction. 'Why don't you ring her – see if she can spare you an hour tomorrow first thing? I'd ring myself, but . . . , well, her husband's around. Bit awkward, you know.'

His chuckle was like treacle.

'I see. Been needing a little therapy yourself, sir?' Andrew grinned.

'Mmmm. Not a good topic in the current circumstances.'

'Maybe not. I'll try the number now.'

Andrew felt in his pocket for change, then headed for the payphone.

He returned a few minutes later.

'Did you get her?'

Andrew nodded.

'She'll be here at eight in the morning.'

'Good. Then I'll bid you goodnight. Pop into my office for a word before you leave tomorrow, will you?'

* * *

HMS Truculent.

Lieutenant Commander Tim Pike ran a comb through his short, wavy hair. He always did that before going to bed, a hangover from his prep-school when Matron would inspect them all for neatness before lights-out.

It was after 0100 hrs. He'd stripped to his underpants for the night; there was no room on a submarine for luxuries like pyjamas. He looked at himself in the mirror, wondering if his skin still bore traces of the suntan acquired in Portugal four months earlier. His fiancée had insisted they go abroad to get rid of his undersea pallor.

Pike pulled at the elastic of his briefs to compare the untanned skin underneath with the rest.

'Checking your knob's still there?' Paul Spriggs jibed, lifting the curtain and entering the cabin.

'I don't do that by *looking* at it,' Pike quipped back, swinging himself up onto the top bunk. 'Sandra asked me to leave it behind, this trip. Said it was the only bit of me she'd miss!'

'So, instead you gave her a new battery for her vibrator.'

'Coarse at times, aren't you?'

Spriggs switched off the reading light, leaving the dim glow of the red lamp on the ceiling. The whole submarine was in red-light conditions in the hours of darkness. The men needed night-vision to use the periscope.

Spriggs didn't bother to undress – just took off his shoes and lay down on the lower bunk.

'Can I ask you a straightforward question?' the weapons engineer asked softly.

Pike braced himself to be interrogated on some aspect of his sex-life; he suspected his cabin mate had had little experience of women.

'If you must . . .'

'Well . . . have you *any* idea what the hell's going on. The captain won't let anyone in the wireless room when the signals come in. What's so secret about this change of plan, where the hell are we going, and why?'

Tim Pike lay staring at the ceiling. The answer he wanted to give was a bitter, anguished one, reflecting the offence he felt at not being taken into his captain's confidence. A first lieutenant on a submarine was meant to be the CO's right-hand man, but on this patrol Hitchens had been treating him like a mere sub-lieutenant.

'No.'

'No, what?'

'No, I don't have any idea what the hell's going on.'

They were silent again, the hum of the ventilation fans loud in the tiny cabin.

'Uh . . . , don't you think you *should* know?'

'There's nothing in the rule book that says a captain has to take his first lieutenant into his confidence, unless it's absolutely necessary for operational reasons. Our captain's doing it by the book. That's the *on-the-record* answer . . . Privately, and just within these walls – I'm as pissed-off as hell!'

'What has he told you?'

'Same as he told you and everyone else on the "pipe". Simply that the patrol task had been changed; we have to make all speed to the Barents Sea and he's been ordered to vet all communications personally until after the mission's completed.'

'Bloody odd, that – vetting *all* the comms. Ever happened to you before?'

'Once, maybe. For forty-eight hours or so.'

'But this is open-ended. Supposing World War Three breaks out up there – how'll we get to know about it? Can we rely on our captain to tell us?'

'Don't worry. The Russians'll let us know. They'll tap on the casing with a nuclear depth charge.'

'That's not funny, Tim.'

'Just put it down to experience. It's good training. Submariners are supposed to be lone wolves, operating in the dark. He's passing on the intelligence briefs telling us what else is in the area, so we won't hit anything, I promise you.'

Pike deemed it his duty to be reassuring, but it wasn't how he felt.

'You're sure he's all right, are you?' Spriggs asked with renewed earnestness. 'You don't think he's lost his marbles, or anything?'

'Why do you say that?' Pike snapped, alarmed that he was not alone in his suspicions.

'Well, Hitchens has always been a tight-arse, but he seems twitchier than ever this trip. He has domestic problems, doesn't he? Neurotic wife, or something?'

'Never confided in me . . .'

'Oh, come on, Tim! Stop being so fucking stiff-necked! You know bloody well what they say about him!'

Pike rolled over and looked down onto the bunk below.

'Tell you what, Paul – if you're really worried about

him, then so am I,' he confided finally. 'But we need to be bloody careful. I'm no mutineer.'

'Nor me, for God's sake. But what do we do about it?'

'We start making notes. Independently. Every time we notice something about his behaviour that's not normal, every time he does something that's not the usual procedure – we make a note of it. Just you and me. Nobody else. No conspiracies or he'll have us both by the neck!'

He rolled back, eyes fixed on the ceiling, hands behind his head.

'Okay,' Spriggs eventually acknowledged from below.

For a good ten minutes they lay there, staring at the red glow, disinclined to sleep, searching their memories for things Commander Hitchens had said and done since they'd left Devonport, things different from his normal behaviour. The more they thought, the more disturbed each became.

'The trouble with this game,' Spriggs moaned suddenly, 'is it leads to paranoia!'

'Mmmm. Let's rethink it in the morning.'

'OK. Goodnight.'

''Night.'

Less than a minute later, a sharp rap on the door frame brought them fully awake again.

'Sorry, sir.'

It was the young navigator. He was duty watch leader.

'Tried to raise the captain, sir, but he's out cold. Snoring his head off. Just can't wake him.'

Pike slipped feet-first from the upper bunk and reached for his shirt and trousers.

'What's the problem? What's happened?'

'Sodding great contact, sir. Sound room thinks it's a Russian *Victor* class sub, coming straight for us!'

CHAPTER FOUR

Monday 21st October. 0130 hrs. GMT.

HMS Truculent. The Norwegian Sea.

'Report!' Pike snapped at Cavendish, as he ran into the control room, still buttoning his shirt.

'Depth – two-hundred-and-fifty. Speed – fifteen knots. Course – zero-five-five,' called out the navigator.

'Water under the keel?'

'Plenty. Two-thousand-three-hundred metres.'

Pulling the back strap of his sandals over his heel, Pike hopped to the video displays of the action information consoles. The cross in the centre of the screen marked their own position, the small square box lower down and to the left that of the contact.

'We've been sprinting at thirty knots for three hours. Dropped our speed just five minutes ago for a listen, and then we heard him. We'd been deafening ourselves going fast.'

'Range?'

'Don't know. Could be ten miles.'

'Or more. At this depth and with the noise we were making, he could've heard us forty miles off easily. Another bloody triumph for NATO naval intelligence!'

The lanky figure of Lieutenant Cordell appeared between the periscope standards. He'd handed over the watch to Cavendish half an hour earlier, but had returned to the control room on hearing of the contact.

'Talk to me, Sebastian,' said Pike. 'What does our TAS officer think?'

'Definitely a *Victor*. The last intelligence sitrep mentioned one, but put it much further north. This must be another one. Could've picked up our track anytime during the past three hours. He's coming up astern on our port quarter. We detected him on the towed array when we dropped below eighteen knots.'

'We need to lose him. Where do we go?'

Pike knew the answer to his own question. But Cordell was new to *Truculent* and needed testing.

'He's chasing fast, so his sonar's deaf. When he slows down to listen, we should be invisible to him, now we've cut our own speed. He'll start guessing then, wondering whether we're keeping on the same course.'

'*Control room, sound room!*' The voice of the senior rating in the sound room came from the loudspeaker above the AIS console.

'Yes, Hicks,' Pike answered, keying the transmit switch.

'*Contact's fading, sir. Same bearing.*'

'There we are. *Victor*'s slowing down. When he finds out he's lost us, he'll guess we've detected him,' Cordell concluded. 'Now, will he expect us to keep the same course? If he starts searching left or right, he'll be stabbing in the dark. If he keeps to the same track he may think he's got a better chance of keeping on our tail.'

'So what do we do, brains?'

'I suggest we come left sixty degrees. That'll keep us in the deep Norwegian Basin, and put us at right-angles to him. We should pick him up on the bow sonar too, then – give us a better bearing and range.'

'Depth?' Pike pressured.

'He can go deeper than us, and faster. So why don't we go shallower, above the thermocline?'

The first sign of uncertainty flickered in his eyes. Pike was giving him no help.

'Disadvantages of going shallow?'

'Can't hear him any more. But still worthwhile, sir – I think.'

'What else was in that last intelligence report? Any other "hostiles"?'

'Nothing, sir – at least, not in the dope the captain handed out.'

Cordell's words were a reproach. Pike felt it directed at him. Glancing round, he sensed the attention of several pairs of eyes. They'd all been unsettled by the captain's 'pipe' the previous evening.

Pike wanted to round on them, saying he was as much in the dark about their mission as they were, but he kept silent; nothing should be done to undermine the authority of command at a time like this.

'Navigator, any hazards to the north?'

'None.'

'Right! Planesman, ten up. Keep fifty metres. Port ten, steer three-five-five. Revolutions for ten knots.'

Cordell smiled fleetingly; his advice was being followed to the letter.

Pike took Lieutenant Nick Cavendish to the chart table. Bending over it and pretending to study a detail, he spoke in a whisper.

'I'd better go and see Hitchens. You say you couldn't rouse him?'

'Yup. Knocked on the door, called loudly, shook him by the shoulder even, but he was out cold.'

'Wasn't dead, was he?'

'Don't be daft! I told you, he was snoring his head off. It's unlike him – he's usually a light sleeper. On his feet instantly if you call him.'

'Might've taken some sleeping pills. But he should have bloody told me if he was going to do that!' Pike hissed, resentful at yet another sign of his captain's disregard for him. 'Okay, Nick. You have the ship. And not a word about the captain. Understand?'

'Sebastian knows.'

'Well, keep it to the two of you then.'

Cavendish crossed to the ship control console to check his orders were being followed. Already the decks were tilting, as the submarine banked and climbed to its new depth and course. The planesman pulled back on the control stick, eyes locked onto the indicators.

Pike grabbed at pipework to steady himself as he headed aft. Beyond the control room the red-light glow of the night encouraged a stillness in the boat, even though half the crew was on watch.

Outside the captain's cabin he hesitated, listening for

any sound of Hitchens stirring. Hearing none, he rapped on the door frame and waited. No response. He pulled back the edge of the curtain and looked inside. It was exactly as the navigator had described.

Hitchens *could be* dead, for all he knew. The thin face was turned away from him, mouth open, cheeks hollow. Pike shook him by the shoulder. The body stirred at his touch, taking in a startled breath, and then with a grunt sank back into deep sleep.

Best to leave him, Pike thought. He wasn't needed in the control room, and would be little use if forced out of a drugged sleep.

He stood back from the bunk and looked around for a pill container. He found it inside a small, blue sponge bag on the table. The name on the label was unfamiliar, but the pharmacist's instructions read 'one to two at night when needed'. He pulled off the cap – it was one of those child-proof ones. Inside he counted about a dozen capsules. At least Hitchens hadn't taken the lot.

He looked at the wall-clock: 0200. Let him sleep it off. Even asleep Hitchens' face looked stressed and unhappy. Enough stress to have unbalanced him? How could Pike tell? He was no medic, and they didn't have a doctor on board.

He pulled the curtain shut behind him and returned to the control room. The submarine was levelling off.

* * *

Over the Norwegian Sea.

The crew of RAF Nimrod call-sign Eight-Lima-Golf could hardly believe the drama unfolding below them. The four-engined jet criss-crossed the pitch-black Norwegian Sea at 220 knots, 300 feet up, monitoring and plotting every detail of the duel under the waves.

On routine patrol from its base at Kinloss, the Nimrod had been directed to the area by reports from the Norwegian Air Force, whose P-3 Orion maritime patrol planes had suddenly detected the Soviet submarine south of Vestfjord. Where it had come from, they didn't know.

Somehow it had escaped detection elsewhere in the Norwegian Sea.

The RAF were pleased to get in on the action; at first they'd suspected the target was one of the new ultra-quiet *Sierra* class boats. But then they picked up the characteristic noise signature of a *Victor*, albeit quieter than usual. Must've just come out of refit, they'd concluded.

It had taken time to find the *Victor*; the fix the Norwegians had given was over an hour old. The first line of sonobuoys they'd dropped into the sea had drawn a blank. Knowing the *Victor*'s ability to sprint at forty knots, the airborne electronics officer had gambled that the boat had turned north, to keep away from the shallows of the continental shelf.

He'd been right, but for the wrong reason.

Sixty miles north of the *Victor*'s last known position they'd dropped eight Jezebel sonobuoys two miles apart, in a chevron from east to west. Once in the water the buoys separated into two sections; one part, containing an omni-directional hydrophone, dropped 150 metres while the other section, linked to it by cable, containing a small radio and antenna, floated to the surface to transmit to the aircraft the sounds the hydrophone detected.

The noise of a speeding *Victor* can travel great distances. All eight Jezebel buoys detected it simultaneously. The two operators on the AQS.901 acoustic processor inside the cramped and tatty fuselage of the Nimrod grinned at each other at the strength of the signals they were hearing through their headphones.

To their left, on a large circular TV screen, the tactical navigator was constructing his plot of the water below. The line of sonobuoys was marked by eight small green squares, each identified with a radio channel.

'Fifty and *twenty-seven are top buoys!*'

The voice on the intercom indicated the Jezebels giving the strongest signals, the ones closest to the target.

Looking over the shoulder of the tactical navigator, the AEO saw that the top buoys were at each end of the chevron.

'Spot on! He's coming straight for us,' he shouted with satisfaction.

Suddenly one processor operator jabbed a finger at the top of his sonar display, the green 'waterfall' sound pattern detected by buoy '36' at the apex of the chevron. He was detecting something more than ripples in the pattern created by the distant *Victor*.

'Hey, I've got something!' he snapped into his boom-microphone.

He spun a roller-ball to move the cursor to the low-frequency noise that had caught his eye, a frequency too low to be audible to the human ear.

His fingers flicked switches to focus the narrow-band analyser onto it.

'I'm getting doppler effect on thirty-six,' he snapped again.

'Same on forty-two,' the second operator reported.

A minute reduction in the frequency detected told them something other than the *Victor* had just passed between two hydrophones and was heading away from the line.

The tactical navigator moved a cursor across his video map, to the position of the new target. He pressed a key to fix the co-ordinates in the navigation computer. The aircraft turned on its new heading.

'Prepare DIFARS seven-five and zero-nine,' the TacNav ordered.

In the rear of the plane aircrew selected directional buoys from a storage rack, set the radio channels, and loaded them into the ejection tubes.

A button on his control panel launched the first of the buoys. 'Seven-five, gone. Turn now,' sang out the TacNav. The plane banked sharply to reach the launch position for the second.

The AEO clutched the edge of the processor housing to steady himself. The 'G' force in the sharp turn threatened to buckle his knees.

'Zero-nine, away.'

He crouched in front of the processor screens. The DIFAR buoys, directional and highly sensitive, would give the speed and bearing of the target.

Ten buoys in the water was no problem for the AQS.901. Sixteen could be monitored simultaneously on the four displays.

'*DIFAR* seven-five gives bearing one-seven-zero, and decreasing.'

'Zero-nine gives two-five-seven, increasing.'

'Any classification yet?' the AEO asked.

The operators studied the pattern emerging on their screens. Listening didn't help; nothing but squeaks and crackles from shrimps and other marine life. It was down to the computer to analyse the low-frequency vibration of the target.

'Looks like a bloody *Trafalgar*! That's the noise signature!'

The second operator nodded in agreement.

So that was it. That was why the *Victor* had headed north.

'Bet he's never been that lucky before! A *Victor* tracking a *Trafalgar*? Impossible, according to the bloody Navy!'

'They're both doing nearly 30 knots!'

The bearings from the DIFARs changed rapidly as the target passed between them. The Russian boat was coming up fast through the Jezebel line.

'They'll both be deaf, going that fast,' the AEO remarked.

'Hang on!' called the TacNav. 'Our chap's slowing down.'

'She's sprinting and drifting. This is where he finds out he's picked up a tail. Could get interesting!'

While they waited to see what the *Victor* would do, the AEO grabbed the signaller's clip-board of intelligence signals. Very odd. Not a word about a RN boat being in the area.

The portly, middle-aged AEO chortled inwardly at the chance of embarrassing the Navy. He drafted a brief, sarcastic signal to the joint Maritime headquarters at Northwood, reporting their contact, and asking if they knew where all their own submarines were. The radio operator hunched over his keyboard, encrypting the message from a code card.

HMS Truculent.

Tim Pike was controlling the boat from the 'bandstand', a circular railing in the centre of the control room.

'Depth fifty metres,' yelled the helmsman.

'*Control Room, Sound Room!*' the communications box crackled.

Pike clicked the switch and acknowledged.

'*Contact's gone active, sir! The sod's pinging us!*'

Cordell threw himself at the AIS Console. Sonar data were transferred automatically from the sound room to the AIS.

The intercept sensor projecting like a stubby finger from the upper casing of *Truculent* had detected the faint 'ping' from below the thermocline. The computer gave them a bearing and range.

Cordell saw from the amber lines snaking across the screen that the 'ping' had been too weak to detect them. The sound-absorbing tiles coating their hull would have prevented an echo.

'Out of range,' he called over his shoulder. 'Contact bearing two-six-zero. Range five-thousand-three-hundred yards. Depth three-hundred metres.'

'Closer than we thought,' Pike breathed, leaning over the TAS officer's shoulder. 'Odd! The Soviets don't usually go active – don't want to give away their frequencies.'

The use of active sonar was a last resort for submariners; the signal inevitably revealed the position of the transmitting boat.

'He's just pinged again. Different angle. He's searching for us.'

'Time to show him our tail,' warned Pike. 'Steer zero-eight-zero. Revolutions for thirty knots. Clear the datum.'

'He's dead keen to keep tabs on us,' Cordell mused. 'Perhaps there's a promotion in it for him!'

The submarine banked to starboard; the men in the control room gripped fittings and grab-rails.

Truculent would make more noise going fast, and her

sonar would be deaf, but they needed the distance. Just a few minutes' sprint, then they'd slow down to listen.

'Give us room! Give us room!' Pike muttered to himself, his body spring-tight with tension. 'When he realizes we're not deep any more, he'll come up here looking for us.'

Silence fell in the control room, anxious eyes fixed on dials and screens.

'Still pinging?' Pike checked.

'No, he's stopped,' replied Cordell.

'Are we out of range if he pings again directly at us?'

'Probably not. Stern on, we're a small target, but he might get an echo off the propulsor.'

Truculent's propulsion system was like an aircraft's turbojet, a double row of compressor fans encased in a tube. Only from directly astern could the blades be detected on sonar.

'Another course change,' Pike ordered, swinging round to the planesman. 'Port five. Steer zero-six-zero, and be ready to go deep again.'

'How long now at this speed?' Pike asked.

'Six minutes, sir!' answered the navigator.

Three miles they'd covered; three miles further from the *Victor*, he hoped. Time to listen again.

'Reduce speed. Revs for fifteen knots,' he called.

The instruction was relayed aft to the manoeuvring room. The response from the propulsion plant was almost immediate.

'*Aircraft overhead!*' barked the tannoy.

Coming alive again, the sonar had picked up the roar of jet engines.

'Jesus! What *is* this? A plane too?'

'Because of the exercise?' Cordell guessed. 'The Sovs keeping tabs on Ocean Guardian?'

'Or something else. Something to do with what the captain was talking about. The East–West crisis!'

Pike hurled a silent curse at the sleeping Hitchens. Why hadn't the bastard told him what was going on?

Cordell's head turned, snake-like on his long, thin neck. There was a flicker of fear in his eyes.

108

'You mean the *Victor* was trying for a firing solution?' he asked aghast. 'Wants to torpedo us?'

'That's the usual reason for going active, isn't it?'

'You're joking!'

'Well, I *hope* I am!'

'Shit! The tubes are empty! We're defenceless!'

Pike thought hard. The intelligence reports had let them down. They were on their own. Better play it safe. He grabbed the microphone for the tannoy.

'Watch stand to!' he spoke, steadying his voice. 'We're being shadowed by a Soviet SSN, and will adopt defence watch conditions.'

'Taking it a bit personally, aren't you?' the weapon engineer chided as he entered the control room at a run.

'Taking no chances. Anyway, *you* were the one worrying about World War Three starting. Better bring the bloody tubes to the action state!'

Spriggs raised one eyebrow, but disappeared fast down the ladder to the torpedo stowage compartment below, where the ratings were already wrenching open the tube rear doors and loading the 1½ tonne *Tigerfish* torpedoes. Attached behind each propeller was the drum of guidance wire that would spool out after launch, keeping the weapons under the control of the submarine.

'Where's the target, TAS?' asked Pike.

'Moving away, sir. Bearing one-nine-three. Range ten-thousand yards. Heading one-seven-zero. Still pinging.'

'Good. Let's show him some more leg. Set course ten degrees. Revolutions for thirty knots.'

'Aye, aye, sir!'

* * *

In the sky above, the Nimrod banked and weaved. When the British boat slowed down she became desperately difficult to track.

They'd detected the start of her turn to port, but by the time they'd dropped a pair of buoys on what they thought was the new track, there was no sign of her.

Locating the Russian boat was easy. Its sonar 'pings' set the ink-pens quivering on the hard-copy printers of the acoustic processor.

'Noisy bastard!' growled the AEO. 'Doesn't want to lose our boy, does he?'

The pens quivered again and then a third time.

The AEO began to frown. It was doubly odd; a Soviet sub using active sonar, and a British boat being somewhere it wasn't meant to be.

'I don't know what's going on down there, but I'm not taking any chances,' he told the TacNav. 'Arm up a couple of Stingrays just in case that *Victor* decides to do something nasty.'

The navigator punched buttons to switch on the giros in two of the torpedoes in the bomb bay.

'Getting a reply to that signal, by the look of it,' remarked the radio operator, as the teleprinter began to buzz. He read the cipher as it was being printed and began to decrypt it from his code cards.

The AEO took the handwritten note when it was completed.

'Well, bugger me!' he exclaimed. 'They *didn't* know they had a boat here! They're ordering us to track her, and they're sending a tanker to refuel us so we can stay on task longer.'

'You mean we're not getting home today?' the TacNav groaned.

''Sright, sunshine.'

'My wife'll kill me. It's our anniversary! We'd got a dinner booked!'

* * *

0500 hrs. Soviet time. [0200 GMT]

Severomorsk.

The flight bringing Vice-Admiral Feliks Astashenkov back from Moscow was delayed again; then the taxi bringing him from Murmansk to the naval town of Severomorsk suffered a puncture, so it was four in the morning before he arrived at the comfortable villa that went with the job of Deputy Commander of the Northern Fleet.

He didn't go to bed. Apart from not wanting to wake

his wife, he'd come straight from the arms of another woman, and his conscience pricked him.

It had been a painful farewell with Tatiana. They'd both known they wouldn't meet again, but neither had said it.

He made himself some tea and slumped back in the red-velvet, wing-backed armchair that had belonged to his grandmother.

He felt afraid. Savkin had tricked him into making a personal commitment that could put him at odds with his own Commander-in-Chief, even the entire Stavka, the high command.

He knew what pressure the General Secretary was under from the Politburo. Savkin's survival was by no means certain, and if he lost his gamble to preserve *perestroika* Astashenkov could see himself being pulled down with him.

Why had he committed himself? Because he still believed in the complete restructuring of Soviet society that Gorbachev had begun, and Savkin was struggling to continue. But what if he could see that Savkin was going to fail, and still the call came to honour that commitment? Was he ready to destroy his own career for a lost cause? Better surely to hold his hand, to fight another day. All he could hope was that the call would never come.

His eyes focused on the canvas over the fireplace, an heroic oil painting of the destroyer *Sevastopol*, which his father had commanded in 1943 and in which he'd died. From childhood Feliks' ambition had been to honour his father by reaching the highest levels in the Soviet Navy, and having a warship named after him. At the age of fifty he was on track to achieve that goal – or would be if Nikolai Savkin didn't ask him to throw it all away.

In the dim light from the desk lamp, Astashenkov's eyelids began to droop. He dozed for about an hour.

He came to when the carriage clock on the mantelpiece chimed six. He stroked his chin and decided to begin the new day. Quietly he made his way upstairs to the bathroom.

After a shower and a shave he felt refreshed. His dressing room was separate from the bedroom, so he need not disturb his wife as he hung up his brown civilian suit and donned the dark-blue uniform of a Vice-Admiral with its two stars on the heavy gold shoulderboards, one broad band and two narrow ones on the sleeves.

The smell of coffee told him that his staff were awake and about their business. The house was managed by a middle-aged civilian couple from Leningrad; the woman cooked and cleaned, and her husband served at table, polished brass and silver and acted as valet to Feliks.

He also had a personal driver, who lived in the barracks in the main naval base area, a *starshina* who would arrive outside the house at 6.30 each morning, drunk or sober.

Feliks would take his breakfast in the kitchen, bread, sliced sausage, and coffee. His staff took pleasure in his passing the time of day with them; his wife treated them like serfs.

The kitchen window faced east, overlooking a distant creek where sailing boats lined the jetties of a small marina belonging to the officers' club. The sky was grey, but gold where the clouds broke to reveal the rising sun.

He would start early as soon as the driver arrived, tour the harbour and see who he could catch off-guard.

Severomorsk is a grey, granite naval town, ringed by greenhouse farms to provide fresh vegetables for the Navy. The town's only purpose is to serve as the headquarters of the Northern Fleet. Set on a bay on the east bank of the Kol'skiy Zaliv, the Kola inlet that leads to Murmansk, its piers stretch from the dockyard like outspread fingers. Heavy cranes tower black against the clouds.

They passed a guard post and the duty man hurried back into his hut to telephone ahead that the Deputy Commander was on the prowl.

To Feliks' right lay the sea, grey and choppy in the chill breeze that felt as if it came from the North Pole. The low hills on the far bank of the fjord five kilometres distant were discernible just as an outline in the mist.

Some of the finest warships in the Soviet fleet lined the piers. The twelve-thousand-ton cruiser *Slava* took up almost the whole length of No.3 jetty, some of her long-range missile tubes hoisted ashore for maintenance. Beyond her, at anchor in the bay, Feliks could see the distinctive outline of the aircraft-carrier *Minsk*.

He instructed the driver to stop the car, and wound down the window. The temperature felt below freezing, but he sniffed the air, savouring the odours of oil fumes and rotting fish. It was a smell of which he would never tire.

He was proud of his Navy, which had been expanded and modernized dramatically in the past decade. Yet he prayed it would never have to fight a war. He looked again at the *Minsk*. She carried a dozen vertical take-off jet fighters and a similar number of helicopters, but had none of the striking power of the Americans. The first of his own Navy's big carriers was still on sea trials and there'd be no more built.

Another pier, and a pair of *Sovremenny* class destroyers. They were due to sail any day now, to join the carrier *Kiev* and the cruiser *Kirov* maintaining the defensive barrier north of North Cape. Their departure depended on crew training; three-quarters of the men on board were conscripts. Autumn was the time for a new intake, and all the problems of moulding reluctant, ignorant young men into sailors.

His own submarine service was the worst affected. Greater skills were needed for the complex technology. With a rapid turnover of crews, harbour-time was high; most submarines in the fleet would spend all but a few weeks of the year alongside the jetty.

Feliks envied the professional, volunteer navies of other countries.

'Let's move on, Comrade,' he called to his driver.

They drove along the waterfront road that linked the heads of the piers. There were no submarines in harbour that morning; in fact, there were seldom any at Severomorsk, the main submarine bases being further north around Polyarny, at the mouth of the Kol'skiy Zaliv.

Looking out to the main navigation channel, he watched a fish-factory ship heading south for Murmansk, low in the water with the weight of its catch from around the shores of the British Isles.

Murmansk was an ugly sprawl of a city, whose population had grown to nearly four hundred thousand on the back of the Atlantic fishing fleet based there. The Gulf Stream kept the fjord to Murmansk open all year round with winter temperatures ten degrees higher than other Arctic zones on the same latitude.

To Feliks, however, the whole area was grim. He hated the bare rocks of the coastal zone, and pitied the puny shrubs and birch trees that struggled to survive inland. He longed for the gardened splendour of Leningrad.

The car turned left, past the storage sheds and maintenance workshops essential for keeping the complicated and costly warships operational. Men on bicycles weaved their way through dockyard clutter, as a night-shift finished and the day workers began.

Feliks decided against an unannounced visit to a ship. He'd bitterly resented such treatment from his own superiors when he'd been a submarine commander.

'Take me to the headquarters building,' he grunted. He'd put in an hour or so with the paperwork that threatened to take over his desk, before attending the morning command briefing.

★ ★ ★

0800 hrs. GMT.

Northwood, England.

Andrew Tinker searched the corridor of the Fleet headquarters for the office of the Fleet Psychiatrist. Finding the door, he tapped on it but there was no answer.

It was locked. He checked his watch – just past eight.

Behind him in the corridor he heard the click of high heels.

'Excessive punctuality's a sign of anxiety,' chided a confident female voice.

Andrew turned to see a short, red-haired WRN commander approaching.

'Tell that to those who trained me,' he countered.

114

She took his outstretched hand and held it loosely.

'It's a lost cause with me, I'm afraid,' she smiled.

Commander Felicity Rush was maturely attractive, but she looked weary.

'The thing is, I'm terrible at getting up in the mornings. Never normally see anyone before ten if I can help it. But when an Admiral orders. . . .'

She unlocked the door and led him in. Andrew was expecting it to be more like a consulting room than just another office.

'You *are* Commander Tinker?'

'Indeed I am.'

She placed her briefcase on the desk but left it unopened.

'Pull up a seat. There's nothing very comfortable, I'm afraid. I don't rate an armchair.'

Andrew dragged a typist's swivel seat over to the desk and sat down.

'Now, I've no idea what this is about,' she began, pulling a notepad from a drawer, 'except that it must be exceptionally urgent. Admiral Bourlet knows perfectly well how badly I function at this hour.'

Andrew raised an eyebrow at what he thought was innuendo, but there was no hint of embarrassment on her face.

'Are you the one with the problem?' she pressed, her eyes softening with professional sympathy.

'What? No, thank God! Not me. It's a friend of mine. He also drives a submarine, but the poor sod's just had a bust-up with his wife. We're worried he may have had some sort of breakdown.'

'Oh?'

'Yes. He's not responding to signals from headquarters and is now somewhere under the North Atlantic heading for the Arctic Circle at a rate of knots.'

For a moment her face didn't move. Then she frowned.

'Would you mind saying that again?'

Andrew began to explain. The Admiral had told him to tell her only what was necessary for her to form a medical opinion.

'This is utterly confidential. I can't give you all the details, but the blunt facts are these; the CO in question discovered his wife had been regularly unfaithful while he was away. That was bad enough, but then he found out one of her lovers was a Soviet agent.'

'Wow!'

'And it's beginning to look as if he's decided to get his own back on the Russians, using the weapons on his submarine.'

'Crikey!'

His words had shaken her out of her morning stupor.

'But that's appalling! Surely he'll be stopped by his crew.'

'Yes, but only if the other officers can see something's wrong and do something about it. That's why I'm here. I'm hoping you can give us some idea of how he'll be behaving down there.'

'I see.' She looked flustered. She'd never met a situation like this before. 'You'd better start again. Tell me what you know, from the beginning.'

As she listened, she took a note from time to time, usually just a single word to jog her memory.

'It's difficult without knowing the man himself. What you've described is a tragically common state of affairs. Infidelity is part of the human condition, and when the offended partner finds out about it, the effects can be devastating. It can tip someone over the edge into doing something wild, but that's usually a spur-of-the-moment thing. If I understand you correctly, you suspect that this man has planned some quite elaborate revenge. That implies a certain rationality – an irrational rationality, if you follow me.'

'Er . . , not altogether.'

'Let me explain. The initial reaction to marital breaks is the obvious one – anger and despair. That can lead to a depression which can become clinical – a sense of helplessness, loss of self-esteem, crying, physical disorders, thoughts of suicide. Now, if that's what your man is going through, it should be obvious to the other officers on board. He'll be unusually irritable, off his food, and above all indecisive. What sort of a CO is he, by the way? Easy-going or a stickler for discipline?'

'Definitely the latter, I would say. Not the most popular of captains. Gets the respect of his crew, but not their affection.'

'Pity. That'll make it more difficult for his first lieutenant. If he was a more relaxed type, his irritability would be more obvious. But it's odd. I'd expect a man like that to stick to the rules, whatever his personal problems. He might even find some comfort in the familiarity of discipline and order. Yet he's not doing that, you say. He's scrapped the rule book and taken matters into his own hands. He faces a court-martial for what he's doing, and if he does something nasty to the Russians, he's risking his own life and those of his crew and a great deal else besides. That suggests something much more serious than depression. He may be psychotic – unable to distinguish between reality and fantasy. But again, that should be pretty obvious to his junior officers . . .'

She was thinking aloud, tapping one end of her ballpoint on the pad, turning it over and tapping it again.

'Tell me more about him. I don't have a picture of the man yet. I'd get his file from the registry, but it's too early in the morning.'

'He's a year younger than me, and I'm forty. We trained at Dartmouth together – shared a cabin. He worries; always thought I had the edge on him because I'd spent a year in the big, wide world before joining up, even though I'd only driven a delivery van most of that time.

'Anyway, he'd come straight from school. A bit unworldly, I suppose; still is. Nervous of women, very few girlfriends before he met Sara. Certainly prefers the company of men, so he should be well suited stuck in a steel tube for months at a time!'

'Latent homosexual perhaps?' she asked casually.

'Oh, no. I don't think so. We slept in the same room for nearly a year; I just don't think he's very interested in sex.'

Commander Felicity Rush knew that no man was uninterested in sex and wrote down the words 'acute sexual repression' followed by a question mark.

'Are his parents still alive?'

'I seem to remember his father died when Philip was a kid. He was in the Navy, also a submariner. His boat disappeared up north, somewhere. I'm not sure they ever discovered what happened.'

'How old was Philip when that happened?'

'Don't know. Quite young, I think.'

'That's very interesting. A tragic loss in childhood can sensitize you; if you face something similar later you can react much more dramatically than normal. What about his mother?'

'I don't know anything about her. He never mentioned her. Funny, that. Used to talk of "going home", but never said who was there.'

'What about his work? He's respected as a commanding officer, you said; what's his attitude towards the Soviets?'

'Pretty sceptical, like most of us. Thinks they're a devious bunch of opportunists. Come to think of it, he's harder than most. Rants and raves in high glee when they get caught out.'

'So he hates the Russians?'

'Well, yes. He probably does.'

She arched her eyebrows and sat back, arms folded.

'All I can say is that you'd better stop him. And soon.'

'That may not be so easy. But that's why I want your advice. If we can get close enough to *Truculent* I'll try to talk to him – by underwater telephone. But if I say something wrong, I could make things worse.'

'Whatever you say may be wrong, as far as he's concerned. Look; if his mental disorder were just the result of a broken marriage, either he'd have had an emotional breakdown, which would be obvious to his crew, or he'd have come to his senses and given up any daft idea of revenge. Since neither of those things has happened, apparently, I can only assume he may have some sort of psychopathic condition, that's been dormant up to now.'

'Phil? A psychopath? That's ridiculous!'

'A psychopath isn't just someone going berserk with a

118

meat cleaver,' she explained. 'It's to do with attitudes. I'm sure Philip knows that launching an attack on the Russians is morally wrong, yet if he can't resist doing it, that's psychopathic. Such a person would be unaffected by anything you said to him. No. Your best bet is to talk to his first lieutenant. Tell him to relieve his captain of command.'

Andrew let out a deep sigh. The task ahead looked increasingly complicated.

Commander Rush suddenly leaned forward, elbows on the desk, her green eyes earnest.

'Suppose that doesn't work. What will you do then?' she asked.

Andrew looked away. He had always had an irrational fear of psychiatrists, that they could read his thoughts.

'That's something I haven't dared contemplate,' he lied.

* * *

0900 hrs. GMT.

Whitehall, London.

A black Mercedes turned into Horseguards Parade, and stopped at the rear entrance to the Foreign Office. The driver showed a pass to the policeman in the sentry box, who peered into the back of the car, recognized the passenger and waved the vehicle on.

The driver swung the wheel to the right and let the limousine roll easily up to the Ambassadors' entrance. The Soviet diplomat got out, glancing sideways towards Downing Street, conscious that it was there his message was directed.

A junior official received him on the steps and led him to the Foreign Secretary who had just returned from his monthly breakfast with the Diplomatic Press Corps.

Twenty minutes later the ambassador had delivered his protest about 'Ocean Guardian', and was back outside. He paused briefly for a news agency photographer to take his picture. Then the Mercedes sped him back to Kensington Palace Gardens.

12 Noon [0900 GMT].

The Kremlin, Moscow.

The news, that Monday morning, was not good. The Soviet leader could see the abyss opening before him. Strikes were spreading and he was in the throes of re-imposing full censorship on the media to prevent the situation snowballing out of control.

'*Perestroika* came too late for our people,' Nikolai Savkin muttered, half to himself, half to Foreign Minister Vasily Kalinin. The General Secretary had summoned Kalinin to his private office deep inside the Kremlin walls.

'Thirty years too late, maybe. Too many generations have been taught by the Party to believe the State will do everything, and that they, the people, need do nothing.'

'Such despair is not in your character, Nikolai,' Kalinin soothed. 'All is not lost; and don't allow yourself to think so.'

Savkin laughed self-deprecatingly. He knew he was the wrong man for the job. He silently cursed the Aeroflot mechanic whose carelessness allegedly caused the tragic and untimely death of his predecessor in a plane crash. Personally he'd always suspected the KGB had a hand in it.

Mikhail Sergeyevich Gorbachev had been in a different league from himself. He'd had the personality of a giant; if he were still alive the strikes would be short-lived. He'd have stormed onto the factory floors and argued the toss with the workers. If Savkin tried that tactic himself they'd spit on him.

Then there was the minority problem. Armenians, Latvians, Tartars; all were using the new freedom of expression under *glasnost* to voice the grievances of forty years. The KGB had played it cleverly; opposed to the new openness, they'd let the regional protests get out of control, so the politicians would be humiliated and have to turn to them to sort out the mess.

His control of the Politburo was on a knife edge; the

small majority still supporting his reformist views was being whittled away. He could only retain their support by buckling to pressure for the *perestroika* programme to be further diluted.

There were those in the Politburo who'd proclaimed their commitment to his predecessor's ideas, but without the man himself to hold the line now the going was tough, they'd begun to distance themselves from the policies. They had the rest of their lives to think of; if *perestroika* collapsed, and the old system of economic feather-bedding returned, Savkin thought, holding on to their jobs would be their number-one priority. Without the privileges that went with their status, life wouldn't be worth living in the chaos that followed.

He tugged at the bushy, white hair at his temples, then beat at his head with his knuckles, as if to drum sense into it.

'You're right, Vasily. I'm thinking like a defeated man. And if I think like one, soon I'll act like one. You must stop me.'

Kalinin was more than a foreign minister; he was also Savkin's oldest friend, an ally whose loyalty he believed he could count on for ever. A curious choice for a foreign minister, many thought; Kalinin had never travelled outside the Soviet Union before taking up his appointment. Yet he had an insight into the thinking of western leaders that Savkin found remarkably astute, all the more valuable because Savkin had little insight of his own.

It was Kalinin who had had the original idea of using the threat from the West as a goad to keep the Soviet economy on course for modernization. Previous regimes had used the fear of attack from abroad to tighten belts at home. What had been done before could be done again. The armada of Western warships currently on course for the Kola Peninsula provided just the threat that was needed.

'You know the irony of our plan, Nikolai?' Kalinin grimaced. '*Perestroika* is meant to curb the military budget and redirect funds to consumer goods. But if we make too much of the military threat from NATO, our beloved generals will be demanding the expansion of their arsenals again!'

'It's already happened. Admiral Grekov was here last night. Says he needs more ships to match the NATO navies.'

'I hope you told the Comrade Admiral he was pissing into the wind?'

'Yes . . . but not in those words. Something a little more refined. But tell me, what's the latest from Washington? Are they tugging at the bait?'

'It's too early to say. The predictable reactions have already occurred. Half a dozen Republican senators and the media have been raging about a new threat from Cuba. But McGuire hasn't commented yet. Our ambassador has been given a flat denial that the American helicopters posed any sort of threat to the *Rostov*, and the administration has had nothing at all to say about the MiGs.'

'And Castro?'

'He'll play ball. He's desperate for the aid we've promised him.'

'Is McGuire clever enough to know what's happening?'

'He knows little of life outside Middle America, so he takes advice. Tom Reynolds is the one he'll be listening to. And Tom's a cautious man. "Take no action until you have to" is his motto. They may be waiting to see what we do next.'

'And what will that be, I wonder,' Savkin ruminated. 'Every day that passes, the bigger the distraction needed to jolt our people back into line.'

'The Department of Naval Aviation is taking the television teams out this morning. Their film should be on *Vremya* tonight, and on the American networks. And Admiral Grekov is holding a press conference this afternoon for the foreign journalists.

'He'll condemn NATO strategy, call it provocative and dangerous. He can be pretty aggressive when provoked. And what he says is sure to get the American TV reporters on their hind legs baying at him. He'll call on NATO to abandon their exercise. By the end of the day the West'll be digging its heels in.

'Our own television will of course present the press conference in its true light: Grekov – the voice of reason; the American press – the hyenas of the West ready to bite into the soft and vulnerable throat of Russia. By the end of the day no one should be in any doubt there's a crisis.'

'We'll see,' the General Secretary answered doubtfully. 'It may not be enough.'

In his heart he knew it would take more than TV pictures and a press conference to jolt the Soviet citizenry out of their sloth. With sadness, resignation and fear, he realized it might take war.

* * *

1230 hrs. GMT.

Downing Street, London.

Every time he met the Prime Minister, Admiral Waverley was struck by her small stature and her femininity, which hid a steely determination. Both he and the Foreign Secretary were in a state of some trepidation about the meeting that lay ahead.

'Gentlemen, good day,' she greeted them in the hall. 'We'll go straight in and sit down, if you don't mind. I've got to be in the House at two-thirty.'

She led them into the dining room, where a small table was set with just three places, a large bottle of Malvern Water in its centre.

'You sit here, Admiral, and Nigel, there.'

The Prime Minister placed herself facing the door and nodded to the butler that he could begin serving.

'Now, Stewart, the Defence Secretary has told me about *HMS Truculent* and Commander Hitchens. It's appalling. And the Home Secretary's briefed me on what happened in Plymouth. This KGB officer – he's still on the loose. *Most* unsatisfactory!

'But it's the implications I'm concerned with. Lucky we had this little lunch arranged. Now, first of all, remind me about Ocean Guardian. As you know, the Russians are making the most extraordinary fuss. Heaven knows why; they've never bothered about it before.'

'That's right, Prime Minister,' Waverley answered. 'But the exercise has never been quite like this before. We hold them every two years; dozens of warships from several NATO countries deploying to the North Atlantic, but we've never taken the exercise right round the tip of Norway into the Barents Sea before, right to the doorstep of the Russian Navy's main harbours. That's why they're squealing. It's international waters of course, so they've no right to complain. And Norway *is* NATO's northern frontier.'

'So the Russians could conduct their manoeuvres off the coast of Scotland if they wanted to?' the Foreign Secretary queried. 'We wouldn't like that.'

'So long as they stayed in international waters, we could do nothing to stop them.'

'The idea is to be able to bottle up the Soviet fleet at the start of a conflict, correct?' the PM asked.

'That's right. The Americans took the initiative. They felt defending the Atlantic further south had become too difficult. The Soviets have so many new, quieter submarines.'

'Ambassador Bykov placed another protest on my desk this morning,' Sir Nigel remarked. 'Argued in most reasoned terms. Said this was a time of peace and improved east-west relations, and that such an "aggressive rehearsal for war", as he put it, was quite unacceptable.'

The PM waved him to silence.

'How big is our involvement? How many ships have we got up there?'

'About twenty. The Americans have eighteen, the Canadians, the Dutch, the Norwegians, Germans and French bring the total to over a hundred.'

Just then the door opened and a waitress brought in a tray of soup.

'Carrot soup,' the PM announced. 'My mother's recipe. I do hope you like it.'

The two men made polite, appreciative noises, and reached for their spoons. The waitress closed the door quietly behind her.

'Do continue, Admiral. You were interrupted.'

'Thank you, Prime Minister. Our main task is to provide an anti-submarine force centred on the carrier *HMS Illustrious*. With four escorts, she provides a screen ahead of the US strike fleet – the *Eisenhower* group. Our carrier will keep well away from the Russian coast, but two of her frigates will steam into the Barents, together with two of our submarines.'

'But *Truculent* had a special mission. Those new mines.'

'Exactly. She was due to break away from the exercise, to try to slip through the Soviet defences and get to the sort of position where the mines would have to be laid if war threatened.'

'Inside Soviet territorial waters?'

'Er . . , yes.'

'And the Americans are doing the same?'

'Further east, Prime Minister.'

'And the mines themselves? They're a great advance on anything we've had before?'

'Very much so. Anglo-American development. Launched from a torpedo tube in deep water. Very difficult for the enemy to detect. It's a two part device, with a sonar sensor – very clever – which can be programmed to look out for one particular type of ship or submarine, and the explosive bit which is really a high speed homing torpedo that gets launched once the target's been designated. And the whole thing can sit on the bottom for up to a year, doing nothing, then be activated or reprogrammed by sonar signal from up to forty miles away.'

'Right. We know what *Truculent* was *meant* to do – what is Commander Hitchens *really* going to do, Admiral?'

Waverley sighed uncomfortably.

'We just don't know, Prime Minister. We've had no response to any signals. He's ignoring orders, but appears still to be heading for the Kola Inlet. An RAF Nimrod picked up his track off Norway this morning, but lost it again. There was a Soviet submarine in the area, too.'

'But what about the rest of his crew? Are you telling me they're also ignoring orders?'

'Certainly not! But you see, Prime Minister, Hitchens could well say he's acting under secret orders issued to him personally. Often happens. Submarines operate in extreme secrecy. Frequently most of the crew haven't a clue where they are or why.'

The colour began to drain from the Prime Minister's face. She turned to Sir Nigel. Their looks met, each realizing for the first time the full implications of what Waverley had said.

'What . . . ah . . . what could he actually *do?*' Sir Nigel asked, clearing the frog from his throat.

'At worst, he could sink about a dozen Soviet warships . . .'

'Christ Almighty!'

'But that's improbable. To launch torpedoes and missiles he'd need the co-operation of his crew. He'd have to convince them war had broken out. Impossible, I'd say. But he has got those mines on board, four of them. It's just possible he could lay them . . .'

The Foreign Secretary put his hands up to his face.

'Just when Savkin's accusing us of undue aggression!' he groaned.

The Prime Minister tapped nervously on the table-cloth with her fingernails as she thought of what had to be done. She reached under the table and pressed a bell-push.

'Your soup's gone cold, Admiral. We'll go on to the next course.'

The waitress returned with her tray. While she cleared the plates and served them a main course of roast pork, the three remained silent.

'Now, Stewart. You obviously have a plan. What is it?'

'We've got about three days in which to find *Truculent* . . .'

'It's no good finding her if you lose her again,' the PM chided.

'Our submarines are designed to *avoid* being detected, Prime Minister. Twice he's passed through waters we were monitoring anyway, but keeping track of him when he doesn't want to be tracked is another matter.

'It's not going to be easy. The RAF are searching round the clock, but our best chance lies with *HMS Tenby*. Another SSN. A Commander Tinker, who knows Hitchens and is fully briefed on the problem, is flying to north Norway to join the *Tenby*. We have a good idea where Hitchens will go, and if Tinker can pick up his trail, he should be able to communicate with *Truculent* and stop him in good time.'

The Admiral had spoken in the most confident voice he could muster, but the Prime Minister had not been taken in.

'What if *Truculent*'s not listening?'

'Then we have a very difficult decision to take.'

'To do what?'

'Well, if we can find her, to stop her by force.'

'How would you do that?'

'Attack the *Truculent* with a torpedo. Try to cripple her without loss of life.'

'That's an appalling prospect. Is it possible?'

The Admiral shrugged.

'We've never tried it. Our weapons are designed to destroy boats, not wing them.'

'How many are there on board?'

''Bout a hundred.'

They fell silent again. None of them felt disposed to eat.

'There must be some alternative?' the PM suggested.

'We could tell the Russians what's happened,' the Foreign Secretary remarked. 'Warn them to keep clear of the mines until we can deal with them.'

'And give them a propaganda triumph of unimaginable proportions, Nigel. Just what they need to justify their claim that our manoeuvres are provocative. That's a ridiculous idea!'

'The earlier we pick up *Truculent*'s trail, the better,' Waverley pressed. 'And the more resources we put into the search, the sooner we're likely to find her. Sounds obvious, Prime Minister, but we've got precious few vessels in the right place. If we got some help from our allies – the Americans, the Norwegians, it could make all the difference.'

'No! I don't want any other nation to know about this. The name of the Royal Navy is held in the *highest* regard by friend and foe alike. What *would* people think if they learned that one of our submarine commanders could jeopardize the peace of the whole world? That our command structure has failed to prevent a madman going on the rampage in charge of one of Her Majesty's ships?'

Her eyes bored accusingly into the Admiral's.

'I assume you'll be examining your personnel selection procedures as a matter of urgency, Admiral?'

'That'll be our *second* priority, Prime Minister,' Waverley bristled. 'The first is to find the boat.'

'There'll come a time when our allies'll have to know,' Sir Nigel interjected gloomily. 'If you don't stop Hitchens in time, and he's about to blow up the Soviet Navy, it'd be better if our friends know before it happens rather than after.'

'That's a sound point, Nigel. President McGuire is difficult enough to handle as it is.'

She began to pick at her food and the two men followed suit. She frowned in concentration.

'*Do* you think you'll find him in time, Stewart?' she asked suddenly.

The Admiral swallowed some mineral water before replying.

'The chances are less than even, I'm afraid. Our best hope is that his officers twig what's going on.'

'What do you *think* he intends to do? What are we in for?'

'God knows! But if he lays the Moray mines outside Polyarny, and several Soviet submarines make a run for the open sea at the same time, he could take out four of them before they realize what's happening. Four nuclear reactors exploding underwater, pollution over a wide area, and at least four hundred dead! Not a happy scenario!'

'And all because his wife fooled around with some Russian? It's madness,' Sir Nigel exclaimed.

'A Russian who hasn't been caught,' the PM repeated.

'Perhaps he'll contact Mrs Hitchens again,' the Foreign Secretary mused, half to himself.

His thoughts were moving in a direction quite different from those of his leader. She'd dismissed his idea of warning the Russians, but it could be the only way to avoid catastrophe. It would have to be done with enormous care, and clearly without the knowledge of 'the boss'.

'If the worst does happen, Nigel, what's Savkin going to do about it?' the PM asked. 'He'll hardly declare war, surely?'

'I don't know,' Sir Nigel warned. 'He's making a lot of noise about "NATO aggression", much more than is justified. Got to ask ourselves why. Also this business of a ship-load of MiGs heading for Cuba; that has to have been done for a purpose. If Savkin's intention was simply to supply an ally with new planes, he'd have flown them to Cuba in transporter planes. No fuss that way.

'But to put them on the deck of a cargo ship and to sail it slap through the middle of the US fleet – I ask you! He *wanted* them to be seen! He *wanted* the Yanks to go screaming around in their helicopters and plastering pictures of his MiGs all over their television news bulletins. They're so bloody predictable, the Americans; they did exactly what he wanted! One more example of Western aggression to show to his own citizens on TV.'

'Yes, but come to the point, Nigel. What's Savkin up to?'

'Ah, now that's more difficult to say. The one thing we do know is that he's in big trouble with his economy. He's facing an unprecedented wave of strikes and civil unrest. He may be looking for a distraction, and banking on America, and us, supplying it. It's the oldest trick in the book, but it could be the only one he's got up his sleeve.'

The PM frowned with irritation; she'd foreseen her Foreign Secretary's conclusion, before he'd finished speaking.

'But I return to my point; he'll hardly declare war, will he?' she insisted.

'And I repeat *my* point; I simply don't know. The danger is he'll back himself into a corner; if he whips up enough anti-western feeling at home, and our Commander Hitchens then blows up some of his submarines, he may have no option but to declare war.'

The Prime Minister stared at him aghast. Then she turned to the Commander-in-Chief of the Fleet.

'Commander Hitchens must be stopped, Admiral. At *any* price!'

CHAPTER FIVE

Earlier that morning.

Severomorsk, USSR.

'Guard! Salute!'

The naval infantryman pinned his fingers to his fore-head as the Zil limousine rolled to a halt outside the operations centre, its pristine black paint spattered with mud.

The Senior Lieutenant in charge of the guard opened the car door and saluted too, his eyes fixed on the horizon.

The Vice-Admiral ignored the young officer and strode briskly up the steps to the heavy, blast-proof, iron doors, eager to be out of the arctic wind. He heard the electro-magnetic bolts click back, and the door swung open.

He entered the command centre of the Red Banner Northern Fleet. Built into a rocky hillside overlooking the town, the bunker was deep enough under the granite to withstand the megatons of nuclear destruction which the Americans had earmarked for it.

'Did you get a good catch at the weekend, Comrade Admiral?' fawned the Captain 2nd Rank staff officer. 'Some fine salmon for your dinner, perhaps?'

'No such luck,' Astashenkov growled, remembering the alibi for his weekend in Moscow. 'Nothing you could even feed to a cat! I shan't fish again until the spring.'

'The days are getting shorter.'

'I hate winter. It's at this time of year I wish I was commanding an *Eskadra* in the Mediterranean.'

Their footsteps echoed in the bare concrete tunnel. Ahead was the inner door, beyond which the air was filtered and recycled to exclude nuclear fallout or poison gas.

As they approached, there came again the click of opening bolts and the door swung towards them, driven by hydraulic rams powerful enough to push back rubble if the tunnel collapsed as the result of a direct hit.

Beyond lay another corridor lined with offices; then a corner, and the door to the operations room. The Captain 2nd Rank tapped his personal security code into a keypad, then opened the door for the Admiral to enter.

Two dozen uniformed men and women saluted. Astashenkov acknowledged them with a nod. He strode to the podium in the centre of the room. Admiral Belikov's staff officer hovered in wait.

'Good day, Comrade Vice-Admiral,' the young man bowed. 'The Commander-in-Chief is detained. An important telephone call from Admiral Grekov. He can't attend this briefing. He asks that you report to him in his office afterwards.'

Astashenkov nodded curtly, disguising his unease. Belikov talking on the phone to the Admiral of the Fleet? It must be urgent. Normally Grekov preferred to write.

Had they got wind of his meeting with Savkin?

He sat at the small desk. Another nod. The briefing could begin.

The wall was covered with a map of the northern hemisphere, the Pole at its centre. The Captain Lieutenant briefing officer was young, blond and enthusiastic. Astashenkov remembered himself being like that many years ago.

'This was the situation at 06.00 today,' the youth began, using a torch to project an arrow onto the map. *'Podvodnaya Lodka Atomnaya Raketnaya Ballisticheskaya*. We have eight PLARBs on patrol.'

These were nuclear-powered, ballistic-missile boats, their rockets targeted on the major cities in the United States. The newer ones were *Taifun* class, at twenty-five thousand tons the biggest submarines ever built. Each boat carried twenty missiles with a range of four thousand eight hundred miles, seven warheads per missile. Each boat could destroy one hundred and forty American towns or military bases.

This was the main reason for the Northern Fleet's existence; to keep operational forty submarines, carrying six hundred missiles with two thousand warheads.

So, eight were at sea. Not bad, Feliks thought, considering the maintenance they needed and the amount of shore leave for the crew.

'Four in the Barents Sea, four under the Arctic ice.'

The torch pointed to eight rings on the map. No precise positions, just the areas where the boats would patrol slowly, waiting for the orders they hoped would never come.

'*Podvodnaya Lodka Atomnaya*,' the briefing officer went on. PLAs were the nuclear-powered attack boats. 'Fifteen operational.'

Out of fifty? Not so good, thought Feliks.

'Three are in the Mediterranean, and two are currently returning from there. One is to the west of Scotland gathering intelligence on the British Navy, and one returning. Two more are on long-distance Atlantic patrol off the United States coast, and two transitting home. One of those is shadowing the US aircraft carrier *Eisenhower*. That leaves four on the barrier between North Cape and Greenland.'

'Four PLAs to try to stop the NATO SSNs from tracking our missile boats? It's not enough!' exploded Astashenkov in exasperation.

They all knew it wasn't enough; they also knew that the American *Los Angeles* class submarines and the British *Trafalgars* were so damned quiet, it would be difficult to detect them, however many PLAs they had on patrol.

'Permission to continue, Comrade Vice-Admiral?'

Feliks raised a hand.

'The surface fleet. In defensive positions facing the west, the *Kiev* and the *Moskva* are co-ordinating anti-submarine tactics, with five escorts.'

'What about the two *Sovremenys* in the harbour?'

'Due to sail tomorrow morning. Taking on final stores.'

The Captain Lieutenant rattled off a list of ships deployed further afield, then handed over to the intelligence briefer. Astashenkov concentrated his attention.

'The tactics in NATO's Exercise Ocean Guardian are

as predicted – what we'd expect them to be in the prelude to war.'

The boy had learned the jargon well, Astashenkov mused.

'The US carrier battle-groups have yet to threaten the *Rodina*. One is in mid-Atlantic, the other closer to the motherland, but still near Iceland. It's the British who are nearest our shores. Our radar satellite is tracking the *Illustrious* group in the Norwegian sea. And we have reports locating one or two of their submarines in the past twenty-four hours.'

Astashenkov's eyebrows arched in anticipation.

'The first came from a *Vishnya* intelligence vessel, north of Scotland. It heard a British helicopter trying to radio a submarine. There was no response and in desperation the pilot broke the code. He called "in clear" to *HMS Truculent*.

'The second may have been the same boat or another *Trafalgar*, west of Trondheim, travelling northeast at speed. A PLA tracked it for over an hour.'

'A PLA near Trondheim?' Astashenkov growled. 'I don't remember anything from last week's. . . .'

'Admiral Belikov, sir. The boat is under the personal orders of the Commander-in-Chief.'

'Ah, yes . . .' he nodded, pretending to know. 'And what do you conclude from these two – unusual – reports?'

'The communications security breach was carelessness,' the Captain Lieutenant answered a little too quickly.

'Or deliberate. . . .'

A silence hung in the air as they pondered the significance of the Admiral's remark.

'Indeed, sir.'

His eyes searched the chart. It was rare for NATO submarines to be detected so easily; he'd have liked to capitalize on the situation, and maintain the tracking, but the PLA near Trondheim had lost the target. He wasn't surprised.

Admiral Andrei Belikov, Commander-in-Chief of the Northern Fleet, had a square, lined face, with dark hair, thick at the sides but absent on top. He pushed his heavy-framed spectacles onto the bridge of his nose as Astashenkov entered his large, windowless office in the command centre.

Belikov gestured to a chair.

'Sit down, Feliks. Interesting briefing?'

'Nothing you don't know already, I imagine,' Astashenkov replied pointedly.

Belikov looked momentarily discomfited.

'Meaning?'

'I'm sure you know what's going on without having to attend a briefing, Andrei.'

'You're annoyed that you didn't know about that PLA in the Norwegian Sea. I'm not surprised; I would be too, in your place. But Grekov insisted on secrecy.'

He removed his spectacles and rubbed his eyes. He'd planned to involve his deputy in the KGB operation, but later rather than sooner. The chances of failure had always been high and if the plan came to nothing, the fewer who knew about it the better.

'Feliks, there's a little scheme underway, involving us and the intelligence departments which, if it's successful, could be the most significant since James Walker gave us US Navy submarine secrets.

'The British and Americans have developed a new mine which they believe is undetectable and unbeatable. If it came to war, they'd use them to close our harbours. They call them "Moray" mines, after that eel with the sharp teeth . . .'

'Yes. I know about them, of course.'

Belikov paused for effect.

'We think we're about to get our hands on one!'

'What? How?'

'The boat detected near Trondheim was *HMS Truculent*. We were expecting her. That PLA you hadn't been told about – it was there to pick up her trail, so we'd be ready to receive her and her little gift!'

'A British submarine? Coming here?' Astashenkov gasped. 'To *give* us a secret weapon?'

Belikov folded his spectacles.

'We *need* that mine, Feliks! They say it's undetectable by sonar. If the Americans and the British were to seed our coastline with those weapons, they could destroy the Northern Fleet before it fired a shot!

'Grekov himself ordered the KGB to give it top priority.'

'But how has this been done?'

Andrei Belikov savoured his reply.

'The key's in the hands of a very old man who lives near here – *exists* might be a better word. A prisoner of the State. He's close to death now, but he has a son. A son who'll do almost anything to see his father free before he dies.'

* * *

Murmansk, USSR.

The Moscow correspondent of the American Broadcasting Corporation couldn't stop the grin spreading across his fresh, Nordic face. *Glasnost* had opened countless doors for foreign journalists in the Soviet Union, but he'd never imagined the day would come when he'd be sitting inside the long, silver fuselage of a TU-95 maritime reconnaissance bomber, wearing the flying suit of a Soviet naval aviator.

Known as the *Bear-D* to NATO, the plane carried four giant turboprop engines, with double rows of contra-rotating propellers. The nose of the aircraft was glazed for observers to watch the sea below, and large bulges below the fuselage contained radar for locating shipping.

The pilot introduced himself simply as Valentin. He led the correspondent and his cameraman up a narrow, aluminium ladder into the cramped interior, followed by a technician from Gostelradio.

'When there's something to see, I'll tell you,' Valentin explained. 'Your camera can film through the glass.'

The compartment was crammed with radar scopes. There was nowhere to sit.

'Until then, you will be more comfortable in the back. There are seats there.'

He pointed to a narrow hatch.

'Jeez! Are we sure 'bout all this, Nick?' the American cameraman whispered from the side of his mouth.

'I guess we do as the man says,' the correspondent replied.

Passing the video camcorder ahead of them, they squeezed through the tunnel across the top of the bomb bay to the compartment behind the wing, which was equipped with seats as the pilot had promised.

It was going to be a long day. They'd left Moscow at 5 a.m., flying to Murmansk on a scheduled Aeroflot run. It was now 8.30 a.m. and they had to be back in time to catch the 3pm flight to Moscow, for a press conference with Admiral Grekov. Their material had to be on the satellite to New York soon after midnight if they were to make the evening news programmes on all four US networks.

It had never happened before – American journalists taking pictures of the US Navy from a Soviet spy plane. When offered it as a pool facility the networks had jumped at it.

They strapped themselves in as the first turboprop fired. The crewman thrust headsets into their hands, indicating that it was going to get noisy in there.

They were facing rearwards, and the seatbelts bit into their stomachs as the *Bear* accelerated down the long runway. Heavy with fuel for the long flight, it seemed to race ahead eternally before lifting sluggishly into the air.

There was no window in the rear compartment – just one dim, neon tube set into the roof. Claustrophobia gripped the two Americans, and from the expression on the face of the Russian cameraman, they knew he was similarly affected. It wasn't going to be fun, this assignment.

They slept a little. Two full hours passed before the pilot called them.

Forward of the crawlway, the radar operators turned from their screens to stare with unrestrained curiosity. Having Americans aboard their plane was an idea as alien to them as to the TV team.

'In five minutes you'll see something,' Valentin shouted through the intercom. He'd connected their headsets to the internal circuit.

'Where are we?' the correspondent called back.

'About five hundred kilometres east of Iceland.'

'There's a lot of water down there. Looks pretty empty to me.'

'Empty to you, but not to me,' the pilot boasted. 'We can *always* find your ships when we want to.'

'Oh, yeah?'

The two cameramen squeezed onto the single seat in the forward observation bubble and adjusted their lenses.

'You have a little microphone?' the pilot enquired.

'I've got a neck mike, if that's what you mean.'

'Put it inside your earphone. I'm switching to the frequency the Americans use. If they speak, you will hear.'

Nick fixed the microphone to his headset.

Suddenly the plane banked to the left and dived towards the sea.

'Sheeit!'

Nick grabbed for a hand-hold.

'Three ships in front!' called the pilot.

The journalists peered through the glass, seeing nothing but the grey sea flecked with foam.

Then both cameramen moved at once, eyepieces jammed to their faces. They'd seen the long lines of the wakes.

'Got them!'

The pilot dived and turned, skilfully keeping the American warships ahead of the plane's nose. Five hundred metres from the water, he levelled out, overshot and began a long slow bank round to make another pass.

Nick was no expert, but he knew a carrier when he saw one.

'Is that the *Eisenhower*?'

'No. The *Eisenhower*'s much bigger. That's the *Saipan*. Amphibious. For invasion. With her are one *Spruance* and one *Ticonderoga*.'

Nick felt uncomfortable at the ease with which his

nation's navy had been detected and identified by the Soviets.

'One more pass. Okay?'

'Yep.'

This time the Bear had slowed considerably. It banked over the *Ticonderoga* cruiser with its boxy superstructure housing the long-range, high-performance Aegis radar, and its deck covered with round hatches concealing Tomahawk and Standard missiles.

On the flight-deck of the *USS Saipan*, Nick counted six large helicopters. They flew low enough to see the deck crew gazing up at the circling plane.

'Those guys'd go ape if they knew a US TV team was up here,' he thought to himself.

'Enough?' Valentin's voice in the headphones.

'Well, I wouldn't mind . . .'

'But this is nothing. Don't you want to see your big ship?'

'Sure. Okay, we got enough here.'

The pressure was knee-buckling as the pilot pulled the TU-95 up steeply. A tighter, more intense vibration came from the engines as the propeller pitch sharpened, blades biting harder into the air to give them power for the climb.

Nick looked round. The radar operators ignored their screens, watching everything the Americans did.

'How d'you know where to look?' Nick asked into the microphone that pressed against his lips.

'National Technical Means.'

'What's that?'

'You don't know? You Americans invented the words.'

'Okay, but I didn't. I'm no expert.'

The pilot found that hard to believe. The Americans must surely have given special training to the man given the unique chance to fly in a Soviet warplane.

'Satellites. We have a radar satellite. Shows everything, even us.'

'So you don't need to use your own radar?'

'That's right. If we did, your sailors would know we were here.'

'They know now!'

The plane levelled from the climb. The pilot's fix for the *Eisenhower* was twenty minutes out of date. He'd guessed where she should have steamed to, but was wrong. There was no sign, not even a wake. He wouldn't get a new fix from the radarsat for another ten minutes. It would look bad not to be able to find the big ship before then.

The radar operators turned back to their scopes, hands reaching for the control knobs.

'*Soviet Naval Aviation TU-95!*'

The voice in the earphones was Texan. Nick's cameraman looked round at him and frowned.

'*This is US Navy Tomcat on your port wingtip. Please acknowledge! Over!*'

Heads whipped round to the left.

'Sheeit!'

Just beyond the end of the wing a dull-grey fighter floated upwards, US Navy markings emblazoned on the side. Inside its long perspex canopy, two sinister black visors and oxygen masks were turned towards them.

'*Soviet TU-95 – you're approaching a US Navy aircraft carrier. Please maintain a distance of five miles from the ship. Acknowledge. Over.*'

'US fighter plane,' Valentin's voice answered, high-pitched with tension. 'This is international airspace. Keep your distance! Over.'

'*Soviet aircraft –* ' The Texan voice sounded tired. '*The US carrier has a hot deck. For your safety, please make a left to maintain five miles from the ship. Acknowledge. Over.*'

Nick braced himself for a sudden change of course, but there was none. The Tomcat rose and banked away, ostentatiously showing off the racks of missiles under its wings.

Suddenly the *Bear* lurched to the left. From the right came another Tomcat, streaking past their nose, scarcely feet away.

'Christ! Somebody tell those guys there are US citizens in here!' the cameraman yelled in alarm.

The radio had gone silent. There was no point in posturing any more. Each side knew what the other was about.

The nose went down. The rush of air past the fuselage grew louder as they gathered speed.

'The *Eisenhower* is straight ahead. Soon you will have your pictures,' Valentin barked through the intercom. He sounded angry. 'They are very aggressive, your pilots. This is international airspace!'

Nick opted to say nothing.

Having failed to deflect the Tupolev from its course, the Tomcats settled one on each wingtip, indicating unmistakably that if the Russian showed the slightest sign of hostility towards the *Eisenhower*, they'd blow him out of the sky.

Ahead, the carrier came in view. The plane levelled off and dropped its speed. Nick guessed they were at about two thousand feet, but it was difficult to tell. The Tomcats dropped back to watch for the Tupolev's bomb-doors opening, ready to rip open the Russian plane with their 20mm Vulcan cannon.

'I will pass to the left of the ship, turn in front, and pass back on the other side,' the pilot told them, calmer now.

'She sure is big,' Nick whistled.

'Ninety-thousand tons. Eighty-five fighter planes on board. Nuclear weapons, too. Your navy has fifteen ships like that, our navy has none. They are a big threat to us.'

The microphone in Nick's headset was recording every word.

Fighters of different types were packed on the forward deck, wings folded, leaving the angled flight-deck clear for operations. Two machines were poised for launch on the steam catapults.

Past the ship, the two Tomcats closed in again, like guards pinioning a prisoner. The *Bear* attempted a turn but abandoned it just short of a collision.

'American Navy fighters! You are flying dangerously close! Please move away. This is international airspace. Acknowledge! Over.'

Neither fighter flinched from its wing-tip position. The radio was silent.

'American warplanes! You are violating the international rules of air safety. You have put my aircraft in danger!'

Silence. The cameraman grinned. The shots were terrific – big close-ups of the US markings. The foreshortening effect of the zoom made it look as if the wingtips were touching. In one of the Tomcats the navigator was taking pictures with a stills camera.

'*Soviet aircraft!*'

The Texan drawl was back.

'*Okay, guys; this is where we say g'bye. We're five miles from our mother. Keep at least this distance, and we won't have to meet again. Have a good day now, y'hear. Over.*'

The two Tomcats banked and accelerated away in perfect unison. From underneath came a third fighter, pulling up ahead to let them know he'd been sitting on their tail all the time, missiles armed.

'You have enough pictures now? Our time is up, I think.'

Nick looked at his watch. It was nearly noon. Time to head back to Kola.

* * *

Plymouth, England.

Patsy Tinker put an armful of carrier bags on the back seat of her car and closed the door. She was pleased with her purchases; it was high time she had some new things, and if Andrew complained about how much she'd spent, she'd say it was compensation for his disappearing again so soon after returning home.

She started the engine and crunched the gears, then looked over her shoulder as she eased out of the parking bay. She paused to let a silver-coloured Volkswagen Golf pass, then pulled out behind it.

Hang on, wasn't that Sara? She vaguely remembered the Hitchens had a silver VW.

'Keep an eye on Sara', Andrew had said. Okay, she'd follow; if Sara was going home, she'd drop in for a chat.

But the car turned up one of the Victorian terraces that led to the Hoe, then turned left, and left again into the close dominated by the modern tower of the Holiday Inn. There was one parking space free, which she took.

Patsy hesitated. She hadn't meant to follow Sara like a spy. Sara might be meeting a man.

She drove past the hotel and found a space. Sara was walking slowly up towards the Naval War Memorial on the Hoe.

Patsy got out, pressing herself against the car to avoid a dusty, red Ford Escort that pulled into the bay ahead.

Climbing the slope, Sara suddenly felt dizzy, her leaden limbs and dull headache the result of too little sleep for the past few nights.

Why had she come, she asked herself? Retracing her past? Trying to make sense of it? She'd walked here with Simon when he was younger.

She glanced back at the Holiday Inn, remembering the view from the sixth floor. She'd had a lot of fun with Gunnar in the hotel's big double beds, but now she was paying the price.

The weather was glorious, for a change – an autumn sun bathed the Portland stone of the monuments in mellow gold. As she reached the crest of the hill, she felt a breeze on her face, warm for October.

Ahead, the waters of the Sound sparkled in the sun. A white-sailed yacht made its way towards the marina, its wake stretching to the farthest shore.

Sara turned to look up at the weathered bronze statue of Sir Francis Drake, then bent her head to read the inscription. She'd been here so many times before, but had never read the words.

'Hello, Sara!' exclaimed Patsy, catching up with her. 'Fancy seeing you!'

Sara jumped.

'Patsy . . .' she gasped. 'You startled me.'

'Sorry. Didn't mean to. Such a lovely afternoon, I was passing and thought I'd stop to admire the view. You too?'

'I suppose so.'

Sara avoided Patsy's eyes. She found her self-confidence intimidating.

'Are you heading for the lighthouse? Perhaps we could walk together.'

'Why not,' Sara shrugged.

'Look, if you'd prefer to be on your own . . .'

'No . . . ,' she answered, puzzled at the sudden solicitude. 'Has Andrew told you?'

'You mean . . . , about you and Philip? A little. Just that there'd been a row.'

Sara gave a short, sharp laugh that caught in her throat.

'That could be an understatement,' she half-whispered.

They crossed the grass towards Smeaton's Lighthouse. A few couples had spread rugs on the turf to protect themselves from the moist ground while they enjoyed one of the last warm days of the year.

'D'you know, for years I thought that was a real lighthouse?' Sara remarked. 'I used to bring Simon here and tell him that at night the light shone right out to sea, to guide the sailors home – guide his daddy back to us. I never came here at night until recently . . .'

'It was real once.'

'Oh?'

'It was out on the Eddystone Rock for a hundred-and-twenty years. Then the rock began to crumble, so they brought it here and built a new Eddystone light on firmer ground.'

'Being a teacher, you'd know that sort of thing,' Sara sniped.

Patsy felt her scalp prickle. She and Sara had never liked each other much.

'Philip's gone to sea again, I gather.'

If Sara wasn't going to raise the subject, she would.

Sara stopped and eyed Patsy suspiciously, her face grey, her eyes red and ringed.

'This meeting's no accident,' she snapped. 'Who sent you?'

'No one sent me,' Patsy replied, edgily. 'Andrew said things were a mess – suggested I should say hello if I happened to see you. That's all.'

'How much of a mess, did he say?'

'Look, all he said was that you'd been seeing someone else, and that Philip had found out and was devastated. That's all.'

Sara looked away, embarrassed.

'He didn't say who?'

'Nothing like that, no.'

They began walking again, heading for a vacant bench by the lighthouse.

'I'm not really allowed to talk about it,' Sara said. 'I think it's an official secret.'

'What on earth do you mean?'

Sara chewed at her lower lip.

'I've been incredibly stupid,' she whispered. 'I can't believe how stupid I've been. You know, when I was nineteen, there was one sort of girl I used to really despise. Half drunk at a party – some boy with his tongue down her throat and his hand up her jumper. You knew that within the hour she'd be on her back and the next night it'd be with someone else. Well . . , they all think *I'm* like that now!'

'Nonsense! Who thinks that?'

'Philip. Andrew. The police.'

'The *police?*'

'Oh God, I shouldn't have said that. They're probably an official secret too.'

'You're not involved in anything . . . *criminal*, are you, Sara?' Patsy whispered anxiously.

'Criminal? I don't know. I hadn't thought of it as criminal.'

Sara looked round, checking no one was within earshot. Patsy found herself doing the same. They both ignored the nondescript, brown-haired man in a fawn windcheater sitting on another bench some twenty yards to their right.

'There were lots of men. I used to get so bloody *lonely* . . .' Sara's voice had become so soft as to be almost inaudible. 'One of those men worked for – a foreign government.'

'Oh. I see . . ,' Patsy answered, but didn't.

'Don't tell Andrew I told you.'

145

They stared in silence at the distant horizon. The aggressive outline of a frigate had come into view round the headland, making a sweeping turn towards the dockyard.

A foreign government? Patsy chewed at the words. God almighty! Sara meant a spy!

'Philip brought me here on our first afternoon in Plymouth, about ten years ago,' Sara digressed, half to herself. 'Wanted me to know where I could come to watch, when he set off in his submarine. We'd never been apart for more than a few days up to then. I had no idea what it was going to be like.'

Sara turned to Patsy, who found the digression aggravating.

'You're tougher than me, but it must upset you too, the separations?' Sara asked.

'Appalling. Particularly in the early days,' she answered briskly. 'But I learned to accept it, most of the time. There wasn't any alternative.'

She'd meant to sound matter-of-fact, but Sara took it as a reproach.

'The alternative's bloody obvious!' she snapped. 'Patsy, you're so *organized*, so bloody virtuous, I'm surprised you allow yourself to be seen in public with me! But surely, even in your well-ordered existence there must've been times, when Andrew was away, when you were desperate for . . . for *something?* I don't just mean sex; I mean emotionally?'

Patsy felt her neck and face begin to burn.

'You make me sound like a nun,' she laughed uncomfortably.

'Of course I get lonely, too. Of course . . .'

Patsy hesitated.

'I've never told anyone this. But I did have an affair, once. You must never, *never* repeat this. Andrew doesn't know, and he never will. It was a man I work with, a nice man. I shall always be fond of him. But one day I weighed what I was doing against my marriage and my children. And I ended it.'

'Blimey,' Sara whispered. 'So you *are* human!'

Patsy stiffened. A pair of gulls swooped screeching over their heads, one chasing the other.

'Is it our own fault, the way we end up? The sort of people we become?' Sara demanded. 'It can't be, can it? Our parents must take some of the blame.'

'I don't know. I suppose it's a bit of both . . .'

'My mother used to have one lover after another. Destroyed my father. I hated her, but now I'm just like her.'

Sara's eyes began to fill with tears.

Reminding herself why she'd engineered this meeting, Patsy decided she had to pull their conversation back on track.

'What did you mean just now? About your lover being from a foreign government?'

'I shouldn't have said that! You mustn't ask!'

But Patsy persevered, 'When politicians use that phrase, they mean a spy!'

Sara's face crumpled.

'A Russian?'

Sara nodded.

'Oh, God!'

Patsy felt chilled. This wasn't just a matter of infidelity; it was a betrayal of everything.

'Did you talk to him about Phil's work?'

'Of course not. At least, not in any way that mattered,' she insisted. 'Anyhow, I don't know anything about it, except what it does to me.'

'I see. But . . .' Patsy searched for something to say.

'Philip found out. And he flipped, literally. Something seemed to snap in his mind. Andrew was scared he might do something daft. I think they're trying to bring him back, but nobody's telling me anything. If *you* know what's happening. . . .'

'Not a thing. It's all news to me. But what did you mean about him doing something daft?'

'Blowing up the Russians? I don't know – some sort of revenge.'

'You can't be serious!'

'*I* don't know . . . !' Sara wailed, and burst into tears.

'It's not just because of what I did, though! I'm sure there's something else.'

'Like what?'

'I don't know. There's been something churning round in Phil's mind for months. Something to do with his work. He never said. Always denied there was anything wrong.'

Patsy felt deeply alarmed. She decided she'd better sound reassuring if she could.

'Well, let's hope they get Philip back soon. You'll have to talk the whole thing out with him, I suppose. But what about your marriage? Do you want to save it? You might still be able to.'

Sara shut her eyes and groaned. Patsy hadn't understood.

'It's too late for that! Don't you see?'

'Oh, I'm sure it's not. Andrew'll talk to him. Philip can get a job ashore, so he won't be away so much.'

'Patsy! *Listen!* He's not . . . coming . . . back! Ever!'

A shiver ran down Patsy's spine.

'It was in his eyes as he left. Philip is going to die!'

Patsy felt cold all over. The wind had got up.

* * *

Northwood, England.

'Are you there, Anthony?' the Commander-in-Chief shouted, pushing open the door to the room occupied by the Flag Officer Submarines.

Admiral Bourlet rose to his feet.

'We need to talk. About Hitchens. Can you come along to my office, and bring his file with you?'

'Of course.'

Bourlet had spent much of the morning studying the file. It had not made comfortable reading.

He closed the C-in-C's door and sat in the leather armchair to which Waverley directed him.

'Never seen the PM more alarmed. She's horrified at the very idea that world stability could be threatened by an officer in Her Majesty's Navy.'

'She's ahead of herself, in that case. It hasn't come to

that yet. We've still a good chance of stopping him, sir,' Bourlet announced, with contrived confidence.

'What I want to know is how such a lunatic managed to end up as the captain of an SSN. They're supposed to be our top talent, for God's sake!'

Sir Stewart perched a pair of half-moon spectacles on the bridge of his long, thin nose. He reached across for the file.

'To be frank, sir, he's been bloody lucky. Twice,' Bourlet explained as Waverley read. 'He scraped through his "Perisher" with the recommendation that his ability to command had yet to be proven. They said he should be given the chance to show his worth as an Executive Officer. Then one of the Gulf sultanates bought a fleet of small diesel submarines, remember? Offered enormous sums tax-free to our submariners to work five-year contracts training Arabs to drive them. We lost four COs in a month. Three from *Oberon* diesel boats, and one from an SSN.'

'And suddenly Lieutenant Commander Hitchens found himself in demand.'

'Exactly. Got an "O" boat to drive. Did all right for a couple of years. Not much flair, but no mishaps either. Then came his second lucky break. Look at his S206 dated a couple of years back – his Officer's Confidential Report, at the time he came up for promotion to Commander – Section 3, the General Report, says "A competent commanding officer of an 'O' boat, but a man obsessed by petty rules and regulations. Holds the respect of his men through firm discipline rather than any degree of affection. Not a team player. Could create unnecessary tension on board".

'Yet Section 5 recommends him for immediate promotion. The explanation comes in Section 6 – written by my predecessor. As you'll see, sir, he says that although Hitchens hadn't displayed the usual flair and leadership required for the command of a nuclear boat, the sudden shortage of SSN COs which occurred at that time made it essential Hitchens be considered for promotion.'

'Ah! It's coming back to me. There was some frightful accident. . . .'

'That's right, sir. Up at Faslane. Three SSN COs driving off base for a stag night. One of them was getting married the next day. Hit a petrol tanker. Went up in flames. All dead.'

'And suddenly we had three boats without skippers. Mmmm. That explains some of it. So, we've got an obsessive nit-picker on the loose, obsessed at the moment, it seems, with a personal grievance against the Russians. Anything else in the file, further back?'

Bourlet riffled through the pages.

'He came from a naval family. Father and grandfather. His father had a curious end to his career. Could be relevant. Remember the old *HMS Tenby*? A diesel submarine that disappeared in the Barents Sea in November 1962? All hands lost. No trace of her ever found.'

'Oh, yes. I remember vaguely.'

'Philip Hitchens' father was her second-in-command.'

'I remember it now; I was at Dartmouth at the time. But I can't remember the details. . . .'

'She was on an intelligence mission, monitoring Soviet torpedo trials. We believed some of them were nuclear-tipped. There was always a suspicion that the Soviets had sunk her, but never any evidence. Some boffin down at the naval architects' department in Bath came up with a theory that a fire on one of the mess decks could have flashed through into the torpedo room. Proved it on a test rig. The enquiry concluded that's what must have happened. Magazine explosion causing total loss. They changed the design of the class after that.'

'Hitchens the younger must've been still at school at the time. Traumatic for him.'

'Early teens. There's nothing in his file about his thoughts on the matter, except a curious line in his original application to join. He said he saw himself as "continuing the career which his father had been unable to complete".'

'That obsessive streak again. There, right at the start, and no one saw the danger in it.'

150

'To be fair, it's not an uncommon characteristic in the Navy, sir.'

'Hmmm. So what you're saying is that there's nothing in the man's record that could've led us to predict something like this.'

'Absolutely, sir. The file shows he's a weak link in the chain, slipped into the system out of temporary necessity. But there's nothing to suggest he'd ever defy orders. Just the opposite, if anything.'

'But how come he got chosen for this special mission with the Moray mines? We should've chosen a top operator for that job.'

'It's just the way the cards fell, sir. *Truculent* was already being fitted out as the trials boat for the mines when Hitchens took command. She's the only boat equipped to use the mines so far. It had to be him. There was no alternative.'

'Jesus! What a shambles! I don't think the PM'll swallow much of this. She's already looking for someone to blame,' Waverley concluded miserably. 'What's the latest on the search for *Truculent?*'

'Nothing new, sir. The Nimrods haven't made contact again, and at present *Tenby*'s not in the frame yet. Ironic that the name of the sub we're sending to look for Hitchens should be the same as the ship in which his father died.'

'God! If he ever finds out, it'll probably drive him clean round the bend!'

* * *

The Arctic Circle.

The mountainous spine of Norway turned a sinister grey as the RAF HS.125 executive jet flew steadily north. When the sun dipped below the horizon, the snow-covered tips of the peaks glowed pink. Directly below them the water in the fjords looked inky black.

Andrew felt restricted by the narrow cabin. They'd been flying for over three hours and he was desperate to stretch his legs. Even to stand up meant stooping to prevent his head striking the roof.

The landscape below had been dramatic to watch for a while, but the more he gazed down at the vast expanse of the Norwegian Sea stretching away to the left, the more pessimistic he became about the difficulties involved in finding the *Truculent*.

The captain eased his portly frame through the cockpit door. A surprisingly elderly man, Andrew thought, in his late fifties at least. A former fighter pilot, perhaps, who couldn't live without flying, but who'd grown too old for fast jets?

'More coffee, Commander?'

'No thanks,' Andrew answered. 'It just makes me need to pee, and the heads you have on board isn't the easiest to get in and out of!'

The RAF man grinned. 'We just call it "the can". Not a lot of room, I agree, but the plane's a delight to fly. Want to come up front?'

Andrew followed the pilot forward and ducked through the doorway. The second officer grinned a greeting. There was no room to enter the cockpit, so he just leaned in, supporting himself on the doorframe. The control panel was dominated by a multi-coloured radar screen in its centre.

'I've just spoken to Tromso. Should be there in about twenty-seven minutes,' the second officer announced. 'They said they were expecting you. Mentioned a Sea King.'

'That's right.'

'Going to join a ship, are you?'

'Yep. A submarine.'

'Rather you than me, on a night like this.'

'Heard a weather forecast, have you?'

'Force five, I'm afraid.'

Andrew grimaced. He disliked helicopter flights at the best of times, but to be lowered on a wire towards a conning tower, which was wobbling about like a wooden toy? Not pleasant.

'What does that radar screen show you?' Andrew asked.

'It's mainly for weather. Storm warning, but it maps the ground if you point it downwards.'

152

He indicated the green and yellow shapes interspersed with blue.

'That's the fjord where we sank the Tirpitz,' he pointed. 'Tromso's just on the shoreline. We'll start our descent in a couple of minutes.'

Andrew nodded, and studied the multitude of dials for a while. Then the radio crackled and the captain pulled earphones over his head. Andrew made a gesture of thanks and returned to the main cabin.

Cross-winds buffeted them as the main wheels touched the runway. Andrew peered towards the terminal building, where two helicopters were silhouetted against the lights of an open hangar. Then he strained to study another shape further away.

'Bloody hell, that's a Nimrod,' he muttered. 'What's the RAF doing here?'

The HS.125 jolted to a halt. Andrew unbuckled his belt and zipped up his holdall. The whine of the jets died as the pilot cut the engines. From the cockpit came the sound of switches being turned off, and the giros spinning to a standstill.

'Did you see that?' the pilot called over his shoulder. 'One of ours. Nimrod. Probably got a technical hitch.'

Andrew suspected its presence at Tromso was more significant than that. He stretched out his hand to shake the pilot's.

'Well, goodbye, and thanks for a nice flight.'

'Is that bag all you've got? No other luggage?' the RAF man asked.

'That's all.'

'Just staying overnight then, are you?'

'I've everything I need in here. S'long now.'

Andrew hurried off the plane, anxious to avoid further questions. On the tarmac was an officer in the grey-blue uniform of the Norwegian Air Force.

'Commander Tinker? I'm Major Mjell, the Station Commander. Welcome to Tromso.'

His Norwegian accent seemed to dip in and out of the words like a wading bird.

'Thank you. I'm glad to be here.'

'We should hurry. The weather will get worse. Even now the helicopter pilots are not sure they can land you on your submarine. We might have to try tomorrow.'

'I'm ready now. Let's get a move on. I must get aboard tonight. Is the helicopter ready?'

'Yes, but there is someone you must speak with first. Please to come to my office.'

He hurried across the tarmac to the far end of the terminal. The wind was icy and cut through the thick navy blue pullover Andrew was wearing.

'Ah, that's better. It's warm in here. Now I'll leave you three alone for five minutes. That should be enough?'

Andrew saw a whey-faced young man in a flying suit rise from a leather armchair to greet him. His shoulder insignia marked him as an RAF Flight Lieutenant.

'Five minutes should be fine,' the pilot acknowledged in a strong Scots accent, then introduced himself. 'Alex McCringle. I expect you saw the grey beast on the tarmac?'

'Nimrod MR2, unless I'm much mistaken.'

'Exactly. Just come off patrol. This is my AEO, Stan Mackintosh. He's the boss. Northwood told us to land here so we could report to you.'

'Picked up some curious activity which they said you'd want to know about,' Mackintosh explained.

'Oh? Did they say why I'd want to know?'

Andrew was curious to know how much the RAF had been told of the Navy's problems.

'Said it was to do with the exercise *Ocean Guardian*? You're involved in a special operation code-named *Shadowhunt*? Playing the part of the Soviets, trying to track one of our submarines?'

'Something like that, yes.'

He could tell they hadn't been convinced by the cover story.

'Odd sort of operation, when Northwood doesn't even know where its boats are,' the AEO needled. 'Anyway, let me tell you what we got.'

The flight lieutenant spread a chart on the office table.

His finger drew a square shape over the sea about two hundred miles west of Trondheim in southern Norway.

'We began a box search of this area at about one o'clock this morning. Beautiful clear night. Getting worse now, though. Anyway, we dropped a sonobuoy barrier looking for a *Victor* which the Norwegians had been tracking. Well, we found it but he wasn't on his own. He was chasing one of yours, a bloody *Trafalgar*.'

He pointed northeast on the chart.

'And what happened?'

'We tracked them for a bit, then suddenly your boy got wise and slowed right down. The *Victor* didn't realize what had happened at first, but then he slowed up too. We lost your boat at that point. They're bloody quiet when they're not rushing about, the *Trafalgars*. The *Victor* must have lost him too, because he suddenly went active! Practically deafened us!'

'Pinged him, did he? They don't often do that.'

'Exactly. Must have been pretty bloody eager to keep tabs on your boy, don't you think?'

'Well, they don't often get a chance like that. We're normally too careful for them. But this time. . . .'

Andrew searched for the right words, that would give nothing away.

'This time it's different tactics,' he added cautiously.

'Well, the sooner you get back to the old ones, the better, I reckon!'

'So what happened after that?'

'We never picked up the T-boat again. Nor did the Russian. He went pinging around in all directions, up and down, changing depths, but he never found him again. Northwood told us to try to track your man; we dropped buoys all over the place, but he'd gone. And that's it, Commander. Any use to you?'

'Very much so, thank you. Now show me again on the chart exactly where you lost her.'

The AEO pointed and Andrew made a note of the co-ordinates.

'So where are ye off to now, then?' McCringle asked,

making no effort to restrain his curiosity. '*Hunting the Shadow* underwater, are ye?'

'That's right. Trying out some new equipment . . .' Andrew lied.

'Hidden in that wee bag, is it?' he joked, pointing at Andrew's holdall.

''Sright. Don't need much space for a floppy disc . . .'

'Well, we'll see how good it is, then. We've been told to stick around here for a few more days. See if we can be of some help. My fiver says we'll find him again first!'

'If you do, I'll happily pay you ten times that.'

'You're on!'

They shook on it.

'When do you plan to fly again?'

'Tomorrow at eight,' said Mackintosh. 'They're flying in a Herc from Kinloss with a load of sonobuoys – we've almost run out.'

The door clicked open. Major Mjell poked his head round.

'You must go now to the briefing room, Commander. It's the last chance to get off tonight.'

'Good luck,' McCringle called as Andrew followed the major out.

He followed the Norwegian out onto the tarmac again. The wind was even stronger. They passed the HS.125, refuelling for the return journey, and walked on towards the big, brightly lit hangar with the two helicopters parked outside.

'This is the regional search and rescue headquarters,' Mjell explained. 'The Coastguard use it too.'

Warm air enveloped them as they stepped inside the flight office.

'Klaasen,' announced the pilot, introducing himself.

'Tinker.'

The three-man aircrew for the Sea King were dressed in drab green immersion suits that would keep them dry if they ended up in the sea.

The loadmaster took a quick look at Andrew, assessing his size, and took from a rack a larger rubber suit in day-glo red.

'You'll be familiar with this equipment, Commander?'

Andrew pulled down the heavy zip and stepped into the legs of the suit. Floppy black rubber boots encased his feet. He forced his arms into the sleeves, taking care not to rip the soft rubber at the end which made a water-tight seal with his wrists.

'We need the suit back,' Klaasen reminded him drily. Andrew knew how expensive they were. 'After you're safely on board the submarine, we'll lower a bag for you to put it in. And the life-jacket too.'

'Fine.'

Andrew slipped the life-preserver over his head and pulled up the strap under his groin.

'Now, if you're ready, I will start my briefing.'

The aircrew stood in a semicircle and checked their watches. Klaasen spoke in Norwegian for the first minute, outlining the flight plan. Then he broke into English.

'The rendezvous with the *Tenby* should be seventy kilometres west from here. It will take about half-an-hour to the area, and then we have to find her. She should be surfaced, but we have not been able to contact her on VHF. Some hills are in the way. We can try again in the air.

'The sea is high and the wind getting stronger, so we'll put you on the fin. We lower a guideline first, so that they can pull you to the right place as you go down. You use the same system, I think?'

'Yes. I've had the misfortune to go through this several times!'

'Then we'll waste no more time. We can go to the aircraft now, and the loadmaster will give you the safety brief. You have heard it all before, but we insist.'

'Fine by me.'

Major Mjell gripped him by the hand and wished him luck.

Andrew clambered into the helicopter, and felt his way into one of the aluminium-framed canvas seats that lined the fuselage. Klaasen flicked the power switch and a red light came on in the roof, just bright enough for Andrew to make out the layout of the interior.

'The door close while we fly. I open when the pilot finds the ship.' The loadmaster's English wasn't up to the standard of the pilot's. 'When I say, you unfix seat belt and sit on the floor. Very careful, it's a long way down. Then I put cable harness on you, you know?'

'Yes, I know,' Andrew answered patiently.

'Emergency exits.' The loadmaster pointed to the door itself and to two other panels in the fuselage sides. 'If we go in the water, you must wait until the rotor stops, otherwise . . .'

He made a sign of slitting his throat.

'Let in the water first. Then swim out as it sinks. Then pull life-jacket. Not to inflate before leaving aircraft.'

'Yes, yes. Fine.'

The pre-flight briefings made Andrew more nervous than the flight itself. It was all pointless anyway. Few people survived helicopter crashes – they all knew that.

With a muffled roar the twin jet engines lit and built up their revs to a high-pitched whine. The loadmaster gave him a thumbs-up sign, which Andrew returned. Then with a bowel-churning grind, the gearbox was engaged and the rotors began to turn.

It was almost pitch black inside the helicopter. From time to time as they flew, the loadmaster pulled out a flashlamp and shone it along the bare pipes of the hydraulic system, checking for leaks.

The two aircrew were bulky, anonymous shadows against the amber glow of their instruments; for the next thirty minutes his life lay in their hands.

He thought of home. Patsy. The children: Theresa, Mark, and Anthony struggling to cope with boarding school.

A change in the engine pitch; his heart beat faster.

He cursed himself for being so nervous. Eyes closed, he thought of the task ahead. The Nimrod could cover a greater area than a submarine, although its small sono-buoys lacked the sensitivity of the bigger, more powerful systems in the *Tenby*.

The tail of the machine dipped, slowing down, it banked right, then left, spreading the search. The loadmaster extended his hands forward and swayed from side to side, indicating the roughness of the water below.

For a good ten minutes they hovered or flew slowly backwards and forwards.

Suddenly the loadmaster touched Andrew on the knee and gave him the thumbs up. They'd found his boat.

The nose dipped, the machine banked and sped in a new direction. Three minutes later Klaasen eased it back into the hover. The loadmaster crouched by the door and wrenched it open, letting in an icy blast. Then he busied himself with the winch, unstrapping the harness, checking the cable and controls.

Klaasen manoeuvred the machine inch by inch. The loadmaster beckoned. Andrew unclipped his belt and slid forward onto the floor, clutching his holdall firmly. The loadmaster slipped the harness over his head. He tightened the strop under his arms and winched the cable taut.

Ahead and below was blackness. Then he saw green and red navigation lights, close together. A boat. A pencil of light from the helicopter pierced the dark, picking out white wave-crests in its search.

It found the smooth, shiny curves of the submarine. The beam followed the casing forward, a sparkle from the foam breaking across the steel, then the fin reaching up. On the top, the pale dots of faces looking up.

He had to land on that? Jesus, it looked so small! As he watched, the periscope and radio mast slid down into the fin so as not to obstruct his descent.

The loadmaster lowered a thin handline, weighted at the bottom. Through his microphone, he directed the pilot until the line was grabbed by a sailor on the bridge. Then he secured the line to Andrew's harness.

He was ready? Andrew nodded and pulled the rubber hood over his head. It was wet down there and bitterly cold.

A final thumbs up; Andrew felt the winch cable jerk the strop tight under his armpits. He sat on the ledge, legs over the edge. The downdraught from the rotor tugged at the loose folds of his survival suit. A firm push in the small of his back and he was in mid-air.

The cable jolted and jerked. The winchman lowered him a few metres at a time. Arms by the side; that's what they always tell you. Do nothing; just hang there; leave it to the other guys. It was an act of faith. It had to be.

The wind tugged at his feet; he felt salt spray on his face, or was it rain? Something pulled him sideways against the wind. He remembered the handline.

Suddenly his shins cracked hard against metal. He gasped at the sharp pain. Rough hands grasped his legs, then his waist. The edge of the bridge grazed his buttocks; he was down. The steel grating felt firm underfoot, and the chest-high rim of the conning tower supported his back.

He lurched against it. The submarine rolled like a plastic duck.

'Welcome to *Tenby*, sir,' the burly rating shouted in his ear.

'Thanks!' Andrew yelled, trying to beat the din of the machine overhead. 'There's a bag to come, and they want this kit of theirs back!'

He slipped the harness off and the rating held the strop to one side to show the winchman it was clear. Within seconds it was gone.

'Best take the gear off here, sir!'

He unstrapped the life-vest, then struggled with the zips of the survival suit; the rating helped him. In a few moments he was free from the gear and, ducking, began to make his way below. A young officer greeted him at the top of the ladder. As he climbed down inside the tower, a warm blast of air came up to greet him, carrying a familiar smell of machinery and cooking.

He emerged into the control room. A ring of faces greeted him.

'Hello, I'm Peter Biddle.'

The CO looked no more than a boy, smooth-skinned, fair-haired, waxy pale from the rolling of the boat. Andrew checked the gold bars on his epaulettes to be sure.

'Andrew Tinker. Glad to be aboard.'

'Ah, this looks like your kit.'

He glanced past Andrew at the sub-lieutenant carrying the holdall.

'Good. The sooner we get below in this weather, the better we'll all feel.'

Andrew heard the clunk of the upper hatch being closed.

'Upper lid shut and clipped,' the rating called.

'Officer of the Watch. Dive the submarine. Let's clear the datum!' Commander Biddle ordered.

Shortly afterwards, with the submarine at 180 metres, Biddle led the way to his cabin.

'Now take a seat,' he suggested to Andrew, 'and put me out of my misery. What the hell's this all about?'

* * *

Washington DC, USA.

President John McGuire entered the 'bunker', as he called it, and closed the door. He was a short man with wavy brown hair, blue eyes, and a nice smile. His National Security Adviser Tom Reynolds was already there, waiting for him.

The room was a new addition to the White House, just big enough to seat a dozen if necessary. Special wire mesh embedded in its walls, floor and ceiling prevented electronic eavesdropping.

'Okay, Tom. What've you got?'

McGuire was nervous. Newly elected, he was still feeling his way through the complexities of foreign policy. He hailed from a midwestern state where he'd built a reputation as a tough and efficient governor, but where Russians were still thought of as hostile aliens from another planet.

'It's thin, John. Real thin,' Reynolds drawled, stroking his long, angular chin.

A former US Air Force General, he'd spent much of his professional life studying the Soviet mind. The President relied on him to read the Russians, but this time he was unsure, and that made him nervous. He clasped and unclasped his hands.

'The Defense Intelligence Agency has confirmed they're MiG-29s on that ship, and that it's called the *Rostov* . . .'

'Goddammit, Tom! I knew that much yesterday! Where are they headed, that's what I need to know?'

'And that's what none of our agencies can tell us yet. It's weird. Real weird. We've not had a whisper out of Cuba or Central America to suggest they're expecting new fighters. There's been nothing on the satellites either. The latest pictures from the KH12 over Cuba, Nicaragua, and El Salvador yesterday – the sky was clear, the pix are great, but there's not the slightest sign they're getting ready for new planes.'

'So where are they going with those things? I got no feel for this, Tom. You've got to help me.'

'Could be just about anyplace. Angola, Mozambique, Libya – you name it.'

'Do those places matter to us? I mean, if they get the planes?'

Reynolds shrugged.

'We sure as hell would care if they went to Libya. But I don't think they will. Savkin and Gaddafy ain't speakin' much these days. No. I still think it's Cuba – if it's anywhere at all.'

'What the hell's that supposed to mean?'

'It's weird. Those planes are built just outside Moscow. The easiest way to get them anywhere is to fly 'em. So why take them all the way up to Murmansk to put them on a ship?'

'Maybe he hoped no one'd spot them that way.'

Reynolds shook his head.

'You don't steam right past a US Navy flat-top if you want to keep secret a deck-full of jet fighters.'

'So what're you saying? It was bait? And we took it?'

'Could be. We can't say for sure.'

'So, Savkin wants to wind us up, huh?'

'Could be. Maybe he thinks if he can make us look real mean, it'll strengthen his hand in the next arms talks. Don't forget, they want naval forces on the agenda this time. And we've got a lot more at sea than they have.'

McGuire stood up, spun round the chair so its back

was against the table. Then he straddled it, resting his arms on the top.

'Suppose you're wrong, and those planes go to Cuba. What do we have to do about it? What can this MiG do? Is it a threat?'

Tom Reynolds pursed his thin lips.

'Militarily? The MiG-29's like our own F-18. Good all-round fighter. But there's only six of 'em on the ship, so far as we know – peanuts.

'But politically? That's different. Any strengthening of communist forces so close to the US is bad news. You've seen what the media are doing with it. Watch the news-casts tonight and see how many congressmen have picked up the ball. I can name a handful who're guaranteed to be running with it.'

'Mmmm,' the President mused, calculating the political advantages in the various courses of action open to him.

'I guess the smart money's on not doing anything too fast,' he concluded, eyeing his National Security Adviser for his reaction. 'Just so long as the rednecks in Congress don't see it as weakness.'

He stood up and thrust his hands into his pockets.

'If Congress kicks up a fuss, I'll tell 'em the Soviets know damn well what to expect if they do anything that threatens the USA.'

'And if you're asked if the MiGs are a threat?'

'I'll tell 'em I don't know yet. Savkin hasn't told me where he's sending them!'

The President laughed, but was cut short.

'Then the media'll give us shit because the CIA and DIA haven't found out where they're goin'.'

'Okay! Then I'll be enigmatic. Say they're not a threat where they are right now!'

'Sure.'

Reynolds leaned back in his chair, hands clasped behind his head.

'You're right about keeping it cool, John. What I'm worried about is what *could* happen. Eighteen of our biggest and best warships are steaming into what the Sovi-ets think of as their own home waters. Savkin means to use our exercise for his own ends. I can see some of what he's after, but not all of it. With those MiGs, we flew into a trap. We've got to look out for the next one and avoid it.'

'First thing is to muzzle the media on the *Eisenhower*,' McGuire growled. 'The only pictures of Russian ships I want to see from now on are the ones that come in from the Pentagon. Make sure the Navy knows that, will you, Tom?'

'You got it. And what do you want State to do about the protest from the Soviet Ambassador?'

'Throw it back at them. But do it diplomatically!'

The President stood up again, indicating their meeting was over, but Reynolds stayed seated.

'Anything else?' McGuire demanded, looking anxiously at his watch.

'Well . . . , I don't rightly know.'

'What's that supposed to mean?'

'Well, it may be nothing. Just something that's come from a US Navy Commander doing NATO duty at the east Atlantic headquarters at Northwood, England. He's talked about it to the Defense Intelligence Agency. Says the Brits have got big trouble with one of their submarines. Doesn't know what, but there's a lot of important people over there looking real worried. And they're not telling us about it, which is odd, since the sub's in the exercise.'

'Some kind of accident, you figure?'

'Nope. They'd be after our rescue vehicle if it was.'

'What then?'

'All the guy knows is, the boat ain't doing what it's supposed to. So there may be a joker in the pack, and if you're going to play poker with Savkin, you ought to know that.'

The President eyed Reynolds silently for what felt like a full half-minute.

'Thanks, Tom.'

* * *

At six that evening Washington time, the four main American television news channels went on the air with their world news bulletins. All of them led on the remarkable report from ABC Moscow correspondent Nick Hallberg, the first western journalist ever to fly on patrol in a Soviet warplane.

The sight of American jets flaunting their weaponry at the Russian plane made some viewers' hearts flutter with pride. It left others feeling apprehensive, however. Amongst the latter was Tom Reynolds.

By putting curbs on the US Navy's media facilities, he'd hoped to control US TV pictures from the North Atlantic. He kicked himself for his naïvety.

After the pooled Hallberg report, each network other than ABC switched to their own Moscow correspondent's despatch from the press conference given in Moscow that evening by Admiral Grekov, Supreme Commander of the Soviet Navy.

Grekov spoke no English. His words were relayed in the exaggeratedly American tones of the official Soviet interpreter.

The US Navy pilots had violated international law, he railed. They'd jeopardized the lives of the crew of the 'unarmed Soviet reconnaissance plane'. The aggression they'd displayed was symbolic of the whole tone of the NATO exercise about to be enacted close to the Soviet coast, he insisted.

The Admiral then stood up, resplendent in his uniform, and pointed with a stick to a chart comparing NATO and Warsaw Pact naval forces in Atlantic and European waters.

'Aircraft carriers: NATO has twenty-four, the Warsaw Pact just four small ones with no strike power. Submarines: about two hundred each. Frigates and destroyers: NATO has three times the number in our navies. With such odds in the West's favour, why does NATO need to mount aggressive manoeuvres in Soviet waters?' he demanded to know. 'It can hardly be for defence, so is it for war?'

Grekov directed his final query to the camera, his wrinkled face a picture of affronted innocence.

Tom Reynolds was watching four channels simultaneously in his room in the Old Executive Office Building next to the White House. Under his lean jaw, a nerve twitched.

The broadcasts finished with a brief commentary from the networks' Pentagon correspondents, confirming that the figures Grekov had quoted were fundamentally correct.

Reynolds snatched up the green telephone.

'Could you tell the President I need to see him again,' he barked. '*Right now!*'

CHAPTER SIX

Tuesday 22nd October. 0400 hrs GMT.

HMS Truculent.

Lieutenant Sebastian Cordell couldn't sleep. The night was nearly gone; three more hours and he'd be back on watch.

The bunk was too small; his head touched one bulkhead of the four-berth cabin, his feet another. He was alone; the three he shared with were on watch.

The cause of his insomnia wasn't the size of the bunk, however, but the turmoil in his mind.

In the past thirty-six hours, conversation amongst the officers had reduced to a single topic – speculation about their captain's highly irregular orders.

They'd all remarked on his heightened irritability, snapping at them one minute, icy calm the next.

The others could only guess what had got into the old man, but Sebastian – he reckoned he knew. And it had nothing to do with secret orders from CINCFLEET.

Whether to tell someone, that was the question churning round in his mind. He'd seen the first lieutenant and the WEO whispering secretly in corners. Had to be talking about Hitchens. Should he tell them their captain had flipped, and why?

He'd been dodging Hitchens' eyes, which seemed to burn with pain and anger. Sometimes he'd caught the captain looking at him across the control room; his expression seemed to say: 'I've got your number, you bastard!'

Sebastian cursed his luck for being posted to *Truculent* – for being brought face to face with the man he'd innocently cuckolded two years ago.

Sara Hitchens was the first woman he'd spent the night with – the first time he'd made love in a bed. Before that

167

it had been fumbles in the back of his car – awkward, and hurried.

They'd not expected to strike lucky, that night in the restaurant two years ago. He and another midshipman had been celebrating his twentieth birthday, when two women had begun eyeing them from another table.

Bold as brass, one of the women had asked them to join them for coffee.

He'd suspected they were tarts; nice girls waited for men to make the first approach. But he'd soon realized he was wrong. These women had class.

They'd only used their first names – made it more mysterious. The women were ten or fifteen years older than them. Divorcees, the boys had reckoned.

'Come home and we'll have a little party!' the women had insisted, after a few liqueurs.

Back at Sara's old house out in the wilds, Sebastian had sensed she was still married. He didn't care, though; he'd drunk plenty by then.

It was the other woman who'd got things moving; she'd been all over Sebastian's chum, and dragged him off to a bedroom. Sara had been more hesitant, nervous even. Sebastian had liked her for it.

They'd had another drink, alone. Then, emboldened, they'd gone to her bedroom. It had smelt of perfume. He could still smell it when he closed his eyes.

She'd seen he was inexperienced, and took the lead; he could still picture the mischief on her urchin face as she began to unbutton his shirt. Her breasts had felt hot, so unbelievably soft. Skin as smooth as cream.

They'd made love, and for the first time for Sebastian the words had had meaning.

Then morning had come. A dry throat, a throbbing head – and the sight of her husband's photograph on the bedside table.

He'd not dared ask about him, not wanted to know Sara's surname. But on a pewter tankard next to the photograph, were engraved the words 'Congratulations to Lieutenant Commander Philip Hitchens'.

Two years later he'd been told to join *HMS Truculent*;

he'd thought of asking for a different appointment, but without a good reason, a man would damage his career that way. Anyway, TAS Officer was exactly the job he'd wanted.

When he'd first joined the boat, Hitchens had shown no sign of suspicion. Sebastian had relaxed, believing his secret was safe. Until the start of this patrol. On his return from shore leave this time, Commander Hitchens' attitude to him had changed radically.

Now the whole boat was in turmoil. Because of him, so he believed. Sebastian pressed his fists against the deckhead. The steel seemed to crush downwards.

How much had Sara told him? Everything they'd done that night?

He'd never seen her again – hadn't dared to. For months she'd haunted his thoughts. He'd never been so in love before.

He almost wished Hitchens would come out with it. Tell him what he thought of him and have done with it. But it was as if Hitchens had decided Cordell had ceased to exist. That look in his eye was of a man betrayed by his closest friends. A man whose mind had been turned by it.

He ought to warn them; tell them what he knew. But what if he were imagining it? Supposing there really were secret orders? He'd have made a fool of himself. It'd go on his file.

Best to hold his tongue for the time being. Just one more day. See what developed. But should he wait, when the whole ship's company might be heading for appalling danger?

He banged his fists against his head. He had to tell someone. He'd talk to Pike. That's what a first lieutenant was for.

Philip Hitchens checked in the small mirror that his hair was groomed. Doubt plagued him; he panicked even, at the thought of what he'd taken on.

The day ahead would be critical. No more wavering. He had to weigh his options – decide what to do.

He looked long and hard at his reflection. The strain was less noticeable now. Two nights of deep, drug-induced sleep had worked their beneficial effect.

He'd apologized to Pike for not telling him about the tablets. But he hadn't realized they'd put him so far under. He'd imagined he'd still be rouseable in an emergency.

His crew had done well handling that *Victor*, though he'd torn a strip off them for not waking him at the time. That was when Pike had rounded on him in the control room.

He'd realized then how close he was to wrecking everything. He'd taken stock rapidly, wrenching his emotions back under control. Now, after a second night of deep sleep, he felt ready.

Calm and consistent; that's how he must appear to his men if they weren't to doubt his authority. Whatever the outcome of his mission, he needed them to obey his orders without question.

Taking a deep breath to steady himself, he left his cabin and stepped into the wardroom for breakfast. Seated at the near end of the table was a short, stocky figure, shovelling bacon, egg and sausages through a small gap in his bushy black beard.

'Stoking up, Peter?'

'It's all fuel, sir,' answered the marine engineer officer, Lieutenant Commander Peter Claypole. 'Body's just like a machine.'

'Standard, sir?' asked the steward.

'Yes, please,' answered Philip. 'I can just about manage it this morning.'

'Standard' was egg, bacon, sausage, tomato and fried bread.

Further down the table sat Sub-Lieutenant Smallbone, the radio officer, and Lieutenant Cordell.

'Are you going on or just off watch, Sebastian?' Philip asked, pouring himself a cup of tea.

'Off – I mean, just going on, sir,' Cordell stammered.

There's something wrong with Cordell, Philip thought. The boy blushed whenever he spoke to him. He hoped he wasn't gay.

170

'This morning – and this affects both of you lads – we need a SSIXS. Scheduled at 1130, isn't it, Hugo?'

'That's right, sir.'

SSIXS stood for Ship to Shore Information Exchange Satellite.

'We'll need to take extra care this far north, Sebastian. The Russians are everywhere.'

'Yes, sir. I know that.'

The steward placed the greasy breakfast on the table. What would Sara say about all that cholesterol?

For a split second nothing happened.

Sara. Oh, Jesus!

The hurt hit him like a gloved fist. Eyes closed against the pain, he swayed and gripped the table.

'Everythin' okay, sir?'

The steward's voice sounded distant, as if deep in a tunnel.

From the far end of the table Sebastian and Hugo stared at Hitchens open-mouthed.

'Back to the stoke-hole,' muttered the marine engineer, noticing nothing and heading for the door.

'Yes . . . fine,' Philip managed to reply.

He forced down a sip of tea, and felt better for it.

He gripped the knife and fork and began to eat, forcing the food down. He mustn't give way like that again.

'If you'll excuse us, sir . . .'

Cordell and Smallbone were heading for the door.

'Of course.'

Lieutenant Commander Peter Claypole was brushing his teeth in his cabin, when the phone call came from the chief of the watch, aft. Trouble with a pump in the reactor's secondary cooling system.

Claypole looked like the popular idea of a submariner, stocky and bearded. He was a man of routine; three meals a day, regular as clockwork and never a problem with his health. Bodies were like machines; keep them fuelled and maintained and everything should run smoothly. He thought of submarines in much the same way.

But now a pump was playing up.

Passing through the control room, he glanced at the dials on the power panel. They were doing thirty-one knots.

'I may have to slow you down, Tim,' he warned.

Pike had been in command most of the night, and looked weary.

'Trouble?'

'Maybe.'

'Serious?'

'Let you know.'

With that he was on his way. Claypole never used two words where one would do.

He reached the tunnel over the reactor and pulled the lever on the airlock door. Before entering, he checked his radiation monitor card was clipped to his belt.

He hurried down the tunnel that led aft. Beneath his feet was the reactor compartment with its primary cooling circuits and steam generators.

Through the second door, and he was into the machine-spaces. He entered the manoeuvring room, the reactor control centre, where every aspect of the power plant and propulsion system was monitored. His eye went straight to the gauges showing the temperature in the pumps. The needle was high for pump three in the number two steam loop.

'Where's the chief of the watch?' Claypole asked.

'Three deck, sir.'

Logical. That's where the secondary circuit pumps were. He gripped the rails of the ladder and slid below.

The secondary circuit carried superheated steam from the reactor compartment through the turbines that drove the propulsor and the electrical generator. After the steam had released its energy it passed through a sea-water condenser; then, as water, was pumped back into the reactor heat-exchanger to start the process all over again.

Two deck. One more ladder, and he'd be there.

CPO Gostyn was crouched beside the silver-grey pump. He wore headphones connected to sensors built into the pump casing, listening to confirm his suspicion that the grinding noise from inside was getting steadily worse.

They were two of a kind, Claypole and Gostyn, yet separated by rank and status. Both men lived for their machines, knew the workings of them intimately. But Claypole, with his engineering degree ranked as an officer; Gostyn with his 'O' levels and an engineering diploma would probably never rise above warrant officer.

Gostyn removed his headphones and passed them across. 'Bearing, sir. Almost certain.' In a war, machine noise could be the death of them all. The smallest extra vibration or rumble could transmit itself to the water outside and pinpoint their position for an enemy.

Claypole pressed the phones to his ears.

'Not much doubt. Bloody dockyard was supposed to have checked that last time we were in!'

They both knew the fault probably lay with a microscopic flaw in the steel used in the bearing, but it helped to have someone to blame.

'We'll have to shut it down,' Claypole decided. 'If we leave it running, it'll seize. Captain'll go bananas.'

'Can't be helped, can it, sir? Not our fault.'

There were four pumps in each coolant loop, mounted on rubber rafts to absorb noise. Shutting down one pump meant the loss of about five knots.

'He's not going to like it. Wherever it is we're going, he's in one hell of a hurry to get there. What d'you think? If he won't play ball, how long can we keep it running before it seizes?'

Gostyn shrugged.

'Fuck knows! If the fucking bearing breaks up, he'll fucking 'ave to slow down!'

Claypole smiled. He couldn't have put it better himself.

'Right. Wish me luck.'

In the control room Tim Pike was desperate to get his head down, but had hung on to hear what the marine engineer had to say.

'Don't baffle me with jargon, Peter,' he began. 'Words of one syllable please. Two at the most.'

'Got a duff bearing in a pump. Simple enough for you?'

'And you're proposing. . . . ?'

'Shut it down. Means you'll lose a few knots.'

'That'll knock us back on our schedule. Captain won't like it. Do you have to?'

'The bearing could go at any time. If it does you'll be down to twenty-five knots anyway. Shut it down now and you'll still have it in reserve – turn it on again if you really need it.'

'Sod it! We'll need to talk to the captain. This is his mission we're on. Only he knows our deadline. You'd better come with me.'

At that moment Philip entered the control room.

'Problem, Tim?'

'Trouble with a pump, sir. MEO wants to shut it down. We'd lose five knots.'

'We can't do that! We need the speed! And *why* is there trouble with a pump?' His voice began to rise. 'They're not supposed to need attention from one refit to the next. If one of your men's fouled it up, Mr Claypole, I'll have him on a charge!'

Philip's eyes blazed.

'Nobody's fouled anything up, sir,' Claypole bristled. 'Leastways, not any of *my* men. There's a bearing that's noisy and overheating. Ship's engineers don't have access to them. Dockyard job. But it must be shut down.'

'Don't tell me what *must* be done! You're being too bloody cautious, MEO. If we were at war you wouldn't be talking about stopping a pump.'

'I bloody would, sir!' Claypole growled.

Hitchens flinched. He could smell mutiny.

The men were staring. He suddenly realized he'd been shouting. Careful! He swallowed hard.

'All right, Peter. What's the percentage chance of that pump failing?'

'Oh, it'll fail. Hundred per cent. The only question is when. The bearing's got a rumble. Low-frequency. Probably not bad enough yet to be heard outside the hull. But it'll get worse. Could go very quick. If the bearing breaks up and bits of metal get into the lubricating system, then we could write the whole pump off.'

'What's the chance of failure in the next forty-eight hours?' Hitchens pressed.

'God knows!'

'Give me your considered judgement. You're an engineer, aren't you?'

Claypole frowned, as if deep in thought. Sod the bloody CO! Why couldn't he just accept that something was wrong and let them put it right? He tried to remember a previous incident that would give him a clue. He'd never heard of a bearing actually disintegrating on one of these pumps. Still, there was always a first time.

'Outright failure? I suppose the chance of that is low,' the MEO conceded. 'But deterioration, with the pump overheating and the noise level becoming detectable outside? The chance is higher. Much higher.'

'In forty-eight hours?'

'Can't guarantee anything, sir,' Claypole concluded sullenly.

'We'll risk it. We have to,' the commander decided. 'You can have a couple of knots if it'll help.'

'Every little bit . . .'

'Twenty-eight knots then, Tim.'

'Aye, aye, sir,' Pike acknowledged as Hitchens turned to the chart table.

'And I want reports every hour, MEO.'

Lieutenant Sebastian Cordell had just taken over the watch from Nick Cavendish, and was leaning over the chart. He eased to one side as Hitchens appeared next to him. Their course had brought them closer to the Norwegian coast, but they were still one hundred and fifty miles west of the nearest land. The Lofoten Islands were well to the south. Beneath them the ocean plunged two-thousand-five-hundred metres to total darkness, and a sea-bed of ooze and rock.

'ETA abeam North Cape?' Hitchens asked. 'At twenty-eight knots?'

Cordell picked up his brass-handled dividers, set them against the latitude scale and measured out the distance.

'About three-hundred-and-thirty miles to run . . .'

He pulled the calculator towards him and punched at the keys.

'2200 tonight, sir. And that allows for some slow running for comms.'

'Mmmm.' Hitchens looked reassured. He picked up the dividers and measured the distance for himself.

'We'll be crossing the edge of the continental shelf in about four hours. You'd better start plotting sea-bed soundings. When we get round the Cape there'll be Sovs everywhere. Won't be able to poke a mast up to get a satellite fix.'

'Yes, sir.'

Navigating by reading the topography of the ocean floor was a difficult art dependant on finding large features, like underwater mountains. There weren't too many of those in the shallow waters of the Barents Sea.

Hitchens pulled out the chart showing the northern tip of Norway and the western half of the Soviet Kola peninsula.

'Where are we heading after North Cape, sir?' Cordell queried nervously.

'You'll know when you need to,' Hitchens snapped. He slid the chart back into the drawer. 'Just make sure we get there.'

Unnerved by Cordell's question, he turned for the door. 'Call me when it's time for the satcom.'

'Sir.'

Philip felt panic rising. It was the tension in the control room that did it. They were all suspicious – all watching him. He had to have solitude to think things through, make decisions.

He slid shut the door to his cabin, and slumped into his chair. What was truth, what was lies?

Those KGB bastards! They'd led him by the nose. He'd believed their 'evidence', succumbed to their blackmail, agreed to their plan. But was it true, what they'd told him? How the hell could he tell, down there in the dark silence of the ocean.

And poor Sara. The way they'd used her – trickery,

176

lies. And all to make sure of him, as though the other thing weren't enough.

He remembered his stunned disbelief when a completely strange woman had stopped him on the cliff footpath, earlier that year, to tell him his father was still alive. The father whom he'd worshipped and whose disappearance thirty years ago he'd never been able to accept.

The letter and the photograph the Russian woman had produced as evidence – he could still picture them. The cheap paper covered with his father's still familiar scrawl had torn a little in the summer breeze.

It had poleaxed him, shattered him. At that moment, he'd become a boy again, a boy on the edge of his teens; a child who'd idolized a father all too often absent, a boy who craved paternal approval.

The words in his father's letter had cut into his heart, pleading, begging that he should do something to end his suffering. The handwriting had been uneven and shaky. They'd broken his father in the labour camp – the woman had admitted it. She'd even apologized; blamed it on the Stalinists.

She'd waited until their third meeting before revealing the price to be paid for freeing the sick old man. She was sure of Philip by then.

It was the second letter from his father that had sealed it; the handwriting strayed down the page and told of incurable heart disease. Did he have grandchildren, the old man asked; believing that one day he'd see them had kept him going all those years. He begged that before he died, Philip would make the dream come true.

Treason was the price to be paid for his father's freedom. Betrayal of his country's secrets to the KGB. Betrayal of the Navy which was his whole life.

Until that moment Philip had never questioned the meaning of 'loyalty'. It was absolute. Handing British naval secrets to the Russians was unthinkable. But now he faced a choice; loyalty to his country – or loyalty to his own flesh and blood.

It was only a small thing they asked, the woman had said. Just a small favour.

A small thing. To lay an inert Moray mine at a precise location off the Kola coast, so it could be retrieved by a Soviet submersible. Retrieved and dismantled, so that the most potent anti-submarine weapon ever devised by the West could be understood, and rendered impotent. A small thing.

His mind had rejected the treachery; but his heart hadn't.

Would it really do so much harm? The Soviets themselves must have similar technology. If they didn't learn the secret from him, they'd get it from someone else. They'd bribe some underpaid technician at the factory, perhaps. There'd never be a war anyway, so what did it matter?

It would be difficult, he'd warned her. There'd be no opportunity.

Yes, there would, she told him. They knew he commanded *Truculent*, the trials boat for the Moray mines. The thoroughness of the KGB's research had startled him.

A few months later, as she had predicted, he was ordered to the Kola, on the ideal mission to fulfil the KGB's plan. Although just a simulated mine-laying, he would be carrying war stocks, they told him.

Suddenly he had the means to free his father. It was fate; it had to be.

He met the KGB woman in Plymouth that night. She gave him the chart coordinates for the laying of the mine, and said his father would be moved immediately to a clinic in a neutral country, where he would be cared for until other arrangements could be made.

How he would explain the loss of a mine when he returned to Plymouth, he couldn't imagine. He'd think of something. The plan had to proceed.

Then suddenly, the whole thing had exploded in his face. He'd found out about Sara.

He'd been a puppet all the time. There wasn't just a KGB woman pulling his strings; there was a man too. A Russian who'd seduced Sara months before to make her talk. Talk about him, his obsession with his father, his vulnerability.

The bastards! They'd invented the whole thing! Faked the letter and the blurred photograph. They hadn't let him keep them, of course. Couldn't risk them falling into the hands of the British authorities, the woman had said.

It had been bloody clever. He cringed at the thought of how he'd fallen for it. *God*, how he hated them, and their evil masters in the Kremlin. Okay, he'd give them a bloody Moray mine. Right up the backside of an *Oscar* class submarine!

Thus he had begun the patrol blinded by anger and a thirst for revenge.

But now the doubts had come back. Supposing they *had* been telling the truth after all? Why shouldn't his father be alive? The writing had looked like his, the words and the expressions had been right. And the photograph – well, who could tell after so many years?

He sank his head in his hands. He must decide; go through it all again, all the evidence for and against. The reports he'd read of the catastrophic 'accident' nearly thirty years ago – think back through them. Remember what the Russian woman had told him about the survival of just two men, who'd escaped the destruction of the old *Tenby* because they'd been ashore on the Soviet coast when it had happened, taking photographs of a radar site.

He wanted the story to be true, wanted desperately to bring his father home to England, back to life. But he had to guard against self-deception.

Think. Think hard. Then decide. He mustn't have doubts when the time came.

The last time he'd seen his father had been in Guernsey in August 1962. Philip had been fourteen. That summer he'd felt closer to his father than ever before.

That's how he remembered it anyhow. Had it really been like that?

His father had been such a confident man, with firm views on everything – never a moment's doubt in his own judgement. Whenever he came home from sea, Philip would follow him round the house like a dog, he remembered, drawing strength from being close to him.

His father had been an aloof man, however, and in

truth there'd been few occasions when the two of them had been really close.

It had rained most of that summer. Much of the holiday had been spent indoors playing Monopoly, or even bridge whenever his father managed to bully a fellow holiday-maker into making up a four. Philip had no brothers or sisters; his mother had confided once that giving birth to him had been such a ghastly experience, she'd determined never to repeat it.

He'd sensed an unusual tension between his parents that summer. Perhaps his mother had known his father was about to embark on a spying mission; perhaps it was something personal. He would never know now.

When the news came that his father's boat was Missing Presumed Lost, his mother retreated into extended mourning, bitter at the world for taking away her husband.

Philip shuddered. Looking back on his unhappy boyhood would do nothing to answer the questions in his head.

What would Andrew do in his situation?

He often asked himself that – an old habit acquired soon after the two of them began their naval training together at Dartmouth. To Philip, every decision Andrew Tinker took seemed effortless; the man knew instinctively what to do, while he himself floundered in uncertainty and self-doubt.

He'd used Andrew as a life-raft when they were students; uncomfortably aware of it, he'd wondered that his room-mate tolerated him so gladly. One day in a flash of insight, he worked out why; for all Andrew's decisiveness and competence, there was one ingredient for a naval career which he lacked. Background.

And that was something Philip had plenty of. With a dead hero for a father, and a grandfather who'd been a Rear Admiral, it was 'background' that had brought him into the Navy and 'background' which he'd hoped might offset any lack of brilliance as an officer.

Coming from a family with no naval connections,

Andrew had hungered for the true taste of the Navy and its traditions. It was a knowledge Philip could provide.

The complementary nature of their original friendship had turned later into good-natured rivalry in everything they did – even marriage. Philip knew it had been Andrew's engagement to Patsy that had spurred him to find a wife for himself.

He and Sara had been wildly in love when they married. Dreams, all dreams. A nightmare now.

* * *

HMS Tenby.

Andrew Tinker sat huddled over the wardroom table of *HMS Tenby* and chewed his thumbnail. Spread before him were charts of the underwater landscape north of Norway and inside the Kola inlet.

'What we really need is a mind-reader,' Andrew sighed.

'He's been sitting in that boat for nearly a week,' Commander Biddle reminded him. 'Even if he were planning to blow up some Russians because a KGB man poked his wife, surely he'd have thought better of it by now?'

Andrew nodded. His own thoughts exactly.

'And if he hasn't, he must be really off his head. Somebody on board should have twigged.'

'But they haven't,' Biddle said. 'There's just been a signal in from FOSM. No news at all. No sign of the *Truc* since the "crabs" found and lost her yesterday.'

'The Nimrod should be airborne again by now.'

'That's confirmed. They're starting at twenty degrees east and working west.'

Andrew found the longitude line on the chart and nodded.

' 'S' about right. Couldn't have got any further than that if he'd gone flat out. Where are we?'

Biddle's finger traced a line northeast from where they'd picked up Andrew the previous evening.

'We're doing eighteen knots. Means we can listen on sonar and still end up in front of him. We'll sit tight off North Cape and wait for his signature as he comes steaming up behind us.'

'I can't for one moment believe it'll be that easy.'

Andrew pulled towards him the chart showing the Kol'-skiy Zaliv, the Kola Inlet where the Soviet Northern Fleet had its headquarters.

'We can't be sure that's where he's going,' Andrew continued.

'Best place if he's looking for Sovs to shoot.'

'Ah, but is that what he's planning? I've known Phil a long time. This picture we're painting of a man ready to risk war to avenge his wife's indiscretions – it just doesn't fit.'

'No? What about the mental breakdown theory?'

'I've thought a lot about that, and I don't buy it either. If Phil had a breakdown, he wouldn't be able to conceal it. He'd just go to pieces. Tim Pike's his first lieutenant; he's a good hand and he'd soon sort him out.'

'But he hasn't.'

'Exactly. Which is why I'm convinced there's something else behind it. Something much more complicated.'

'Such as?'

'Christ! If I knew that . . .' Andrew spread his arms wide and stretched.

'Would it be worth getting FOSM to look in his personnel file?'

'Maybe. I'll send a signal. Trouble is, I don't know what they should look for.'

They fell silent. *Tenby*'s wardroom began to fill up with officers finished with the night watch, but not yet ready to get their heads down. There were thirteen officers on board, but the dining table only had seats for ten. In a corner by the door was a small refrigerator containing beer and soft drinks. Andrew had been offered a beer the night before, but had noticed none of Biddle's officers drank when at sea, and had declined it.

'We've got a satcom slot at 12.20. But we can do an HF burst sooner than that, if you want.'

'Okay. I'll draft a signal.'

Instinctively Andrew made as if to return to his cabin, but checked himself in time. His sleeping quarter was a mattress pallet, clipped to the torpedo rack in the forward weapons compartment. Biddle had offered the use of his own quarters as an office, but it was desperately small, which was why they'd chosen to sit in the wardroom. He pulled out a small notebook and turned to a clean page.

'*Captain, sir!*' the loudspeaker crackled.

Biddle stood up and pressed the microphone key.

'Yes, Murray.' It was the executive officer.

'*Got a contact. At least, TAS says we have.*'

'On my way.'

They both headed for the sound room.

'The trouble with being the trials boat for a new sonar system,' Biddle explained, 'is the shortage of background data. Without more experience with the gear, we don't know whether we've really got a contact or whether the transputer analyser's imagined it!'

The green-glowing sonar displays in the big grey, shock-mounted cabinets looked the same as the ones on his own boat, but Andrew had been told that both the hydrophones trailed astern and the computer that analysed and categorized the different sounds had been developed a step beyond his own equipment.

'This is Algy Colqhoun. A very enthusiastic TAS. Says this new gear's so sensitive it can pick up the moaning ghosts from World War Two shipwrecks! Now then, TAS; what're you up to!'

The tactics and sonar officer pointed to the VDU at his shoulder. Vertical bands of green shading moved slowly up the screen. He pointed to a very narrow line running up the screen between two broader bands, and spun the screen cursor onto it, using the roller-ball control on the console.

'We've got a line at 370 Hz., sir,' he explained, grinning. 'Can't hear it on headphones, but it's definitely not part of the natural background.'

'Okay, so what is it?'

The TAS officer punched a few keys and displayed the frequency of the noise in a window at the right of the screen. Then the picture changed to a table of data, on the left a list of known sounds in that same frequency range. He pointed to a paragraph on the right.

'Closest thing in the classification guide is the main coolant pump in one of these.'

'A *Trafalgar*?'

'We don't often make that sort of racket, thank God, but if we had undetected pump trouble it'd be somewhere in that range. Must be going fast not to hear it on his own sonar.'

'Where do you think it is?' Andrew interjected.

'It's very faint, sir. Right on the edge of the capabilities of even this equipment.' He patted the console. 'We've got an ambiguous bearing of eighty degrees relative to the array. My guess is it's on our port bow, but I'd like to alter course twenty degrees to starboard to eliminate the ambiguity.'

The initial bearing from the towed array was always ambiguous; the hydrophones couldn't tell which side the sound was coming from. By altering course and taking new relative bearings, one fix would remain constant, the other would diverge further, clearing up the ambiguity.

'Well, hang on to it. It's all we've got,' Biddle ordered.

Andrew hurried to the chart table.

'There's nothing on the intelligence plot about any of our subs being in this area, so it could well be our man.'

'Starboard ten. Steer zero-two-five,' ordered Lieutenant Colqhoun. The blue-shirted rating switched off the auto-pilot and turned the steering column, glad of something to do.

It would be several minutes before the array steadied again behind them, after which they could get their new bearing.

'Exactly right,' Andrew breathed, laying the protractor on the chart. 'If it's confirmed as a portside contact, it puts him precisely where the Nimrod's searching! We may just have struck lucky!'

He took up the dividers and measured the distance between their present position and the track he imagined the *Truculent* was following.

'About three hours! That's all it would take!' he remarked.

Lieutenant Colqhoun called across from the Action Information Display.

'Got a confirmed bearing, sir. Two-eight-six degrees. Range – probably between fifty and a hundred miles.'

'Thanks.'

Biddle settled himself at the chart table. He would calculate an intercept course to close the range. They'd have to guess the speed of the target. Thirty knots probably, making that much noise.

He pulled the keypad of a small computer across the table and tapped in the figures. A split second later its narrow liquid-crystal screen displayed the course to follow.

'Steer three-five-six. Keep seventy metres, revolutions for fifteen knots!'

Andrew scribbled down his radio signal to FOSM. It was in two parts. The first gave their own position and the bearing and possible range of the suspected target, to be relayed to the Nimrod overhead; the second was to ask for a search of Philip's file for clues.

'We'll come to periscope depth for the transmission in ten minutes,' Biddle told him.

Then the commander leaned an elbow on the chart table. He didn't want the navigation rating to hear what he said next.

'If this *is* the right contact, Andrew . . .'

He didn't need to complete the sentence. Andrew beckoned and led the way out of the control room.

'Can we talk in your cabin?'

'Of course.'

Biddle pushed open the door for him. Andrew sat on the narrow bunk.

'My orders are to stop him,' he declared simply.

Carefully, he watched Biddle's face for his reaction.

'How we do that, I don't know yet. I hope to God it's easy and a few words on the underwater telephone will be enough to let Pike take over.'

'And if not?'

'Then I'll need fresh orders. But in the last resort – we're supposed to hit him. That's what they told me.'

He expelled a long breath.

'You can't do that!' Biddle almost shouted. 'There's a hundred guys in there, Andrew. I know most of them. You couldn't pull the plug on them.'

'Depends on the alternative, doesn't it,' Andrew countered sharply. 'If he's about to do something that'll make the Russians turn my children into nuclear cinders, then a hundred lives is a small price to pay. We let over twice that many die in the Falklands, for Christ's sake!'

'But how will you know what he's going to do?' Biddle persisted. 'Who's to be the judge of what effect his action'll have? We can't know down here, that's for sure. Will CINCFLEET decide? Or Downing Street?'

'You have a point . . . We're going to want to be in contact with base when the moment comes. But if we keep bobbing up to the surface to transmit, we'll risk losing him.'

'So in the end it may be down to you . . .'

Andrew's eye was drawn to the photograph on Biddle's desk. Two little girls aged about three. Twins, probably.

'I just hope to God it doesn't come to that.'

* * *

HMS Truculent.

Chief Petty Officer Gostyn was not a happy man. Not only did he have a defective pump in the number two steam system of *HMS Truculent*, and an unsympathetic Commanding Officer, he also had a bad apple among his mechanics.

He knew who it was. But could he prove it? Could he hell!

It was bloody Percy Harwood again, had to be. None of the other five sods whose job it was to check and maintain the steam system would have been so flaming stupid as to drop an eighteen-inch wrench down behind the defective pump and then pretend it hadn't happened.

Anybody else, any other bugger on the entire submarine, would have known what a disaster it was to do something like that and not report it.

Millions of pounds had been spent on inventing ways

to make all this machinery silent. Mounting individual pumps and piping on rubber, developing low-speed bearings, all of it to reduce the noise detectable outside the hull to a bare minimum. And all it took was Percy bloody Harwood to leave his spanner resting one end against the pump, the other on the deck, thus building a bridge across the sound insulation so that the rumble coming from the defective bearing could be transmitted straight out into the deep sound channel of the North Atlantic.

Gostyn had spotted it himself, while making his hourly rounds. Harwood had denied it was him, of course, but it couldn't have been anyone else. It was he who'd drawn the wrench from stores.

The question now was, should he report it? He was the chief down here; it might reflect on him. Lieutenant Commander Claypole might be sympathetic, but with this dodgy mission they were on, he'd probably report it to the captain. And Commander Hitchens could be bloody vindictive.

Something wrong with their captain, this patrol. The whole boat was talking about it. Some of the CPOs had even heard a rumour the other officers were plotting to relieve him of his command. Bloody riot that would cause, when they got back to Devonport. It'd never happen of course. They hadn't got the guts.

So he decided to say nothing about the wrench, nothing about the fact that their secret presence in the area had been revealed for a couple of hours to any passing ship or plane that had cared to listen. With any luck there hadn't been any.

All over with now. No more noises escaping to the outside world. And the pump bearing was holding up despite his fears.

* * *

Northwood, England.

Rear-Admiral Anthony Bourlet was on his third cup of coffee. At his insistence the WRNS who was his personal assistant had installed a filter machine when he took over the job of Flag Officer Submarines. He looked across his office to the brass ship's clock on the wall next to the barometer.

Nearly eleven. The 'crabs' should have been airborne for several hours already. The RAF hated the Navy's nickname for them, but Bourlet thought the tag apt. Airmen did seem to do everything sideways.

He downed a cup of Kenya blend and headed for the staircase.

'Going down the "hole",' he growled to his trim, smartly-uniformed PA as he passed the outer office.

'OPCON's on the line, sir. There's been a signal from *Tenby*.'

He swerved into her doorway and grabbed the outstretched phone.

'FOSM here,' he barked, then listened. 'Aha! Bloody good news!' He listened again.

'His file? Already been through that. Still, no harm in another look. On my way.'

He passed the phone back to his PA.

'Hitchens' file – we've still got it here, haven't we?'

'I think it's with Commander Rush, sir. She asked to look at it first thing this morning.'

'Ah. Get her to come and talk to me about it in an hour, would you? Or maybe a little later. Say twelve-thirty, and fix us some sandwiches – smoked salmon – and, er, a bottle of the Sauvignon, nicely chilled?'

He winked at her, which made her smile self-consciously. She knew he was a frightful lecher but she liked him anyway.

It took him three minutes to walk to the entrance of the bunker, and another three to descend to the computer-filled cavern of the OPCON centre. Thousands of signals a day were dealt with here, and stored for months on computer files.

'It's all happening, sir,' the duty operations officer saluted. 'We've just had the Nimrod on. They're in contact with a *Trafalgar* at this very minute. It has to be *Truculent*.'

'Bloody good news!'

'She's got a dodgy pump apparently; making a hell of

a racket. But she's doing twenty-eight knots and can't hear herself.'

'Where is she?'

The ops officer picked up an illuminated pointer and turned to the giant wall map.

'About two-fifty miles west of North Cape, heading northeast.'

A signals warrant officer tore a sheet from a printer and thrust it into the Ops officer's hand.

'Eight Lima Golf again, sir.'

'Thank you. Our Nimrod, sir,' the Ops officer explained to the Admiral.

'And . . . ?'

'They seem to have fixed the pump, sir. Noise signature's almost back to normal. She's slowed down to twenty knots. The Nimrod's asking if you want them to let the boat know they're there.'

'No! Absolutely not! They must stay with her – keep tracking until the *Tenby* can get close. She'll do the talking.'

'Right, sir. I'll send that off.'

'And fast, before the "crabs" bugger it up.'

* * *

HMS Truculent.

Philip stood in the 'bandstand'. They were getting close to Soviet waters. Time to go 'invisible'. He'd ordered a cut in speed to eighteen knots and told the MEO he could shut down the pump with the worn bearing. At their slower, quieter speed, Philip had ordered rapid changes of course to lose any hunters who might have tracked them while they'd been moving fast.

Philip looked at the control-room clock set on Zulu time – GMT. In ten minutes precisely, a communications satellite would beam down a stream of signals. The closer they came to Soviet waters, the more he needed the intelligence data it would include.

The sound room had reported nothing except the propeller cavitation of a couple of merchantmen butting their way round the craggy north Norwegian coast about forty miles away.

The information had not reassured him. Both his own Navy and the Soviets were bound to be looking for him. So, where were they?

At first the intelligence reports had listed the *Truculent*, but no more. *HMS Tenby* had received the same treatment. On Sunday she'd been west of Tromso, but on Monday there'd been no mention of her.

So was it the new *Tenby* they were sending after him? How ironic that it should be her, of all boats.

'Revolutions for six knots! Ten up. Keep periscope depth!' Cordell ordered.

Philip looked at the clock again, anxiously. Five minutes to their satcom slot.

* * *

RAF Nimrod, Eight-Lima-Golf.

Over the north Norwegian Sea.

Flight Lieutenant Stan Mackintosh was uncomfortably aware of his hangover. The night before, after discovering the price of Norwegian beer, he and his crew had retired to a hotel bedroom with some six-packs of lager and bottles of scotch, bought at NAAFI prices before leaving England.

'Tosh' had come to the conclusion that he was a bit too old for the heavy drinking the younger men could manage. His brain hurt and his stomach churned alarmingly as the Nimrod banked and turned, trying to keep track of the suddenly elusive submarine below.

He didn't know what had prompted the *Truculent* to take evasive action. They'd certainly not given away their presence. They'd dropped passive buoys only, and had kept above five-thousand feet so the boat wouldn't hear them through the water.

It had been easy at first; 'spearing fish in a barrel' was how he'd described it when they'd detected the boat's noisy pump over fifty miles away. But now the AQS.

901 acoustic processor was struggling to separate anything from the normal background noise.

He peered over the shoulders of the operators at the green screens. Even on the narrow band analyser none of the buoys they had in the water at the moment had kept a hold on the *Truculent*'s noise signature.

'We've lost the bastard,' yelled the Tactical Navigator in exasperation.

The big round screen showed the plot disintegrating. Bearing lines from the buoys, which had converged neatly to give the boat's position, now diverged wildly.

'Last seen heading north but believed to be turning west. We've got buoys still listening on that side, and there's nothing.'

'Perhaps the bugger's coming up to periscope depth,' the AEO suggested. They hadn't used their Searchwater radar so far. No need, and anyway its transmissions would give away their presence to any warship within a hundred and fifty miles.

Mackintosh swung his burly frame down the narrow tube of the aircraft to the radar operator's position. The bored flight sergeant was idly turning the pages of the Searchwater manual.

'All fired up?' the AEO asked.

'Red hot, sir!'

Tosh reflected for a moment. If *Truculent* stuck her periscope above the surface, she'd soon know the Nimrod was there. Northwood had told them to keep their presence secret. Yet if they didn't use the radar they might never find the boat again.

'Oh, what the hell! Give it a burst.'

The radar operator flicked the switch that brought his screen sparkling to life.

* * *

HMS Truculent.

Cordell checked the control room clock. Just minutes to go.

'Course zero-four-five. Reducing to three knots. Returning to periscope depth!'

The zig-zag they'd been following should have confused any trackers, in the unlikely event there were any. Their sensors had detected none. But you couldn't be too careful in these northerly waters; the Bears were everywhere.

'Periscope depth, sir!'

'Up ESM!'

The Electronic Support Measures mast, covered with radar detectors, slid upwards, its dome just breaking the surface. Shaped to reflect radar beams no more strongly than a wave-crest, it scanned the electromagnetic spectrum for emitters.

Cordell leaned over the shoulder of the CPO at the Action Information console.

Printed on the amber VDU screen was the data processed by the ESM computer.

'Four radars detected, but none of them a threat, sir.'

Cordell ran his eye down the list. The first trace was from the Soviet RORSAT ocean surveillance satellite, passing 180 kilometres above their heads. *Truculent*'s periscope wouldn't be large enough to register. Two other traces were the navigation radars of passing freighters, the fourth from a Soviet TU-95 *Bear-F* reconnaisance plane, too far away to matter.

'Raise the search periscope! Standby, wireless room!'

The search periscope came hissing up from the control room deck. Mounted atop its optical system was a conical satellite antenna.

Cordell pressed his face to the eyepiece and swung the viewfinder through 360 degrees.

'Nothing in sight!'

He looked away to the control room clock. It was time.

In the wireless room, Hitchens hovered behind the signaller, waiting for the burst of satellite data to be received and stored in the communications computer. At that point he would expel the others from the room, so that he could print out the signals unobserved.

The digital clock completed the hour. On the dot, a red l.e.d. on the satcom panel began to flicker. The signals were being sucked in. Within fifteen seconds the transmission would be over.

'*Aircraft overhead!*' bawled the Action Information rating.

'Searchwater, sir!'

'Bearing?'

'One-nine-two, sir.'

'One of ours. Thank God for that! What's he doing this far north?'

'What's happened?' Hitchens had heard the shout and came running from the wireless room.

'Nimrod, sir. South of us. Detected its radar.'

'What?' Hitchens screamed. 'Get the masts down, you stupid sod! Go deep! Go deep! Get this bloody boat out of the way!'

'But the aircraft's friendly, sir,' Cordell gaped.

Hitchens' eyes almost burst from their sockets. He looked ready to kill. Fists clenched, he advanced on Cordell.

Then he checked himself, Cordell's face, open-mouthed, inches from his own. All around him he sensed a stillness, the men watchful.

Unnoticed, Tim Pike had entered the control room. He saw the expression change on his captain's face. Rage became fear, then bewilderment; then the mask was back in place.

'Depth under the keel?' Hitchens demanded, breaking the silence.

'Two-sixty metres, sir!' called the navigator.

'Keep two hundred metres, come left, steer three-two-zero.'

Still struggling to control emotions which seemed not to belong to him, Hitchens took Cordell by the arm to one side of the control room. The boat heeled to port as the planesman responded to the orders.

'That aircraft. It's on the exercise. But we're not any more, see?'

Cordell didn't see, but nodded as if he did.

'Now, get us away from the datum. Evasion tactics. Lose the bloody Nimrod!'

Philip pushed past Lieutenant Smallbone and Radio Operator Bennett and closed the door firmly behind him.

Tim Pike caught the eye of the weapon engineer, Paul Spriggs. This was one more incident to add to the list.

Cordell took a grip on himself.

'Sound room! Call the best evasion depth when we reach it!' he barked into the intercom. 'Planesman! Call out the depth every thirty metres!'

'Sixty metres, sir!'

Built into the outer hull, a water sampler constantly measured the temperature and salinity of the sea, feeding a computer in the sound room which calculated the best conditions in which to hide and distort their underwater sounds.

'Ninety metres, sir!'

Pike joined Cordell at the chart table.

'The bastard was gonna hit me! Did you see?'

'Forget it. Sort yourself out. Concentrate on evading.'

'I'm not going to bloody forget it! There's more to this than you know about, sir.'

'One-hundred-twenty metres, sir!' the planesman yelled.

'What d'you mean?' asked Pike.

'The reason he's so bloody bolshie, sir. I know what's behind it.'

The two men leaned over the chart, so as not to be heard.

'What?'

'Well, it's er . . . , look it's dead personal, sir. Can we . . . ?'

'Okay. Tell me later. Now, let's think what the bloody "crabs" are going to do.'

* * *

Nimrod Eight-Lima-Golf.

'Riser, bearing zero-one-two!'

'Got it!'

The tactical navigator tapped the key which brought the radar data onto his display.

'Turned half a circle from his last position. No wonder we lost him.'

The flight navigator gave the new course to the pilot, and the plane banked sharply. They'd be overhead the submarine in two minutes.

'Prepare Barra 9 and Difar 20.'

In the rear of the aircraft the air electronics operator selected the directional buoys, set them and loaded them into the ejection tubes.

'Radar's cold! He's gone deep again!'

'Here we go,' Mackintosh groaned.

'I need a bathy-buoy, fast.'

'Bathy 34 ready in the multilauncher,' crackled the voice from the rear of the plane.

'Bathy away.'

'Barra 9 away.'

They'd just flown over the last known position of the submarine. The tacnav put one buoy to the west and south, told the pilot to turn hard right, and launched the other buoy to the north and east. It would take about a minute for the buoys to start transmitting their information.

'Difar 20 away.'

'Can't we go active?' the tacnav asked Mackintosh. 'Best chance of finding him.'

'Need clearance from Northwood for that, and there's no time. Just have to keep our fingers crossed.'

One of the processor operators called, 'Best evasion depth one-hundred-and-fifty metres, the bathy says.'

The bathythermographic buoy had measured the temperature and salinity of the water down to the sea bed. Up here the North Cape Current could produce sudden changes in water conditions that could affect drastically the passage of sound through the water.

'Touched bottom at three-hundred-and-fifty metres.'

'Thanks. Anything on the Barra yet?'

'Nope. Barra and Difar both cold.'

'Sod him! We'll have to put a circle round the area. Ten mile radius. And we'll be out of Lofars by the time we've finished.'

'Time to signal Northwood again,' Mackintosh sighed. None of this was making his hangover feel any better.

* * *

CINCFLEET, Northwood, England.

Rear-Admiral Bourlet cursed himself for having been so stupidly optimistic. When the earlier signals had come in saying *Truculent* had been detected, he'd called the Commander-in-Chief to tell him. Admiral Waverley said he'd ring Downing Street immediately with the good news.

Arse-licker! If it weren't for Waverley's bum-crawling he wouldn't now be facing the humiliation of having to tell the PM they'd lost the boat again.

There'd been no further signals from *Tenby*, but she was still over fifty miles from the search area, and if the Nimrod had lost track of *Truculent* while sitting almost on top of her, *Tenby* wouldn't stand a chance of hearing her at that range.

He finished scribbling a note.

'Store that signal for *Tenby* on the satellite, so she'll get it whenever she calls,' he ordered, and headed back along the tunnels and up the stairways to the surface.

It was always good to get into real air again. Underground the atmosphere smelled filtered and artificial.

He strode up the tarmac road to the office block by the entrance to the headquarters. The wind had got up and tugged at the White Ensign flying from a mast in front of the doorway.

He took the stairs at a run, and his heart felt surprisingly light considering the crisis he faced.

The reason for his headiness stood waiting outside his office, chatting to his PA, Hitchens' file tucked under her arm.

'Ah, Felicity, my dear. Thank you so much for coming,' he greeted her.

Commander Rush smiled saucily.

'I took it as an order, sir.'

As she followed him into his office, she turned to his PA and winked. The young WRNS raised an eyebrow.

* * *

The long, black submarine passed undetected from the Norwegian Sea into the Barents. She'd zigged and zagged, alternating thirty knot bursts of speed with periods of near immobility. For the Nimrod to have kept up with her progress would have taken more than skill; the RAF would have needed extraordinary luck and an almost limitless supply of sonobuoys.

Without closing with the surface again, they'd never know for sure that they'd thrown off their shadow, but Sebastian Cordell was confident they were safe when he handed over the watch at lunchtime to Lieutenant Nick Cavendish.

'We got a satellite fix before the old man panicked,' Cordell confided to Cavendish. 'It showed the SINS is still spot on. We're here, at this moment.'

He pointed to a position half way between the shallows of the Fugley Bank and the pinnacle of rock thirty miles northwest of it which rose from the ocean floor like an aberration in the almost flat underwater landscape.

'Course-change due at 1315. New course zero-nine-eight. Next stop North Cape. All aboard for the mystery tour!'

Cavendish shook his head.

'He thinks we're a load of bloody schoolchildren,' he scoffed, 'not old enough to be told the facts of life! It's not on, you know. Bloody dangerous if we don't all know what we're up to. Did you get an intelligence summary on the satcom?'

'Yep.'

He pushed across the page of teletype.

'Still no mention of *Tenby*. Odd that. Nothing since Sunday, as if she'd disappeared.'

'Perhaps she's doing the same as us. Covert op,' Cavendish suggested. His eye ran further down the page to the Soviet deployments. 'Christ! That's quite a barrier for the Sovs. They don't usually get that many ships out for us.'

'Mmmm. I think we'll be looking for some little friend to help us through, don't you?'

Sebastian patted Cavendish on the shoulder and left him to it.

Lieutenant Commander Tim Pike was waiting for him in his cabin. The first lieutenant looked tense, and tugged at the short tufts of his ginger beard.

'Okay. Let's have it. What is it you wanted to say about the captain?'

Cordell felt a hot flush creeping up his neck.

'Oh, sit down, Sebastian, for heaven's sake.'

Pike pointed at the spare chair.

'As I said, sir, it's rather personal. But . . . , well . . . , about a couple of years ago I met a girl – a woman – in a restaurant, and we . . . , we went to bed together. I only knew her by her Christian name, you see. But it turned out she was Mrs Hitchens,' Sebastian concluded miserably.

'What? You've been knobbing the captain's missus? You rotten little sod!'

'I didn't know at the time, sir. She did all the picking up, not me!'

'I can believe that,' mocked Pike. 'Bloody hell! And you think the captain's found you out, is that it?'

'Yes, sir.'

'And that it accounts for his um . . . , overreaction this morning?'

'Exactly. And not just this morning. He's been pretty odd the whole patrol.'

'And you think it's all down to you?'

'Well, yes. I suppose I do.'

Tim Pike frowned. *Could* it be as simple as that? He doubted it. Rumours about Philip Hitchens' marital problems had been circulating for months, yet it hadn't affected his professional conduct before.

'Okay, Sebastian. Thanks for telling me about it. It's right that I should know. And I shan't tell anyone else, don't worry.'

'Thank you, sir.'

'Now, you'd better get along to the wardroom, or there'll be no lunch left.'

'Right, sir.'

Why would Sara Hitchens want to seduce a boy like Sebastian, Pike wondered? *Did* women fancy kids just out of school?

He spun the combination lock on the small wall-safe beneath his desk and took out a notebook. He looked through the list of things that had concerned him about Commander Hitchens on that patrol.

Each incident of jumpiness, aggression or secretiveness looked small and insignificant on its own, but a picture was beginning to emerge. But a picture of what?

Evidence of mental instability? Or just the tension of working under highly secret, highly sensitive orders?

But Hitchens had been on the point of strangling Cordell in the control room earlier; Pike had seen it with his own eyes. He'd lost his self-control, and that was dangerous. If he did it again when they were in contact with the Soviets he could put all their lives at risk.

The curtain across the doorway was brushed aside and Paul Spriggs came in. He spotted the notebook.

'Something new happened?'

'Could be.'

They'd each been making notes on Hitchens since the previous morning, keeping their writings separate. That way, if it came to anything, each man's evidence would have some claim to validity.

Suddenly the tannoy crackled.

'Do you hear there! Captain speaking.'

Both men looked at one another in surprise. Pike was expecting to make 'the pipe' himself in a few minutes' time.

'Thought you'd like an update on our situation. We've just altered course to the east. Should be abeam North Cape sometime later tonight. We're heading on into the Barents Sea. Things are pretty tense up on the surface, so we'll all need to be very much on our toes from now on.'

'Things are pretty tense down here too, old chap,' Pike muttered.

'*According to the World Service News summary,*' Hitchens' voice continued, '*there was a little confrontation yesterday between one of the American flat-tops and a Soviet Bear bomber that got too close. The Yanks came within an inch of shooting it out of the sky.*'

'Fucking Americans! Always overreact,' snarled Spriggs.

'*The Soviet Northern Fleet has mustered a pretty strong ASW barrier to protect their bastions. We've got to get through it tomorrow, undetected, and close with the Kola Inlet before all their SSNs get loose. Can't say any more than that at the moment.*

'*Ahead of us we can expect up to two Victor IIIs and two Sierras, according to the intelligence report. With a bit of luck three of those will be well to the north of us, but we're sticking close to the coast – we have to because we're in a hurry – so there'll be a few SSKs around and a lot of aircraft.*

'*I'm sorry we didn't manage to take in any family-grams this morning. We had to put the mast down before we'd received them – for operational reasons.*'

'Huh,' Pike mocked. 'In case our own side finds out what we're up to.'

'Do you mean that?'

'Shh!'

'*In conclusion . . .*'

Hitchens' voice sounded unsteady, almost emotional.

'*I just want to say how terribly important this mission is. There's a lot depending on it, believe me. That is all.*'

'So bloody important, he won't even tell me what it is!'

Pike pushed back his chair and stood up, bristling with anger.

'I've had enough! I'm going to have it out with him!'

Spriggs pushed Pike back down into his seat.

'Cool it Tim! If you go blazing in like that, you'll be up on a charge!'

'Fuck him! The bastard's got right up my nose!'

'Okay. But talk sense for a minute. That crash-dive this morning, to get away from one of our own planes? You think we're not *meant* to be here? The plane was looking for us, is that what you're saying?'

'Yes. That *is* what I'm saying, but I've no way of proving it.'

Spriggs was aghast.

'But why? Hitchens is a rule-book man. He'd never chance his arm . . .'

'Sure? Do you know what's going on in his mind? I don't. The man's a closed book to me.'

Paul thought of the explosive power stacked in the bow compartment of the submarine. Harpoon missiles that could devastate surface ships over fifty miles away; Tigerfish torpedoes that could rip through the double-hulls of Soviet submarines; and Moray mines that could lie dormant in the depths before darting from the dark to cripple the unsuspecting. He shivered.

'If you really believe he's acting against orders, Tim, then we've got to do something about it. And fast!'

'We need proof, Paul. And how the hell do we get it?'

CHAPTER SEVEN

Plymouth, England.

Tuesday 22nd October. A.M.

Two security men sat next to each other on a commuter flight to Plymouth. They spoke little.

Hillier was SIS, the Secret Intelligence Service or MI6, controlled by the Foreign Office. Black was MI5, a Home Office man. Hillier was tall and gaunt with a fine-boned nose, Black stocky with a tendency to sweat. The former styled himself a diplomat, the latter a policeman.

'Nearly there,' Hillier declared in a voice edged with boredom, glancing at his gold wrist-watch.

John Black pulled back his sleeve to reveal his own timepiece, digital and stainless-steel. It was a quarter-to-nine. They'd been served breakfast on the flight.

'The watchers'll have just changed shift,' Black mumbled. 'Boring bloody job, that is.'

'Did well yesterday, your man.' Hillier's voice was patronizing. 'Spotting Gunnar like that. Very timely.'

'Except that Gunnar spotted him at the same time. He'll get a reprimand.'

'Don't be too hard. He's probably given us an extra twenty-four hours. We needed that.'

The previous evening, Hillier had been halfway out of his office in the Soviet Department at Century House, when he'd received the summons to the Director's office. The instructions he'd been given were highly irregular. He didn't know where the orders came from, but it had to be the Foreign Secretary himself. And that meant the PM. He couldn't believe Sir Nigel would take a flyer on a thing like this.

The Director had been uneasy about the whole business. Doubted the wisdom of it. He refused to use their

Moscow agents to plant the information about *HMS Truculent*. The call from MI5 to say the Russian had been seen again, sniffing near Sara Hitchens' home, had been timely. Very timely.

Normally, feeding information to the Russians was an MI6 job, but handling Soviet spies on British soil was MI5. Hence the two of them were on the breakfast flight to the West Country. Their meeting with Mrs Hitchens was fixed for nine o'clock.

'Remind me what you've got on Gunnar,' Hillier asked wearily as they turned from the airport road onto the Plymouth by-pass. Black was driving the hired car.

'Not a lot,' Black grunted, braking sharply as a motor-cyclist weaved in front of them. 'Knew nothing about him until all this blew up. Found out where he lived by accident. Sharp-eyed neighbour saw the man and his missus moving their stuff out of the house in the middle of the night. Called the police the next day.

'In too much of a hurry – they were. Got careless. Left some coding pads. We assumed they'd have got out of the country, but we kept a watch on Mrs Hitchens just in case. Yesterday he suddenly turned up. Drove straight past her house. It was us he was looking for. Saw us the same moment we saw him. Off like a rocket. Our man put out a call to the local police, but Gunnar disappeared.'

'Bit daring, isn't he, coming back to the house? She must've been giving him something special!' Hillier sneered.

'Probably wants to shut 'er up. Thinks she's the only one who can identify him. Do her in and he could slip back into the undergrowth for a year or two, then emerge with a new cover.'

'Well, she'll be safe enough with your brave boys parked at the end of her drive!'

Black felt the back of his neck prickle. Hillier was needling him because his watcher had failed to conceal himself properly.

'Have you met her?' Hillier asked.

'Mmm. Came down here when the case broke. Temperamental bitch.'

Hillier looked about him as they drove through the first of the grey stone villages to the southeast of the city. Some pretty properties here, he thought to himself.

'Will she play, d'you think?'

Black thought for a moment. He took out a cigarette and lit it. Hillier pointedly wound down his window.

'Tell her her old man's life could depend on it, and she might. Curious that; she says she still loves him despite all the stuff she got up to behind his back.'

'Ah, women! Where *would* we be without them!'

Black cast him a sideways glance.

'Some of us manage very well, thanks.'

Sara had been awake most of the night, worrying. The MI5 man had given no reason for needing to see her again. During the night she'd thought she could hear someone outside, prowling round the house.

She watched unseen from a window as the two men got out of their car, then waited for them to ring the bell before she let them in.

'Hello, Mrs Hitchens.'

Black tried to sound jovial.

Sara nodded a greeting, eyeing Hillier with suspicion.

'You'll have to make do with the kitchen, I'm afraid. That's where I live when I'm alone here,' she said, leading them in.

She switched on the kettle and pointed to the old pine table.

'I'm not sure why . . .'

'Let me introduce myself.' The SIS man extended his hand. 'Hillier from the Foreign Office . . .'

'I've already told Mr Black everything I can remember . . .'

'So you want to know why we're here? Naturally.'

Hillier spoke to her as if she had a mental age of five.

'Glad you've got the kettle on. I could do with a cuppa.'

Sara became increasingly nervous. She lit a cigarette and inhaled deeply.

'Tea or coffee?'

'Coffee, please.'

'Tea, if you don't mind,' added Black.

Sara reached for a cupboard.

'What a delightful kitchen.'

Hillier's comment annoyed her.

'Isn't it just?' she answered abruptly. 'But let's skip the polite conversation, shall we? Would you mind telling me what you want?'

Hillier's eyebrows arched upwards.

'Very well . . .'

Tread carefully with this one, he told himself.

'This man who called himself Gunnar . . ,' he paused. 'We're anxious to know if he's contacted you again?'

'Certainly not! He won't come back after what I said to him.'

She searched their faces for clues. Their blank expressions made her shiver.

'You think he will?'

The footsteps round the house last night . . .

'We think he might, yes.'

'He'll be in Moscow by now, surely?'

'We believe not, Mrs Hitchens,' Black chipped in. 'A man fitting his description was seen near here yesterday.'

'Oh . . .' Her voice caught in her throat.

'The fact is, we're keen that he should contact you,' Hillier added.

'Why?' she snapped defensively.

'We want you to tell him something; give him a specific piece of information.'

'What sort of information?'

'We'll come to that in a minute. But do you agree to help us?'

Hillier's face was friendly, Black's hard. In the familiar warmth of her kitchen the two men seemed enormous, threatening.

'I don't know. Why should I?'

Hillier folded his arms and sighed, like a schoolteacher whose patience was reaching its limits.

'I'm told you're an intelligent woman, Mrs Hitchens. I

don't need to spell *everything* out, do I? Suffice it to say, your husband is approaching the coast of Russia with a boatload of sophisticated weaponry. He's not behaving normally. Thousands of lives may be in danger, his being one of them.'

'Oh, God!'

Her worst fears were suddenly being confirmed.

'But what can *I* do about it?'

'Within forty-eight hours your husband may trigger off a spot of genocide. Now, of course all sorts of things are being done at official levels to ensure it doesn't happen. But it's just possible the Navy may not stop him in time. So, we – that's you and us – we're like an insurance policy. To give the Soviets an inkling that we've a problem we may not be able to handle. Have to do it indirectly, though. And that means you.'

Sara swallowed. Her heart was racing. Genocide? For God's sake!

'But . . , how's that going to help, if the Russians know about the problem?' she demanded.

'It means they'll keep well out of the way, if they've any sense,' Black answered briskly. 'They don't want a war any more than we do.'

Sara felt sick. To think she'd started all this!

'Now, there are things we need to know,' Black continued. 'When you were seeing this man, how did you make contact?'

'He would ring when he came to Plymouth. If I wanted to contact him, I'd leave a message at the Holiday Inn. Even when he wasn't in Plymouth, they'd take calls for him.'

'I'll bet he's not using them any more,' Black growled. 'We think he'll contact you soon. A phone-call or a message of some sort.'

'But what does he want? I told him I'd never see him again.'

The two men shifted uncomfortably.

'He's obviously very fond of you, Mrs Hitchens,' Hillier said in an oily tone.

'There'll be no risk to you in all this,' Black explained. 'You've got protection. Twenty-four hour cover.'

Sara looked startled.

'Protection? From Gunnar?'

'Just a precaution,' Hillier soothed. 'One of John Black's men is keeping an eye on the house. You'll be quite safe.

'Now, this message you're going to give him. You mustn't say it's from us, of course. Pretend it's based on something your husband said to you, just before he sailed.'

'What?'

'That he intends to lay mines at the entrance to the main Soviet submarine base at Polyarny.'

'Poly . . . what?'

'Think of Polyanna. Tell him that, in fact. Mis-remembering the name will make it more convincing.'

'Is this true? How do you know what Philip's going to do?'

'We don't,' admitted Black. 'It's a guess. But if the Russians send submarines to sea from Polyarny, and they're blown up by your husband's mines – that'll be war, Mrs Hitchens.'

'What we need is time,' Hillier took over. 'If the Soviets keep their boats out of the way, it'll give our Navy more time to find your husband and bring him back.'

'But supposing Gunnar doesn't make contact, or I don't convince him?'

'Doesn't bear thinking about, does it?' answered John Black.

'I'm sure you'll do your very best. You must want to – after what's happened,' Hillier added pointedly.

Eventually they left. They gave Sara a card with two telephone numbers on it. One was Hillier's desk in London, the other a Plymouth number for the local watchers.

The silence in the house terrified her. She wandered from room to room trying to peer from windows without being seen. Somewhere out there were two men. One to protect her, the other . . . ? What did he want? Why had Gunnar come back?

It was unreal. Soon she would awake and the nightmare would fade.

And there was a third man, Philip. What wild obsession had gripped him? It wasn't just because of her – it *couldn't* be! The security men were blaming her for everything, but that was unfair!

There was much more behind it. If only she knew what.

Outside in the garden, a pigeon took flight with a clatter of wings. Somewhere upstairs an unfastened window banged shut in a sudden breeze. She shivered.

She was scared to be in the house alone, but they'd told her to wait.

Waiting for Gunnar. A title for a melodrama.

Suddenly there was the crunch of tyres on gravel. Her heart pounded. He wouldn't just arrive, would he?

She strained to see out.

Patsy Tinker. What did she want? If Gunnar came and saw the car he'd be put off.

She'd pretend not to be in.

Too late. Patsy saw her and waved.

'Thought I'd drop in,' Patsy explained. 'You seemed so down when we met on the Hoe yesterday . . .'

'Oh, I'm okay. I'm expecting someone, that's all.'

'Oh, I'm sorry.' Patsy looked embarrassed. 'Should I . . . ?'

'No, no. Come in. Have some coffee or something.'

They moved to the kitchen.

'Oh, you've had it done since I was last here,' Patsy exclaimed admiringly. 'New units. Very smart.'

'That was last year. Shows how long it's been.'

Sara busied herself with the kettle and mugs.

'That was pretty startling, what you told me yesterday,' Patsy ventured. 'All that security business. I'd be scared to death living out here on my own with all that going on.'

'Well, with kind neighbours like you dropping in to get all the juicy details, I don't have time to be scared, do I?'

'Sara, that's *not* why I came! I simply thought you might

208

want someone to talk to. It's bad for you, keeping it all bottled up. All those feelings locked up inside you. You'll burst.'

Sara was on the point of doing exactly that. She shook with anger at being lectured.

'Look, sod off! I didn't ask you here!'

And she burst into tears. It was what Patsy had hoped would happen. The tension was broken.

Patsy let her cry, saying nothing, until Sara's shoulders had stopped shaking.

The kettle began to whistle.

'I'll do that,' Patsy said. Coffee and tea had been left out, and there were unwashed cups and saucers in the sink. So, there'd been other visitors that morning.

Sara pulled a handkerchief from the handbag on the table.

'I'm sorry,' she sniffed. 'I know you mean to help. But really there's nothing you can do.'

Patsy placed a mug on the table next to Sara, and sat down.

'Thanks.'

'Is Simon all right? Have you been able to keep it away from him, all the problems?'

'Hardly,' Sara laughed bitterly. 'It was through Simon that Philip found out.

'I'd been very silly. A little while back, there was a man I . . . used to see. He came round here quite often. I let Simon meet him. Then, ten days ago, he and Philip bumped into the man in the city. Suddenly Philip had found the key to my little box of secrets.

'Simon was back at school when it all came out, so he missed the awful rows. I think he sensed it was coming, though; that's what's been behind the trouble at school this term.'

'Vandalizing microscopes?'

'That's it. I'm sure there's worse to come. Perhaps I'll bring him home for a while . . .'

'Why don't you? That could be good for both of you.'

'I think I will.'

209

They fell silent and sipped at their coffee. Patsy took a deep breath, and started the conversation again.

'This man you were seeing . . . The one you said worked for a foreign government . . . the Russian . . . did you . . . tell him anything at all that you shouldn't have?'

'I don't *think* so, but then I'm not sure what he wanted to know. Nothing really secret, that's for sure. I don't know anything secret. Do you? I mean, does Andrew talk about his work?'

'Never.'

'It's . . . , it's not my fault, Patsy,' Sara pleaded. 'Whatever Philip's doing – it's unfair to blame me for it. It's much more involved than people think.'

'How do you mean?'

'This "revenge" they think he's planning – they imagine it's just because of me and Gunnar, but it isn't. It's more than that. It has to be.'

Wishful thinking, Patsy wondered?

'They really think he's going to attack the Russians?'

'Yes. They told me this morning.'

'What? Who did?'

Sara scraped back her chair and stood up. She grabbed a transistor radio from the worktop next to the kettle, and turned it on at full volume.

'We may be bugged,' she explained in a whisper.

'Who by?'

'MI5. They were here this morning.'

The pop music was deafening. Patsy found it unbearable.

'Couldn't we walk in the garden? It's a nice morning,' she suggested. Sara led the way to the back of the house.

The garden was walled, sheltering it from the wind. Roses and honeysuckle clung to the old brickwork. The last of the season's apples weighed heavily on the branches of young trees which Andrew had helped Philip plant the previous year.

'We should be safe out here.'

'You must think I've gone mad.'

'I'd be the same, I assure you.'

Sara reached out and held one of the apples, giving it a tiny twist so that it parted from the branch. Perfectly ripe. She held it out for Patsy.

Patsy took a bite. 'Gorgeous.' Sticking her hands determinedly into her trouser pockets, Sara turned to face Patsy squarely.

'Do you know about Philip's father?'

'No. Should I?'

'Philip hero-worshipped him, but he died when Philip was just fourteen. *HMS Tenby*? Does that ring a bell?'

'Vaguely. One of the SSNs is called *Tenby*.'

'This was an earlier one. An old diesel sub. Disappeared on patrol in the Barents Sea in 1962. All a big mystery. Philip's dad was her first lieutenant.'

'Oh, yes. I remember something. An accidental explosion, was it?'

'Not according to Philip. He's convinced the Russians sank her.'

'What? I've never heard that said before!'

'It was an open verdict at the official inquiry. No wreckage was ever found. No survivors. Just theories. The one they settled for was that there'd been a fire on board and the torpedoes had gone up. They even made changes to the way the things were stored on board after that.'

'But Philip didn't buy that idea?'

'I suppose he may have done at the beginning; he was only a boy. But he overheard someone talking to his mother about it, a few years later, saying the *Tenby* had been in the Barents to keep an eye on Russian torpedo trials. Nuclear torpedoes.'

'Crikey! And was it true?'

'I don't know. But Philip thinks so. He became convinced the Russians tested a nuclear torpedo on the *Tenby* and vapourized his father along with the rest of the crew.'

'But that's madness! The Russians would never have done that. They'd have risked starting a nuclear war, wouldn't they?'

Sara shrugged. She'd never given much heed to Philip's theories before now.

'It was November 1962, the Cuban missile crisis,

remember? All very jumpy. The Americans and Russians on the brink of war – Philip reckoned the White House put pressure on Britain not to make an issue of the *Tenby*.'

'Oh.'

Patsy racked her brains to remember what that crisis had been about.

'What is it you're saying? That this revenge Philip's planning is to do with his father's death?'

'I don't know exactly. But I'm sure it's involved.'

'*Why* are you so sure?'

Sara hesitated over how much to say.

'This summer we went on holiday to Guernsey, all three of us. It was Philip's idea. He used to go there as a boy, but hadn't been back since. I didn't know before, but it was in Guernsey that he'd last seen his father. Straight after that holiday in 1962, the *Tenby* sailed north and never returned.'

'Oh, I see.'

'Something happened this summer, to Philip. We'd been there a few days, staying in an absolute dump of a hotel. He'd been a bit moody – memories and all that – then one afternoon he came back after a walk on his own, looking as if he'd seen a ghost. Simon and I were by the pool; I expected him to join us, and when he didn't I went up to our room to look for him. Well . . .'

She frowned.

'Go on . . .'

'He was – I didn't go into the room, because he seemed to be . . . crying. I could hear, through the door. I . . . I didn't know what to think. Philip's so – undemonstrative. So, I just stood there, listening to this awful croaking noise, sort of frozen. And then he said something, in a strangled voice. Out loud. He said "Dad, Dad, what have they done to you?" '

'Good Lord! But you still didn't go in?'

'I thought he'd be upset – embarrassed that I'd heard him. So I went down again and waited for him. He didn't appear for hours. Claimed he'd fallen asleep. I asked if anything was wrong, but he said no. So I just put it down to his being back in the place where he'd last seen his father. Something deeply buried coming to the surface.'

'And that was that?'

'Well, no. He didn't sleep at night, tossing and turning; always desperately short-tempered and wanting to be on his own. Then a couple of days later, some other mother I got talking to at the hotel was telling me about a beautiful walk she'd just been on, lonely clifftops and all that, when she mentioned having seen Philip up there, sitting on a bench – with a woman.'

'Oh, really?'

'I thought the obvious at first. That evening I asked him about it. It shook him that he'd been spotted, but he dismissed it; said the woman had just been another walker who'd stopped for a rest. He was lying; I can always tell – he does it very badly.'

'You think she had some connection with his father?'

'I don't know. We came home at the end of the holiday; life returned to normal, except that Philip had closed up. I couldn't get through to him at all. He was like a man facing a crucial decision, unable to make up his mind.'

'And he was still like that when . . .'

'When he found out about Gunnar. Yes. But that's just it. Afterwards – after all the screaming and recrimination – he was different. It was as if he *had* finally made up his mind, finally decided what to do about the problem that had dogged him since Guernsey.'

A blackbird began to sing shrilly from a heavily-laden pear tree further down the garden. They began to walk again, Sara bobbing down to pull a long tuft of rye-grass from a flower bed.

'Have you told anyone about this? The authorities?'

'Hardly! It's just the imaginings of a silly woman, isn't it?' she snorted scornfully.

'It could be rather more than that. I think you should tell someone.'

Suddenly Sara clutched at Patsy's arm. The noise of a car at the front of the house had startled her.

'Sounds like you've got another visitor. Shall I go and look for you?'

Sara shook her head.

'We can go round the side.'

A trail of paving stones led to the front of the house. A small green van was parked in the drive. Its driver stood outside the front door cradling a bouquet of roses.

'Ah,' the youth turned. 'One of you Mrs Hitchens?'

'Yes, me.' Sara advanced towards him.

'Could you sign here, please?'

She did, and took the flowers from him. As the van reversed down the drive, she stood quite still staring at the blooms, as if they were poisoned.

'Aren't they beautiful? No one ever sends me flowers,' Patsy complained.

Sara looked petrified, eyes fixed on the envelope pinned to the cellophane.

'Do you know who they're from?'

'I think so,' she answered in a whisper. 'I must find a vase.'

The front door was latched, so they walked the path back to the kitchen, Patsy feeling awkward. Greetings from a new lover or an old one, she wondered?

Sara gingerly unpinned the envelope and pulled open the flap.

Patsy tried to see. The card was almost covered with writing; Sara's hands trembled as she read it. The message continued on the back.

'Nothing wrong, I hope.'

'I'm sorry . . ,' was all she could say. She looked at her watch. She was plainly very scared.

'You want me to go?'

Sara nodded. Tears welled up again; she pulled a tissue from her sleeve and blew her nose.

'All right. But look. Ring me whenever you feel like it. D'you promise?'

'Yes, I will.'

Patsy clasped Sara by the shoulders and kissed her on the cheek. For the first time in her life she felt some kinship with her.

''Bye, now. I'll drop in again soon.'

Sara forced a smile.

'Thanks for coming. I mean that.'

Patsy turned her car into the road and headed for Plymouth. What Sara had just told her was immensely important. It was what Andrew must have had in mind when he'd asked her to get talking with Sara.

She decided to ring Norman Craig from a phone box, and arrange to see him at the Naval Base.

At the front of the old rectory, overlooking the road, was a small bedroom used to store junk. Sara unlatched a small window at the top of the frame and pushed it open. This was the signal she'd been told to make when Gunnar made contact. The room smelled stale; it could do with ventilation anyway.

She prayed the watcher was watching.

She still clutched the florist's card. The words, written in Gunnar's foreign script, had terrified but excited her.

He'd deceived her, taken advantage of her loneliness. He was an enemy of her country, who'd used her cynically. Yet he'd loved her with a passion she'd never known before, a passion which surely no man could fake.

The words seemed to smoulder on the card.

> My darling. I *have* to see you again. For me
> it is not over between us and can never be.
> My heart is broke, and you must mend it.
> Please!
> Big news! I'm leaving my employer, and need
> your help to make friends with the people
> you know. I depend on you. Please don't fail
> me!
> Cannot meet at old rendezvous, but you go
> there now. Don't delay. *Tell no one.* I'll
> know if you do. The H.I. desk will have a
> message for 'Mrs Mathews'. That will tell you
> where I am.
> Please do it! I long to kiss you again.
> G.

'Leaving his employer'? He wanted to defect?

Or was it another deception? Perhaps she should contact

Hillier first. If things were changing, would they still want her to tell Gunnar about Philip?

But she dared not delay. They'd told her to do nothing to make Gunnar suspicious. Was *he* bugging her phone? Would he be watching her from a distance as she drove into Plymouth to meet him? Possibly. She could take no risks.

She opened the wardrobe in her bedroom. She'd have to change. Couldn't drive into Plymouth in an old pair of jeans.

She'd wear the plum-coloured skirt and blouse, with the black jacket.

She looked at her watch; eleven-thirty. The traffic wouldn't be bad; she could be there by twelve. Her face was a mess. Anyone could tell she'd been crying. She splashed on some cold water, then applied some makeup.

Handbag, money, car keys, then she closed the front door and checked it was latched. She'd left the upstairs window open as instructed, but it made her uneasy. Burglaries were rife in the district.

A South West Electricity Board van was parked fifty yards from the Hitchens' house. The engineer sitting behind the wheel was eating a sandwich and drinking coffee from a flask.

The silver Volkswagen drove past him at speed, heading for Plymouth. The watcher picked up a microphone to report that Mrs Hitchens was on her way.

He finished his coffee. There was no great hurry; another car would pick her up at the next crossroads. His instructions were to follow at a distance, and hold himself ready for new orders.

At the junction with the Plymouth road Sara noticed the car behind her. A red Escort. Was it following her?

She turned left and the Escort followed, but two minutes later it turned off to the right. Unknown to her, the trail had been taken up by the green Vauxhall in front.

At the outskirts of the city she slowed down. The car she was following pulled into a filling station. Her heart

216

raced as she neared the rendezvous. Fear gripped her, fear and excitement.

Left into a side street, up to the Hoe. She didn't notice the green Vauxhall following fifty yards behind. Left again into Citadel Road. She was in luck; a parking meter bay was just coming free.

The Vauxhall slid past her and disappeared. Sara locked her car and paused for a moment to compose herself. Her legs felt like jelly. Two deep breaths, then she started towards the Holiday Inn. She looked up to the sixth floor. It was where Gunnar had always stayed; a room with a view of the Hoe. Was he there now, watching her?

As she mounted the hotel steps, the red Escort drew up opposite. She was through the swing door and approaching the reception desk, when its driver began to cross the lawn to the hotel.

'Do you have a message for Mrs Mathews?' Sara asked the girl behind the desk, as calmly as she could.

'Oh, hullo!'

The receptionist had recognized her. Sara smiled; she was sure the girl had never known her name.

'Yes, here it is.'

'Thank you.'

Sara took it and walked towards the bar and the lifts.

My darling! We must be very careful! You are
being folowed.
Take the lift *alone* to the fifth floor. Make
sure you are alone in the lift. On the fifth
go strait to the fire stairs. Down to the
basement – the garage. Be sure no one
follows! In bay 16 is a Black VW. The door is
open, the keys inside. KEEP THE WINDOWS SHUT.
Drive out on the Exeter road. After 3 miles
take the left to Stumpton. On the edge of the
village is the Red Crown pub. Stop in the car
park and wait for me. If I'm not there after
twenty minutes, go inside and ask for the
phonebox. I'll ring you there.
I love you, rember.
G.

There was something endearing about Gunnar's spelling mistakes.

The lift came; the doors closed behind her. From the lobby, the man who had driven the red Ford Escort watched the lift indicator stop at number five.

They'd told him to protect her, but not to compromise her rendezvous with the target. Stupid bloody instructions! He couldn't do both.

He hurried to the payphone at the other end of the lobby and punched in a number. It answered instantly; he spoke for no more than five seconds and replaced the receiver.

Sara's heels clattered on the stone stairs. On every other flight she stopped to listen, but hers were the only feet she could hear.

The basement garage stank of petrol. It was dimly lit. At first she couldn't see the bay numbers, but recognized the car, a VW like her own but black.

The engine fired at the first turn of the key. She slipped it into first and drove up the ramp into daylight, realizing then that the windows were of dark-tinted glass. The Electricity Board van was parked opposite.

The watcher wasn't sure. It could've been her. Sod those blackened side windows! Better report it, just in case.

Sara found the pub with ease. It was lunchtime and the car park was already half-full. She swung the VW round to face the road. There was little traffic; just a green Vauxhall cruising past and up the hill to her left.

She re-read both his notes. She could almost hear him speaking the words in the fake Scandinavian accent he'd cultivated. She ought to hate him, yet she didn't. Evil? Dangerous? But he wanted her help to defect . . .

Doubts set in. Sara closed her eyes and prayed it wasn't a trick.

Behind the Red Crown a wooded hill rose steeply. From the car park a path led diagonally up it through beech and oak trees. A wooden railing lined the path.

Concealed amongst the beeches stood a man, himself built like a tree, training binoculars on the black VW below. This was Viktor Kovalenko, known to most of those he'd met in recent months as 'Gunnar'.

Kovalenko stood over six feet tall, his frame broad with muscle. His hair had been almost blond, but today it was dyed a dark chestnut. As a 'Swede' he'd let it grow long, but now it was neatly trimmed.

He worked for the First Chief Directorate of the KGB. His role was to establish an identity in Britain, to build an information network, and to identify targets to be assassinated if the Soviet Union went to war with the West.

Until a few weeks ago his mission had gone according to plan. He had lived with his 'wife' Elena in a London suburb; they'd blended well into the background. Now their cover had been broken, and he was to blame.

Elena had been picked to work with him by the First Chief Directorate, without thought to their personal compatibility. They'd experimented with a physical relationship, but it had only heightened their dislike for one another. The problem was a serious one for Viktor Kovalenko, a man with an inexhaustible sexual appetite.

He searched the road below for signs of watchers, but saw none; he'd give it another ten minutes to be sure.

He brought the binoculars to bear on the VW and cursed the black glass which prevented him from seeing Sara, the woman whose welcoming body and child-like hunger to be loved had given such a pleasurable edge to his duties. He and Elena had been activated in the summer. A naval attaché at the Soviet Embassy in London had learned the name of the commander of the trials boat for the new Moray mines. KGB headquarters in Moscow had then made the stunning discovery that a man with the same surname was a prisoner in a labour camp on the Kola. Checks at Somerset House confirmed they were father and son.

Keeping watch on Sara Hitchens' activities for a couple of weeks had been enough for Viktor to know she was a natural target. It had been easy.

At their second date, she'd talked of her unhappy marriage and mentioned the plan for a family holiday in Guernsey.

It was Elena who'd targeted Philip on the Channel Island clifftops. She'd handled it well, Viktor had to admit.

He knew he'd been careless. He'd made the unforgiveable mistake of letting a woman mean more to him than easy sex. A week ago, when Sara had told him Philip knew about their affair, and that she'd guessed he was a spy, it had shaken him. Years of training and preparation thrown away for allowing personal involvement to cloud his brain!

He'd told Elena by phone they'd have to leave the house before dawn, and driven fast back to London that night.

They'd moved to Bristol, a contingency plan ready prepared. The London house had been raided – they knew that – but how much of their scheme had been uncovered? Were their identities known? Had he been photographed? And above all, did the security services know what Hitchens had agreed to do for the KGB?

That was why he was here today; he had to find out even if it meant risking his neck.

She'd been waiting fifteen minutes. Time to say hello.

Sara glanced at the dashboard clock every minute while she sat there. Alone in the car, she felt conspicuous and vulnerable.

The sharp tap on the window made her jump in her seat. She didn't recognize him at first with his short, dark hair, but then came the familiar smile. Trembling, she unlocked the passenger door.

'I was afraid you wouldn't come,' he breathed, slipping into the seat beside her, and tossing his small rucksack into the back.

'I . . . I don't know why I did . . ,' she stuttered. 'You look so different with that hair.'

'The change is superficial, my darling,' he grinned, putting his arm round her. 'Underneath I'm the same!'

'Don't touch me!'

He pulled a face like a scolded child.

'Nothing's changed since last week,' she warned him.

'Except that you said you'd never see me again, and you're here now.' There was a twinkle of triumph in his eyes. 'But we can't talk here.'

'Why not?'

'Someone might come. Were you followed?'

'Not that I noticed. But then, I'm not trained to spot these things,' she goaded.

'One mile up the road. There's a parking place at the top of a hill. It'll be more private. Drive there please, my darling.'

She noticed his accent had changed. He'd dropped the Swedish lilt.

'All right.'

At the edge of the road she paused to allow a red Escort into the car park, then she sped off up the hill. Kovalenko kept his eye on the wing mirror, but there was no one following. The lay-by was signposted, and she pulled in behind a clump of bushes. The car park boasted public toilets.

'This isn't very nice,' Sara complained.

He was silent and didn't look at her.

'I want to know your real name,' she demanded.

'Don't you know it already? Haven't *they* told you?'

She realized he meant the security men.

'I don't think *they* know it.'

He smiled inwardly. She'd told him some good news.

'You can call me Viktor.'

It was okay to tell her now.

'I meant what I said in the letter,' he told her, then added eagerly, 'Did you like the flowers?'

'Yes.' She allowed herself a brief smile. 'They were lovely.'

'They were to say sorry for deceiving you.'

'You admit you're a spy. That's an advance; you were still denying it a week ago,' she answered tartly.

'What did you expect? But it's different now. You must listen to me, my darling.'

He edged closer to her, but without touching.

221

'When we first met it was for one reason only. Not because I'm a spy and your husband . . . I didn't know anything about that when we met,' he protested. 'Believe me. There was nothing in what you told me that was any use to Moscow.'

Sincerity blazed from his eyes.

'The reason . . , the reason we met was that we both wanted the same thing. Love. Why does a woman go to a restaurant alone? Because she wants a man. Why was I there alone? Because I needed a woman. We were looking for each other. And then you came back to my hotel, and we weren't just any man and any woman; we were *magic*!'

His face lit up and the grin spread from ear to ear. Sara laughed. It moved her when he looked like that; he was like a big child.

He took hold of her and this time she didn't resist. He kissed her mouth. Guiltily she sensed the arousal of her body.

'You are such a woman! So loving, so generous! What we have together is too good to lose!'

She pulled back and shook her head.

'No.'

This was dangerous. There was a purpose in meeting him again. A deadly purpose.

'I told you what I'm going to do,' he pressed. 'I hate my work. I want to stay in England, to prove to you that you can trust me.'

Sara shook her head again.

'Why did you come here if you don't believe me?' he snapped.

'Maybe I do believe you. I don't know. But the reason I had to see you is that I'm frightened.'

His eyes softened as if on cue.

'Not of you. Frightened of what's about to happen,' she blurted out.

Viktor slipped his arm round her shoulder. She accepted it.

'Philip – he knows what you are.'

'I know. You told me last week.'

'Yes. But I didn't tell you the way he reacted. He hates

222

you – he hates all Russians. For all sorts of reasons, good and bad. He wants revenge. He's on an exercise in the Norwegian Sea – I'm sure you know.'

'Of course.' He began to frown.

'Well, he's not doing what he should be doing. He's ignoring his orders. The Navy's got no control over him. His submarine's loaded with mines. They think he's going to blow up the Russian fleet!'

Viktor froze. His eyes turned cold; his jaw set like stone.

'How do you know this?'

'Philip said something before he sailed,' she blustered. 'He was so angry he just blurted it out about the mines. Then, I heard from someone else he's ignoring his orders.'

'How many mines?'

'I don't know.'

'Where do they think he's going exactly?'

'Philip said a name. Poly something, could it be?'

'Poly something?' He frowned. 'You came here today to tell me this? Why?'

'Because I'm so afraid of what might happen. Our Navy may not be able to stop him. Someone should be warned. Someone on your side. I don't want a war to start! If it did, it'd be partly because of you and me! Do you realize that?'

Viktor stared straight ahead through the windscreen. Instead of laying an inert mine for the Soviet Navy to recover, was Hitchens now going to use them in anger? He must signal Moscow urgently. But first he needed the rest of the information he'd come for.

'I'll make a deal. I'll warn Moscow. You must promise me something in return. To speak to your security people, on my behalf, so that I can defect.'

'I'll try.'

'Who d'you think could help? Who've you spoken to?' he asked innocently.

'There's a Mr Black . . .'

'Ah, MI5, I think.'

'And Mr Hillier. He's Foreign Office . . .'

Sara instantly knew she'd said too much. Viktor had gone very still.

'What have they said about me?' he asked softly.

'Well, nothing at all, not to me. They just ask questions all the time,' she stammered.

'Mr Hillier, too?'

'Yes.'

He could tell she was lying. What was this all about? Hillier was Secret Intelligence Service, not counter-espionage. Why should he be involved? This message about the mines. Was the SIS behind it? A false story? For what reason?

'Please find out more for me. Your Mr Hillier and Mr Black – I need to discover if they know who I am, and how valuable I could be to them. I need to know if they'll be sympathetic.'

'I'm not sure they'll tell . . .'

'Just try,' he insisted. 'We can meet again here tomorrow, or the day after. Listen carefully. I'll phone you each morning. I'll pretend to be arranging an appointment to mend your TV set. If *I* need to see you, I'll suggest a time; if *you* have news for me, you propose it.'

He smiled his broad smile at her. For the first time Sara realized he could do it to order. He leaned across to kiss her. Suddenly she felt frightened again.

'I want to go home now,' she told him.

'Yes, my darling. Return this car to the hotel car park and leave the keys.'

'How will you . . . ?'

He pointed to where a motorcycle was parked three spaces away. He reached to the back seat, pulled his rucksack onto his knee and extracted a crash helmet.

'I'll ring you in the morning. And remember – trust me.'

He pushed open the door and got out. Sara started the engine. A green Vauxhall parked near the toilets looked vaguely familiar, but she gave it no further thought.

Viktor Kovalenko pulled the chinstrap tight and swung his leg over the Kawasaki 750cc twin. He flicked the starter button and the twin cylinders burst into life.

Out on the road he headed back to the main route for Exeter and the north. He worried about the van that followed him to the junction, but relaxed when it turned right for Plymouth.

He turned left and settled down for the three hour ride to Bristol, checking constantly in his mirror to ensure he was not being shadowed.

He was oblivious of the helicopter flying two thousand feet above him.

CHAPTER EIGHT

Washington DC.

The briefing room at the White House simmered with suppressed excitement. The previous evening's TV news reports from Moscow had stung President John McGuire into calling an extraordinary press conference.

Over sixty reporters crowded the room; the walls were lined with TV cameras, their operators elbow to elbow. It was hot; already those in the front rows had begun to perspire under the lights.

President McGuire was a reluctant briefer of the press; he thought it better to say nothing than to risk saying too much. But the sight of the Soviet *Bear* pretending to be threatened by US F14s, followed by the injured innocence of Admiral Grekov had been too much for him. If America's own TV networks couldn't see when they were being manipulated, then it was time someone told them.

The press spokesman stepped up to the podium.

'Ladies and gentlemen, the President of the United States.'

There was a scraping of chairs as the reporters stood up; their chatter subsided expectantly.

'Please sit down. And thank you for coming here at such short notice. I have a statement to make, and then I shall be glad to take your questions.'

The podium in the briefing room had been lowered in height when McGuire took office. He stood just 5 feet 9 inches tall.

He smoothed the wave of hair on his forehead and took stock of the faces watching him.

'The Soviet Union has accused the United States Navy of aggression. I refute that. Soviet General Secretary and President, Nikolai Savkin, has described the NATO manoeuvres in the Norwegian Sea as provocative. They are not. The Commander-in-Chief of the Soviet Navy, Admiral Grekov, asks if the manoeuvres are a preparation for war. The answer is an emphatic NO. And Admiral Grekov. . . .'

McGuire pulled a sardonic smile. In front of him pens scribbled furiously.

'. . . is a distinguished naval commander, and knows better than to make such an asinine suggestion.

'Let me first deal with what happened yesterday, those pictures on TV last night, showing our fighters intercepting a Soviet warplane, which – it turned out – happened to be carrying an American camera team. The aircraft carrier *Eisenhower* – on a regular NATO exercise, notified in advance to the Russians – was in international waters, flying aircraft off of its deck. To comply with international safety rules any plane approaching a carrier with a hot deck is warned of the danger, and asked to keep a safe distance.

'The Soviet *Bear* reconnaissance bomber was asked that yesterday, but refused. In the interests, presumably, of producing the sort of TV pictures screened last night.

'Now, the question of the exercise itself. It's not provocative. It's defensive. It happens every two years, and the Soviets have not made a fuss about it before.

'How come it's defensive? First – and I've got to give you some figures here – first, because the Kola Peninsula is home to seventy-five per cent of the Soviets' submarine-launched nuclear missiles. Over two thousand nuclear warheads, capable of wiping out most of the USA, are installed in submarines operating from the Barents Sea. It is the right and duty of our navy to try to ensure those missiles could never be fired at us.

'Second – the Kola Peninsula provides bases for over eighty per cent of the submarines the Soviets would use to try to sink US ships reinforcing Europe in wartime. Ships that would be laden with US soldiers, airmen and their equipment needed to save Western Europe from a Soviet invasion. It is the right and duty of NATO navies to ensure those reinforcements would not end up at the bottom of the Atlantic Ocean. And the best way to do that is to stop those Soviet subs from ever getting into the Atlantic.

'Third – if the Soviets were ever to start a war, the north of Norway could be their first objective. The way to stop them invading is air power. That's why the carrier *Eisenhower* is in this exercise. To defend a NATO ally.

'Finally, ladies and gentlemen, let me give it to you straight. The United States will never be the one to start a war with the Soviet Union, but if *they* start one, we will be prepared.

'Now, if you have any questions. . . .'

Hands shot up in the front row. McGuire pointed to the dark-haired doyen of the White House press corps.

'Yes, Sam.'

'Mr President, is it true that NATO submarines are exercising closer to Soviet home waters than ever before? And if that's the case, isn't it open to interpretation as provocative at a time of greater East-West military détente?'

'Now, Sam. You know I can't talk about where our submarines patrol. I've just told you about the threat we face from nuclear missiles. The subs do what they have to do. But the Soviets can't see our subs – so how can they be provocative.'

A ripple of polite amusement swept the room. He pointed to another hand.

'Talking of provocation, Mr President, what about the *Rostov* and the MiGs headed for Cuba?'

'Is that where they're going?'

'What're you going to do about it, Mr President?'

'The Soviets haven't said where they're sending those fighters. They know our views about changing the military balance around the USA. The MiGs don't threaten us yet. If they become a threat, then I'll do something about it.'

'What . . . what'll you do, Mr Pres . . .'

McGuire cut him short and smiled at a woman from the Washington Post.

'Laura . . .'

'Why do you think Mr Savkin is so concerned about the naval exercise this year?'

'You'll have to ask him that.'

'He says we're being unneccessarily aggressive. Have you given instructions to the Navy to avoid doing anything which the Soviets might interpret as provocative, Mr President?'

'No. The Navy's doing what it does every two years or so. Normal manoeuvres. No special instructions.'

'But if Mr Savkin's out to make trouble, some people feel it'd do no harm to hold back a little, Mr President . . .'

'I don't accept your premise . . .'

'What about the other navies in the exercise? The British, for example. Can you be sure they won't do something to provoke the Russians?'

His blue eyes locked onto hers. What did she know? Reynolds had told him the Brits had a submarine gone AWOL. Had she heard it, too?

'Our NATO allies are at least as experienced as us in handling the Soviets,' was his non-committal reply.

'Last question, ladies and gentlemen,' the press spokesman called from behind the President's shoulder.

'Sir, d'you think President Savkin's trying to deflect attention from the problems he's having with *perestroika?*'

'I'm sorry. That's one for him to answer, not me. Thank you, folks. Have a good day.'

McGuire glanced at the cameras and turned to leave. He knew he'd disappointed them, but he'd had one simple message to put across, and he'd given it them.

'That was one goddam wasted morning!'

The bored male voice came from somewhere in the middle of the room, loud enough for McGuire to hear. But he didn't care.

* * *

'Press conference okay?' Reynolds asked anxiously, back in 'the bunker'. Presidents had a habit of being provoked into unwise statements by the media.

McGuire shaped his thumb and index finger into a bullseye.

'They got what I wanted, not what they wanted.'

Reynolds grinned, then pulled a folder from his brief-case and spread the contents on the maple-wood table.

'Intelligence agencies have been working nights,' Reynolds joked, flicking the pages of the files in front of him.

'First the easy bit,' he continued. 'Defense Intelligence Agency reports the *Rostov*'s going slow. Still headed for the Caribbean, but not in any hurry. Still nothing from the satellites that tells us it's Cuba, but humint sources in Havana say Castro's pretty happy about something, and he's not got much else to smile about right now.'

'They threw me a question on the MiGs. Some time I'm going to have to change my line. The question is, when *do* those fighters become a threat? That's when I'll have to say something different.'

'The Pentagon's working on an options brief. They'll have it for you tomorrow.'

Reynolds sounded impatient. He shoved the *Rostov* file to one side.

'Listen. The CIA's got something new out of Moscow. This stuff's hot!'

'Give it to me, Tom.'

'Savkin's just lost his majority on the Politburo. Only he doesn't know it yet. The faction that supports his reforms of the economy is now in a minority. Secretly the opposition to Savkin has decided to put the brakes on. They want to freeze prices, reintroduce subsidies on food, and break the link between pay and output. Strikes are spreading like crazy; they reckon it's the only way to stop them turning into riots.'

'Is that reliable information?'

'Copper-bottomed, the Company says.'

'And how come Savkin doesn't know what's going on?'

'It's one of his closest friends that has changed sides, and he's still choosing the moment to tell him. But the CIA thinks Savkin's seen it coming – that's why he's been sounding off about "American aggression". Wants a distraction. Needs one – at any price, John.'

His final words hung like a thundercloud. Their eyes met, unblinking.

'How far would he go, Tom?'

'That's the sixty-four-thousand dollar question. The Soviet section chief at Langley thinks Savkin wants a shooting-match – a little one – just so long as it's us that starts it.'

'He's not going to risk that!'

'I said "a little one". A small, contained conflict. A few shots fired, maybe one or two people killed – enough to make one hell of a big story back home to take the workers' minds off the bread queues, and to hold together any splits in the Politburo.'

'And how the hell do you arrange a "small, contained conflict" between the USA and the Soviet Union, for God's sake?'

'At sea. It already happened, a few years ago, in the Black Sea. One of our warships got rammed by one of theirs while we were exercising our right of innocent passage through Soviet territorial waters. If you take that scenario a step further, you'll get shots being fired.

'Right now Savkin doesn't reckon he has much to lose. He's just as committed to *perestroika* as Gorbachev was. If it fails, the Soviet Union heads back to the dark ages – that's his line.'

'For dark ages, read "cold war".'

Reynolds shrugged. It was a bleak picture. If the Politburo had its way, Russian relations with the West would take a dive. Yet for Savkin to hold on to power, he'd have to sacrifice all the east-west détente that had been built up in recent years.

'So, what's your advice, Tom?'

'Keep it cool. Like we've done with the *Rostov*. Don't give them the chance to pull us into a fight.'

'And the exercise?'

'You mustn't be seen to be changing any of it. But let's check the game plan. It won't be the surface ships that cause trouble; they'll keep west of North Cape, the way they always do. It's the subs that worry me. They got something different planned, but I don't remember what it is. You got the Chairman of the Joint Chiefs coming to see you in an hour. Just time for me to call him, to make sure he's briefed.'

'Okay. Do it, Tom.'

McGuire looked at his watch. He could grab a sandwich lunch before the Admiral arrived and have everything straightened out before he called the British Prime Minister at 4pm.

* * *

Northwood, England.

Rear-Admiral Anthony Bourlet was thunderstruck. He let the telephone receiver drop onto its rest. What Captain Norman Craig had just told him had given Operation Shadowhunt a ghastly new dimension.

Suddenly they faced the possibility that Hitchens wasn't suffering a breakdown after all, but was acting under some sort of duress, presumable from the KGB.

Bourlet checked his watch. 1700 hrs. There could still be someone at the registry. He jabbed a finger at the intercom button.

'Do something very urgently for me, will you?' he called his WRNS PA. 'Get onto the registry and see what you can dig up on *HMS Tenby*. Not the SSN. The old T-class with the same name, back in the early sixties. Disappeared in the Barents. I want to know when, where, and preferably the inquiry report, too. Hurry now. I'm just going along to the C-in-C.'

'He's just left his office, sir.'

'Well, see if you can catch him. Ring down to the security desk.'

The door to the C-in-C's outer office was open.

'Has he been gone long?'

''Bout half a minute, sir. Just missed him,' replied Waverley's staff officer. Just then the telephone rang.

'Oh, yes, sir. He's here now.'

The lieutenant commander passed the phone across.

'Is this really urgent, Anthony? I'm in a hurry,' came the irritated voice of Admiral Waverley.

'Vital, sir.'

There was a pause. Bourlet heard a sigh at the other end.

'Oh, all right. I'll come up again.'

Within two minutes Bourlet was explaining about the unknown woman who had met Philip secretly in Guernsey earlier that summer.

'Craig's been onto the security services. They're going to see Sara Hitchens again. Apparently the Russian who's been screwing her has a wife. MI5 suspects there was some sort of double-act going on.'

'I'm lost. What exactly do we suspect now?'

Waverley was hollow-eyed at the thought of having to break news of further horrors to the Prime Minister.

'Remember those words of Philip's that Sara overheard; "Dad, what have they done to you?" – something to that effect? Suggests Philip's father is still alive. If that's the case, the Soviets could be offering to free him – in exchange for something.'

Waverley swallowed hard.

'Like what?'

'Dunno. A *Trafalgar* class sub?' Bourlet joked grimly.

'Bollocks! His crew would never let him.'

'Well then, something else. . . .'

'A Moray mine?'

'Exactly!'

'Oh, Christ!'

Waverley pressed the flat of his hand against his brow, rubbing it back and forth as if to muffle the alarm bells ringing inside his head.

The implications were horrendous. The Moray was a British–American development. He could imagine the bad-mouthing that would pour from Washington if this nightmare came true.

'But, but even if Hitchens had been blackmailed into giving them a Moray, what about his wife's affair with the Russian? Are you saying he accepted that as just something else he had to put up with if his father was to be freed? Surely not.'

'According to Sara Hitchens, when Philip found out about her and the Russian, it seemed to make up his mind for him. Make of that what you will.'

'In other words, we haven't a clue what he's going to do.'

'That's about the size of it.'

Waverley stood up and smoothed his uniform jacket.

'I'll have to tell Downing Street. She's not going to like this, you know.'

Bourlet took a certain malicious pleasure in seeing the misery engraved on the face of his Commander-in-Chief.

'And you'd better signal Commander Tinker in *Tenby*, particularly as it's his own wife who's brought all this to light. . . .' Waverley frowned. 'What an extraordinary coincidence – the name of the SSN we've sent to find him. D'you think it means something?'

Back in his own office Bourlet opened Hitchens' file, and began to read. His own memories of the events of 1962 began to return. He'd been a sub-lieutenant then, on his first posting.

The official report had been a bland document for public consumption, making no reference to the spying mission that *Tenby* had been engaged in at the time. But a secret annexe to the report suggested the very real possibility that the Soviets had vaporized the boat with a nuclear torpedo.

But if Lieutenant Commander Hitchens, Philip's father, was still alive, that theory didn't fit any more.

* * *

Downing Street, London.

The Foreign Secretary, Sir Nigel Penfold, arrived at Number 10 at 8.30 p.m., half-an-hour before the call from Washington was due. In his briefcase were the notes from MI6, which offered an assessment of Soviet affairs almost identical to that provided by the CIA to President McGuire.

In the House of Commons that afternoon the Prime Minister had faced tough questions from MPs, suggesting the NATO manoeuvres were indeed provocative at a time when President Savkin needed all the help he could get. In reply she'd slammed into the 'blatant propaganda' emanating from Moscow, and trumpeted the right of NATO navies to exercise in the Norwegian Sea.

'I've had three calls from Admiral Waverley today,

Nigel,' she announced. 'The first to tell me they'd located the *Truculent*, the second to say they'd lost her again, and the third just this moment, to tell me that it now looks as if Commander Hitchens could be a Russian agent!'

'What?'

'The KGB may be blackmailing him. Something to do with his father. I've just launched a rocket at the security chiefs; I should have heard about it from them, not the wretched Navy!

'And Sir Stewart had the cheek to tell me that because the Royal Navy has the quietest submarines in the world, they may not be able to stop Commander Hitchens doing whatever he intends to do!

'Pour me another whisky, would you? It's been a long day.'

The Foreign Secretary obliged, but kept the measure small. He'd noticed the PM losing her concentration recently after too many whiskies.

'What's President McGuire going to say? Not a word to him about this business, Nigel.'

A buzzer sounded in the secure communications box. The PM picked up the receiver, and nodded to Penfold.

'We're ready. Put him through.'

She replaced the receiver and keyed the conference switch that operated a loudspeaker and microphone.

'Good afternoon, Prime Minister. John McGuire here.'

'Good *evening*, Mr President. How nice to hear your voice. I have Sir Nigel with me. Are you accompanied at your end?'

'Tom's here.'

'Good evening, ma'am, Sir Nigel,' came the voice of the National Security Adviser.

'Perhaps you'd let me make the opening shots,' McGuire's voice had an edge to it. 'Our intelligence assets think Savkin's on the way out. The conservatives on the Politburo are getting the upper hand and want to turn the clock back. Our assessment is that he's spoiling for a fight with the West as a distraction. Just a little fight, but something, nonetheless. Do you go along with that view?'

'We agree as to what's happening in the Politburo, and

your assessment of Savkin's actions is certainly a distinct possibility,' the PM answered.

'Our view is that Savkin's lost his hand anyhow. There's no way we can save him. All we can do is pray they don't turn the clock right back to Brezhnev's time.'

'You're more pessimistic than we are, John. But we agree in general with what you say.'

'So it's a time for the Western Alliance to keep its head down. Which isn't easy with about a hundred NATO warships steaming towards the Kola peninsula! Now, we've just discussed this with the Chairman of the Joint Chiefs of Staff. On his advice, we feel there's only one aspect of Exercise Ocean Guardian that needs to be modified to ensure we don't risk mixing it with the Russian Navy . . .'

'Mr President!' the PM interrupted. 'On no account must the Alliance be seen to be backing off in the face of blatant propaganda from the Soviet Union. At times like this we need to show strength, not weakness!'

'If I may continue . . . We won't be *seen* to be backing off at all! It's the submarine operations that should be changed. Their activities are secret anyway, so no one'll know we've given them new orders.'

This was dangerous ground. Penfold's concern grew as the PM reached for her glass.

'Go on, Mr President,' she said.

'I'm talking of two subs in particular, Prime Minister. One of ours and one of yours. Their exercise task, as you know, is to try to penetrate the Soviet surveillance barriers and simulate the planting of the new "smart" mines at the entrances to two major Russian submarine bases. Normally that sort of operation is fair game; we don't admit we're doing it, and the Russians don't admit it if they manage to detect us doing it. But with Savkin looking for a fight, they might just blow those boats out of the water.'

'Yes. I hear what you're saying. But that's an essential task for our submarines, in case a real war threatens. They've got to try it out, see what's possible and what isn't.'

'Let me put it this way. This afternoon I gave orders

that the *USS Baltimore* should turn back from her mission, and join the exercises with the Surface Fleet west of North Cape. There will be no United States submarines operating within a hundred miles of the Soviet coast for the immediate future. If your boat goes in there, she'll be on her own.'

The PM's expression froze.

'I earnestly recommend you to withdraw that boat, Prime Minister. We're all fully agreed on this side that it's the right thing to do. The operation can be set up again in six months when the Kremlin's settled down.'

'I hear what you say, John. We'll give it most urgent thought, I promise you.'

'Say, ah . . . there won't be any problem in recalling that boat, will there? No communications difficulties?'

'The Commander-in-Chief Fleet communicates regularly with all the ships under his command, Mr President. Now, if there's nothing further we need to discuss, I'd like to end this conversation so that I can pursue the points you've raised.'

'Fine by me. Glad to have talked with you. We'll stay in close touch.'

'That would be prudent. Goodnight, Mr President.'

The PM immediately picked up her internal telephone.

'Could you get me CINCFLEET on a secure line urgently, please?'

The Foreign Secretary suddenly thought of the orders he'd given the Secret Intelligence Service, to warn the Russians of the danger from *Truculent*. It now appeared the Soviets were expecting the boat anyway, and for some quite different reason. He hoped to God the PM never found out what he'd done.

* * *

Severomorsk, USSR.

Vice-Admiral Feliks Astashenkov found it impossible to sleep. His heart was racing from too much cognac, and his wife, who had a heavy cold, was snoring fitfully.

The green digits of his alarm clock told him it was just before one.

Despite his wakefulness, the knock at the door startled him.

'Admiral Belikov wishes to see you immediately at his home, Comrade Vice-Admiral,' came the grumpy voice of his valet who'd been woken out of a deep sleep. 'He's just telephoned.'

'All right. Order the car,' Astashenkov whispered, hoping his wife hadn't been woken. He could have walked it in five minutes, but the wind was bitter, and if he was to be deprived of sleep he didn't see why his driver shouldn't suffer, too.

The heavy smell of spirits in the car almost made him change his mind. But even if the *starshina* driver was drunk, he shouldn't come to much harm on the short drive.

'Left here, halfwit!' he yelled as they overshot the turning.

When they reached Belikov's house the driver slammed on the brakes, hurling Astashenkov against the seat in front.

'Right, you animal! Give me the bottle!'

The driver turned and shrugged, feigning bewilderment.

'That's an order!'

Grudgingly the *starshina* fished in the pocket of his heavy greatcoat and pulled out a flask. Astashenkov grabbed it from him, and emptied the contents onto the road.

'Wait here!'

He left the car door open and marched up to the portal of Belikov's villa. The guard had been watching for him and opened the door before he could knock.

The Commander of the Northern Fleet was waiting in his study, a large brandy bottle and two glasses on a tray on the desk.

'My apologies for this, Feliks. It can't be helped. No one's getting much sleep tonight. Grekov called me from Moscow an hour ago. He'd been woken by the KGB. Come and sit down. Brandy?'

'I'd prefer tea, if you don't mind.'

'Of course. So would I.'

Belikov signalled to the guard to arrange it.

'What's happened?'

'The operation we talked about yesterday – the British submarine that's bringing us a "Moray" mine . . .'

Astashenkov nodded expectantly.

'Damned KGB! Arrogant bastards! You know what they've done? Screwed up the whole plan! That's just the word for it, too; *screwed up!*

'Their man in Plymouth had to end up in bed with the wife of the British commander who's working for us! The commander found out and is so goddamned angry he's coming here to blow our Fleet to pieces!'

'What?' Astashenkov cried. 'I don't understand!'

The guard brought in the tea, giving Belikov time to cool down.

'All right, I'll explain the whole story,' he went on, when they were alone again.

Feliks listened with growing astonishment and anger. After five minutes he knew as much as Belikov.

'We must find that boat before it finds one of ours,' Belikov insisted. He was a surface-ship man, ill-versed in the details of undersea warfare.

'We must also face facts, Andrei. Our submarines make more noise than theirs. If we send out our boats to look for *Truculent*, it could amount to suicide. Do we want to risk that?'

'The *PLA* I sent south managed to intercept it. It could do so again.'

'The British boat was moving fast then. Now it'll be slow. Very slow and silent. We can hunt it from the air. It'll be safer that way.'

Belikov cursed and poured himself a cognac. He cocked an eyebrow at Astashenkov.

'All right. I'll join you after all.'

'Can we be certain he plans to attack us?' Feliks demanded. 'He might still be intending to give us the mine so his father can go free.'

'Nothing's certain. But we have to be prepared.'

Astashenkov's brow furrowed.

'If he wants to catch us with mines, he'll have to lay them at the choke points, where he knows we have to pass. That almost certainly means close to the mouth of this very inlet.'

'He could go further east, to the *Taifun* base at Gremikha . . .'

'Unlikely. The further east he goes, the greater the risk we'll catch him. No. He'll come here. I'm sure of it. What was the original plan, Andrei? Where was he going to deliver the mine? To the harbourmaster at Polyarny?'

The Commander-in-Chief glared. It was no time for jokes.

'He was to lay it about twenty kilometres off-shore, in less than one-hundred-and-fifty metres of water. The KGB promised to unite him with his father in Helsinki, after the mine had been recovered.'

'Hmmm. Not bad. A pity it may not happen now.'

Belikov swirled the brandy in his glass.

'Maybe it still will, but differently.'

'Meaning?'

The Commander-in-Chief leaned forward, clasping his glass globe between the palms of his hands. His words came as a hoarse whisper.

'If he comes into our territorial waters, we can sink him. The wreckage of *HMS Truculent* will give us a whole harvest of secrets – *and* a Moray mine.'

* * *

The north Norwegian Sea.

Midnight, Tuesday.

The Gulf Stream sweeps its warm water round the northern tip of Norway, keeping the fjords free of ice in the winter months, almost as far east as the entrance to the White Sea.

Off North Cape, Europe's most northerly outpost, the current flows eastwards at a steady half-a-knot carrying with it the smaller marine life like shrimps and krill that form the smallest components in the food chain, and create much of the background noise underwater.

HMS Tenby, 5,000 tons of steel packed with electronics, machinery and men, dipped in and out of that current deep below the surface, trailing her sonar array hundreds of metres astern. She was travelling at ten knots and heading east, hoping to hear *Truculent* coming up behind, but with no certainty the boat hadn't already passed her, further out to sea.

'I don't bloody well believe it!' growled Andrew Tinker, folding the signal in half and tossing it onto the wardroom table.

'May I?' inquired the commander, reaching across.

'Yes. See what you think of it. Sodding signal makes no sense to me at all.'

Biddle whistled softly.

'Shit! That's a bit strong! Phil Hitchens recruited by the KGB? Are we sure this isn't a joke?'

Andrew stuffed his hands in his pockets and waited for Biddle to finish reading.

'Huh! The cheek!' exploded Biddle. 'This bit at the end – "Decided you should know this, not because it materially affects your task, but to impress upon you the seriousness of the situation".'

'Bourlet's a pompous ass!' snapped Andrew. 'I can just hear him dictating this crap! Does he think we're treating it as a game?'

He dropped into a chair and took back the signal.

'You know, something I've realized in the last few days is that you can know someone for twenty years – think of them as a close friend, even – and yet not really know them at all. I'm stating the obvious, but it's sad, isn't it?'

Biddle nodded. It was approaching midnight and he was dog-tired.

They'd sped north and east after losing contact with *Truculent* earlier in the day. Every hour or so they'd risen to periscope depth, to receive messages from the satellite.

Two Nimrods were laying Jezebel barriers far to the north and east of North Cape. *Tenby*'s instructions were to stay close to the Norwegian coast, listening in Norwegian waters where the Nimrods couldn't search without prompting awkward questions.

'If you wanted to deliver a Moray mine to the Soviet Navy, how would you do it?' demanded Andrew.

'Explosively!'

'Seriously, how can Phil do it? Without the conscious support of his crew?'

'I'd say it's impossible. He can hardly go alongside in the Kola Inlet and hand one over. And if he's going to pop one out of a torpedo tube, his WEO would have to prepare it and take part in the firing. No. I just can't see it.'

'With the other plan we envisaged – to lay mines and activate them later – it's just possible he could convince his crew. But if he's trying to pass one of the mines to the Sovs, it'd have to be totally inert, otherwise the anti-handling devices would blow it up as soon as they tried to pick it up off the bottom. And to persuade a WEO to discharge a mine that hasn't been switched on? He'd never do it. Not in a month of Sundays.'

'It's mission impossible, isn't it? He'd have to place the mine with incredible precision, otherwise the Russians would never find it. It's supposed to be almost undetectable on sonar.'

The wardroom door opened. First Lieutenant Murray Watson stared at them in surprise.

'Sorry. Thought there'd be no one here. Just wanted a cuppa before turning in.'

'Pickles your liver, all that tea,' Biddle answered. He glanced at the wall clock. 'There's a watch change in a few minutes. Wardroom'll be busy. We'll continue this in my cabin.'

* * *

To the east of North Cape is Porsangen Fjord. Floating motionless in the middle of its ten-mile-wide mouth, 100 metres below the surface, was a *Kobben* class submarine of the Royal Norwegian Navy.

One of the midgets of the submarine world at just over 400 tons, the *Storm* was less than a tenth the size of *Tenby* and *Truculent*. Crouched inside were just eighteen crew, trained to say very little and to talk in whispers when they did.

242

Her task was to slowly criss-cross the North Cape current, silently and undetected, listening to the world go by. At this she was extremely effective. Powered by a 1,700 horse-power electric motor, she was completely noiseless when moving at a mere five knots.

Every twelve hours or so, within the shelter of the Norwegian coast, she'd raise a breathing tube for her oxygen-hungry diesels to recharge the batteries.

Tonight there was excitement on board, suppressed but still almost tangible. The young conscript crew had heard things they'd never heard before.

Sea creatures and passing tramp steamers were the normal acoustic diet of their bow-mounted sonar, but tonight there'd been submarines, friendly boats whose details should have appeared in the day's intelligence summary, and hadn't.

Norway's navy co-operated closely with Britain's, and expected to be informed when British boats passed through Norwegian waters.

The first contact had passed from west to east at about fifteen knots, two hours earlier. The noise signature had been that of a *Trafalgar* class submarine.

They'd guessed it passed within four miles for them to have heard it at all. *Trafalgars* were notoriously quiet.

The *Storm* had turned south again.

Then came the second surprise – an almost identical signature, moving more slowly this time, but on the same eastbound track.

The commander of the *Storm* smiled to herself and guessed they were heading for the Kola Inlet.

They must be on an intelligence operation, nothing to do with Exercise Ocean Guardian. That's why the British had said nothing.

This was the sort of thing her own navy would never indulge in. Living right next to 'the bear', caution and correctness were the catchwords for neighbourliness.

Another twelve hours and their patrol would be over. She'd report what they'd heard to her intelligence officer, but it would go no further. An ally's secret would be safe with them.

* * *

Peter Biddle spread a chart on his bunk.

'Nothing from the sound room. Not a trace. Looks like we've missed him. Hope to God the Nimrod does better.'

Andrew sighed.

'Look, if the Russians are ever to find the mine, Phil's got to give it to them on a plate.'

'Eh?'

'So, let's look at the chart, and see if we can find a plate.'

Biddle frowned. 'I'm not with you.'

The sheet covered a fifty mile stretch of the Soviet coastline, with the Kola Inlet at its centre. The main Soviet naval bases were clearly marked in the bays around the fjord. A peninsula to the west curved north and east creating a natural shelter against the Arctic storms.

'That's the place!' Andrew exclaimed, pointing to a mark east of the Inlet. 'Has to be. That rock, ten miles off the coast, "Ostrov Chernyy". The chart shows a radar site on it, nothing else. But there's an underwater spit running north from it, covered with fine sand. Water's sixty or seventy metres deep, and the spit's not more than a hundred metres across. It's easy to find with bottom contour navigation; large enough for him to lay the mine safely; and small enough for the Russians to search with their bottom crawlers.'

Mission impossible? Not so impossible, after all.

He pushed the chart to one side and sat down on the bunk. Biddle dropped into his chair.

Andrew closed his eyes trying to remember exactly what had happened to the old *HMS Tenby* all those years ago, and to imagine the effect on a teenage boy of losing a father in such circumstances.

'It's an odd feeling, being on board an *HMS Tenby* in circumstances like these.'

'Bit spooky, really,' responded Biddle.

'Phil must've been shattered to lose his old man like that.'

'No corpse to grieve over.'

'What do you mean?'

'They say you can't complete the process of grieving unless you have the body to bury or burn. Makes it final. In Phil's case, perhaps the grieving process never finished.'

'And now he finds his father's alive. It's enough to send anyone nuts. Do you know the story of the old *Tenby?* You must have a potted history on board, Peter. Previous ships that've borne this glorious name, etcetera.'

'Sure, but it's all pretty bland. You won't learn much from that. Tell you what, though; Murray Watson's done some digging. I think he got a look at some secret files at Bath, once. Keeps threatening to write a book on it and tell the "real" story.'

'Pull him in here, can you? Before he gets his head down.'

Biddle stepped into the corridor and reappeared a few moments later with his first lieutenant, looking puzzled.

'I gather you're a historian, Murray,' Andrew explained.

'Far too grand a title, sir. But I know a bit about the old *Tenby.*'

'All I remember is that she disappeared in the Barents without trace, and they concluded her torpedo magazine had gone up.'

'Yes, well; that was a load of cobblers. But they were so mystified by the disappearance, they spent a fortune on analysing the design. A sharp engineer, keen to make a name for himself, calculated that there was a theoretical fire hazard. The scenario he dreamed up only had a 1 in 100,000 chance of happening, but it was the only conclusion the enquiry was able to reach. So, they spent millions refitting the boats.'

'But you don't reckon there was a fire?'

'No.'

'So what did happen to *Tenby?*'

A shutter seemed to close on Watson's face.

'I don't know, sir.'

'Listen, Murray. What happened in 1962 is connected with what's happening to us at this very moment.'

'Oh?'

'I'm not going to give you all the details; there's no need for you to know. But *Truculent*'s commander, Phil Hitchens: his father was first lieutenant on the old *Tenby*.'

'I knew that, sir.'

'Of course. You would if you've studied the case. Well, whatever Commander Hitchens is doing with *Truculent*, it seems directly connected with the death – or disappearance – of his father on *Tenby*.'

'Ah . . .'

Watson was intrigued.

'So, what I want to know is what the old *Tenby* was doing in the Barents Sea, and what you guess happened to her.'

'Well . . . she was spying. But the stories about watching Soviet nuclear torpedo trials are only half true. That was a cover for her real task.'

'Which was . . . ?'

Watson hesitated, as if he'd said too much.

'If I tell you, sir, you must never let on you heard it from me. I saw some documents once that I shouldn't have, see? And if the security people ever found out, they could trace it back to the bloke who showed me.'

'Agreed. We won't tell.'

'Well, then . . . *Tenby* was after a new Russian radar site. The intelligence bods suspected it was a long-range over-the-horizon type that could track NATO warships 1500 miles away. The installation was on a tiny island, no more than a rock really, about ten miles off the Kola coast.'

A little flag went up in Andrew's brain.

'The boat was to stay out of sight,' Watson continued, 'while a small reconnaissance team went by inflatable onto the island at night. It was to have been two marines from the Special Boat Squadron, but one of them got ill. Appendicitis. Lieutenant Commander Hitchens said he'd go in his place. We know that because the sub sent a signal just before the operation began. Last signal she ever sent –'

A second flag went up.

'The two of them were to get onto the island and hide. Then in daylight they'd take pictures of the radar, hide again, and escape the following night. Nobody knows if they ever made it.'

Andrew and Peter Biddle sat spellbound.

'What . . . what was the name of the island?'

'Ostrov Chernyy.'

The two commanders looked at one another.

'I can show it to you on the chart, if you like.'

'Thanks,' growled Andrew, 'but we've already found it.'

CHAPTER NINE

Wednesday 23rd October.

Moscow 0900 hrs.

The President and General Secretary of the Soviet Union Nikolai Savkin knew that the endgame was at hand.

His efforts to use the media to project a threat from the West had fallen flat. Ever since he'd re-imposed censorship, the Soviet people had treated everything in the newspapers or on television with deep suspicion.

In two days there was to be a full meeting of the Politburo. Without a genuine foreign relations crisis to rally its members, he knew he'd be outvoted and forced to end what was left of the economic and political reform programme.

The head of the KGB sat across the table from him.

Savkin mistrusted Medvedev; it was the Politburo who'd appointed him, demanding a new strong-man at the KGB after the organization's failure to control the secessionist riots in the Baltic republics earlier that year.

Savkin was only half-listening to Medvedev, who was reeling off a long list of arrests and deaths during the disturbances of the past week, expressing satisfaction that the figures were falling. That showed most of the ringleaders had already been disposed of, he claimed.

Savkin gave Medvedev a watery smile when he eventually left, relieved at his departure.

Admiral of the Fleet Sergey Grekov was waiting outside. A stolid, non-political seaman, Grekov owed his promotion to Gorbachev's early efforts to separate the military from politics.

Their meeting had been hastily arranged that morning. The Admiral had insisted on seeing Savkin at the earliest opportunity.

'Please come in, Comrade Admiral,' Savkin welcomed him.

'It's good of you to see me at such short notice, Comrade President, I know how busy you are. I'm sure you'll understand the urgency when I . . .'

'Yes, yes, Sergey Ivanovich,' Savkin answered impatiently. 'Sit down, and get your breath back.'

The Admiral was sweating from the haste of his arrival at the Kremlin. Savkin had heard he'd been having heart trouble lately.

'It's an intelligence matter,' Grekov puffed. 'Disturbing information we received from London last night.'

The Admiral paused, trying to guess from Savkin's expression whether the KGB chief had already told him about the Englishman Hitchens.

'Oh?'

'Yes. Concerning a British nuclear submarine.'

'Really? Well, go on. I'm not telepathic . . .'

Grekov relaxed. Savkin's apparent ignorance meant he could simplify the details.

'A *Trafalgar* class submarine, according to information gathered by one of our agents in Plymouth – that's the home port for the boat – is heading towards our main submarine bases in Kola, intending to attack us.'

'What? That's ridiculous!'

'Her commanding officer is disobeying orders. He appears to have a personal grudge against the Soviet Union. It's possible some of his officers support him.'

'Are you sure? Has it been checked?'

'The British are searching for him. Their maritime aircraft are operating in the Barents Sea – that's almost unheard of, so far north. It means the submarine must be close.'

Nikolai Savkin's heart was racing. He struggled to control himself. If he believed in God, he'd have said his prayers had been answered. Grekov mustn't see his excitement.

'This is terrible! What are you doing about it?'

'We, too, are searching. Aircraft and helicopters are out at this moment, covering the widest possible area.'

'And what of your navy, Admiral? How many ships and submarines are also searching?'

'Comrade President, we have to take care. If the British commander wants our blood, we must not make it easy for him. The *Trafalgar* submarines are very advanced. Their technology makes them hard to find. In a contest with even our newest *PLA*s, the chances are the *Trafalgar* would win.'

'What are you saying, Sergey?' Savkin growled. 'That you dare not confront him?'

'Of course not, Comrade President. But when you know a trap's being set, but not where it is, you move cautiously. We must assume he's now close to the mouth of the Kol'skiy Zaliv. Nearby, there are six submarine bases; he could be lying in wait at any one of them.'

'Are you saying the Red Banner Fleet of the Soviet Navy is hiding in its harbours, for fear of one single British submarine?' Savkin bellowed in mounting fury.

'That's an insult, Comrade President!' Grekov hurled back, hauling himself to his feet. 'An insult to me and to the brave men under my command! It would be an act of the utmost foolishness to send out submarines which are now in harbour, without knowing whether the enemy has blockaded the ports. No military man of any experience would take such a decision.'

'All right. Simmer down, Sergey!'

Savkin drummed his fingers on his desk, his mind hyperactive.

Admiral Grekov felt his heart beating uncomfortably fast. The doctors had told him to avoid situations which excited him.

'What ships are already at sea?' the President continued.

'An anti-submarine barrier. Surface ships and submarines. They're to the west, facing the NATO fleets – the Ocean Guardian exercise. It's possible they'll find the British boat. He won't dare attack out there. Too many of us.

'The danger is inshore. He has mines of a new type. We know little about them . . .'

Grekov hesitated. Should he tell Savkin the KGB had bungled the operation to get hold of one? He decided not.

'If he lays the mines close to our submarine bases, it'd be suicide for any of our boats to leave harbour. We need time, Comrade. Just a few days, to find the *Trafalgar*, and neutralize the threat.'

'Has it occurred to you the British might be bluffing? That, far from disobeying orders, the submarine could be the spearhead for a NATO attack on our Northern Fleet? Under the guise of their manoeuvres?'

'We considered that, of course. It did seem possible; their naval strategy is very threatening. But all the intelligence information we have suggests the British are themselves close to panic. They're desperate to get their submarine back under control, but at the same time don't want their allies to know anything's wrong. The British claim to have the best trained, best disciplined Navy in the world. It could be damaging to their reputation.

'Also, our radar satellites show the NATO warships are no longer moving towards the Barents. They're manoeuvring off the coast of Norway, as in previous years. Perhaps our protests have had some effect.'

Savkin would have felt triumphant at the West backing down, if these had been normal times, but Grekov's words were like a body-punch. A diminishing threat from the West meant the crumbling of his last hope of using fear to bring the unruly Soviet people back to heel.

His last hope but one. There was still the submarine.

Savkin swung his chair round to face the window. The sky was a watery blue. He could see the top of the Spassky Tower on the Kremlin wall, crowned with its big red star.

'I want reports as soon as the submarine is traced,' he said, just loud enough for Grekov to hear. 'Whatever happens, keep me up to date. We may be on the brink of war.'

'It won't come to that, I can assure you, Comrade President.'

'No? We'll see. Thank you, Admiral.'

Grekov levered himself from his chair and saluted curtly, and left without another word.

Savkin sat almost motionless for a full two minutes. Then he pulled a diary from his jacket pocket, and opened it at a page of telephone numbers. A capital 'A' had been written beside one number. 'A' for Astashenkov, Vice-Admiral Feliks, Deputy Commander of the Northern Fleet at Severomorsk.

Looking at the number struck terror into his heart. Savkin was no natural gambler. Now he faced the most perilous decision of his entire life. If he chose to play the one card he had left, the odds on him winning or losing were impossible to calculate.

He faced two choices; he could yield his power to the forces of conservatism and accept that it was impossible to reform the monolith of the Soviet economy; or he could provoke a naval war in the North Atlantic, in the desperate hope that it would sober the Soviet workers into knuckling down to further hardship and belt-tightening.

The problem was how to provoke a conflict large enough to have the desired effect, but small enough to be contained without the risk of escalation.

The burden of making such a choice seemed to crush him. Alone, he found it impossible to decide, yet was it fair to entrust it to anyone else?

He picked up the telephone. His secretary answered.

'Would you call Foreign Minister Kalinin, and ask him to come to see me immediately?'

It was half an hour before Vasily Kalinin arrived from the Foreign Ministry, annoyed at having had to postpone a meeting with a delegation from Poland.

'Vasily!'

Savkin grasped his friend by the shoulders.

'The most powerful man in the Soviet Union is also the most lonely at times, my friend. It's an old saying, but truer than ever at this moment. I'm glad you're here.'

'They told me it was most urgent.'

'And so it is; so it is.'

They sat in a pair of high-backed, brocaded armchairs beside the window that overlooked the Kremlin courtyard.

'The Americans are holding back their fleet. Grekov says they won't come anywhere near our Kola bases.'

'Ah! That's unfortunate. President McGuire is showing

more maturity than we expected. The way he reacted to the *Rostov* affair has made it a dead issue in the American media. The "crisis" we'd anticipated hasn't materialized. I'm sorry.'

Kalinin had been joint architect of their plan.

'And at the Politburo meeting on Friday? I'll lose? The reformists will give up the struggle?'

'It's possible. I can't say.'

Kalinin was lying to his friend. He knew it was already decided.

'There are many who admire what the KGB has done in the Baltic,' he explained. 'They feel the old firm hand of authority at the centre is the only way to control our country. What the KGB has done to bring the dissidents into line, Gosplan must again do for the economy. That's what they think.'

'And you, Vasily? What do you think now?'

'Me? I'm with you, carrying high the banner of change and reform first lifted aloft by Mikhail Gorbachev.'

At the flowery words, Savkin looked hard into Kalinin's eyes. There was cynicism there and, he suspected, a hint of pity.

'But, Nikolai, my eyesight is good enough to see that the tide changed long ago, and we are going to be cut off.'

The President sensed he was about to be abandoned. There was a weariness in Kalinin's tone he'd not heard before.

'Don't give up just yet. There is one high rock that could save us from the tide. One you've not yet seen.'

Savkin's voice had sunk close to a whisper.

'Oh? Be sure it's not a mirage.'

'This came from Admiral Grekov. He's not a man to imagine things.'

'So, tell me about your rock.'

'A British submarine is approaching our Kola naval bases, intent on attacking us. The commanding officer has taken leave of his senses and is defying orders. The British are unable to control him.'

Kalinin's eyebrows arched.

'If this is a joke, it's a feeble one, Nikolai.'

'Grekov doesn't tell jokes.'

Kalinin whistled softly.

'Wheew! Then I'm beginning to see what you mean. And Grekov? What's he doing about it?'

'Nothing! Wants to wait to see what happens. But he's wrong. We must be ready to confront it.'

'That could be dangerous. Very dangerous.'

'Yes, but history shows it's a risk that can be justified. Remember 1982? Mrs Margaret Thatcher's regime was deeply unpopular. Heading for defeat. Then the British had their Falklands war. A small, limited war. Afterwards Mrs Thatcher and her reformist policies were transformed.'

Kalinin's eyes appeared to grow ever wider.

'You want a war? With the British? That would be most reckless.'

Savkin felt disappointment. He'd expected a more positive reaction.

'But the British would be shown to have started it. Think of the impact on our people. They'd rally behind us, as we justifiably fight off the aggressor and give him a bloody nose!'

'Possibly.'

'What's the alternative? To let our country turn its back on the chance to compete with the capitalists on equal terms? To lock our people away for another twenty years until someone else has the courage to look for change?'

Savkin paced back and forth, waving his fist to emphasize his point. Kalinin watched coolly. He admired his leader's devotion to the cause of reform, but recognized that whatever Savkin decided, it would be out of desperation, and that made him apprehensive.

'You may be right, Nikolai. It may be the answer. But openly to seek a war is not a gamble I'd have the courage to take. If the British commander is crazy enough to attack us, then we have every right to respond. But I suspect you have a different plan in mind – some way of provoking a fight. If that's the case, then it's better you don't tell me about it. I'd have to advise you against it.'

Savkin's pacing had brought him to the window.

So, he was on his own. He would have to take the decision alone, after all. He'd known it would be so. Supporting him in such a gamble was too much to ask of any friend, however close.

'Then I must ask one last favour of you, Vasily,' Savkin ventured, spinning round.

'Yes?'

'To forget that this conversation ever took place.'

* * *

Severomorsk 1000 hrs.

Inside the command bunker of the Red Banner Northern Fleet, Vice-Admiral Feliks Astashenkov listened to the briefing officer with close attention.

The lights were dimmed in the cavernous room, and a fine beam from the pointer in the briefer's hand highlighted the areas on the wall map where the search for the *Truculent* was being conducted.

From longitude 32 degrees, in a line north of the Soviet border with Norway, the anti-submarine surface force stretched its tentacles westwards. The carriers *Moskva* and *Kiev* were operating their helicopters round the clock, the Captain-Lieutenant told him, dunking sonar transducers into the sea.

Feliks doubted it was truly like that; few of the pilots were qualified for night flying from a deck.

Several possible contacts had been made, over a wide area, the briefer said. Feliks doubted that, too. Whales probably.

The British Nimrod aircraft were already operating east of the *Kiev/Moskva* group, almost due north of the Kol'skiy Zaliv. That's where the *Truculent* would be now. Almost at the sanctuary gates of the Northern Fleet.

If they'd known her intentions earlier, Astashenkov would have ordered four submarines to sea immediately. He'd have given them each a sector in which to wait, drifting in total silence, listening intently for the faint, narrow-band sounds that could give away the approach of the British submarine.

But now it was too late for that; he agreed with Grekov

and Belikov that it would be foolhardy to send out sub-marines, now that mines could already have been laid outside their harbours. Aircraft would do the job almost as well.

On the wall map, blue boxes in an arc north of the mouth of the Kol'skiy Zaliv showed where the IL-38 patrol aircraft had sown a dense sonobuoy barrier. *Truculent* would have to pass through soon, unless she had already done so.

Inside the barrier the sea was further divided into sec-tors, each constantly searched by a rotation of helicopters, dipping their sonar transducers into the water.

So far there'd been dozens of possible sightings, but nothing that could be called a target.

Astashenkov was glad he was not Hitchens. The British submarine was entering waters of which it had limited experience, waters the Soviet Navy knew in intimate detail.

Soviet survey ships had charted every square metre of the sea-bed outside their harbours to find the best place to lay their own hydrophone intruder alarms. They kept their charts updated so the minehunters could tell when anything new appeared on the bottom.

If they'd not been warned a submarine was heading their way, *Truculent* would have a ninety per cent chance of getting in and out undetected. But with Soviet anti-submarine forces on full alert, Astashenkov rated the Brit-ish boat's chances as less than even.

'Comrade Vice-Admiral?'

It was his acting secretary, a Captain 3rd Rank.

'There is an urgent telephone call for you. In your private office.'

His tone made it quite clear the call was from someone who should not be kept waiting.

'From Moscow. On the encrypto-phone. They won't identify the caller, but I think it's the Kremlin,' the sec-retary explained in a whisper, and then left Astashenkov on his own.

The phone had an electronic security device. Feliks inserted a magnetic card which controlled access. The calls were scrambled and de-scrambled at each end of the line which linked Severomorsk with Moscow. Both the Stavka (the Supreme Military Headquarters) and the Kremlin were linked to the system.

'Feliks?'

The voice was as clear as if in the next room.

'This is the President, Nikolai Savkin.'

'Good Morning, Comrade President.'

Feliks felt an uncomfortable dryness in his throat.

'I'm calling with reference to our conversation last week, Feliks.'

'Yes. I assumed that was it.'

'I warned you then that I might need to ask a service of you. If the future of *perestroika* was at stake.'

'You did, Comrade President.'

'I'm afraid that moment has come, Feliks. I'm sorry. I'm placing the future of the Soviet Union in your hands.'

* * *

Helsinki 1034 hrs.

The TU-134 jet, unmarked except for the Soviet red star on its tail, taxied to a halt. Immigration and customs officers boarded the aircraft to complete the brief formalities.

Within minutes an ambulance drew up beside it. The steps were pulled aside and an hydraulic platform positioned in their place. Two men in blue hospital overalls wheeled a stretcher out through the narrow aircraft doorway and opened umbrellas to shelter it from the driving rain.

Once on the ground, the stretcher was lifted from its trolley and eased into the ambulance. One of the Russian nurses accompanied it, the other stepped into an embassy limousine which had pulled up behind, joining two men in suits who'd also come off the plane.

Sedately, the small convoy drove from the airport, escorted by two Finnish police motorcyclists.

Inside the ambulance, the KGB nurse felt the pulse of the ashen-faced, withered, old man in his custody.

Still with us, just, he thought to himself.

Lieutenant Commander Alex Hitchens DSO (posthumous) Royal Navy, drifted in and out of consciousness. He had no idea where he was being taken. All he knew was that he had left the clinic in Leningrad which had been his home for the past few months, and that the pain in his chest was getting worse.

For the last four months people had been kind to him, and he was grateful. Grateful to have been taken away from the bleak and bitter prison camp on the Kola. Grateful to be given food that wasn't just broth and bread. Grateful to be allowed medicines that relieved the pain.

In his lucid moments he knew he was soon going to die. The last thirty years had been a living death, and he had often longed for the end.

But then they'd told him about Philip. Now he was desperate to live just a little longer.

'Is my son here?' he whispered in shaky Russian. He'd never perfected the language.

'Try not to talk. It'll tire you,' the nurse answered, not understanding what the old man had said.

Clouded eyes stared wildly from wrinkled hollows. His erratic memory suddenly recalled the photographs of Philip and his grandson they'd shown him in Leningrad.

At the time, in his confusion, he'd thought he was looking at a thirty-year-old picture of himself with his own son. Once he had been a tall fair-haired good-looking man like that; and the boy, Simon, was the spitting image of Philip when he'd last seen him.

His eyelids closed again as the memory slipped away.

The ambulance turned off the main road and up a cobbled hill to the clinic. The tyres on the stones set up a drumming inside the vehicle.

Alex Hitchens turned his head fretfully. The drumming of the wheels was like the throbbing of the diesels in the submarine. The noise triggered memories, ones that had dogged him since 1962.

He'd been broken on the wheel of those memories, time and time again, broken by the guilt of knowing all the men on board had died because of him. He no longer remembered their faces or names. Time had been kind to him in that respect.

He'd gone ashore with one other man, a Royal Marine. They'd been captured together. The marine had been trained to resist interrogation, but Alex hadn't. He was only there because the second SBS man was ill. He remembered the marine – a short, stocky, silent figure, reduced to a bloodied corpse by the torture, preferring to die rather than talk.

Alex had not been so brave; the beatings had been relentless, the pain unbearable. He'd been terrified of death.

He'd confessed to spying; then, as they began to break his fingers, he'd told them the time and place for the offshore rendezvous with *Tenby*.

Later, they'd stood him on the cliff-top to listen to the explosions of the torpedoes and depth charges as they blew his submarine to pieces.

The resonant detonations had sounded like the slamming of the gates of hell. He'd imagined he could hear the screams of dying men borne on the wind. The noise haunted his sleep to this day.

The ambulance stopped. The rear doors opened, and different faces appeared – new men to carry out the stretcher.

'Where am I?'

His voice was barely audible. The KGB nurse heard it, but not the words.

'It'll be all right. Don't worry. You're safe.'

His enfeebled eyes saw a blur of lights and faces about him. A hand gripped his wrist for the pulse. Suddenly there were urgent words in a language he didn't understand. They began to hurry, along the corridor, into a small room. A nurse unbuttoned his pyjama shirt and placed suckers on his bony chest. Another rolled up his sleeve. He felt a pain as they tourniqueted his arm, raising his vein for the needle.

'Phil?' he called softly.

His mind spun like a catherine wheel, faster and faster. His child, his boy. The men he'd betrayed; the men who'd died because of him. Did Philip know what he'd done? Did they *all* know of his shame? How could he face them if they did?

The Finnish nurse taped the intravenous needle in place and connected the sedative drip. She looked up at the old man's face and noticed a tear roll down one cheek.

Poor old bugger, she thought to herself. Shouldn't have been moved in his condition. Why had they brought him? Nobody would say. All very odd.

★　★　★

HMS Truculent 0600 hrs GMT.

Philip Hitchens was summoned immediately the bow sonar on *HMS Truculent* detected the *Victor III*.

He'd not been able to sleep anyway. In the red-light glow of his cabin, panic had engulfed him in successive waves. This was the day when everything would be decided, one way or the other.

He cut their speed to three knots. The plot on the Action Information Console showed the Soviet hunter/killer crossing their path about five miles in front of them, heading south.

The towed array was picking up the heavy sounds of large surface ships belonging to the Soviet anti-submarine task force strung out along the unmarked western perimeter of the Barents Sea, well to their north. Intelligence reports had listed the *Moskva* and the *Kiev* as being in the task force, but identification was impossible; the sounds were being distorted by reflections from the uneven sea-bed.

This was the moment Philip had been dreading, the moment when the hunters began closing in from all sides.

They weren't going to find him, however; no one was going to stop him doing what he had to do.

Hatred for the Russians, and anger at the misery they'd inflicted on his family, surged inside him, but he suppressed it, forcing himself to concentrate on the immediate threat; the *Victor* might hear them if they got much closer.

Philip ordered a turn to port, taking them northeast,

and increased their speed to ten knots. It would give them sea-room.

Thirty minutes later their Paris sonar-intercept sonar detected distant 'pings' from transducers dipped by helicopters from the Russian carriers. Too far away to be any threat. Yet.

The *Victor* was well south by now, so they headed southeast again, back on course for the Kola Inlet.

At 0700 Sebastian Cordell took over the watch from Nick Cavendish, who looked relieved to be escaping the control room.

'Bugger's jumpier than ever this morning,' he confided.

Cordell glanced uncomfortably at Hitchens, who hovered by the AIO console, checking the display and the speed and depth gauges.

'Morning, TAS. Nick filled you in?'

The voice was strained, artificially brisk.

'Yes, sir. I'm just going to check on the sound room, with your permission, sir.'

'Yes, please.'

Sebastian scuttled forward, glad to be away from Hitchens.

'Morning, Chief. What's the equipment state?'

'Hundred per cent, sir. So far as I know,' CPO Hicks reported. 'I've just come on watch, sir.'

'How many contacts have we got?'

'About a dozen, sir. Most of 'em merchantmen. Three Sovfleet warships to the north, between fifty and a hundred miles. We lost the *Victor* on the LOFAR, but picked up a transient from the south about ten minutes ago. Could have been the *Victor*'s rudder moving. She was due to turn about then; have to, or she'd ground on the coast.'

'Well done. So she's probably coming back our way again?'

'If she does, she'll be nose-on this time. More difficult to hear.'

'Okay, Hicks. Anything else close to us I should know about?'

'Couple of freighters within twenty miles, sir. One's

heading west so we won't be tracking him much longer. The other's ahead of us. Big single diesel. One shaft. Four blades.'

Hicks pointed to the green waterfall display, and a ribbed smudge on the left of the screen.

'Fundamental frequency 4.7 Hz. Shaft revs 282 per minute. Could be one of their big supply ships heading back into Murmansk. Might find some useful broadband noise close up.'

'Mmmm. You're working well this morning, Hicks. How much of this is on the AIO?'

'Thirty mile radius, sir.'

Back from the sound room, Sebastian was studying the screens of the Action Information Organization. The senior rating aligned the display with the compass points to superimpose chart data on it.

'Depth's two-seventy metres here, sir. We're at two hundred. Oceanographics give an initial detection range of four miles, sir.'

Automatic analysis of the water conditions around them predicted the maximum distance at which they could be detected by the most sensitive sonar known. The nearest contact was well beyond that range, but Sebastian wasn't happy.

'Aircraft. That's what we've got to worry about.'

Hitchens was standing in the bandstand, watching him.

'I'm worried about the *Bears* and *Mays*, sir. This close to their coastline, the sky could be full of them.'

'What d'you suggest we do about it?'

Cordell was thrown. Hitchens sounded unsure, humble even.

'Well, sir, some sharp manoeuvring. Sprint and drift. To throw them off, just in case they've got a line on us.'

'Yes. Carry on. You have the ship. Call me if there are any new contacts.'

With that he stepped from the bandstand and abruptly left the control room.

Surprised to find himself so suddenly in charge, Sebastian hurriedly checked the chart and the AIO again.

'Steer zero-four-five. Revolutions for eighteen knots!'

The ratings at the engineering panel repeated the order back to him. He was going to put more distance between *Truculent* and the invisible *Victor* that could now be heading directly for them.

Just for a few minutes, then he'd alter course again. And again. Weaving and circling in a pattern so random no airborne tacnav would be able to follow him. He hoped.

Philip hurried to the officers' heads. His bowels were rumbling volcanically.

After relieving himself he returned to his cabin for the shave he'd not had time for earlier. His hands shook uncontrollably, and he nicked his neck with the razor.

He knew he should eat; there was a long day ahead. But the thought of food made him retch. He'd forgo breakfast. Drink some tea. That might help.

His brain felt paralysed by the conflict of his thoughts.

Revenge was the passion that had taken control of him again. To get back at the bastard Russians for seducing his wife, for murdering his father, and for forcing him to betray his country for a lie.

But was he right to believe his father dead? The KGB's efforts to prove him alive, had they *really* been a trick? After all he'd believed them at first, totally. The evidence – the letters, the photograph – *had* convinced him. Then he'd discovered how they'd used Sara and her knowledge of his vulnerability, his obsession with the fate of his father. An obsession powerful enough to blind him to reality.

Every piece of their evidence could have been fabricated. But he couldn't be certain.

What if his father really was in Helsinki waiting for him? If Philip set the Moray mines in the Kola Inlet, as he intended, several hundred Russians might die, but so would his father.

How the hell could he decide? Two hundred metres below the surface of the icy, grey-green waters of the Barents, isolated from his own people, isolated even from the bloody Russians, it was too late to ask for clarification. Too late for a lot of things. Too late to return to base and pretend there'd been a communications failure. Too late to save his career. No, he had to press on, give the Russians what was coming to them.

A sharp rap on the door frame made him jump.

'Yes?'

'May I speak to you, sir?' It was the first lieutenant.

'Yes. Yes, of course.'

Tim Pike slid the door shut behind him and stood awkwardly.

'I'm anxious that you should brief me on our mission, sir,' he blurted out. 'We're in hostile waters; I'm your deputy, sir. Not knowing why we're here or where we're going puts me in an impossible position.'

His short, ginger beard quivered as he spoke, his grey eyes staring at a point above the commander's head.

'I've told you, Tim, that the orders are top secret. For my eyes only. That's still the situation. Nothing's changed.'

'But there will come a point, sir, when a large sector of the ship's company will have to be told your orders. You can't operate the boat on your own, sir.'

'I'd caution you not to be impertinent, Lieutenant Commander.'

Their eyes met. Pike saw that behind the arrogance, Hitchens was afraid.

'May I sit down, sir?'

Philip gestured to the bunk, and turned away to fumble with a pen on the desk. Pike was right; he'd have to tell them something soon. But what?

'And there's another thing, sir. I hesitate to mention it. Don't want you to think I'm prying. But there's been some talk on board that you've been having some problems at home. Now, I don't know if that is the case, sir, but sometimes it helps to talk. . . .'

'How bloody dare you! Spreading malicious gossip about your Commanding Officer? That's an offence under Queen's Regulations. I'll put you on a bloody charge if you don't watch it!'

'Sir, I've not spread any gossip . . .'

'Well, who has? I want their names. Come on!'

He thrust the pen towards Pike.

'Write them down. All of them!'

'Sir, you're being unreasonable. You must understand – the men are uneasy. This patrol has been unorthodox, to say the least. The secrecy with the communications routines, the need to avoid contact with our own side as much as with the Soviets, the mystery about our ultimate mission – it doesn't make for a happy ship.'

'Are you challenging my authority?'

Philip's voice had risen in pitch. Pike looked at the redness in his eyes, the veins standing out from his neck. Was this rage? Or panic.

'Well?'

Now it was Pike's turn to be afraid. Was this the moment to take command?

He funked it.

'No, sir,' he muttered. 'I'm not challenging your authority.'

Philip subsided, relieved.

'Just as well,' he said drily.

'Just trying to help, sir. Do my job.'

'Mmmm,' Philip grunted, his temper now under control. 'Well . . . , don't think I haven't realized the difficulties you're all facing.'

He struggled to decide how much to say.

'You see, things are looking pretty bad, with the Russians. There may be some action. That's why I can't say much yet. Don't want to alarm the men. We're going in close . . . , that's all I can say. Very close to the Soviet submarine bases. You know what weapons we have on board. I hope it won't be necessary to use them. But I don't know how things'll turn out.'

'How will you get your final orders, sir. On the broadcast? The trailing wire antenna?'

'There'll be no more orders. I already have my rules of engagement.'

Pike was stunned. He could tell that Hitchens knew he'd said too much.

'That'll be all, Tim. What I've just said is in confidence. Just for you. Not to be passed on. Understood?'

'If you say so, sir.'

'I do. Now carry on.'

The conversation had disturbed Pike deeply. Already had his rules of engagement? Christ! That meant the decision to fight or not to fight was down to Hitchens, and Hitchens alone. Close contact with the Russians needed a CO with a cool head and a rational mind. The way Hitchens had just behaved had revealed no sign of either.

He headed for the wardroom and breakfast. Suddenly, the submarine banked sharply and Pike had to steady himself. Why the manoeuvre?

Breakfast could wait. He made for the control room. Sebastian Cordell stood in the bandstand, gripping the rail and calling out orders.

'Steer one-eight-zero! Keep 260 metres. Revolutions for twenty-five knots!'

'Why so deep? What's going on?' Pike demanded.

'Active sonobuoys. Someone's pinging us. I just called the captain. He said I should ask you. He didn't sound very well, sir. I think he was throwing up. He left the key down and I could hear him.'

'I see.'

Pike studied the Action Information screen. Depth of water 300 metres.

'I hope to God the inertial nav. system hasn't drifted. It can get pretty shallow around here.'

'We've a bearing on the buoy, sir!'

'Yes?'

'Zero-three-zero, sir! Range two-thousand-eight-hundred yards.'

'Steer two-one-zero! I'll shake the buggers off,' Cordell muttered. 'Take a depth sounding. The sods know we're here now. Making a bit of a noise won't matter much. Ident on the sonobuoy?'

'CAMBS, sir,' came a voice from the AIO.

Pike and Cordell stared at one another open-mouthed. CAMBS was one of their own.

'A Nimrod? Up here? Must be forward-basing on the sodding Kola Peninsula!' Cordell exploded. 'I don't get it. We're right inside a Soviet ASW area, and there's a bloody Nimrod operating. If things are as tense as the captain says, the crabs'll be shot down!'

Pike ran his hand over his beard. The boy had never spoken a truer word, if only he knew it.

'As the captain says'. That was the trouble. Everything they knew down there came from just one source; the captain. And God alone knew how reliable *he* was!

'And why's the Nimrod gone active? Does he *want* us to know he's there?' Cordell blustered.

'Maybe he does,' mused Pike under his breath.

'Thirty metres under the keel, sir!'

'I'd like to go deeper.' Sebastian's face glowed with excitement. 'The crabs' CAMBS may still be able to separate us from the echoes off the sea bed. Just a little bit closer to the mud and we'll be invisible.'

'Too risky at this speed,' Pike cautioned.

'Cut the speed to five knots?'

'Okay.'

'Keep two-seven-five metres. Revolutions for five knots!'

The helm responded and the deck tilted downwards.

'I'll change course back to the south again,' Cordell decided. 'Then ease round to the east so we get back on our original track. There's a big surface contact heading for Murmansk. If we can close with it, we can hide in her shadow.'

'Sounds good to me,' Pike agreed. The boy was doing all right for his first run as tactics officer.

Suddenly all heads turned towards the door. Ashen-faced, Philip Hitchens entered the control room.

'Everything all right, sir?' Pike asked softly.

'Fine. Cordell can brief me, then I'll take over,' he snapped.

'Right, sir. I'll leave you to it.'

Pike hurried to the wardroom. There were two men he needed to collar before they disappeared into the bowels of the submarine.

Claypole, the stocky, bushy-bearded marine engineer, was one of them. Pike stopped him as he was heading towards the tunnel over the reactor.

'We need to talk,' he whispered urgently. 'You, me and Paul. Confidential. In my cabin at 0900?'

Claypole shrugged, showing no curiosity.

'Sure. I'll have finished my rounds by then.'

Paul Spriggs was downing the last of his coffee. Pike dropped into the seat beside him and delivered the same message.

'Excuse me, sir. You 'avin' Standard, sir?' The voice came from behind his shoulder.

The steward looked at his watch to make the point that the first lieutenant was late for breakfast.

'Yes. Standard,' Pike glared.

When the rating was out of earshot again, Spriggs responded.

'You've spoken to him?'

'Yes. Just now. We need to get our act together. I think we're about to hit the shit!'

* * *

HMS Tenby.

'Active sonar, sir! Forty mile range. Bearing northwest.'

The call from the sound room brought Andrew Tinker, hard on the heels of Commander Peter Biddle, squeezing into the cramped sonar compartment.

'Frequency shows it's a buoy from the Nimrod, sir.'

'Could mean a change of plans, Peter,' Andrew breathed over Biddle's shoulder.

They'd been moving fast towards Ostrov Chernyy, hoping to reach the island ahead of *Truculent*, to head her off.

Andrew pulled Biddle out into the corridor, where they could talk privately.

'The Nimrod wouldn't want to go active with so many Sovs around,' he whispered. 'If he's pinging, he's trying to warn the guys on *Truculent* that something's up. And to tell us that he's found her.'

'So we close in?'

'We need more data. If the crabs are tracking her, they can vector us. We'll have to risk putting a mast up.'

'Mmmm. Don't like that much. We're only forty miles from the Russian coast.'

'Got a better idea?'

Again the rating called out from the sound room.

'Submarine contact astern, sir!'

Biddle poked his head back through the doorway.

'Classification?'

'Looks like a *Victor III*. It's suddenly come on quite strong. Must've turned up the power.'

'Going to investigate our pinger maybe,' Andrew suggested.

Biddle pushed back into the control room to order a change of course.

'Steer zero-eight-five!'

The towed array was giving ambiguous bearings for the *Victor*. The change of course would clarify it in a few minutes.

'The sooner we try communicating with the Nimrod the better,' Andrew insisted. 'In a few hours we'll be smack in the middle of the main shipping lanes into Murmansk.'

He crossed to the wireless room to alert the operators and to prepare a signal for CINCFLEET.

Biddle checked in the sound room again. The CPO confirmed that the *Victor* was to the west and heading north. Safe to ignore for the time being.

'Keep 30 metres!' Biddle ordered. 'Sound room, plot all surface contacts on the AIO!'

Andrew joined Biddle at the chart table.

The navigator had their position plotted half-way across the thirty mile wide mouth of Varanger Fjord, east of the Norwegian/Soviet land border. Soon they'd be on their own; the Nimrod would go no further east, for fear of trespassing in Soviet airspace. It'd be one submarine against another.

Commander Biddle studied the Action Information plot. North of them in the main shipping lanes there were several contacts, the largest identified as a naval supply ship based in Murmansk. He needed to be further from them, for safety.

'Steer one-six-zero,' he ordered. 'Revolutions for fifteen knots.'

Then he turned to Andrew.

'Ten minutes, and we'll stick the mast up.'

* * *

Varangar Fjord.

The pilot of the Mil Mi-14 helicopter was not a happy man. He'd been scrambled, along with every other available aircraft, despite having a defective radar.

How the hell was he supposed to look for enemy submarines when only half his equipment was working? The squadron commander had given him the Varanger Fjord to patrol, assuring him no foreign submarines would enter the bay; there was nothing there worth spying on.

Operating from the Bolshaya Litsa naval base, the Mi-14 had an endurance of four hours; with a forty minute transit flight each way, the pilot could afford two hours on station and still have fuel in reserve for a diversion.

They'd been on station for an hour already, criss-crossing the bay, dipping the sonar transducer as they went, and hearing nothing but seals and porpoises for their trouble.

Soviet time was three hours ahead of GMT, so for the helicopter crew it was late morning. The *michman* loadmaster handed out ration packs.

Grey and showery at first, it had become a fine morning. The sun had broken through, casting silver-gold shafts onto the sparkling water. On the horizon was silhouetted the traffic of the shipping lanes. Closer to them, there was nothing but unbroken sea.

Suddenly the pilot did a double-take. Smack in the middle of a patch of light a thin mast protruded from the water. He nudged his navigator and pointed, flicking the intercom switch on the control stick.

The navigator nodded excitedly and pointed to the chart to show where they were. Deep water. No rocks nearby masked with warning posts. It had to be a periscope.

The two men in the cockpit laughed at their incredible

luck. It was difficult enough to spot a periscope with radar, but with the naked eye? Astonishing!

The pilot pulled the machine back into a hover. They were nearly a kilometre away from the target; if they got closer the submarine might see or hear them.

The Captain Lieutenant commanding the aircraft from the sonar suite in the rear cabin called his base by radio, and was startled to find his call being routed straight to the operational control centre at Severomorsk.

He was even more startled when, after a pause of a few minutes, his sighting report was answered by a very odd question. Did he speak English?

He could manage a few words, he replied.

Suddenly the pilot alerted him that the submarine had dived. The Captain Lieutenant reported the fact by radio. The orders he received a few minutes later left him stony-faced with astonishment.

The nose of the helicopter dipped. They began to race ahead of the spot where the periscope had been seen. They flew on for a kilometre, then hovered low over the water. The winchman released the safety lock on the cable and the bulky sonar transducer dropped through the hole in the helicopter floor, entering the water with a slight splash.

* * *

HMS Tenby.

The communications had worked well. The encrypted VHF call to the Nimrod revealed the plane had lost contact with the *Truculent* but the RAF gave them the last known position of the boat, less than fifteen minutes old.

In a burst transmission of the SSIX satellite, they'd passed back to CINCFLEET their theory about *Truculent*'s destination, and picked up a string of signals stored for them.

Andrew and Peter Biddle consulted the chart, trying to guess the direction *Truculent* would have taken to avoid the Nimrod.

Ping.

'Shit!'

The sonar transmission had been so loud they'd all heard it through the casing.

'Bloody hell, sound room! Where's the contact?' Biddle screamed.

Ping.

'Dead ahead, sir! Less than 500 yards.'

'Helm hard-a-port! Ten down. Keep one hundred metres. Revolutions for maximum speed!'

Biddle glared round at Andrew, as the submarine banked hard to the left.

'Told you this would happen!'

'We have no sonar contact, sir,' yelled the CPO in the sound room. 'Classified as active sonar from a *Haze* helicopter.'

Suddenly a high-pitched whistle issued from the loudspeaker at the back of the control room.

The underwater telephone!

The men froze.

The whistle stopped. A voice spoke, in a heavy Slav accent.

At first the words were terrifyingly incomprehensible, but then became mystifyingly clear.

'Helsinki is arranged. Helsinki is arranged.'

The voice repeated the words about ten times and then ceased.

'What the fuck's going on?' exploded Biddle.

'God knows!' Andrew answered, his mind racing.

Biddle stood over the Action Information console like a predator, pre-occupied with getting his boat away from the Russian aircraft that had so dangerously and embarrassingly found him.

Andrew felt himself in the way, and walked to the empty wardroom, where he slumped into an armchair.

The message from the Soviet helicopter could not have been meant for them. The Soviets wouldn't have known they were the *Tenby*. Yet it was intended for an English boat. The voice had spoken English.

Truculent. The Russians thought they were *Truculent*.

Suddenly the unbelievable possibility that Philip Hitchens had done a deal with the KGB seemed more real.

Helsinki. Was that where Phil was to see his father again, after leaving a Moray mine at Ostrov Chernyy?

The Russians had taken a hell of a risk with that underwater message, a risk of giving it to the wrong boat, or of arousing suspicion in the control room of *HMS Truculent*. Why would they do that?

Because they were scared. It had to be that. Scared that Phil intended to renege on their deal, because of the KGB's seduction of Sara.

Andrew looked up from his thoughts. The communications officer walked in to the wardroom.

'Signal for you, sir. Came in on SSIX. Just finished unscrambling it.'

'Thanks.'

He took the page of printout and the youth left.

FLASH 230630Z OCT

FROM CINCFLEET
TO HMS TENBY

TOP SECRET
PERSONAL FOR CDR TINKER
STILL CONSIDER IT MOST LIKELY CDR HITCHENS
UNDER PRESSURE FROM KGB TO DELIVER NEW
MINE.
ALTERNATELY HE MAY USE MINES TO ATTACK
SOVIETS. UNCLEAR. CONSIDER ALL POSSIBILIT-
IES. CANNOT ADVISE FURTHER.
INTERNATIONAL SITUATION VERY TENSE. ANY
OFFENSIVE ACTION BY TRUCULENT WOULD BE
SERIOUS THREAT TO WORLD PEACE. DOWNING
STREET ORDERS YOU STOP HITCHENS. IMPOSS-
IBLE TO GIVE YOU OTHER SUBSURFACE ASSETS AS
BACKUP.
ALL NOW UP TO YOU. USE WHATEVER RPT. WHAT-
EVER MEANS NECESSARY TO STOP HIS ACTIONS.
GOOD LUCK. GODSPEED.
FOSM.

Andrew swallowed hard. All up to him, now, the signal said. To stop an old friend from doing something unspeakably stupid.

'Phil! What have you got into?' he moaned. 'You crazy bastard!'

He strode back to the control room. Peter Biddle looked puzzled.

'That *Haze*. He's made no effort to track us, as far as we can tell.'

'Perhaps he doesn't need to. If the Sovs think we're the *Truc*, they may reckon they know where we're going.'

'Ahh. Got you.'

Biddle took him by the elbow across to the chart table.

'We're heading for a position thirty miles northeast of Nemetskiy Point.'

He indicated the tip of the Rybachiy Peninsula, the most northerly point on the Kola. South of them lay the densest concentration of military bases anywhere in the Soviet Union.

Andrew shivered as a wave of fear swept through him, from seeing on the chart just how close they were to the Russian bases.

'The *Truc* has to be west of us,' Biddle continued. 'She won't be doing more than eighteen knots, and taking a line from where the Nimrod lost contact puts her somewhere here.'

He indicated a wide arc of sea. Without the help of aircraft, it was a hopelessly large area to search. *Tenby* would need to be within five miles for her sister boat to have any chance of hearing her.

'We have to narrow the search area,' Andrew decided.

He moved his hand down the chart to the mouth of the Kola Inlet, which led to the Coastal Defence Headquarters and main submarine base at Polyarny, and the Soviet Northern Fleet HQ at Severomorsk.

To the west of the inlet the approach was narrowed by the protruding mass of the Rybachiy Peninsula. Twenty miles east of Rybachiy, beyond the main channel into the inlet and about ten miles north of the main Kola coast lay the island of Ostrov Chernyy.

'That's where Philip's going; into that gap. And that's where we've got to be, Peter. Looking straight up the nostrils of the Russian bear!'

Biddle chuckled, nervously.

'Bit heavy on the melodrama?'

'I'm not so sure. The Sovs are waiting for Philip. They don't know whether he's going to give them a mine, or try to sink some of their submarines. They're going to be using every asset they've got to keep track of him. We've got to find him before they do.'

'There's plenty of cover about. The AIO plot's filling up.'

They crossed the control room to the Action Information display.

'Talk us through it, Algy.'

The TAS officer pointed to the symbols on the screen.

'All surface contacts. We've lost touch with the *Victor III*. That's the main shipping lane into the inlet. Most of it's civil, freighters and fishing vessels probably going up river to Murmansk. But there's at least one military vessel identified. A naval supply ship. She'll be astern of us when we turn east. She's listed in the NISUMS.'

These were the Naval Intelligence Summaries carried on board every submarine.

'She's based at Severomorsk. Going home, I presume.'

'Mmm. If I was Phil Hitchens, I think I'd have found a comfy spot somewhere underneath that one. They'd never hear him with all that racket going on.'

Andrew agreed.

'And we need to keep ahead of her?'

Biddle nodded. When *Truculent* reached the target area, they had to be waiting.

Andrew pulled Biddle to one side, out of earshot of the others.

'Look, we've been ordered to stop him by any means possible. If we don't get close enough in time to use the underwater telephone, or if he takes no notice, then it'll have to be a torpedo.'

Biddle winced.

'You've got the new ones on board here, haven't you? The Hammerfish?' Andrew asked.

'That's right. We're still doing trials. They're supposed to be very clever, but their reliability's not proven yet.'

'Tell me what they can do.'

Biddle led him to the firing display next to the AI consoles.

'They're like Tigerfish, in that they're controlled from the submarine by wire. Guided either by the boat's sonar or by the torpedo's. But there are two big differences. First, they're much faster. Seventy-five knots they can do! And second they have a high-frequency, high-definition sonar that turns on two-hundred metres from the target.'

'What's the point of that?'

'Gives us a precise outline of the target, on this display here. It means the weapon operator has a couple of seconds to choose the precise spot where the torpedo will strike. Soviet subs are well protected, but if you can hit the right place on the hull . . .'

'Clever. Very clever. And that could be just what we need. Not to ensure we *destroy* the *Truculent*, but to ensure that we don't!'

Andrew's face brightened at the discovery.

Biddle looked at him doubtfully. It was the one aspect of the torpedo's performance they'd been unable to cover in training.

* * *

HMS Truculent 0900 hrs GMT.

There was hardly room for three men in the first lieutenant's cabin. Paul Spriggs hauled himself onto the top bunk to make room for the MEO Peter Claypole.

All Lieutenant Commanders, they were the three most senior men on board after the captain.

Tim Pike told them he no longer considered Commander Hitchens to be in a balanced or responsible state of mind. He listed his reasons; the secretiveness, the overreactions to crises, and the unorthodox communications orders. There were now physical signs the captain was under abnormal stress; he was taking sleeping pills and there had been evidence that morning of vomiting and bowel problems.

'D'you think any of us is qualified to make a judgement?

We're engine drivers, not bloody doctors!' Claypole growled.

Pike was startled at encountering resistance from the engineer. After his brush with the captain the previous day, he'd expected support from him.

'If we suspect the captain's condition is a threat to safety, then we're bloody well entitled to our opinions,' insisted Spriggs.

'Oh yes. Opinions are all right. It's the next step that's the problem.'

'What're you proposing, Tim?'

Pike looked flustered as he answered.

'Since we left Devonport, there isn't a man on board who hasn't begun to wonder if the captain's gone off his head. You know that, Peter, as well as I do.'

'Aye. Wondering's one thing. Doing something about it's another.'

'Are you saying we should ignore these warning signs?' Spriggs interjected, his voiced tinged with exasperation.

'I'm saying we should be damned careful! There's precious little precedent for first lieutenants relieving their captains of command. It's not popular with the Admiralty Board. In a court-martial, even this little meeting could be seen as conspiracy to mutiny.'

'It might also be seen as senior officers using their brains to avoid a disaster!' Pike countered angrily.

'What disaster?' Claypole demanded.

Pike looked at his cabin-mate for support.

'Paul and I have been closer to it than you, Peter. You've only had the one row with him. For me, the friction's been there the whole trip. You ask "what disaster?" I don't know. *Why* don't I know? Because the bugger hasn't told me what his orders are. But . . .'

He hesitated. Hitchens had told him not to pass on what he'd said. Pike decided he had to.

'We're going close to the Soviet submarine bases, and Hitchens is saying there may be some action. What he means, Peter, is he may take us to war!'

Claypole scratched pensively at his bushy black beard.

Pike went on, 'He told me he's already got his rules of

engagement. He's not waiting for any more orders from CINCFLEET. It's for him to decide if we go in fighting. Now, if he orders the firing of a salvo of Harpoons, or the launch of a pair of Mk 24s, would you be happy to pull the trigger?'

'Well, put like that . . . But it's still only surmise,' Claypole cautioned. 'It's not enough if you're thinking of pushing him out of the bandstand now.'

'But if he orders weapons to be readied, then you'll back me?'

'In those circs you've got the right to see the orders, the rules of engagement and the target listings. Yes. If he won't show them to you, then I'm right behind you.'

'And you, Paul?'

'Oh, yes. I'll be with you.'

Pike expelled a deep sigh of relief.

'Let's hope we're imagining all this,' he concluded.

The three men went their separate ways, Claypole to the propulsion section aft, Spriggs forward to check the arsenal of missiles, mines and torpedoes, and Pike to the control room, where Lieutenant Cordell met him.

'We're heading for the Kola Inlet, sir. Captain's orders. Tucked ourselves under the *Boris Bubnov*, bound for Severomorsk. Plenty of broadband noise from her. Should make us invisible. I sodding well hope so.'

Tim Pike stepped past into the control room.

Hitchens stood in the bandstand; with his chiselled features and ramrod straight back, he looked like a figure from an heroic painting.

The image made Pike shudder; a captain clinging to the bridge of his ship – as it sank beneath him.

CHAPTER TEN

Bolshaya Litsa, Kola Peninsula.

1147 hrs.

The Kamov Ka-32 helicopter flew slowly along the line of jetties. Astashenkov, sitting beside the pilot, was struggling to differentiate one submarine from another. There were six of the broad-beamed 7000-tonners in harbour.

Then the pilot saw the orange armbands of the ground controller, on the fourth pier along. The machine circled once, feeling for the wind direction, before setting down gently, within a few metres of the companionway from the pier to the submarine.

The pilot saluted, and Astashenkov stepped down onto the concrete, clutching his cap to prevent it blowing away in the downdraught.

The Captain 2nd Rank who welcomed him on board the boat was well known to the Vice-Admiral. He'd been executive officer on Astashenkov's last command – a strategic missile submarine.

The commander of the newly commissioned *PLA* saluted, then offered his hand.

'You're most welcome, Comrade Vice-Admiral,' he shouted above the whine of the helicopter.

Astashenkov glanced admiringly at the rounded black hull with its coating of rubber to deaden sonar reflections. The submarine had a fat pod mounted atop the rudder, containing a towed sonar array, and was the newest in what NATO knew as the *Sierra* class.

'You're ready to sail?'

'We'll shut the hatches as we go below.'

Astashenkov took a last, quick look at the Bolshaya Litsa submarine base, his home port in younger days. He could be seeing it for the last time.

The piers for the big, nuclear-powered attack submarines were on the eastern shore of the fjord. Cut into the cliffs behind the quay that linked the piers were caverns for stores, spares and weapons.

To his right beyond the cliffs, the bleak granite rose two hundred metres in contours smoothed by the arctic ice of an earlier age.

A cutting wind came in off the sea, and Astashenkov shivered. Time to go, before the phones started buzzing between Bolshaya Litsa and the Severomorsk headquarters.

Astashenkov had been on board the *Ametyst* at her commissioning the previous year, but was again impressed by the size and comfort of her interior. Captain 2nd Rank Yury Makhov had a spacious day-cabin as well as his sleeping quarters. Fixed to the wall in the day-room was a photograph of President Nikolai Savkin. Feliks pointed to it.

'I'm acting on the direct instructions of the President,' he declared in answer to Makhov's unspoken question. 'But without the knowledge of the Commander-in-Chief, Admiral Belikov.'

'I see.'

The captain's pale face seemed to grow paler still.

'There is a British submarine attempting to penetrate the waters of the Rodina. We are to intercept and destroy it.'

'We've all been aware of the search going on. Never known so many aircraft operating at one time. I was beginning to wonder why we'd been left out,' Makhov answered.

Astashenkov decided not to tell him there was still a ban on submarines putting to sea. If Makhov knew of the risk that British mines had already been laid outside the harbour, he'd have the right to refuse to sail.

Nikolai Savkin's telephone call earlier that morning had almost caused Feliks to renege on the pledge he'd made him in Moscow the previous weekend. Savkin told him the nation needed a military confrontation with the West.

Sending a submarine to sea to confront the British intruder was the only way it could be made to happen.

He'd not been specific. He didn't need to be. They both knew of the danger from mines.

The implication of the President's request was clear; a Soviet submarine and the men on board were to be sacrificed, if need be, to secure the unity of the USSR.

Feliks knew he could never order one of his own commanders on a suicide mission. He could never live with his conscience.

There was only one way he could fulfil his pledge to Savkin – take the submarine to sea himself.

'Have you given the order to cast off?'

'It's being done at this moment, Comrade Vice-Admiral. Er . . , you said the Northern Fleet Commander Admiral Belikov doesn't know of our mission? He cannot fail to know within a very few minutes. Our departure from the dock will be reported.'

'I know. Do you trust me, Captain?'

'Of course, Admiral.'

'Then you mustn't ask political questions. I'm forbidden to tell you why we're acting alone. The situation in Moscow is tense; the Politburo threatens to tear itself apart. What we're doing is for Nikolai Savkin and may help save our country from chaos.'

His sombre words silenced Makhov.

'I understand. What are my instructions?'

'The *Truculent* was detected earlier this morning by a helicopter crew. The boat had a mast up, west of Nemetskiy Point. We believe, from our intelligence sources, that the captain of the British boat was receiving final orders to launch a provocative attack. To sink one of our major warships or submarines!

'The West wants to exploit the political crisis in Moscow, you see. A surprise attack from an unidentified aggressor. Something the West can deny responsibility for; they reckon it could shake the confidence of the Soviet people in their leaders and in us, their military protectors.'

Makhov's jaw gaped open. Astashenkov's bland delivery of the 'facts' had done nothing to conceal the impact of what he was saying.

'That's madness. It's unbelievable.'

'I'm not lying,' Astashenkov lied. 'If the *Truculent* is successful in her mission, it could be a disaster for the Soviet Union. We've got to stop her. And we have to do it alone. No communication with headquarters. Nothing that can ever be traced. We too must be totally "deniable".'

'I understand, I think. But where do we look? We need to know what the aircraft have found out. They may be tracking the boat by now.'

'Can you listen in to their radio transmissions? Before we dive?'

'Their stuff's all encrypted. We don't carry the right decoder.'

'Then it's up to us, isn't it?'

They both felt a slight jolt as the submarine nudged itself away from the pier. Normally tugs would assist a boat as large at the *Ametyst*, but not today. The 40,000 horsepower produced by her twin, pressurized-water nuclear reactors would need careful control to prevent damage as she eased her way out of the dock.

The Zapadnaya Litsa Fjord emerges into the sea twenty miles west of the main Kola Inlet. Within a mile of the shore, the waters of the Barents Sea plunge 250 metres to a sea-bed of black mud.

'We'll dive when we've passed Ostrov Kuvshin,' Makhov announced. This was an island at the mouth of the fjord. 'Then we can unreel the array. It's noisy when we do it, so let's hope the English boat isn't close already. D'you have any idea of her exact target?'

'No. It could be any of the naval bases. All we can do is patrol between here and Ostrov Chernyy. Sixty kilometres of sea. She has to cross our path if she's to complete her mission.

'The name of the boat, by the way – *Truculent* – I looked it up in a dictionary. It means "of merciless temper"!'

'How fitting. But if we are to destroy her, then we must be of even more merciless temper, mustn't we?'

* * *

Admiral Belikov took off his heavy-framed spectacles and polished them with his pocket handkerchief. The waiting was dragging on his nerves. In the command bunker, the big screen was marked with dozens of triangles, denoting contacts detected by the maritime patrol aircraft and helicopters.

They couldn't all be *Truculent*, scattered widely over 4000 square kilometres of sea. The question was whether any of them were. None of the contacts had been confirmed, since the chance discovery of the vessel west of Nemetskiy Point. Infuriatingly the helicopter had had no spare fuel to give chase, so they'd had to start the search all over again. The Royal Navy was damnably good at silencing its boats.

It had been a gamble, ordering the message about Helsinki to be transmitted to the boat they'd discovered. He hoped it was clear enough to persuade Commander Hitchens to adhere to his arrangement with the KGB, but sufficiently mysterious for the rest of his crew to ignore it.

They'd know soon. Four helicopters were dunking transducers into the waters round Ostrov Chernyy. If Commander Hitchens delivered the Moray mine there, they'd be sure to hear the submarine's bow caps opening. If he didn't, they'd know he had a more sinister intent, and would concentrate the search closer inshore.

All aircraft had now been loaded with homing torpedoes or depth charges.

He replaced the spectacles and looked again at the screen. A fresh symbol had appeared, at the mouth of the Zapadnaya Litsa fjord – a circle this time, denoting one of his own submarines.

'Captain Lieutenant!' he spluttered. 'What the hell is that?'

The briefing officer hurriedly checked his computer terminal.

'The PLA *Ametyst*, Comrade Admiral. Sailed from Bolshaya Litsa an hour ago. Vice-Admiral Astashenkov is listed as being in command.'

Belikov stared at the small circle on the screen, transfixed. He dared not speak, knowing his voice would betray his horror; dared not reveal that his own deputy was acting without his knowledge!

A red flush spread upwards from his neck. He was conscious of a dozen pairs of eyes turned towards him. Every man and woman in that room knew the instructions that had been issued to all shipping in the Kol'skiy Zaliv, including their own submarines; to stay in harbour until the enemy boat had been located and neutralized.

What the hell was Astashenkov playing at? Trying to rid the Rodina of the submarine threat single-handed? Playing the glory seeker, at his age?

Suddenly he sensed the dabbling hand of Moscow. Someone was playing for power.

For his own deputy to risk everything, the orders must have come from the very top. From Sergey Grekov, Admiral of the Fleet of the Soviet Union, or Nikolai Savkin – the President himself.

But why? What was their plan? They knew the risks. It was Grekov himself who had ordered boats confined to port.

It had to be Savkin. If the *Ametyst* were destroyed by a Western mine, he'd have an international incident of mighty proportions to exploit for political ends. And if she found the *Truculent* and sank her, Savkin would also have a political feather for his threadbare cap.

He couldn't lose.

And himself? He needed an insurance policy.

His eyes focused on the screen again, looking north of the Rybachiy Peninsula.

'All the ships inbound to Kol'skiy Zaliv – have they hove to, as ordered?'

'Yes, Comrade Admiral,' answered the Captain Lieutenant. He pointed with a light pen to the northeast tip of the Ribachiy. 'The supply vessel *Boris Bubnov* is waiting off Voronkovskiy Point. She's the closest to harbour.'

'And the PLA *Ladny*? What's her position?'

This was the *Victor III*, detected by *Truculent* and *Tenby* earlier that morning.

'At last report she was following the *Boris Bubnov* in case the *Truculent* was using her as cover. She's due to report again in half an hour.'

'When she does, I have new orders for her,' Belikov intoned. 'Tell her that if she finds the *Truculent* within five kilometres of the Kol'skiy Zaliv, she's to sink her!'

* * *

Plymouth, England.

0900 hrs GMT.

John Black took a cigarette from the half-empty packet that had been new that morning, and offered one to Sara Hitchens.

She lit it and inhaled hungrily. Her face, ghostlike from sleeplessness and emotional stress, paled yet again when he told her what they wanted her to do.

They were closing the net. Orders from on high.

The day before, a police helicopter had followed Gunnar on his motorbike to Bristol, Black explained, but the Russian had abandoned it in a public car park there, and vanished on foot.

He wouldn't use the machine again, Black guessed. He'd be too careful for that, now he knew they were looking for him. The only chance they had of catching him was for Sara to lure him into a trap.

'You're sure he didn't say what time he'd ring you?' Black pressed for the third time.

'Quite sure,' Sara snapped, exhaling smoke. 'He just said it'd be this morning. But he's probably thought better of it. He could be on his way to Moscow by now.'

Privately she hoped he was.

For Sara, waiting was an agony. John Black would tell her nothing. She'd not recognized the MI5 man when he'd knocked at the door clad in blue overalls and clutching a tool bag. His Electricity Board van was parked out in the drive.

As she moved about the room, her right shoe felt heavy with the weight of the small radio transmitter fitted inside the heel. She was terrified it would show, despite Black's insistence that it didn't.

'You got your words sorted out?' he pestered. Women couldn't be trusted. 'You know what to say when he rings?'

'No, Mr Black. I've forgotten!' she answered sarcastically. 'I think *you'd* better talk to him!'

He turned away, embarrassed at the sharpness of her tone, then looked at his watch.

'I'll leave you to it, then. I've been here quite long enough to have fixed your cooker. Remember, we plan to grab him after your meeting's over, but we may need to move sooner than that, so if you hear me shout, do whatever I say and do it fast. Okay?'

'What are you going to do to him?'

Black picked up his toolbag, and stubbed out the remains of his cigarette.

'Ask him a few questions. If he doesn't co-operate, we'll throw the book at him.'

'He told me he wanted to defect.'

'We'll see, won't we?'

Sara watched as he climbed into the van and reversed it into the road.

With the MI5 man gone, the house became eerily silent. She could almost hear the walls breathe.

At night, during the past week, she had lain awake for hours, ears straining to catch the sounds of the darkness, imagining footfalls and twigs breaking. She could stand it no longer, being alone in the house. She would telephone Simon's school and persuade his housemaster to let him come home for a few days.

Philip would never return from his crazed voyage to the Arctic Circle, her certainty of that had grown stronger. It was time Simon knew what had happened, time for her to prepare him to understand that he'd never see his father again.

The shrill ring of the telephone had her leaping to her feet. She closed her eyes tightly, trying to stem the panic.

The phone rang four times before she picked it up, praying that her voice wouldn't fail her.

'Hello?'

'Mrs Hitchens?'

'Yes.'

'It's the TV man. The repair to your set? You wanted to fix a time for me to do it?'

Viktor Kovalenko had gone back to his Swedish accent.

'Oh, yes. That's right. This morning some time?'

The steadiness of her voice surprised her.

'Ten o'clock. As we discussed yesterday.' The voice was tense, clipped. 'Please make sure there are no other tradesmen with you. I like to work alone. Understood?'

Sara almost choked.

'Yes, of course,' she whispered, but the line was already dead.

He'd guessed it was a trap. He must have.

She ought to tell John Black, but there was no time. She had to get to the same car park they'd gone to yesterday, on the far side of Plymouth. It was already nearly half-past-nine. It would take nearly thirty minutes to get there. She'd have to leave immediately.

As she turned out of the drive, she was gripped by an urge to flee, to head away from Plymouth, anywhere to escape.

The MI5 man had bullied her mercilessly before she'd agreed to help, threatening her with prison if she didn't co-operate.

It was a ridiculous threat; she'd done nothing illegal. Nothing really wrong either, she decided. Whatever appalling plan Philip had conceived, the cause lay way back in his own past. Her infidelity couldn't have provoked that strong a reaction.

And Gunnar – Viktor, as he called himself now? She believed he really had loved her; maybe he still did. Perhaps she'd even loved him too. And now she was going to betray him.

She braked the car gently into a sharp bend, beyond which was a turning into a farmyard, disused since the farmer gave up milk production. She rounded the corner.

Suddenly, a figure leaped into the road waving. Sara braked hard and swerved.

The man had long, straggly hair and wore an old rain-coat. He banged on the bonnet of the car and shouted as she tried to avoid him.

'Sara!'

The voice was Gunnar's; so was the face beneath the greasy wig. She stamped on the brake. He wrenched open the passenger door and threw himself inside.

'Drive on! Left into the farm!' he barked, twisting round to see if any car was following.

Sara obeyed, heart thudding.

A rutted track led to a group of farm buildings which had fallen into disrepair.

'In there,' he pointed to an open-sided barn. 'Next to the van.'

The car bumped over a broken brick floor; the van belonged to a firm of feed-merchants.

'Who knows you're meeting me?' he demanded, grip-ping her arm so tightly she thought he'd break it.

'No . . . no one,' she stammered. 'I came straight here after you rang.'

'You had a visitor this morning.'

She felt her lower lip trembling.

'The cooker. A man came to mend it. A hot plate had burnt out.'

He was frightening her. His eyes had never looked so cold. She squirmed.

'That wig. It's awful. Can't you take it off?'

'Not yet. Come. Get out. Into the van.'

He pulled open the rear doors and looked her up and down. She was wearing jeans and a dark blue guernsey.

'In those clothes you'll be all right in the back. There's some sacking to sit on.'

'Why? Where are we going?'

'Not far. Somewhere safe. Just a few minutes. Get in.'

She knew he'd accept no argument. The sacking smelled of fertilizer. He closed the door behind her. The only light came through a small window to the driving compartment.

He reversed backwards over the bumps. Where the track met the road, he turned right, back to the village.

She thought of the electronic bleeper in the heel of her shoe. The MI5 men were expecting a rendezvous miles away. Would they be able to track her here? Half of her hoped they wouldn't.

They passed her house. She strained to see it through the small pane, half expecting to see John Black's van parked in the drive. Nothing there.

Viktor turned right. She had to think for a moment where they were going. It was a narrow tarmaced road, little used, that ran round the back of the village, re-entering the main street beyond the church, and just short of the quay. Along the way they would pass a farm and three labourers' cottages, she remembered; one of them was for sale.

After less than a minute the van turned left off the road and jolted its way down a short track. Viktor swung right again and stopped. She heard him get out and walk round to the back.

'Okay. Out now,' he said softly, as he opened the door. He took her by the arm to help her to the ground.

She looked round. They were behind a cottage, hidden from the road.

'I was thinking of buying this house,' he smiled. 'To be near you.'

He led her round to the front. A large 'For sale' sign was fixed to the gatepost. From his pocket, he pulled a key attached to a label.

'Very trusting, the estate agent.'

The rooms were bare, and smelled of rot.

'Wait here.'

He climbed the steep, narrow stairs to the upper floor.

After a few moments he called to her to come up.

He was leaning against the wall, to one side of a window.

'You stand the other side and tell me if you see anyone coming. This way we look both ways at once.'

She did as he asked, conscious of wanting to calm her own breathing, but not being able to.

'Now we can talk.'

He pulled off his wig, folded it carefully, and pushed it into a pocket. He still looked strange to her with his hair, that had been long and blond, dyed brown and trimmed short.

'That's better,' she smiled.

'Have you heard anything more? About Philip?'

'They haven't managed to stop him; that's all.'

'And I risk this meeting, just for you to tell me that?'

His voice grated. His eyes flicked back to the window nervously.

'I was lonely. I wanted to see you again,' she heard herself say.

For a few moments he was silent, then he chuckled.

He pulled her away from the window. She felt limp, paralysed.

'You're a child,' he told her, putting his arms round her in a tender embrace. 'A beautiful, sensual woman. But also a child.'

Then he crushed his mouth to hers and, cupping his big hands round her behind, he pressed against her hungrily.

Sara struggled for breath. She wanted to stop him, warn him it was a trap, yet she felt powerless.

'Please, no,' she protested feebly.

'Please, yes. It's the last time I'll see you.'

His voice grated in his throat like gravel.

'I have to go away. It's dangerous for me here. But I can't go without feeling you again. Having you one more time.'

He pulled up her guernsey and tugged her blouse free of her jeans so he could slip his hands underneath to caress her.

'Gunnar . . . don't.'

He teased at her mouth with his lips, silencing her, and began to fumble with the zip of her jeans. He tore at it, breaking the button.

He unclasped the belt of his trousers.

Then he heard the helicopter.

He froze.

Sara whimpered. She'd heard it too.

Viktor seized her by the shoulders and held her so he could see her eyes. She looked away.

'You? You knew?' he whispered.

'I'm sorry . . .'

'Your police? Coming for me?' he hissed.

'I'm sorry.' She began to cry. 'They . . . made me.'

He let out a howl of rage. '*Bitch!*'

Drawing back his right hand, he balled it into a fist, and smashed it into her face.

Sara crashed to the floor, blood spurting from her mouth. Her midriff was bare, pullover pushed up, trousers on her hips.

Kovalenko darted to the window. The noise of the helicopter was deafening; it was landing in the meadow behind the house. They must not take him. Moscow's orders.

In terror and pain, Sara began to scream for help.

Kovalenko stared in shock at the woman whose sweet body had blinded him so fatally. Anger overwhelmed him. He calmly re-buckled his trousers and reached into the side pocket of his coat.

The first bullet ripped into Sara's groin, the second into her chest. The scream froze in her throat.

Wide-eyed and open-mouthed, she stared. She looked suddenly surprised.

Viktor aimed again and blasted a hole in the centre of her forehead.

He flung himself down the stairs. At the back of the house he could hear voices, and the helicopter turbines still whining.

The van started at first turn of the key. He slammed into reverse and swung the vehicle round to face the road. Left or right? It didn't matter.

He turned left, away from the village. He raced up through the gears, foot jammed hard down on the accelerator. There was a bend ahead. He rounded it, barely keeping the wheels on the road.

Just fifty yards ahead a South West Electricity Board van was slewed across the road.

His mind raced. Could he stop? No room! His foot

moved to the brake, touched it lightly, then swung back desperately to where it was before.

John Black crouched behind the van, an automatic pistol in his right hand. The expected drop in the engine note never came.

'Fucking hell!' he exploded, and hurled himself sideways into the ditch, as the van carrying Viktor Kovalenko smashed into the roadblock and exploded in flames.

★ ★ ★

HMS Tenby 1240 hrs GMT.

'Contact confirmed, sir. It's a *Trafalgar* ahead of us.'

'*Watch stand to!*' called Commander Biddle on the loudspeaker. Then he said to the weapons engineer, 'All tubes to the action state! Hammerfish torpedoes.'

'Aye, aye, sir!' The WEO looked startled, but scuttled down the companionway to the forward weapons compartment.

Biddle stood next to Tinker.

'At bloody last!' he hissed.

'We're only eight miles from the Rybachiy Peninsula. Well inside their twelve-mile limit,' Andrew warned. 'If we don't get it right, and we cripple him here, the Soviets'll have a whole *Trafalgar* class submarine to play with!'

'It's your decision, Andrew.'

'Don't I bloody know it!' he replied drily. 'We need to know the distance.'

'Steer zero-nine-five, revolutions for fifteen knots!'

The course change was to compute the range.

'*Aircraft overhead!*' squawked the communications box. '*Sounds like a MAD run!*'

MAD stood for Magnetic Anomaly Detector. A tail 'sting' on the Soviet IL-38 anti-submarine aircraft could pick out a large metal submarine from its interference with the earth's magnetic field.

'Steer zero-three-five!' Biddle called. 'Keep one-hundred-and-seventy-five metres!'

They'd need to go in for some fast evasive action.

'That's all we sodding well need!' Andrew cursed.

'*Stony ridge ahead, sir, rising to one-two-five metres!*' the navigator shouted. *'Distance on the new course, about three miles!'*

'Got that, thank you,' Biddle answered calmly.

They'd been navigating a deep-water trench some six miles wide, which led southeast into the Kola Inlet. Turning at a right-angle to evade the aircraft, they now risked smashing into the ridge at its northern edge.

The two commanders made the calculation simultaneously. Twelve minutes before they hit the rocks.

Andrew bit his tongue. He was in command of their overall mission, but Biddle was driving the boat.

'Revolutions for twenty-five knots!'

Biddle looked at the clock. He'd take no chances; just two minutes on this course and speed, before weaving east again.

Andrew stepped into the sound room to talk to the TAS, Algy Colqhoun.

'What's the maximum range of the underwater telephone here, d'you reckon?'

The lieutenant checked the Sound Path Predictor computer, linked to probes on the hull that analysed water samples.

'About three to four miles, sir. And at a guess, at least a dozen Soviet sonobuoys would hear it too, and get a nice fix on us!'

Andrew didn't need reminding. He went back to the control room.

'Revolutions for fifteen knots! Starboard twenty. Steer one-three-five!'

The deck lurched sideways with the violence of the new manoeuvre.

'Where's the range on the bloody target, TAS?' Biddle growled, knowing Colqhoun would be working on it without his telling him.

'New contact, sir!' the sound room announced. *'Astern. Submarine contact on the towed array.'*

'Classification?'

'Working on it, sir. Looks like a Victor.'

On the Action Information screen, contour lines marked the edges of the deep-water channel. Ahead of the symbol for their own boat, a small square representing *Truculent* changed to a diamond, signifying its range was now known.

The operator hit a key to open a window with the target data on the right of the screen.

'Range eight miles, heading one-four-zero, speed eight knots,' Andrew read. '*Eight* miles? Are we sure? That's beyond the normal detection range for a *Trafalgar*.'

'Told you the sonar fit on here's bloody brilliant,' Biddle answered. 'The *Truc*'s got the older set. Phil won't know we're here yet.'

'Eight more miles, and he'll be at Ostrov Chernyy,' Andrew grimaced. 'If he maintains that speed, he'll be there in an hour.'

'Target's changed course, sir,' the AIO rating called across.

'Dodging planes, like us, I guess,' Andrew commented.

'Steer one-eight-zero!' Biddle ordered, changing course again so the towed array could compute a bearing on the second contact, behind them.

'We've got to catch up with him, Peter,' Andrew insisted, 'before he gets there and lays a Moray mine on the shelf, like a bloody Easter Egg. Ten minutes at thirty knots might put us close enough to talk to him.'

'But we'd be deaf for those ten minutes. We're surrounded by Russians. And they've got sea-bed arrays somewhere around here. The noise we'd make could give them a firing solution.'

'Tow a decoy. Make them think we're one of their own.'

Biddle hesitated. The decoy would make even more noise – make them easier to track. Would it fool the Soviets if they tuned it to sound like a *Victor III*?

'*Second contact confirmed, sir!*' came the voice from the sound room box. '*Victor three astern. Heading one-two-seven degrees. Range ten miles, range decreasing. Estimated speed twenty knots!*'

'Okay, Andrew, you've got it,' Biddle decided. 'Time's running out. But hang on tight. It's going to be a bumpy ride.'

Philip Hitchens gripped the padded rail of the bandstand, picking at its blue imitation leather cover with his fingernails.

'Steer zero-six-zero. Ten down. Keep two hundred and twenty metres,' he snapped.

The sound room kept reporting aircraft noise. The sky must be full of planes. What the hell were the Russians up to? If they wanted the damned mine, they'd do better to leave him in peace.

Had they decided he'd renege on the deal? Perhaps they were right. Doubt still paralysed him. He was acting on instinct now. Survival – that was all. Had to get away from those planes.

'Charted depth two-hundred-and-fifty metres, sir,' cautioned Lieutenant Nick Cavendish.

The chart was all they had to go on. They dared not use their echo-sounder, for fear it would be detected and give away their position.

Faces in the control room were tense and sombre. The day before, they'd found it hard to accept the Captain's warnings that the world above them was close to war. But today they were beginning to believe him.

A few hours earlier, Sebastian Cordell had summoned Tim Pike to the sound room, and clamped headphones on his ears so he could hear the sudden silence. The sonar had been tracking over fifteen surface contacts, from tankers to trawlers, but one by one they'd disappeared.

It was eerie. All around them, ships had cut their engines; propellers hung idle.

There was only one explanation; the Russians knew they were there. They'd ordered silence, to make it easier to find them.

Deprived of the *Boris Bubnov* as a noise shadow, they were now on their own in hostile waters, lacking the most important weapon a submarine can have – surprise.

The Action Information display was uncomfortably empty of contacts. Tim Pike felt like a goldfish in a bowl, surrounded by hungry Soviet cats.

Every post on the submarine was closed-up now, ready for action. Pike's task was to follow his captain's every move, ready to take over if ordered – or if he felt the time had come.

'It's almost as if they were expecting us, sir,' Pike murmured to the captain. 'They'll have sonobuoys everywhere.'

'Yes.'

'What're we going to do, sir?'

'Complete our mission,' Philip said icily, yet feeling as if someone else had spoken. He swung round to address Paul Spriggs.

'WEO. Bring all tubes to the action state. Load two tubes with Mark 24 torpedoes. Make ready three Moray mines.'

Spriggs shot a glance at Pike for support.

'What exactly are our orders for the mines, sir?'

There was a moment's silence, but Hitchens was ready for them.

'Very shortly, Paul, I shall be in a position to tell you. Tim? Take over. I shall be in my cabin.'

* * *

Severomorsk.

Admiral Andrei Belikov snapped his fingers for some more tea. He'd sat in the operations room in the underground bunker since the moment he'd learned of Astashenkov's 'freelance' mission on board the *Ametyst*, and his eyes were feeling gritty and tired.

Reports from the IL–38s had produced nothing but confusion; suspected contacts had been 'detected' in six different areas. Most of them were caused by malfunction in the equipment or by excessive optimism on the part of the crew, Belikov believed.

But there had been persistent traces of a submarine, northwest of Ostrov Chernyy. It was in the right place and on the right heading if Commander Philip Hitchens was intending to carry out his contract with the KGB. The trouble was that there had also been strong reports of another contact twelve kilometres further west.

The Captain Lieutenant seated in front of him turned from his communications panel.

'A request from one of the maritime aircraft, Comrade Admiral. The intermittent contact it was tracking now sounds to him like one of our own *PLAs*. He's asked if we can confirm it's the *Ladny*.'

'Which track is that?'

'Number four.'

The Captain Lieutenant shone his light pen at the more westerly of the two strongest contacts.

'Send *Ladny* a signal. Tell her to report her position.'

The submarine towed a communications buoy. The antenna could only receive, but she'd reply within minutes by raising a VHF mast above the waves.

Belikov drummed his fingers on his desk as they waited until the printer began to chatter. The Captain Lieutenant tore off the sheet, noted the contents and, with eyebrows raised, passed it to the Admiral. Then he tapped the keys on his computer terminal.

On the large wall-screen in front of them, a red circle appeared for the *Ladny*, well to the left of the triangle which was the contact reported by the aircraft.

'Hah! So the *Ladny* has a ghost!' Belikov exclaimed.

'I've asked the IL-38 to re-confirm the position of its contact, Comrade Admiral.'

'Where's the *Ametyst* got to? Could it be *her* the aircraft's tracking?' Belikov demanded.

'Not out there. She was detected close to the Kol'skiy Zaliv, half an hour ago.'

The printer spewed out more paper.

'Reconfirmed,' declared the Captain Lieutenant. 'The IL-38 reports the contact has headed east at speed, conducting evasive manoeuvres. They've lost it now. Should they try to track it?'

'Tell them, yes. And put out a general alert that the British submarine *Truculent* seems to be using a noise generator. She's pretending to be one of ours.'

* * *

Submarine *Ametyst*.

Feliks Astashenkov heaved a sigh of relief when he checked on the chart the position of the *Truculent* that the Severomorsk headquarters had just transmitted. If she was still that far out the chances were she'd not yet laid her mines.

The thought of the undetectable threat that might be sitting on the sea-bed anywhere in their path had terrified him since leaving port. Against another submarine they could fight, but a mine gave no warning, no possibility of retaliation.

Suddenly, he was filled with hope. There was a chance, after all, that they could complete their mission, that the British boat could be destroyed inside Soviet waters and the wreckage brought up so that the Soviet people could be shown how NATO threatened the security of the State.

'There you are, Yury. Those are the co-ordinates of the target,' he said, putting his arm round the younger man's shoulders. 'Let's go and look for it!'

* * *

Helsinki, Finland.

The young, white-coated doctor crashed through the swing doors with a trolley carrying a cardiac-arrest emergency kit.

Ahead of him he could see the Russian nurse holding open the door to the small, private room.

He swung the trolley inside; one of the clinic's own female nurses was pressing rhythmically on the breastbone of the old man on the bed.

They hadn't been told his name; they knew him simply as 'the patient in room 112'. But a nurse had heard him speaking English.

'He must be kept alive, doctor,' whispered the Soviet official who'd been guarding the room since their arrival earlier that day.

The Finnish doctor ignored the remark. Goddamned KGB! He could smell them a mile off.

He grabbed the old man's wrist. No pulse. The trace on the electrocardiograph screen was flat.

'How long?'

'Two, three minutes,' answered the nurse.

The doctor uncoiled cables and placed two electrodes either side of Alex Hitchens' immobile heart, removing the ones connected to the electrocardiograph.

'Stand back,' he instructed, and pressed the switch.

Four times he repeated the process, checking after each shock for some sign that the heart had restarted. There was none.

The ECG was reconnected. The trace stayed flat.

'He's dead,' he announced.

'Not possible,' hissed the Russian guard. 'He has to live!'

The doctor suppressed a desire to seize the Russian by the throat.

'He was half-dead when he arrived here this morning. You gave us no medical records for him. But he had clear signs of heart failure. You must've known that before you brought him here. You knew the risks. He should never have been moved in his condition.'

With that he began to pack up his equipment.

The Finnish nurse looked down at the wrinkled old man, his sunken eyes hidden beneath closed lids. No name. No past. No future. It was sad that anyone should end their days in such anonymity.

Then she noticed something that gave her a certain comfort – a trace of a smile on the old man's thin lips.

* * *

HMS Truculent.

Philip's mind was made up. The decision had come quite suddenly, as if placed in his brain by some outside agency.

His father was dead; he was suddenly certain of it. He'd been dead for years probably, though exactly when it had happened was irrelevant. The 'evidence' that he was alive, which the KGB woman had produced, was fake. The whole scheme was a trick. He knew he had been stupid, but it no longer mattered.

Now the Soviets would pay the price for destroying his father, destroying his marriage and eventually destroying him too. They were going to get what was coming to them.

'*Captain, Control Room!*'

'On my way,' Philip said into the communications box. He hurried to the control room.

'Two submarine contacts, sir,' Pike told him. 'Both approaching from the west, both appear to be *Victor Threes*.'

On the chart he pointed to the island of Ostrov Chernyy with the underwater spit of sand extending from its northern shore.

'We're four miles from the island itself, two miles from the edge of the shallows. The first contact is five miles behind us on a bearing of three-one-zero. Coming straight at us. Fifteen knots. She may be tracking us, or else getting a steer from an aircraft.'

'Our speed?'

'Seven knots, sir.'

'And the second contact?'

'Less of a threat. Twelve miles distant.'

'Right. Spriggs, over here!' Philip ordered, suddenly sounding decisive and confident. 'We've got to be quick. They could be about to attack. Our task, gentlemen, is to lay three Moray mines close to their submarine lanes. Set the fuses for any submarine target, WEO, but with remote triggering. The mines won't be activated until later – by sonar burst. When, and who by, that'll be up to CINCFLEET. Is that clear?'

Pike hesitated. Spriggs was looking to him for a sign.

'The orders, sir . . . , they specify geographical co-ordinates for the mines? You'll give us the signal you received?'

Philip ground his teeth, determined to keep his nerve.

'The co-ordinates I was given no longer apply,' he snapped. 'It was supposed to be right in the mouth of the Kola Inlet. We'll never get there now. The fall back plan was to place them somewhere else. That's down to me.'

He prodded the chart.

'There. Just on the edge of the shelf, where it rises up towards Ostrov Chernyy. That's where we'll put them.'

In his mind's eye he imagined the spot; a slope of mud and fine sand, 150 metres down; protruding from it – the twisted metal of the old *T-class* boat, *HMS Tenby*. Soon, very soon, two Soviet *Victor* class submarines would be joining that pile of wreckage, if all went well.

'Right, gentlemen. Get on with it. We only have minutes to put those mines on the bottom and get the hell out of here!'

And Philip strode off to the sound room.

'Well?' asked Spriggs.

'Shit! I dunno! They won't be armed when we lay them. He says it'll need further orders.'

Spriggs raised an eyebrow.

'Look. I'm the one that'll get the chop if I'm wrong!' Pike reasoned. 'It's not the moment, Paul. We just haven't got enough evidence for me to relieve him. You'd better get the mines ready!'

* * *

HMS Tenby.

'Target's altered course, sir,' called Lieutenant Algy Colqhoun. 'He's heading for the shelf north of Ostrov Chernyy.'

'Christ!' breathed Andrew. 'The moment of truth! He's going to bloody give them the mine!'

'I'll proceed with the firing sequence?' Biddle suggested.

'Yes, but hold the final order,' Andrew told him.

'*Open bow caps!*' the WEO ordered the weapons compartment crew below.

Andrew looked hard at the AI plot. *Truculent* was five miles ahead. Too far for the underwater telephone.

'That *Victor*'s after us, Peter. Eight miles astern. We've not fooled her with our decoy. All we've done is given her something loud enough to track.'

'Dump the decoy!' Biddle shouted, swinging himself into the bandstand. 'Let it swim right here!'

He glanced rapidly at the plot.

'Starboard ten. Steer zero-nine-zero. Standby to fire!'

They were turning away from the decoy, weaving, almost certain the Soviet boat wouldn't detect them.

So, Philip was going to do it – betray his country – hand over technology that could be ten years ahead of anything the Soviets had.

A Hammerfish torpedo would take just four minutes to reach the *Truculent*. There was a chance, just a chance he could use it to stop the mine-laying and still let the hundred men on board survive.

'Get the bloody thing into the water!' he barked to Biddle.

The CO gave the order.

'Fire!'

From the nose of the submarine the Hammerfish shot forward, propelled by its miniature gas turbine. Trailing behind, a thin wire linked it to the submarine.

The weapons controller had his eyes glued to his screen. The target was at the centre; a green symbol approaching it from below was the torpedo. Guidance was from the submarine's bow sonar to start with, but shortly the weapon's own sensors would begin to track the target.

Andrew hovered at his shoulder.

'When the range is down to two-hundred metres, and the high-definition sonar goes active, we're going to have to move bloody fast,' Andrew warned. 'If we get it wrong, all the men in that boat are dead.'

The operator swallowed hard, hand hovering over the joystick that would guide the torpedo on its last few metres of flight.

* * *

HMS Truculent.

'*Torpedo! Torpedo! Torpedo! Torpedo bearing red one-five-zero! True bearing two-nine-five!*'

'Shit!' Pike hissed.

'Starboard thirty! Steer two-nine-five! Ready the mines!' Philip bellowed.

'Only one mine ready in the tube, sir!' Spriggs called.

The control room heeled over as the submarine turned on its tail to face the threat.

'Fire a decoy!'

Forward of the control room a rating slipped a Bandfish decoy into a launch tube and tugged at the lever that propelled it into the sea. The cylinder of electronics hovered in the water emitting a high intensity signal to lure the torpedo.

'Course two-nine-five, sir,' Cavendish called as the boat settled onto the new heading.

'Are we tracking the bastard who's firing at us?'

'Bit confused, sir. Thought it was the *Victor Three*, but the transients of the bow caps and torpedo launch came from a different bearing.'

'Lay the mine!'

The forward weapons compartment reverberated to the thunder of compressed air, blasting the Moray mine out of the torpedo tube. It began to sink towards the sea-bed one hundred metres below.

'*Torpedo's gone active, sir!*'

'Give me a firing solution, sonar, for Christ's sake!' Philip screamed, clinging to the bandstand.

'*Torpedo's sonar's classified as a fucking Hammerfish, sir!*' came a yell of astonishment from the sound room.

Philip froze.

'Oh, my God! What have I done?'

* * *

HMS Tenby.

'Three hundred yards to the target, sir!' announced the weapons operator. 'The passive system's swamped by decoy noise, but the active's burning through it!'

'*Just heard the target launch something from a tube, sir!*' yelled the sound room.

'Two hundred yards! High-definition sonar now active, sir.'

'Make it look down! Below the bows,' Andrew hissed in the operator's ear. 'Track what's just come from the tube!'

'If it's a torpedo it'll be gone, sir,' the rating grumbled.

'It's a mine! Just try and track it,' Andrew ordered.

The weapon controller dived the Hammerfish towards the sea-bed. He'd never done this before.

'Got it, sir. Small object, dropping.'

'Spot on! Just one? Sound room! Anything from the other tubes?'

'*Nothing detected, sir!*'

'Fifty yards, sir. Do we hit the mine?'

'Yes. Blow the fucker to pieces!'

* * *

HMS Truculent.

Inside *Truculent*, the double explosion boomed with a terrifying resonance. The blast wave lifted the bows and tossed the boat sideways.

In the control room ratings and officers crashed to the deck. Paul Spriggs gashed his forehead as he fell, blood trickling into his eye.

Tim Pike grabbed the edge of the bandstand and pulled himself to his feet.

'*Oh, God! Oh, God!*'

Eyes closed, the captain was gibbering meaninglessly, his mind a tortured jumble.

The moment had come.

'I have command!' Pike shouted. 'Damage reports!'

Peter Claypole pressed the key on the ship control panel that linked him with the manoeuvring room, aft. He listened, then reassured the first lieutenant.

'No problems with propulsion.'

'Casualties in the weapons compartment!' called Spriggs, pressing a handkerchief to his forehead. 'I'm going down there.'

'Starboard twenty. Steer zero-one-zero! Revolutions for maximum speed,' Pike ordered. 'Nick, give me a safe depth.'

'Two hundred metres for five miles. Then come up to one twenty.'

'Ten down. Keep two hundred metres. TAS, what are the contacts doing?'

'Closing,' Cordell replied. 'Nearest at four miles, now

classified as *Trafalgar* class. Closest *Victor*'s disappeared. Guess it must've been a decoy. Lost track of the other *Victor*. We've a firing solution on the *Trafalgar*.'

'You must be joking! What the hell was he doing firing at us, anyway? And where the fuck's the C.O.?'

The bandstand was empty. Hitchens had gone.

'Hugo,' Pike shouted, spotting the radio officer. 'Find the captain. He's not well. Get him back to his cabin and stay with him. Get a steward to help if you need to.'

* * *

HMS Tenby.

Even four miles away the double detonation of the torpedo and the mine was heard through the hull.

'Bloody well done!' Andrew clapped the weapons operator on the shoulder.

He turned to a grinning Peter Biddle.

'Let's hope Pike's got the message by now. What's the *Truc* doing, TAS?'

'Moving. Fast. Heading north, thirty knots.'

'We do the same? Right?' Biddle checked.

'Right. And keep close. When we're clear of danger I'm going to have a few words with Phil Hitchens on the underwater telephone.'

* * *

Severomorsk.

The operations room of the Soviet Northern Fleet was electrified.

The four helicopters hovering over the waters round Ostrov Chernyy reported the explosions within seconds of each other. Using passive sonar transducers, only one had been close enough to the *Truculent* to hear her bow caps open and the mine being expelled.

Admiral Belikov frowned. They didn't match. The contact discovered by the helicopter and the one the *Ladny* had been following – they were too far apart to be one and the same.

Two foreign submarines? Had the second boat come to

try to stop Commander Hitchens betraying his country? Had the *Truculent* been sunk?

'Tell them to go active. Search the area thoroughly. Put out a general signal to look for foreign submarines. There may be several boats, with the ability to make themselves sound like our own.'

The Captain Lieutenant hastened to relay the order. Using active sonar in the shallow water round Ostov Chernyy would not be easy; reflections from the uneven seabed could make the readings unintelligible.

Decoys. Of course! Belikov snapped his pudgy fingers. The explosions could be a decoy too. To make them concentrate their search round Ostrov Chernyy, while the submarines headed elsewhere! Inshore? To the mouth of the Kol'skiy Zaliv? To lay the new mines where they could do most damage, just outside the main submarine bases? It made sense.

And who would be waiting for them? Felix Astashenkov – ready to claim the military and political glory of destroying the foreign intruder.

Belikov fumed at the thought.

'Send a coded signal to the *Ladny*,' he ordered the Captain Lieutenant. 'Tell her to head inshore fast. I believe the British boats are making for Polyarny.'

* * *

Ametyst.

'The sonar computer puts the explosions at fifteen kilometres northeast of here, Comrade Vice-Admiral,' announced Captain 2nd Rank Yury Makhov.

Mines. And they'd found a target. Feliks had misjudged it. He'd thought the only place the *Truculent* would lay them would be the mouth of the Kol'skiy Zaliv. He'd been fatally wrong.

'The sonar has no submarine contacts yet?'

'Regrettably not, Vice-Admiral. We'll need to be close to a *Trafalgar* to hear her.'

'Then we must close the gap, Yury. Ten minutes at maximum speed will bring us near.'

Makhov disliked driving his vessel fast in inshore

waters, making his sonar deaf. But he could see the anxiety on Astashenkov's face.

'I share your determination. We'll have our revenge on the Englishman!'

He ordered the reactors to maximum power. Imperceptibly the 7,600 ton leviathan began to accelerate to 45 knots.

* * *

HMS Tenby.

'Ten up. Keep one-hundred-and-twenty-five metres, revolutions for fifteen knots!' Biddle directed. They were slowing down to listen, desperate to know what had happened on the *Truculent.*

'Contact bearing zero-four-five. *Trafalgar* class, sir!' the sonar CPO announced. 'Range. . . .'

He waited the few seconds it took the computer to calculate it.

'Two-point-seven nautical miles, sir. No other surface or sub-surface contacts registered.'

'Right. This is it.'

Andrew lifted the handset of the underwater telephone.

'British submarine, British submarine! This is your sister vessel speaking. I am Commander Andrew Tinker. Do you hear me, over?'

HMS Truculent.

Tim Pike spun round, thunderstruck by the voice that suddenly crackled from the loudspeaker. He grabbed the handset.

'I hear you clearly, sir. This is the first lieutenant speaking, Lieutenant Commander Pike. Over.'

There was a lapse of a few seconds before the reply reached through the water.

'Listen carefully, Tim. Commander Hitchens is unwell. You must take command of the boat immediately. I repeat. You must assume command. That is an order from CINCFLEET. Understood? Over.'

Pike felt his shoulders sag with relief.

'I've already taken command, sir. Repeat. I am now in command. Commander Hitchens is being attended to in his cabin. Over.'

Again, a pause for the reply.

'Good news. Give him a message from me, will you? Tell him not to worry. His problems can be sorted out. Tell him I'll help him when we get back home. Now. Get well clear, and when it's safe call CINCFLEET. Over.'

'We have an emergency on board, sir,' Pike continued. 'Two men badly injured. Legs crushed by a torpedo disloged by the explosion. Over.'

'Sorry about that. Better try to get them ashore in Norway. Tell CINCFLEET to organize it. See you in Devonport. Out.'

Tim Pike replaced the handset.

'Clear the datum!' he called. They had to move fast. The Soviets were bound to have heard their conversation.

'TAS. Take control. I'm going to see the captain.'

So, they'd been right about Hitchens all along. The man had thrown a loop. CINCFLEET must have known it soon after they'd left port. Had to send a bloody submarine to get the message through!

He shuddered to think what Tinker had intended when he'd launched that torpedo at them. Had he meant to hit the Moray mine, or had *Truculent* herself been the target?

In the flush of relief that they'd survived, the anger he'd suppressed for days began to boil over.

Hitchens had been happy to risk all their lives in pursuit of some crazy plan of his own. The bastard!

Sub. Lieutenant Hugo Smallbone stood at ease outside the captain's cabin.

'He told me to get out,' Hugo whispered, tapping the tip of a finger against his temple.

Pike pushed into the cabin. The captain's face was like a cast, devoid of emotion.

'There's a message for you, sir. From Commander Tinker.'

Suddenly Pike saw the mask crack. At the mention of the name, Philip's lips began to tremble; a tic set his eyes blinking.

'Said you weren't to worry, sir. He'll help you sort things out when we get home.'

Philip clenched his eyelids to stop their movement. Pike's voice echoed inside his head.

Andrew? Out here? *Andrew* had come after him? The man Sara had named as the first of her string of lovers? *Andrew*, who'd betrayed nearly twenty years of friendship by seducing his wife and setting her on the path to ruin? How could this be the man they'd sent?

'He'll help you sort things out when we get home.' What a mockery! *God*, how patronizing!

'Sir? Sir, are you all right?'

Pike's voice was agitated.

'You're suffering from shock, sir. I'll get the medical assistant to give you something. Just hang on, sir.'

Alarmed at Philip's uncontrollable shaking, Pike hurried to find the steward who'd done a first-aid course. He remembered where he was; he would be attending to the two men with crushed legs in the torpedo compartment.

He clattered down the ladder to the deck below.

'Where's the MA? Quick, get up here with your bag of goodies. Something to sedate the Captain.'

Suddenly Pike heard Hugo Smallbone bellowing for him.

'The captain's gone! Just rushed past me. I thought he was going to the heads. . . .'

Suddenly an alarm bell sounded.

'The forward escape hatch!' Pike yelled and hurled himself along the corridor.

In the escape chamber, the lower hatch was closed, a red light flashing to warn that the chamber was flooding.

Pike wrenched at the hatch. It crashed open, icy sea water drenching down onto the deck. Pike fought his way up through the torrent, gasping for breath. He seized Philip's legs and both men crashed down onto the deck, choking.

The medical assistant and Hugo Smallbone dragged Hitchens to one side so that Pike could get back into the tower. Water streaming past him, he reached up, and fumbled for the flood valve to shut it off.

309

Soaked and shivering he collapsed onto the deck, water swilling away into the drains that led to the bilges.

'Jesus!' he panted. 'Jesus Christ!'

* * *

Neither the *Ametyst* nor the *Ladny* was aware of the other's presence, both deafened by the speed at which they were moving. Their two captains had a single aim; to find the British submarine before it could lay more mines.

The *Ladny* had been ordered to head inshore, the *Ametyst* was bound for the open sea.

The collision came at a combined underwater speed of 72 knots.

The *Ladny* struck the *Ametyst* aft of the forward planes. The protective outer casings of the two vessels crumpled like paper, until the pressure hulls struck with a terrible wrenching of steel and an explosion of escaping air.

The forward weapon compartment of the *Ladny* telescoped, then split open like an egg dropped on concrete, spewing men and oil into the black water. The section of the *Ametyst* ahead of the fin was torn away by the impact. Exploding electrical circuitry jolted the foreshortened hull nose-up, allowing air to escape in a seething column to the surface.

Water surged down through the control and accommodation spaces, stopping only at the watertight hatches through the reactor compartment. Battered and disorientated by the violent movement, the men had no time to don escape masks. Within minutes, more than half the crew had drowned – amongst them Vice-Admiral Feliks Astashenkov.

Devoid of buoyancy, the forward section fell towards the sea-bed fifty metres below, propelled by the still-rotating screw. The aft section of her hull lifted up by the air trapped in it, the *Ametyst* began to somersault.

The safety systems in the two reactors tripped as the hull passed through the critical angle, but it was too late. The hull inverted. Steam percolated back into the reactor pressure vessel, replacing the water which moderated the nuclear reaction. Deprived of coolant, the temperature in the core began to rise. By the time the broken nose of the hull buried itself in the mud of the sea-bed the core was melting.

On the *Ladny*, too, there were no survivors forward of the reactor section. The boat sank to the sea-bed, nose-down, but upright. The engineering crew aft succeeded in scramming the reactors; control rods dropped into the core to absorb the neutron flow and damp down the reaction. Then panic set in.

One hundred metres separated the two wrecks on the bottom. The heat in *Ametyst*'s reactors climbed fast. The molten core burned through the steel of the reactor compartment, then through the hull itself. Ice-cold water surged in and exploded into steam.

The detonation of the reactor compartment released a tidal wave of energy, scattering the shreds of the *Ametyst* like sea-weed, and knocking the *Ladny* onto its side.

* * *

HMS Tenby.

The sounds of the collision, the ripping of metal, and the explosions that followed were heard by the two British submarines twenty miles to the north.

Andrew took the headphones from the sonar rating in the sound room and listened to the brain-curdling racket.

'Where's it coming from, for God's sake?' he asked, suddenly scared that Philip could have laid other mines earlier.

'Bearing one-nine-five, sir. Range twenty miles.'

Andrew hurried to the navigation plot, and picked up the dividers. He measured the distance onto the chart.

'Five miles north of the inlet. Not guilty. *Truculent* never got that far south.'

'It's that *Victor III*,' announced Colqhoun. 'She was sprinting. We tracked her all the way in. Look, it's on disc.'

'Play it back, CPO.'

The sonar chief cued the disc and directed Andrew to the VDU. The phosphor-green wave pattern began to spread up the screen.

'That's the *Victor III*, sir,' explained the chief, pointing to a ridge on the waterfall pattern at the frequency generated by vibration from the Soviet submarine's pumps.

'And what's that next to it?' Andrew asked.

'Just an echo, sir. Shallow water.'

'Couldn't it be another boat?' Andrew pressed.

The CPO keyed the target information into a window on the screen.

'Same bearing, sir. Just an echo.'

'But if there were two boats, and they collided. . . .'

'See what you mean, sir.'

'Spin back five minutes on the disc.'

It took a few seconds.

The chief keyed instructions for the computer to analyse the tracks.

'You're dead right, sir. They were on different bearings.'

Andrew folded his arms. For two Soviet vessels, the submariners' nightmare had come true. A collision at speed.

Peter Biddle appeared at his shoulder.

'We've got to get a signal off fast,' Andrew announced. 'Before the Russians accuse *us* of sinking their boats.'

CHAPTER ELEVEN

Wednesday late.

Journalists in London and Washington were invited at short notice to special briefings at Downing Street and the White House respectively.

They were told the British and US governments had received irrefutable intelligence information that two Soviet submarines had collided accidentally earlier that day, with heavy loss of life. American spy satellites had picked up extensive radio traffic emanating from the major rescue operation the Soviet Navy was mounting.

When asked why they were releasing the information in such an unprecedented manner, the press were told that it was to forestall any attempt the Soviets might make to blame the incident on the West, and more particularly on the NATO exercise Ocean Guardian.

The story made the lead on late-night television news bulletins and would form the splash headline in the newspapers the following morning.

* * *

Moscow. Midnight.

The telephoned report from Admiral Grekov was not the one Nikolai Savkin had expected. The disaster stunned him.

Couldn't it have been NATO mines that had been responsible, he'd asked? Grekov had been adamant. A collision. They'd used the word on open communications. They'd had to; most of the rescue and pollution control vessels had no encrypted communications systems.

Incompetence was the cause, Grekov had insisted. The real culprit was whoever had instructed Feliks Astashenkov to defy orders and take the *Ametyst* to sea.

From the bitter note of recrimination in Grekov's voice, Savkin knew that he knew.

He sat slumped in his chair, in the dimly-lit sitting-room of his Kremlin apartment. Who would they send, he wondered?

An hour had passed since Grekov's call. Then there came a gentle tap on the door.

'Ah, it's you, Vasily,' Savkin sighed with relief at the sight of his Foreign Minister and friend. 'Thank . . .'

His voice caught in his throat as KGB chief Medvedev followed Kalinin into the room.

'There was a meeting earlier this evening,' Kalinin began, unsmiling. 'The vote went against you. You no longer have a majority in the Politburo.'

'Who was it? Which one changed his mind?'

Kalinin dropped his eyes.

'You?' Savkin whispered incredulously.

'It's been too much for you, Nikolai,' Kalinin explained. 'Your sense of judgement . . .' He shook his head sadly. 'And when we learned what happened tonight . . .'

Medvedev stepped forward.

'Comrade Savkin, I must ask you to come with me . . .'

The President of the Soviet Union stared wildly at the two men.

'You could resign on grounds of ill health, Nikolai.' Kalinin added, softly, 'It would be best.'

'Out of the question. We'll meet tomorrow. There'll be another vote.'

'Too late. Your successor's been chosen.'

Savkin gasped.

'What? Who?'

This time Kalinin held his gaze steady.

'It was unanimous. They all insisted it should be me.'

Savkin gripped his shoulders.

'How long have you been planning this, Vasily?'

'The experiment has failed. Our people cannot handle "freedom". We must put the shackles back on. It's the only way if the Union is not to disintegrate. Control from the centre. It'll be better this time. No corruption. More efficiency. We've learnt lessons from *perestroika*, lessons that can never be unlearned.'

Nikolai Savkin turned away, his heart heavy with guilt and sadness.

It had all been in vain. Admiral Astashenkov and the other men who'd died in the submarines had perished to no purpose. If anything, their deaths had now compounded the nation's troubles.

It was over. The collective leadership of the Soviet Union had decided to turn its back on the future.

* * *

Thursday 24th October.

Helsinki.

A small van with Soviet plates drew up to the rear entrance of the clinic, so that the plain wooden box could be slid inside.

The staff at the hospital never knew the name of the man who'd died there the previous day. He'd just been a case number. Now the body was being taken away; the file could be closed.

The van left the city, heading east. It was nearly two hundred kilometres to the Soviet border.

The KGB driver looked at his watch, then pressed his foot to the floor. He'd have to hurry.

Once over the border, there were still another fifty kilometres to drive to deliver the wooden box to the incineration plant.

* * *

Friday 25th October.

The Norwegian Sea.

A two-man Medevac team from the *USS Eisenhower* was lowered by wire from an SH-3 Sea King onto the forward casing of *HMS Truculent*.

They were led down through the forward hatch to the sick bay. The two men whose legs had been crushed in the torpedo compartment were in a bad way. The Royal

Navy medical assistant had done well, but the men needed urgent surgery and intensive care.

Gently they strapped the casualties into stretchers, then organized a team of ratings to lift them through the hatch onto the casing.

Hitchens was groggy from continuous heavy sedation. Tim Pike took his arm and helped him out into the open air.

Anxiously Tim watched him lifted off the casing, the strop held tightly under his arm-pits, arms limply at his sides, until the helicopter crew-chief pulled him backwards into the airframe next to the two stretchers.

They'd feared the commander would try another suicide attempt, and had thought it too risky to lift him off by helicopter, but he'd reassured them. He no longer wanted to die. It was time to get home, to try to sort out the mess.

Andrew was already on the windswept deck of the *Eisenhower* when the helicopter landed. He dreaded Philip's arrival. Pike had sent a signal from *Truculent* warning that after his attempt to kill himself, Philip had raved incoherently, naming Andrew as the man responsible for his troubles.

Andrew could guess what that was all about. Sara. She must have told Philip about their brief affair. Could he explain it to him? Hardly. Probably better to try to convince him it was untrue.

He'd also have to break the news to him that Sara was dead.

* * *

Late Afternoon.

RAF Northolt.

The US Navy Grumman Greyhound approached the runway from the west, skimming low over the dense line of commuter traffic heading home from London at the end of the day.

Philip had made no attempt at conversation during the flight. He'd been glad of the deafening noise that made communication almost impossible. Also, it meant Andrew hadn't been able to hear him when he wept.

When the machine had come to a halt, they removed their survival suits, and walked down the loading ramp into the mild, autumn air.

'Ah. I can see Patsy,' said Andrew raising his arm to acknowledge her wave. She was waiting in front of the old pre-fabricated terminal building. Behind her stood two broad-shouldered men; Andrew assumed they were from Security, waiting for Philip. He could also see the squat figure of Admiral Bourlet and, with Patsy's arm round him, a schoolboy, rather small for his thirteen years.

'Isn't that Simon?'

'Yes,' Philip gulped. 'What am I going to say . . . ?'

'We'll help. Don't worry.'

Patsy rushed forward and flung her arms round Andrew's neck.

'Thank God!' she breathed in his ear. 'The Admiral's told me what you've been up to. Promise me you'll never do it again?'

'Congratulations, Andrew,' Bourlet rumbled. 'Bloody well done!'

Then, uncomfortably, they all turned to the lone figure of Philip.

He was staring at his son, spellbound. Just for a fleeting moment he'd seen himself, thirty years earlier.

In the boy's eyes he recognized the same fear he'd felt whenever his own father had gone away, the fear of being left alone to face the world, unprepared.

Suddenly Simon ran forwards, face crumpling as emotion overwhelmed him.

'Dad . . .' the boy sobbed.

Philip hugged him into silence.

'Hullo, son,' he whispered. 'I'm home.'

SKYDANCER

PROJECT SKYDANCER. The brainchild of the Ministry of Defence – terrifying in its simplicity. New warheads had been designed that could evade the batteries of anti-ballistic missiles the Russians had set up around Moscow. For Aldermaston scientist Peter Joyce, it was the pinnacle of his career.

Until documents from the project turned up in Parliament Hill and he is left with two alternatives: write off a billion-pound project, or approve tests which could give Russia the power to wipe out the West at the touch of a button . . .

'A tautly written, topical thriller' *Manchester Evening News*

EAGLETRAP

He was head of an international drug ring, a kidnapper and a ruthless killer. One night British Sea Harriers reduced his Beirut headquarters to rubble and his evil drug empire to ruins.

But Abdul Habib still had money, and hate, hate enough to spare to construct an elaborate plan which would destroy Gibraltar and the British Aircraft carrier which had committed the fatal strike.

All he needed was luck to thread a nuclear warhead through the complicated network of the Middle East terrorist rings, get it on a Libyan freighter and head west across the Med ... And enough luck to avoid the one man whose hate is even greater than his, Captain Peter Brodrick of the Royal Marines. A man Habib foolishly left alive, though he killed all his friends. A man whose fate is inextricably entwined with his.

'Geoffrey Archer has every reason to consider himself at least first among equals' *The Times*

MORE BESTSELLING FICTION
FROM GEOFFREY ARCHER IN ARROW

☐   SKYDANCER   Geoffrey Archer   £4.99
☐   EAGLETRAP   Geoffrey Archer   £4.99

ALL ARROW BOOKS ARE AVAILABLE THROUGH MAIL ORDER OR FROM YOUR LOCAL BOOKSHOP AND NEWSAGENT.

PLEASE SEND CHEQUE/EUROCHEQUE/POSTAL ORDER (STERLING ONLY) ACCESS, VISA OR MASTERCARD

☐☐☐☐☐☐☐☐☐☐☐☐☐☐☐☐☐☐

EXPIRY DATE............... SIGNATURE..

PLEASE ALLOW 75 PENCE PER BOOK FOR POST AND PACKING U.K.
OVERSEAS CUSTOMERS PLEASE ALLOW £1.00 PER COPY FOR POST AND PACKING.

ALL ORDERS TO:
ARROW BOOKS, BOOK SERVICE BY POST, P.O. BOX 29, DOUGLAS, ISLE OF MAN, IM99 1BQ. TEL: 01624 675137 FAX: 01624 670 923

NAME...

ADDRESS..

....

Please allow 28 days for delivery. Please tick box if you do not wish to receive any additional information ☐

Prices and availability subject to change without notice.